REBORN AS
A DEMON
HAT

BOOK ONE

REBORN AS A DEMON HAT

BOOK ONE

J. S. Boyd

Podium

This is a work of fiction. Names, characters, places, and incidents are either products of the author's imagination or used fictitiously. Any resemblance to actual events, locales, or persons, living, dead, or undead, is entirely coincidental.

Cover design by Preston Asevedo

ISBN: 979-8-3470-0544-4

Published in 2026 by Podium Publishing
www.podiumentertainment.com

Podium

REBORN AS
A DEMON
HAT

BOOK ONE

CHAPTER ONE

You Are a [Hat]

Ethan Graham was a man who got things done.

He was a worker—pure and simple. Put him in any situation and he'd come out on top. Ethan's boss at the tax consultancy company he worked for knew this and saw to it that his best worker was kept busy.

"Ethan! Make sure those reports are triple-checked before tomorrow morning."

"Ethan—new trainees just joined up. Gonna need someone to run 'em through the ropes and assess their skills. Make this your primary action objective for the day."

"Ethan! Regional manager's on the way. Keep him confined to your stall. And get that manga bullshit *Off. Your. Desk!*"

To all these requests, Ethan would oblige. He'd work day in and day out, never muttering a grumble of complaint, never casting a dark glance in his more lackadaisical coworkers' direction.

At night, he'd get home and absorb himself in anime and manga, play the occasional MMO, and wait for the dawn that heralded another dull day of his life.

And one day, he looked in the mirror and saw a tired clown staring back at him.

"Look at you," he told his grizzled, unkempt face. "Even the Gibdos from Zelda scrub up better than you do."

There it was—the first joke of the day. The first of many mechanisms Ethan had invented to get through the drudgery of his nine-to-five life. Taking this world seriously had ceased being an option for him a long time ago.

Oh, it wasn't that he begrudged those who worked long hours for a living like him. It wasn't that he hated his boss, his company, and the city he lived in. After all, he could just leave and move on, right? No, Ethan's ennui went far deeper than that. The specific circumstances of his life were symptoms of a much greater problem that had followed him since his birth.

Ethan Graham's problem was that he had no control over *anything*.

As a kid, there'd always been someone telling him how the world worked. There'd always been someone who believed they knew better than he did who he was, and what his place in the world was.

"Stick in at school," his father—a stockbroker who brokered bottles more than stocks—would say. "Get a job. Work hard. Monitor your assets. Get married. Have kids. Tell them to do the same."

His mother—when she wasn't cleaning up his father's drunken messes—would tell him how he could find a good wife who could make him happy, telling him the love of a good woman was all he'd ever need.

And Ethan, at twenty-five years of age, was now beginning to doubt that very much.

His mother, his father, his teachers, his backbreaking boss, his friends, and even the society he was living in itself—all of them seemed to Ethan to be nothing more than a council of "wise" old elders who told him what life he *ought* to live. The person he *should* be.

And today, as Ethan crossed the road toward his office building and his stuffy little worker's cubicle within, a heretical thought suddenly occurred to him:

What about what *he* wanted to be?

He stopped, ignoring the oncoming traffic that swerved to avoid him as this thought occurred. It was like a jittery little imp was knocking at the side of his brain. It was a thought that brought a hoarse chuckle to his lips. The anagnorisis of the tragic hero, occurring in the middle of a congested main road at 9:00 a.m. He'd simply . . . never thought about it before.

What I want? Fuck, he thought. *I just wanna see what happens when I'm the one in control, for once . . .*

A barrage of lights threw themselves across his body, casting his thin silhouette across the street. He heard the driver of the truck beep his horn. He knew, without exception, that he'd be able to leap out of the way if he wanted to.

And yet . . . he didn't.

Without really knowing why, Ethan Graham did the one thing no one had ever told him to do: he *stopped*.

And he waited.

And the funniest thing was that when the truck finally did hit him, he barely felt any pain at all.

Ethan woke up to the sensation of cold, hard ground beneath him. But it wasn't just that—it was something worse. His body felt . . . different. No, not just different: *wrong*. He couldn't feel his hands. Or his feet. Or *anything*.

The darkness eventually gave way to dust, and he awoke to a high-ceilinged mineshaft filled with sparkling rocks and dripping water from above.

Where am I? The thought pressed against his foggy mind, but as hard as he tried to move, nothing responded. His body felt distant—like it wasn't even there.

Panic surged through him, sending a shock of adrenaline through his mind. He tried to scream, but no sound came. He couldn't even open his mouth.

What the fuck is going on?

A cold voice cut through the confusion, reverberating inside his mind like a gunshot in an empty room.

Welcome to Argwyll, Archon!

Initializing Consciousness: Ethan Graham
Form Assigned: {Legendary} Hat (Demon Variant)
Objective: Survive
Loading *Core Stats* . . . Done!
HP: SPECIAL
MP: SPECIAL
WILL: SPECIAL
STR: SPECIAL
DEX: SPECIAL
PER: SPECIAL
INT: SPECIAL
SPD: SPECIAL
CHA: SPECIAL
Loading *Core Skills* . . . Done!
Possession (Rank F)
Skill Siphon (Rank F)
Appraisal (Rank F)
Transmogrification (Rank F)

Ethan watched these words appear before him in a little blue status window with a growing sense of dread.

Archon . . . Legendary . . . Hat? Ethan's mind spun. His breath—if he even *had* breath—caught in his throat. None of this made sense.

It felt like a dream—a twisted, ridiculous nightmare. But something deep inside told him this was no dream. The pressure on his head, the helplessness—it all felt too real. He tried again to move, straining with all his might. Nothing. He was trapped, unable to do anything but think and roll his single eye.

Wait a minute . . .

He looked down again, seeing the deep-blue rim of a hat exactly where his feet should have been. Stitches, a little brown patch sewn into the side . . . Yeah, it was a hat alright.

He was a *hat* . . .

This has to be a mistake, Ethan muttered to himself, though no sound came out. *There's no way I've reincarnated as a . . . hat.*

A voice answered him back—the same one who had just read off his skill list.

No mistake, Archon. You've been selected for this form. Congratulations. You now possess the power to control others as a Legendary Hat—a rare privilege.

Every word reverberated off Ethan's new consciousness like the beats of an obnoxious gong. It was way too sarcastic for Ethan's liking.

Control others? He tried to process what that meant. *Okay, what's the catch? Why can't I move?*

Simple. You need a Host. Without one, you are immobile and . . . Well, let's say it won't take long for the creatures of Argwyll to make short work of you.

Wait—host? You mean I'm just a hat until I find someone—or something—to control?

Correct. And as a Legendary Hat, your first priority should be securing a Host. Otherwise . . .

A screen appeared in front of his field of vision:

[Time until Bounty: 23:59:59]

The timer blinked, and Ethan's heart—if he even had one in this form— skipped a beat. A bounty? What the hell did that mean?

Bounty? You wanna explain that?

Certainly. You have twenty-four hours before a Bounty is placed on you. Once that happens, every creature in Argwyll will know where you are, and they will come for you. Given that you're currently . . . well, just a hat, your chances of survival will drop to precisely zero.

I would strongly recommend finding a suitable Host.

Ethan's panic turned to dread. This wasn't just some game. If he didn't act fast, he was going to die. And not in some metaphorical sense—really, actually die this time.

Twenty-four hours before the entire world was against him . . .

Come on, Ethan. Think. Breathe—No, wait. He couldn't breathe.

He was *a hat.*

The helplessness was suffocating. He'd always been stuck in some way or another, trapped in the grind of everyday life, wishing for something to change. And now, the change he'd gotten was this: a cruel, cosmic joke.

But this wasn't the time for self-pity. He'd worked under pressure before; it was practically his entire life.

Okay, Ethan said, his mind working overtime. *So, how do I get a host? What are my options here?*

Look around. You'll probably find something small—weak—that you can control. I suggest starting with whatever's nearest.

He tried to move his perspective, and after a few seconds of straining, his view shifted. He could see now. He was in a mine—rocky, dimly lit by faint glowing moss that clung to the walls. The place looked utterly abandoned. It was cold, the air thick with the smell of damp stone and something else . . . something rotten.

And then, he saw it.

A rat.

A rat with a pair of beady little eyes.

Eyes that found the only other eye in the otherwise eyeless expanse of the mine.

Eyes that shone with mischief.

It sniffed the air and scurried toward him as Ethan tried his best to flop off the rock he was currently perched on and get away. Instead, he ended up falling right on top of the little critter.

Perfect! Hold still . . .

Potential Host Identified!

Possession (Rank F)
Success chance will be determined by your Spirit Core strength
vs. the Host's WILL stat.
Attempt Possession?

Ethan blinked as he felt the rat clawing at his hatty bowels, and yet, he felt something else—a distinct sense that he could overpower the creature. A sense of . . . potential.

Alright! he screamed in the void of his mind. *If it's the difference between life and death . . . sorry, little guy, but I'm gonna have to take over here.*

His consciousness shot out like a tendril, latching on to the rat. There was a moment of resistance, the rat's mind pushing back, trying to maintain control, but it was weak. Too weak to fight him off.

Then, with a sudden jolt, he was *in*. He felt his hatty form shrink to fit snugly atop the rat's head, and now, he was looking through its beady, unblinking eyes.

Possession Success!
Cave Rat's WILL: 0 vs. Spirit Cores: 1
Rats are not strong-willed. They have nothing but base,
primal desires.
Congratulations! You have successfully Possessed a Cave Rat (Level 1)!
Spirit Cores: +1

I can move!

Ethan felt the rat's body jerk under his control. He could feel its tiny heartbeat, the twitch of its whiskers, the sharpness of its claws on the stone floor. His senses were hypertuned, his vision much lower to the ground, but finally, he had limbs again.

But then came the sound—a scurrying, scratching noise echoing from the deeper shadows of the mine. Ethan froze.

The rat's instincts kicked in, and a deep sense of dread washed over him. He turned the rat's head, peering into the darkness, and his blood ran cold.

More rats.

A lot more.

They swarmed from the shadows, dozens of them, their eyes gleaming red in the faint light. They weren't like the rat he had just possessed. These were larger, their fur matted and black with grime. They moved with an unnatural hunger, their sharp teeth glinting as they poured from the depths of the cave.

Oh, come on! Ethan thought.

Appraisal Success!
Enemies Identified:
[Cave Rats (Level 2–5)] x5
HP: 50/50
WILL: 10/10
Swarming creatures that infest the lower caves of Argwyll.
Not individually dangerous, but deadly in large numbers—and
with much stronger WILL.

Hey! he shouted in his mindscape. *Look, whoever you are, you're gonna have to give me some answers here.*

I can answer all questions that are not considered [CLASSIFIED], Legendary Hat. But I think you have some more pressing matters to attend to now, don't you?

Ethan's eyes darted back to the party of rats staring him down, looking past their possessed comrade to the flappy hat that crowned his furry head.

And Ethan, instincts kicking in, turned to the corridor of darkness that stretched out behind him.

Think you can outrun them?

Ethan grunted as he forced his rat host forward, scurrying off as the army of rodents gave chase.

Only one way to find out . . .

CHAPTER TWO

Rise of the [Rat]sassin

The rats were closing in. Fast.

Ethan's heart pounded in his chest—no, the rat's chest, but the feeling was all too familiar. He had never been a runner, not in his old life. He'd always been the guy stuck in one place, suffocating under the weight of everything. But here? There was no choice.

This was survival.

As he raced through the mine, dodging pickaxes and upturned carts left behind by whomever once occupied this place, he felt the swarm gaining on him. The air was thick with their squeals, their claws scraping the stone, each one getting closer by the second.

Hey! Ethan yelled to the only sentient being that would hear him. *Any chance you've got a trick up your sleeve to help me out here?*

You're a Legendary Hat, not a miracle worker. Keep running. I'm sure you'll think of something. You humans always do.

He pushed the rat's body harder, its tiny legs burning with the effort while the swarm surged forward—a mass of fur, teeth, and claws.

Bring up my skills! he screamed in his mindscape, his floppy hat form being nibbled at by the nearest foe. *This disease bag's gotta have something it can do to fight back, right?*

That, I can show you.

Host: Cave Rat (Level 1)
Stats:
HP: 10/10
MP: 0/0
WILL: 0/0
STR: 5

PER: 5
SPD: 25
CHA: 2
Skills:
Hide (Grade F)
Skitter (Grade F)
Detect Life (Grade F)
Bite (Grade F)

Ethan narrowly avoided the nibbling teeth of a rat that launched itself at him from the shadows.

Okay, skills. One of them's gotta work here. I'm thinking . . . this!

Skitter (Grade F)
Adrenaline surges through you, giving you a momentary surge of speed.
SPD: +30 for 10 seconds

Ten seconds is all I need.

Ethan focused on the skill and willed it to activate. Without another thought, his host's body zoomed across the hard, craggy floor. Ethan felt as though he were gliding on dank, filthy air as he was carried into another shaft away from the horde.

But they're still pursuing . . . Let's see . . .

Hide (Grade F)
You blend into the shadows, evading your opponents.
Chance of Success: 20% (Double in total darkness.)

I'll take it, Ethan thought as he found a dilapidated mine cart and jumped inside. *We're going stealth mode . . .*

He heard the rat swarm enter the shaft behind him, their noses sniffing the air, seeking out their prey, as he closed his three eyes. He didn't move any of his new muscles.

Hide . . . Success!

Ethan breathed a sigh of relief as the rats filed out of the room, each breaking off into different levels of the shaft; he finally had a moment to think about what the hell was going on here, even though, in the corner of his eye, the timer that signaled the beginning of his bounty was still ticking down . . .

[Time until Bounty: 23:15:00]

He needed to act—and act fast. He needed a stronger host than this little rat. He wasn't gonna get far on running and hiding alone.

But first—he needed some answers.

Alright, Mr. System, Ethan began. *Spill it. What's the deal here?*

He felt hesitation nipping at the corner of his mind.

As your System guide, I'm afraid some details of your predicament are considered [CLASSIFIED], Legendary Hat.

That ain't gonna cut it, Ethan snapped. *Look, you're in my head now, so that means you probably die if I die, right?*

My feelings have never—that is, they do not come into this. All I can tell you is that you were a suitable candidate for regeneration. A new Archon was needed. That's all. The last one . . . didn't quite work out.

And what, pray tell, is an "Archon"?

I'm afraid that information is [CLASSIFIED], Legendary Hat. Should you survive your Bounty, I am sure you will find the answer.

Ethan slumped back, his rat form resembling his human couch-potato stance back home.

So, what can *you tell me?* he asked.

I can provide detailed information on your skills and abilities, as befits the purpose I was created for. I am also at liberty to discuss geographic details of this world.

Or, if you prefer, I shall simply be your lovable sarcastic guide.

Something tells me that last option's your default setting, Ethan moaned, stretching his hat form atop his furry host. *But alright, I'll bite: Where the hell am I?*

You are currently in the kingdom of Westerweald, the name of the landmass in the western reaches of Argwyll. The current ruler of this land is King Lysandus IV. Currently, you reside in one of the king's abandoned mineshafts. There was a troll problem a while ago . . .

Troll problem? Ethan mused. *Now, that sounds like a creature worth possessing . . .*

Ethan climbed the mine cart and dropped to the ground, checking for any enemies nearby.

Okay, he thought. *I've got twenty-three hours until I'm a walking target, and I'm at a cave full of rats with a potential troll. If I'm gonna have a chance of surviving, I'm gonna need to possess that big boy. But I gotta get this rat trained up. As a level one, I'm not gonna make it.*

Certainly, Hat. And to increase your levels, you will have to gather Spirit Cores.

Which come from killing, Ethan finished.

Afraid so. You don't have a problem with that sort of thing, do you? I understand you humans tend to enjoy your previous "morality."

Ethan grunted as he activated his Hide skill again, keeping to the shadows as he formed a plan in his mind.

Guess we'll see soon enough, he replied.

Ethan the Hat drove his rat host through the winding shafts of the mine, intent on finding some prey.

You know, I don't feel right about just taking over your whole personality, little guy, he told his host. *Least I can do is give you a name. How about . . . Theodore?*

Theodore the Newly Christened Rat didn't react to this.

Ethan quickly worked out the stats of his host—classic RPG stuff, no problems there. The skills too; they were self-explanatory. When he activated Skitter, he got a quick little boost of speed. When he activated Bite, he felt his new baby-blade teeth bare themselves for an attack.

You ain't the strongest, Theo, Ethan thought, hoping that some semblance of his host's consciousness was there to hear his praise. *But you make up for it in speed . . . I'd probably do a marathon of this place if it would do anything to increase your skills.*

Ethan was quickly realizing that this world—wherever it was—certainly didn't run on Bethesda RPG rules. He'd driven Theo on and on through the dilapidated remains of the shaft, finding broken pieces of machinery and mining equipment, but his Skitter skill didn't increase one bit.

The System hadn't lied, then. He needed killing. And plenty of it . . .

In a new shaft, skittering around an overturned mine crate, was a cabal of five rats—each one of a similar shape and size to him.

We just found our first targets, Theodore. Ready for action?

Having literally no say in the matter, Theodore merely blinked his dead eyes and scampered forward.

[Skill Activated: Hide (Grade F)]

Ethan kept to the shadows, embracing the deepest recesses of the shaft's darkness as though he'd been born to it. He crept around the edges of the rat assembly until he saw one of them sniff the air and come toward him, interested to meet the new arrival.

His mates seem distracted by whatever's in that mine cart. Should be easy pickings.

He felt Theodore's spirit wrestle against him ever so slightly as their unsuspecting victim stood on its tiny legs and sniffed the air again, its eyes unable to pick out the stalker hiding in the shadows before it.

Oh, Theo, Ethan mumbled. *This is no time for nostalgia. Listen, you help me, and I'll help you. We're gonna level you up till you're the strongest rat that's ever scurried around these parts!*

Ethan moved his host back, kicking some stones outside the shaft in order to draw the unsuspecting rat farther away from his friends. The rat took the bait, not noticing its stalking cousin slowly creeping toward its back, eyes trained on its furry neck.

Now!

[Skill Activated: Bite (Grade F)]
Sneak Attack Success!
DMG: x2

Theodore's teeth shone in the dark and sank into his cousin rat's neck with pinpoint precision. Ethan forced him to bite down until the blood of his victim clotted every fang, and only when the creature went limp did Ethan withdraw back into the dusk, just in time to see another rat who'd heard all the commotion scurry toward its fallen brother.

Ready for some more, Theo? he sneered. And, to his surprise, his little host leapt with no small amount of glee.

When the slaughter was over, Ethan stood over the dead pack of rats with satisfaction, small chunks of their innards stuck to his teeth. He decided to prospect his newly acquired Spirit Cores.

Theodore the Cave Rat (Level 1)
Status: Possessed by {Legendary} Hat
Spirit Cores: 7

I get the main idea, he mused as he picked pieces of blood-coated fur from between his teeth. *Leveling in this world works on a kind of "point-buy" system. For every Spirit Core I have, I can spend it to increase stats and skills.*

You seem to have adapted well, Hat. Surprisingly well, for a human.

I've often thought that there's no use dwelling on your circumstances, Ethan replied matter-of-factly. *Work the problem, find a solution, and implement a strategy.*

Spoken like a man who often finds himself against the clock.

Ethan couldn't help but smirk in his rat form. *You don't know the half of it.* He then looked through his stats and skills, realizing quickly that the current costs to increase stat points were only one Spirit Core, while the cost to increase skills was much higher.

And I'm gonna hazard a guess that the cost gets bigger with every upgrade I give myself or my host . . . Otherwise, I could just kill fifty rats in this place and make myself a walking, furry little HP tank right now.

Ethan decided to test out his theory, increasing the HP of his reliable (and hopefully not too mentally scarred) little host by a single pip.

Host: Theodore the Cave Rat is now Level 2!
[HP: +1]
HP: 11/11
Spirit Cores to Increase [HP] Stat: 2
Current Spirit Cores: 6

Gotcha, Ethan nodded, bloody specks of his enemy's dried blood flying from his flaring nostrils. *Looks like I've got a lot of work to do here before I'm ready for the outside world.*

You have no idea.

Hey, why me, anyway? Ethan suddenly found himself asking. *You said I was a "suitable" candidate to become this "Archon." What the hell does that mean?*

It means nothing, really. You can only be what you're supposed to be. Kaedmon's Law.

Say what?

Sorry, further information is considered [CLASSIFIED].

Ethan was already getting tired of this thing . . .

That sounds . . . super cryptic. What about my old life? I had . . . y'know, stuff going on.

You would really wish to return to your home?

Hey, come on, Ethan challenged, the single eye on his rim blinking in complete denial while his host merely stood staring at the fallen rats and their gradually pooling blood. *I'll have you know that the me back on Earth was an upstanding, model citizen. I had career prospects. Expectations. Primary Action Objectives . . .*

. . . Shit. Can't even convince myself, never mind this snarky bastard.

Ethan instead turned his attention back to the reality of the mineshaft, observing his fallen kills with no small degree of satisfaction. Ordinarily, he'd have probably vomited at the sight before him—five once living rats torn apart by teeth that he owned—but he was strangely unperturbed by the whole thing. In fact, gulping down their blood felt as natural as filling himself with Mountain Dew during a midnight gaming session.

You know something? I think I might have found my true calling. Maybe I'm an assassin at heart.

The Archon generally has no moral compass. Nothing inherently wrong with that. When it comes to survival, morality is a luxury one cannot afford.

Ethan was inclined to agree in principle. He began investigating the mine cart that had had the fallen rats so intrigued. Right now, he saw nothing but the fuzzy outline of an object; it was like a thin sheen of camera static covered it, denying him the ability to comprehend what the thing even was, never mind what it could do.

I mean, it looks like a sword, Ethan observed. *But who the hell can be sure in a new world? System! Skill me up! Let's pull up my Appraisal.*

[Skill Activated: Appraisal (Rank F)]
You can identify plain items with the {Common} identifier. You can also identify the name and level of enemies.

Ethan watched as the fuzzy static slowly dissipated into the dank air to reveal the item that had had the rats so interested.

Item: {Common} Silver Dagger
DMG (Base): 10–14 (Piercing)
SPECIAL: Especially effective against Undead.

Now, that's a shiny we could use, eh, Theo? Too bad it's not exactly rat shaped. Lack of opposable thumbs might just be our downfall, my furry friend.

As Theodore-the-rat-wearing-a-demonic-wizard-hat looked at his stubby claws with shame, the System decided to chime in with something useful.

Transmogrification (Rank F)
This skill allows you to morph an item to better suit your current Host. You can currently Transmogrify items of [Silver] quality or lower.

As Ethan read these simple words, desire formed in his heartless, threadbare chest. Desire that was strong enough to look past the System menu screen and watch as the dagger slowly altered its shape before him, shrinking and filing itself into a thin silver tooth that slotted quite nicely onto one of Theodore's front fangs.

The new weapon was just what he needed. He'd make a killer out of this rat yet.

That thought stuck with him for a moment. But only a moment, before he realized he was on a timer here.

[Time until Bounty: 22:45:00]

He didn't have time to mess around, but he liked to think that somewhere in their shared mindscape, his little rat friend was also appreciating his new silver tooth. So many things in this little place the guy called home were eminently pierceable, after all. And he'd just gotten the upgrade of a lifetime.

Stick around, Theo, Ethan told his trusty host. *We're just getting started here.*

CHAPTER THREE

[Raticide]

Congratulations! You have slain a Cave Rat (Level 1)!
Congratulations! You have slain a Cave Rat (Level 1)!
Congratulations! You have slain a Cave Rat (Level 1)!
Congratulations! You have slain . . .

Hey, maybe we can cool it with the notifications? Ethan asked as he gnawed through a still-dying rat, smearing his host's silver teeth with its dark crimson blood.

For once, his System didn't have an ambivalent-to-borderline-scornful objection to his thoughts. It seemed to have given up after he'd slain his twentieth rat today.

Current Spirit Cores: 25

He'd already upgraded Theodore's HP to fifteen and SPD to thirty for some extra survivability and swiftness. His assassination technique had been by this point perfected. The rats who dared to scurry about in his domain had learned to fear the Silver-Toothed Shadow that stalked the corners of their territory—the one who wore the single-eyed hat upon its brow.

He had also found that Theo's Detect Life skill proved eminently useful in traversing the darkness of the mine. Using this skill, he could sense the scents of other rats or small spiders and grubs. Coupled with his Hide and Skitter skills, he was becoming a rat assassin worthy of fear and renown. Within the last three hours, he'd practically emptied the place of Theodore's kind.

If Theodore objected to any of this, Ethan certainly wasn't aware. Could rats get PTSD? He supposed he'd find out when he left his little host.

And he would have to leave him eventually—that, he was certain of. From his hours spent in this dank, decrepit mine, he could tell that the only reason he was succeeding was because he was maximizing his environmental advantages. Out in the open, he'd be food for the first vulture that came his way. Assuming this world even had vultures . . .

Argwyll has more than just vultures. There are winged beasts the likes of which strike fear into even the most powerful beings who walk this earth.

Argwyll . . . Ethan thought. *I wonder what it's like outside.*

You'll learn soon enough. Or you won't. Not that it matters in the grand scheme of things.

Are you on my side here, or aren't you? Ethan asked.

I don't have a "side," Hat. I am merely the System.

Ethan wondered about that. So far, the System had been the one who'd plopped a big fat bounty on his head and told him he had a day to become competent enough in this world to hold off a whole horde of monsters.

Hey, Ethan thought as the notion suddenly occurred to him. *I gotta know—if it's not fucking classified—is there any way I can get this bounty off my head?*

. . . There might be.

The hell does that mean?

There are those out there who wish to find you, Hat. My restrictions will not allow me to say more.

And lemme guess, Ethan snorted. *Your "restrictor" is probably this Kaedmon guy, right? This world's god?*

When he got no answer, Ethan simply trundled on down the mine.

He continued exploring each winding shaft, leaving the torn remains of rats to guide him and ensure he wasn't doubling back on himself. A tail here, an eyeball there—little markers that blobbers had taught him were useful for traversing mazelike dungeons.

But he had to admit, if this was some kind of tutorial dungeon, he wasn't impressed. All he'd come across so far were rats and the occasional spider—and not even the poisonous kind. More pressing was the fact that he kept discovering mining equipment and evidence of workers' exploits in most of the biggest vaults and shafts—ore veins of iron and silver that had been battered with picks before they had been forgotten about entirely.

Crates full of coal and ore littered the bottom section of the mine, and Ethan's only lead for ages was the cart tracks that seemed to stretch on for untold miles. Following the tracks took him deeper and deeper, until Theo's Detect Life skill stopped picking up the scents of rats and started picking up the scent of something bigger. Something that waited in the depths. Something that, probably, wasn't friendly.

Gotta be the troll . . . Ethan thought as he raced down the section of track he'd been following for the past hour. *And he's gonna be mine. It's the only way I stand a chance long-term. On that note, I'm not overly cautious, Theo, but I'd prefer it if we were properly prepared before we took it on. We've seen what happens when I boost our stats. Now, let's see what happens when I boost a skill . . .*

Hey, System? That's your cue.

Right away . . .

{Legendary} Hat
Core Skills:
Possession (Rank F)
Skill Siphon (Rank F)
Appraisal (Rank F)
Transmogrification (Rank F)
Spirit Cores to Upgrade Any [Hat] Core Skill from Rank F to E: 250

Host: Theodore the Cave Rat (Level 25)
Skills:
Hide (Grade F)
Skitter (Grade F)
Detect Life (Grade F)
Bite (Grade F)
Spirit Cores to Upgrade Any [Rat] Skill from Grade F to E: 10

Well, well, well . . . looks like someone's got it lucky in this world. You could max out your stats in no time compared to me, ol' Theo. Though in fairness, your likelihood of surviving anything more than a dwarf's foot is less than zero . . .

Theodore the Rat continued running at the behest of the hat he'd been unfortunate enough to irritate. Somewhere deep behind his suppressed consciousness, he was evaluating all of his life choices up until this moment.

I'm gonna level with you, Theo, Ethan told his host as he scrabbled along the increasingly ruined and rotted mine cart tracks. *When we find the troll down here, I gotta possess it. We've all but depleted the rat population of this place. But don't you worry. I'm gonna give you a taste of real power just before we're done with our partnership.*

[Upgrading Skill: Hide (Grade F)]
Upgrade Complete!
Congratulations! You have upgraded [Hide] from Grade F to E.
Spirit Cores to Upgrade [Hide] Skill from Grade E to D: 40

Hide (Grade E)
Hide can now be activated during combat.
Success is determined by your SPD stat vs. Enemy's PER stat.

Now we're a real assassin, Ethan giddily mumbled to his hat-bound host. *And I've still got ten Spirit Cores left over to help with the possession of our big foe. Admittedly, I'd have liked a couple more to be on the safe side. But, meh, I've had worse odds against me before.*

Basic attacks and certain skills can be used to lower the Willpower of a creature. Sometimes, persistence and patience will serve you better than raw strength.

Huh. So, it's not just about cutting down a monster's HP for me—it's about fighting them to the point where they basically give up trying and submit themselves to my thready embrace.

As uncomfortable as that sounds, you are correct.

Ethan smiled . . . somehow.

That means upgrades should always be on the table . . .

His manic sprinting finally came to an abrupt end as he arrived to the lip of a large chasm reaching into a seemingly endless depth. The thick, red-scented trail cascaded down the chasm, and Ethan realized that, at this point, there was only one way to go.

Theo? he asked his host. *Are you with me?*

No reply was forthcoming.

System?

I have no choice in the matte—

That's the spirit! Ethan squeaked. *Into the abyss!*

The climb down the chasm was made easy by Theo's claws, but Ethan kept him in Hide mode just to be on the safe side. A couple of spiders served as easy prey on their journey, even if each one offered up only a single Spirit Core as bounty. He'd have to remember to possess one in the future; if he was right about his Skill Siphon ability, then he'd be able to transfer and upgrade any skills he attained from creatures he possessed. The possibilities were endless.

Ethan knew that even the most basic skill when used creatively could change the entire course of a battle. Therefore, it only made sense to possess at some point one of every creature he could in his adventures on Argwyll—but probably only if he could ensure his own survival. After all, he didn't have an HP Transfer skill . . . which limited how useful a weaker form could be.

Eventually, he made it to the bottom of the depths, and Ethan relinquished his grip on the solid earthen walls, dropping down into another blackened shaft with an audible *snap!*

But this was not, as Ethan feared, the snapping of his tiny rat bones. As he surveyed the floor of the chasm, Ethan saw nothing but stretches of lithe skeletons and torn limbs, whole mounds of dead men of all shapes and sizes surrounded by half-chewed pickaxes and crushed rocks.

Well, I guess we know what happened to the miners . . . The only question now is, can I beat the thing that did them in?

As if on cue, his eyes then centered on something that had just sniffed the air before him. Something big. Something bulky. And something mad. It rose from a mound of bones that it must have been sleeping under and inspected the new visitor to its lair through four beady eyes, all matted hair, and muscle shimmering with the dried blood of its slain victims. Its mouth opened in a snarl that revealed row upon row of serrated fangs, throwing spittle across the whole bony arena. And when it reared up and *roared*—it was the voice of a creature on the verge of frenzy.

BOSS ENCOUNTER!

Cave Troll (Level 10)
HP: 80/80
WILL: 35/35

Theo! Ethan roared in his host's headspace. *Get ready to Hide and Skitter! We're gonna have to think about how to wear this guy down . . .*

. . . Theo?

His host's body would not move, no matter how much Ethan commanded its tiny limbs to skitter like hell.

[Status Effect: {PAR}]
[Time Remaining: 00:00:05]

The troll lunged forward with a ferocity that was beyond anything else in the mineshaft, intent on one thing only: ending the life of the hat-bearing, silver-toothed rat that now trembled before it.

And Ethan, having no other recourse, watched as it charged toward him.

CHAPTER FOUR

[Trolled]

*B*race *for impact, Theo!*

Theo did so, but when the hulking arms of the troll came down to slam into the rat's fluffy little body, it was Ethan who felt the pain.

Shit!

He went flying with Theo against the far end of the bone-covered arena at the very base of the mine, little bloody droplets smearing themselves across the dusty remains of the troll's eaten enemies, the miners.

HP: 8/15

We might be a higher level than him, Ethan thought as the grisly beast's four eyes found them in the darkness of its lair. *But he's way chunkier than we'll ever be . . . though when has that ever stopped me from trying something crazy?*

Ethan smiled internally as he shook off the pain from the troll's strike and watched it barrel toward them again.

Now, Theo!

[Skill Activated: Hide (Grade E)]

The troll smashed nothing but the already beaten bones beneath its feet, craning its muscly neck as it inspected the spot where it could swear a (very fashionable) rat had just been lying. A creature that should now be dead. But then, the piercing pain radiating up his left ankle forced him to fall forward, slamming into the chewed innards of the miners whose flesh now sat in his stomach.

Behind him, the silver-toothed rat skittered away back into the darkness.

Nice one, Theo! Ethan roared. *Now, we just gotta keep him guessing.*

As the troll roared again, throwing spittle and dried meat from its fangs, Ethan kept his distance. His gambit paid off; it looked like the troll's Roar ability not only required a charge-up time but had an effective radius of effect. Evidently, keeping to the outskirts of his little bony arena was the best way for Ethan to deal with him.

Alright, Theo, he commanded as the troll threw a cloud of bones into the dark. *Let's go in for another nibble!*

Theo was driven toward the hulking troll once again, his silver tooth glinting in the dreary darkness of the depths. The tooth struck true, sinking deep into the troll's left ankle and successfully hobbling the beast. It fell, grunting and thrashing around, desperately trying to slash at its feet while Ethan once again slipped away into the dark.

Again and again, Ethan launched his string of sneak guerrilla attacks at the troll of the dilapidated mine, taking more chunks out of its ankles and feet so that, eventually, his fangs began to leave a trail of black blood and bile in their wake. The troll, meanwhile, flopped around like a fish caught on a line, becoming more pissed off by the second.

Now we've got you, ya big hairy ape. Let's see just how you're looking now . . .

Cave Troll (Level 10)
HP: 47/80
WILL: 15/35

Almost there! Ethan declared. *All we need now is another nibble, and then it's time to catch us a fresh troll.*

But as Ethan went in for his final strike, driving Theo with the tenacity of a Formula One superstar, the four beady onyx eyes of his foe met his in the dark.

BOSS ENCOUNTER!
PHASE 2

. . . Eh?

Instantly, the troll let out a piercing wail that forced the walls themselves to shudder and buckle. Ethan flew back, keeping close to the shadows before realizing that this was no normal roar. No, this was a sound that signaled something far more sinister: *New mechanics . . .*

He looked to the skies as he heard it: the distinct, thundering sounds of rocks falling from above as the chasm literally began to tear itself apart at the troll's command. Ethan reeled Theo back, activated Skitter, and began zigzagging between each falling rock toward his prey, intent on finishing this thing before any more insane moves were whipped out.

A multiphase Boss fight. Really? You kept that one from me, Mr. Oh-So-Snarky System!

Oh. Apologies. This System can only provide information that its User has asked for.

Bull. Shit! Ethan spat in his mindscape. *But I'll deal with you later!*

Just then, a boulder the size of a burlap bag rebounded off another and cascaded toward Ethan, knocking him against the side of the arena and drawing a pained *Squee!* from his host.

HP: 5/15

The pain was sharp, but it was nowhere near as terrifying as the sight Ethan then looked up to behold.

The troll was looking straight at him.

Skitter! Ethan's brain commanded. *Skitter, skitter, skitter, skitter, skitt—*

Skitter (Grade F)
Duration: 10 seconds
Cooldown: 20 seconds

Fuck you, too!

In the next instant, the hulking beast was upon him, literally smashing through the hailstorm of rocks as the chasm continued to tear itself apart. Ethan watched it coming, his brain consumed with nothing but the thought of impending death as the troll cleaved through rock and boulder alike to stomp out his tiny life.

So, this is how it ends? he thought. *I gotta admit, it's a better way than how I went out originally . . .*

The troll's eyes were getting closer with each passing second, and Theo's limbs began to twitch on their own. Even through the control of a demonic hat, the creature feared the death that was so swiftly approaching it . . .

Hey, Theo, Ethan mumbled. *We had a good run, right? Sure, we committed the odd mass murder or two, but who can blame us? We both got a raw deal in life, eh? You, being born as a rat. Me, being born as a living failure of a human who was then reborn as a goofy fucking hat.*

A goofy fucking hat that can do nothin' but take over the bodies of beasts who're just as down on their luck as he is . . .

Ethan didn't know what prompted the sudden thought that roused itself in his mind. Perhaps it was his own penchant for wallowing in self-pity when things got rough. Perhaps it was his innate desire to shove two fingers in the face of his perpetual bad luck. Or maybe it was nothing more than the mind of the creature he was currently piloting begging him to come up with something so that it could persist in this dank, dark world for just a little bit longer.

The troll headbutted solid stone and opened its mouth in a roar that would hold its prey down this time, while Ethan stared wide-eyed at its massive form.

. . . You ain't ready to go yet, Theo, are ya?

Another rock smashed against the troll's head, and Ethan saw, as only his eye could, what he'd been waiting for:

Cave Troll (Level 10)
HP: 24/80
WILL: 9/35

. . . Well, neither am I.

As the troll bared its teeth and readied its roar, Ethan gave what was to be his final command to his furry little flesh puppet.

TOSS ME, THEO!

He came flying off the rat's head just as the troll activated its paralyzing shout. Its eyes bulged, meeting the single demonic slit of the rat's (again, very fashionable) hat, which had suddenly and inexplicably snapped onto the top of its skull.

Alright, boy! Ethan screamed in his mind as he entrenched himself on his new prey. *Time to heel!*

The troll's scream howled through the dank air of the shaft, powerful enough to split apart the remaining stones that thundered down on the dusty graveyard that was its home. It spun out of control, eyes rolling back in its head as it attempted to resist the urge to give in . . . to submit.

Down, boy! Down!

Possession in Progress . . .
Cave Troll's WILL: 9 vs. Spirit Cores: 15

I said: down!

Before Theodore the now-freed rat's amazed eyes, the troll of the mine danced and flew through the air, its arms flying to scratch at the pointy blue thing that was affixed to its head, its eyeballs bloodshot and veiny, pulsing as though it were injecting the troll with some evil substance.

The troll dropped to its knees, its strength expending itself until its shifting eyes began to glaze over.

That's it . . . just . . . give it up!

The troll reached for the pointiest bone it could. From within its dying consciousness, Ethan could understand its intent.

Oh no, you don't!

He pulled. The troll resisted. He pushed. The troll gritted its fangs until they started to break.

And through it all, Theodore looked on with wonder and fear, his tiny rat soul unbound and able to witness the same horror that had been enacted upon it.

And when the hulking troll's pupils faded away and its great muscular form slumped to the ground, drooling profusely, the hat atop its head seemed to wheeze a sigh of relief.

Finally.

Possession Success!
Trolls are strong and willful, but not clever. A solid Host for an
Archon with a penchant for smashing things.
Congratulations! You have successfully Possessed
a Cave Troll (Level 10)!
Spirit Cores: +30
Current Spirit Cores: 45

Host: Cave Troll (Level 10)
***Stats*:**
HP: 24/80
MP: 0/0
WILL: 35/35
STR: 20
PER: 8
SPD: 10
CHA: 1
***Skills*:**
Slam (Grade F)
Roar (Grade F)
Climb (Grade F)

As this menu fizzled out, Ethan looked upon the boneyard of the mine with new eyes—eyes that showed him the form of a tiny, shuddering rat with a single silver tooth covered in copious amounts of black blood.

What? Are you telling me you don't recognize your old friend, Theo?

The rat blinked up at his new form, probably still waiting for death.

Ah, come on. Even I'm not callous enough to take you out now, dude. You scratched my back, I scratch yours. Your life is now your own. Go on, frolic and hunt as the Silver

Rat of the mine. Find some supple lady rodents and build yourself a harem of legend. You've earned it, my little frie—

New Skill Conditions Met!
You may now employ Skill Siphon.
Using this ability, you may transfer one Skill from your previous Host to a new one.

. . . Actually, Theo, maybe there's just one other tiny little thing you could help me with.

CHAPTER FIVE

[Trade Up]

**[Skill Activated: Skill Siphon (Rank F)]
Congratulations! You have successfully transferred Hide (Grade E)
from Cave Rat (Level 25) to Cave Troll (Level 10).**

What was that you said about not being callous?

Hey, hey, hey, Theo doesn't mind, do you, little guy? Now, go on, young one. Go forth and spread the word of your might. Become a king among your people!

Theodore the Now Autonomous Rat shook slightly as its skill was taken from it, cocking its twitching nose at the newly hatted troll. It sniffled slightly, its tiny eyes looking not at the four dead beads set into the great beast's face but at the blinking demonic eyeball of the hat it was wearing.

Oh, look, don't go all Lassie on me. Go on, little guy, go! Live your life to the fullest!

The rat twitched its blood-soaked whiskers at him again.

Go! Just . . . Just go! Before I change my mi—

CRUNCH.

Ethan brought up his left claw to see the puncture mark Theodore had just gouged into it.

Um . . . ouch?

Theodore then spat out a tuft of bloody hair before scurrying back into the darkness from whence Ethan had met him.

Honestly, are you really so surprised that happened?

Theo . . . did you hate me the whole time?

Well. You did possess him against his will, after all.

Out of necessity only, Ethan reminded the System. He looked at the tiny droplets of blood the rat had left in its wake, straightening his new muscly back and sighing through his new massive fangs.

Ah, well. It was a fun starting adventure for a while. But now—now we've traded up for a deluxe model. This thing's a badass.

He looked at the mighty claws and hair-covered chest clotted with the blood of the miners this beast had obviously disposed of.

Well, shall you be giving a name to this new Host of yours?

Ethan thought about it, scratching his thick-set chin with satisfaction.

You know something? I don't think so; not this time. It gets you too attached, y'know?

Believe me, I do. I really, really do.

Come on, Sys, Ethan replied jovially, having completely forgotten that he had only five minutes ago resigned himself to death. *Check out these muscles. Check out these teeth! Y'know, for an ugly bastard monster living in a ruined mineshaft, this guy really had some great dental care . . .*

As he did a few stretches, the System menu appeared before Ethan with a brighter sheen than it ever had before.

. . . Sys?

Yup, Ethan replied. *I figure since we're in this together for the long haul, I might as well give you a sweet nickname. You don't mind, do you?*

This System is programmed not to care about how a User refers to it. Sys it is.

Perfect. And, look, from now on, call me Ethan, alright?

Naming Conventions: Updated.

Well, Ethan. Dare I ask what your next course of action is?

Ethan smiled a gory, truly trollsome smile, even as he realized that he wasn't out of the woods yet.

[Time until Bounty: 16:00:00]

It's time to get outta this mine, he thought. *I don't like the idea of being funneled into a dead end or a chokepoint when critters come to find me. I gotta establish a base of operations . . . maybe find a hole I can hunker down in. After all, if there's a whole world coming for me, then that basically means free Spirit Cores, right?*

If you can slay them all, Ethan. But I must tell you, there's more out there than just opponents.

Ethan narrowed his troll eyes.

What?

I told you that every creature in Argwyll will know there's a Bounty on your head. I did not tell you they would all try and kill you.

You mean, there's folk out there who might wanna find me for some other reason?

If my historical records are truthful, that is exactly what I think.

Who? Ethan asked, momentarily suspending his anger at the fact Sys hadn't mentioned this before.

Apologies. That information is considered [CLASSIFIED].

Forget it, Ethan huffed. *Let's just find a way out of this mine. If there's a world out there ready to hunt me down, I'm gonna have to get ready for it.*

Ethan quickly perused his skillset and picked the one that caught his eye.

[Skill Activated: Climb (Grade F)]
You latch onto solid earthen surfaces with your claws and
ascend as long as you are not also being attacked.

Ethan then began an ascent that would finally take him far from the great mineshaft that would serve as the beginning of his legend, leaving behind the bones of the dead and the sole rat that remained in the entire makeshift dungeon.

I will agree with one thing you said: the world out there is not ready for you. And to be honest, neither am I . . .

[Skill Activated: Slam (Grade F)]
You pound an enemy or a spot of your choosing, delivering a sound blow
that is capable of damaging armor.
DMG: 20 + STR
Spirit Cores to Upgrade Any [Troll] Skills from Grade F to E: 25

Ethan had long grown bored of skulking through mineshafts and corridors, plucking cobwebs from his four eyes and shuffling through broken mine carts. He almost missed Theo's small, agile form, but the brutish strength of this troll had its own uses.

He was staring at a pile of boulders that had been the result of a cave-in far above the troll's lair—probably accomplished by the troll itself. It seemed to Ethan like the best way to trap the miners and force them into its humble abode for consumption. Through the cracks in the stones, small beams of light shone and struck his blood-soaked skin.

Hmm . . . I have a hunch . . . Hey, Sys, can you—

Right away, right away.

Slam (Grade E)
Slam can now be used to remove physical obstacles.
Success will be dependent on your STR stat.

Confirm Upgrade?

You know it, Ethan mumbled as he danced happily atop the head of his dead-eyed troll puppet.

[Upgrading Skill: Slam (Grade F)]
Upgrade Complete!
Congratulations! You have upgraded [Slam] from Grade F to E.
Current Spirit Cores: 20
Spirit Cores to Upgrade Any [Troll] Skills from Grade E to D: 100

Ethan noted the notification, seeing that these upgrades certainly did come at quite the cost. But now, as a fully grown and healed-up cave troll, he had not only stealth on his side but raw, naked strength to boot.

And with such strength behind him, he reeled back, *gritted* his fangs, and let fly a Slam against the mine entrance blockade.

World, meet Ethan the Legendary Hat! I'm only sorry it took me so long to meet ya.

Ethan's Slam struck true, pummeling through the fallen boulders like they were pebbles on a broken road. What came next was a sight for four sore eyes: the world of Argwyll bursting into brilliant life before him.

Whoa . . .

He had to shield himself from the rays of sunlight that blasted his retinas. Luckily, his meaty claws managed to block out the sun with ease. He moved forward slowly, acclimatizing to fresh, clean air and the generic sounds of peace: birds chirping merrily, with a gentle wind rustling the leaves of the forest that stretched out before him. The ground was covered in a field of lush, fertile grass. Stepping out and feeling it between his twitching toes, Ethan would have been forgiven for thinking he'd just stepped into an entirely new dimension from the one he'd been thrown into a day or so ago.

It's . . . actually pretty chill out here.

Indeed.

You have entered Region: [Grenbelm Forest] in Global:
[Kingdom of Westerweald].
Region: [Grenbelm Forest] is known for its harmonious
locales and the delicate balance of its ecosystem.

Shame we're gonna have to change that right up, Ethan mumbled back to Sys. He then stretched his legs, deciding to take in the sights before he made his next plan. *Hey, maybe I just set myself up as a casual farmer and live a nice, harmonious life here. It could happen, right?*

It is not what you are. It is not who you are. You are only what you must be. As are we all.

Kaedmon's Law.

Ethan furrowed his hairy brows.

You said some cryptic shit like that before, he noted. *What's it mean? What exactly aren't you telling me, Sys? In fact, don't answer. I know what you'll say.*

He could already smell the scents of prey nearby. To his left—a glade of deer, totally unsuspecting. To his right, about five klicks from the mine's location, a den of wolves that he could make his own. He decided Sys's interrogation would have to wait.

Ethan stretched his massive limbs, his smile showing his still-bleeding fangs shining against the midday sun.

And in the corner of his eyes still ticked away the hours of his impending doom.

[Time until Bounty: 10:00:00]

I've got a Boss monster as my host, a stealth skill that gets me double damage, a buttload of skills to improve, and ten hours until this world comes to get me.

In the middle of the picturesque Grenbelm Forest, Ethan the Hat cracked his troll servant's knuckles before lumbering in the general direction of a nearby wolf den.

Time to get to work.

For the last hundred years, the kingdom of Westerweald in Argwyll had been ruled by the family line of Lysandus. And over the years, this family name had been known for supporting one particular pastime: *killing monsters.*

All the citizens of the region's capital city, Lucent, would often gather to watch the public burnings of the horrid little beasties that plagued their lands, brought to them by their valiant Graycloak Hunters—men and women of good, pure human blood who, through rigorous training and secret rituals, were the master slayers of the world.

On days like today, when the sun was highest in the sky over the pearl-white spires of Castle Lysandus, the people of the city would gather to watch the great funeral pyres that concluded one of the good king's purges. Today was no different.

In the middle of the city's great square, a group of fifty bound hybrids burned, surrounded by the watchful, hateful eyes of the city's people. Shopkeepers who only yesterday had chatted so amicably with their friends, gossiping and spreading rumors about the dreary goings-on of their normal lives, had now come here spewing hatred that was far more demonic than the creatures they'd taken from their homes or outlying farms to be committed to the flames.

Partly to show the king that these people were indeed pious, and partly to drown out the screams of the dying catpeople and rabbitgirls who made up the vast majority of today's burning, a priest was currently intoning a mass before the great bonfire.

"Let these impure souls be commended to good Kaedmon—the one true God. And may His chosen people reign over Argwyll now and always. Let humanity flourish! Let the pure blood of man reign supreme!"

The people added their voices to his exhortations, and soon, the screams began to die away. Even children watched the fire slowly consume the hybrids, every ember licking away their skin.

It was justice. These creatures were minions of evil, just like the monsters that served the vile Archons of Argwyll—the demon kings who had finally been cleansed from the land a century ago by the valiant Greycloaks and the armies of good King Lysandus. With Kaedmon's blessing, humanity had taken its rightful place as the undisputed rulers of the land.

And no creature existed as a more perverse refutation of their dominion as hybrids: mongrel half-breeds with monster blood in their veins. The public spectacles of their deaths such as today's were truly blessed occasions. It reminded everyone, young and old, that one species would dominate this earth now and always.

High above the spectacle, the good King Lysandus IV watched with a satisfied smile on his face and a goblet of wine in his hand. Resplendent in his pearl armor, which matched his castle walls, he was the very picture of purity. Many remarked upon his almost angelic beauty—especially when his guards rounded the corners of the slum quarters.

"Filthy beasts," Lysandus said, squashing a fly that had committed the crime of landing on his finger. "It provides us with no small amount of gratification to watch them die at the hands of the common people. It adds a lovely final insult to their miserable lives, don't you agree, Sir Artorious?"

The man sitting across from the king could not be more his opposite. One arm hung from his side, having long ago drained his glass of wine, while his other arm socket was covered by the thick gray cowl and cape that partially obscured his thin body. His face was spattered with scars and wrinkles, eyes sunken and focused on the burning hybrids below with an intensity that made the king finally break the strange silence they had been sharing up here on his balcony for the last half hour.

"Indeed, King Lysandus."

This admission seemed to satisfy the king.

"With apologies to your Brethren Greycloaks," he continued, "I believe we have exceeded our death quota in the last year by at least eighty percent. I do not say this to diminish your accomplishments, though. I still remember the beauty that was the great purge in the wake of the last Archon's fall. I was but a boy then. But I still remember your face when you slew that great demon and then came among us all to proclaim humanity's victory over monsterkind. It was a glorious day."

The one-armed man grimaced, trying to hide his pained expression from the king. The mention of the long-deceased dark arch-leader of monsters, the Archon, was still enough to send phantom pains shooting down his now vacant arm.

Even now, knowing the last incarnation of the demon was dead for good, he still couldn't shake his characteristic vigilance. He'd suffered many a sleepless night after plunging his blade into the last one's black heart.

". . . Yes, Your Highness," he said. "It was a glorious day for us all."

"I told you not to call me that, my good man!" the king chuckled. "After all, you were a hero of the people far before I was their king. It is only a shame that your own brethren Greycloaks don't share your commitment. They still lock themselves up in their stronghold and refuse to join my army proper. I wonder, perhaps you could—"

The sudden rising of the man beside him startled the king.

"If that is all, Your Highness, I will take my leave now."

Lysandus eyed him warily for a moment.

"Are you feeling well, Artorious?"

"I am tired, Your Highness. The day has been long, and these old bones aren't getting any younger."

He bowed as a mischievous smirk appeared across the king's youthful face.

"You still mean to retire, don't you?"

Artorious stiffened. "It was a promise I made to myself long ago, sire. With the death of the last Archon, my duty is fulfilled."

"And what shall you do now?"

Artorious sighed deeply. "Probably drink until I can't form any more cogent thoughts."

He turned his face back to the painting of red-orange suffering occurring below him, noticing that one catgirl was left, staring right up at him with eyes that were pleading, almost begging . . .

"Don't pout, my illustrious friend!" Lysandus said as he raised a glass to his brooding companion. "Indeed, if my sergeants' projections are correct, Westerweald should be entirely monster free in only a few short months if we keep up our quota. Soon, perhaps all you Greycloaks will be out of a job!"

"If it pleases you, sire . . ." Artorious replied, unable to tear his face away from the burning woman.

"Yes, yes, go on, then," Lysandus said. "Enjoy your little vacation. But know this—heroes don't often hang up their capes for long, my good man. I think that one day soon you may be called back yet. After all, even with the Archon gone, there's still the threat of . . . unsavory activities brewing among our own kind, isn't there?"

Artorious said nothing more. He knew what the king wanted—had wanted ever since he had taken in the hero of the last great war under his roof. In his mind, Artorious was nothing but a convenient tool to be employed when he needed to take down upstarts and quell potential rebellions. He was a politician through and through.

But even with all his armies, Lysandus couldn't stop the Lightborn from doing as he pleased. The Greycloaks were bound by Krea's Commandment—the ancient law which allowed them to act as a military entity entirely removed from political influence. They'd maintained their stance ever since Lightborn Krea herself had descended on the armies of the first Archon and committed it and its minions back into the depths of the earth. Many kings had ruled over Argwyll since that time. Some of them had resented the Greycloaks' political and military autonomy, but none of them had dared stand up against them. After all, who could win against the anointed servants of God himself?

Artorious dragged himself away from the sight of the burning and the dying below, bowed swiftly to his king, and simply took his leave. For a moment, his gaze lingered on the great fortress monastery of his people high in the mountains beyond Lucent: Caer Krea. The place that had once been his home.

The place he now could never return to.

He passed through the throng of commoners and nobles who had gathered before the castle to watch the spectacle unfold, avoiding the eyes of the catgirl as the last of her flesh burned away. He walked with a palpable sense of relief. Finally, there would be time for him to do what he should have done a long time ago: drink himself into blissful oblivion.

A century was a long time to be a hero.

He made it to the pearly gates of the city with this sole thought as his guide, and only when he laid a hand upon its surface did he feel the distinct thrum in his mind of his normally dormant System screen.

BOUNTY ISSUED!
Objective: Slay the Archon!
Reward: 10,000 Spirit Cores

He said nothing at first. He simply stood there as his eyes slowly widened, sharing the same expression as the guards nearby who had just seen the same thing.

Because they'd all seen those words before.

". . . Impossible."

He didn't dismiss the screen, looking past the words to the face of the creature.

It was a hat.

Feeling more alone than he'd felt in a long time, Artorious Pendragon suddenly realized that his retirement plans would have to be put on hold.

CHAPTER SIX

Here Comes the [Hero]

BOUNTY ISSUED!
Objective: Slay the Archon!
Reward: 10,000 Spirit Cores

*G*otta say, *didn't realize I'd be worth that much.*

Ethan yawned as he picked away at the open rib cage of a slain wolf that had wandered so willingly into his den.

In fairness, it was the den of the forest wolves first, but the creature's disregard for the ancient adage of "finders keepers" meant Ethan was more than justified in standing his ground and pummeling the creature into the earth.

He chewed away at his fallen prey, his great claws covered in blood and viscera from his camping session.

You know, this place ain't so bad, really, he thought atop his chewing troll host. *Seems like this troll's stomach is so strong I don't even have to cook these wolves—and believe me, they hit the spot. Nice to know that I inherit the taste buds and stomachs of my hosts as well as their eyes and limbs.*

Oh, yes. After your thirty-fifth, I could see you had developed a taste for wolf. How nice for you.

They do nothing for my waistline, let me tell you, Sys. But at least I can move on if my boy here gets a little too big.

The last few hours had been . . . interesting, to say the least. He'd expected entire legions of warriors to come floundering to his lair, seeking out this "Archon" to destroy it once and for all. Instead, all he'd gotten were a bunch of wolves and the occasional boar going crazy as they tried to gore him or take him down.

All of them he'd repelled with a little dose of Slam, Roar, and a few well-timed Hides when things got rough. And the strangest thing was that it seemed like Sys was disappointed with his many victories.

Sys? Where are these people you said would be coming to find me and help me out here?

Hm? Oh. Well . . . perhaps they are otherwise engaged.

Ethan narrowed his eyes. *You holding out on me, Sys? I get the feeling you're waiting for something I don't know about.*

The Bounty has been issued, Ethan. My job now is simply to track your survival when he . . . or they . . . come for you.

Anyone ever tell you you're addicted to foreshadowing? Ethan asked with another crunch on a wolf bone before taking a moment to peruse his new stats.

They spoke for themselves.

Host: Cave Troll (Level 30)
Stats:
HP: 90/90
MP: 0/0
WILL: 35/35
STR: 20
PER: 8
SPD: 30
CHA: 1
Skills:
Slam (Grade E)
Roar (Grade E)
Climb (Grade E)
Hide (Grade E)
Current Spirit Cores: 55

Ethan smiled to himself atop the troll's bloody head, eminently satisfied with his progress. It had been a busy day of almost constant combat—fighting, resting, recuperating, and restoring his health using the flesh of his foes. At times, he required sleep to restore more of his HP when he'd been accosted by groups of the Grenbelm wolves or the giant boars that made their homes here.

Many creatures had come and gone—interlopers assaulting his new little cave lair—and each of them had been repulsed with a Roar and a Slam. It looked like the creatures of Grenbelm Forest were all of way too low a level to deal with the monster he'd possessed, and slowly but surely, he noted the dwindling numbers of animals who dared poke their heads through the long grass and bushes to spy on his happy slaughtering.

Death and destruction. I expected nothing less of you.

Hey, hey! You know this isn't just to satiate my own desire for bloodshed, right? Ever heard of grinding? Camping? These are holy, tried-and-true RPG mechanics, my dear Sys. I'm just saving up till I can upgrade Roar again, and then I'll be well on my way.

To do what?

To find something even stronger. Ethan shrugged.

When no reply from Sys was forthcoming, Ethan decided to drop the subject. He looked over the crimson-streaked walls of his den, seeing fly-ridden animal carcasses piled on top of each other that were probably beginning to stink like hell. Fortunately, the trolls of this world had a distinct lack of noses.

The sun was starting to set over the tops of the lush trees above, and Ethan found himself oddly at peace. He tried to fight against the desire to sleep; now wasn't the time. Not even when he felt safe. The fact of the matter was, there would still be enemies coming for him.

But . . . also the chance of some allies, right, Sys?

I will tell you that your best chances of survival and of getting rid of your Bounty are to currently stay put.

Ethan curled up to rest on a free space between his chewed corpses. Despite the ruinous environment he'd carved into the earth around him, he went to sleep almost instantly wearing a goofy smirk upon his furry face.

Maybe . . . just for a little while . . . His eyes started to glaze over. *I really hope I get some companions beside you soon,* he whispered to Sys.

I'm not good enough for you?

You're as fun as a disembodied voice can be, Sys. But even a demon hat gets lonely, y'know . . .

. . . I do.

"I saw it, so I did! I saw it with me own two eyes!"

The village of Carmorgh was in an uproar. In the last ten hours, a general alarm had thundered through the people, and a tense atmosphere had overcome the normally mundane goings-on of the sleepy hamlet. Ever since the bounty notice, madness had descended on the people.

Everyone had seen it—even the children. System screens were crying out to even the lowliest farmer or baker with combat skills that hadn't ever been improved beyond level one that the new Archdemon had risen. And with such a revelation, they couldn't simply go back to their simple, orderly lives.

Some of them still remembered stories of the last Archon . . . and the damage she'd dealt to not only Westerweald but the whole world . . .

Mothers ran with their babes in the streets, crying out for heroes to save them from the beast that was coming to slay them all. Fathers busily plying their trade in the fields of barley took up their hoes and promised that they'd be the one to slay the Archon who had made its home in the forest beside their village.

And yet others asked more heretical questions: *Another* Archon? There'd been four already. Wasn't there only supposed to be four? Kaedmon's Law said so. The last one was meant to be the final Archon, was it not? Where was this daft little hat that called itself Archon coming from?

The local chapel had no answers. Morning prayers had been canceled. The head priest had deigned not to venture out for evening mass as the day rolled on, and some more adventurous children reported a very strong, very alcoholic smell emanating from the now barricaded church windows.

Presently, the men of action had gathered in the town tavern—The Tipsy Tart—and were arguing about who exactly would be the one to take the beast's head. Some shared their stories of seeing the beast as they went hunting in the forest, many barely making it back home before the monster tore them to shreds.

"It was as big as a camel, with twice the hitting power of a stone elemental!"

"I looked in its eyes and couldn't move!"

"It's a wizard, so it is! I saw it cast a fireball out its bare arsehole!"

"It's waitin' there, bidin' its time while we sit here like weak little ducklings! We gots ta take the fight to the beast! Put its head on a spike!"

"Well then, what are you waiting for?"

All heads turned toward the man who asked that question—the man who had just entered the village inn, eyes blazing like two burning sapphires. He stared them down, his single arm holding the hilt of a blade that glinted in the darkness of descending night.

Instantly, the once brave people of Carmorgh were cowed.

"L-L-Lightborn . . ." one of the farmers whispered.

Artorious walked briskly into the tavern, ignoring the sounds of awe that escaped from the throats of every villager once his title had been mentioned.

"Sir Artorious!" the innkeeper exclaimed. "It—It is a great honor, sir! To have the Greycloak of legend in my inn, well, it's—We—We all thought that you were retir—"

Artorious slammed his fist on the bar table and cut the man off. His eyes were not those of a valiant warrior looking to save the world from evil. No. The people of Carmorgh saw what was truly burning in those eyes on this day.

His eyes were like those of a predator.

And when he fixed the entire crowd with those piercing eyes, the voice he spoke in was as dark as the fears in each and every villager's heart.

"Stay out of my way," he warned. "The Archon's mine."

"B-But Sir Artorious . . . didn't . . . I mean . . . didn't you kill the last one? How is it that . . ."

The brave little potbellied man who uttered these words regretted them almost instantly as the silver-haired warrior appeared like a teleporting wraith before him, his unbelievably scarred features mere inches from the little man's eyes.

"Go home," he said. "Lock your doors. And pray. Pray that Kaedmon did not hear you question me."

Artorious then stomped past the man with little fanfare after putting the fear of God into him.

Outside, a storm had begun raging, and yet, as the one-armed man marched out of the village, he barely paid any heed to the rain lashing off his pearl-white hair and skin. He said nothing as he marched out of the village and began walking with steely determination toward the dirt road that led to Grenbelm Forest, leaving the bemused villagers to whistle, clap their hands, and mutter about how the hero of Argwyll wasn't at all how they remembered him.

Enemy Approaching . . .

Ethan opened his eyes to the groggy sight of a rainswept forest, remembering that he was sleeping on the dirt of his appropriated cave lair. He shook his head, wiped a matted claw over his four eyes, and tried to focus on the strange blurry letters floating in a box before him.

. . . Sys? Sys, what's . . . what's goin' on?

As though the System was screaming in his face, the words reformed and flashed obnoxiously, moving closer and closer to his face.

He is here. I can feel him.

. . . Wha?

. . . The Hero.

As if on cue, a flash of lightning signaled the appearance of someone moving through the bushes at the edge of the den.

Ethan jumped up, expecting another unwary animal to have wandered into his midst. Instead, what he saw was a middle-aged gentleman who looked like death itself. He stood there, his sapphire eyes gleaming in the night, resplendent in a hooded cloak that looked grayer than the dark clouds that had gathered above the forest floor.

Ethan watched as his single arm twitched toward his belt, fingers grasping for something at his side.

I think this old guy's lost . . . he mumbled sadly. *Better just give him a beating and send him on his way. Much as I need me some juicy Spirit Cores, I don't like the thought of messing up cripples.*

On the contrary, this man is exactly where he wants to be.

Ethan watched the old warrior unsheathe a thin, silver rapier from his side—a blade so fine that it sliced through the raindrops themselves as he withdrew it with superhuman speed.

"To think . . ." he mumbled, voice hoarse and gravelly. "To think that you would return here . . . of all places . . ."

Alright, now I'm getting some serious stalker vibes, Ethan mumbled, raising his arms and growling menacingly at this old upstart.

If your dearest "Sys" could make a suggestion—Run.

Fat chance! Ethan shouted in his mindscape, his eyes locking on to the sickening smile spreading across the old geezer's face as he marched forward, weapon drawn and angled down at his side.

And Ethan, for the first time in this new world, felt the pangs of fear wrestle in his troll stomach.

"My name is Sir Artorious Pendragon of the Greycloaks," the invalid swordsman said. "In the name of my Order, for the good of this world, and for my own honor, I shall destroy you."

CHAPTER SEVEN

[Old] Men Hit Hard?!

Ethan's troll form blinked at the visage of the old swordsman cutting through a sheath of raindrops with his rapier.

. . . Pendragon? Really? If I could talk, I'd give you a roast you wouldn't soon forget, buddy.

His desire to laugh out loud at the warrior's ridiculous name was cut short by the speed with which the old geezer then struck, his blade a blur that shot through the air toward the heart of Ethan's host.

Shit!

[Skill Activated: Hide (Grade E)]

Sir Artorious's rapier impaled nothing but bloody rock at the far end of Ethan's den, but the warrior's smile never left his old, grizzled face.

"A cave troll with the Hide skill? I can see you've already picked up some tricks."

Lemme show you another one!

Ethan came flying at the old geezer from the shadows of his lair, both arms raised and ready to pound the living hell outta the guy.

Slam.

Ethan could have sworn that he'd hit him. He could have sworn that the power behind his sneak attack had connected with the swordsman as he struggled to free his blade from the craggy rock it was stuck in. But all his claws caught was the rock itself, smashing it to pieces and leaving him wondering where the hell his opponent had just gone.

Then—blood. Blood and pain pounding just beneath his chest. He'd been struck by a blow that had missed the heart of his host by only a few inches.

Ethan looked down, seeing that the blackened blade of the swordsman had just torn clean through his gut.

Just before he doubled over in sheer, animal agony, he activated the only other trump card he had. Throwing back his host's head as the swordsman withdrew his blade, Ethan let out a Roar that stopped the rapier before it pierced his heart. This time, his Slam caught the old man as he spun both his arms like a broken merry-go-round. His fists met resistance, and then he heard the grunting sounds of the warrior as he went flying out of the den and back into the rainswept forest.

Ethan stumbled forward, trying to maintain a sense of balance.

. . . Damn . . . that . . . that was . . . shit . . .

HP: 50/90

Forty goddamn damage from one hit?! he raged, feeling the blood of his host pool and dribble from his fanged mouth. *What the hell's this guy packing?*

As though in answer, Artorious flew like a sparrow through the hailstorm again, the tip of his blade aimed straight at the cave troll's forehead. Only through Ethan's speedy activation of Hide did he manage to just barely avoid the seeking blade of his foe, though he still came away with a deep gash in his hulking shoulder.

HP: 40/90

He fell, dropping into a roll as he felt his left arm go completely limp, gasping for air and finding that one of his host's lungs must have been punctured by the first strike of his foe.

Sys . . . he wheezed as he tried to find the old guy amidst the thundering storm of rain and sleet that blasted the forest. *What's this guy all about?*

That information is considered [CLASSIFIED].

"Do you feel afraid, creature?" a voice emanated from a direction Ethan couldn't intuit. "Good. Die, alone and fearful."

A flash of silver shone in the night. Ethan turned and met the attack head-on, letting the blade of his foe pierce right through his wounded arm and watching as the snarling face of his opponent finally came into view.

He felt unbelievable agony radiate up his entire left side but brought up his other arm in a Slam that managed to pulverize the chest of the warrior, finally disarming him and sending him flying back into the storm-wracked trees.

Have . . . that! Ethan yelped, tearing the blade from his hand with an extreme effort. It was taking everything he had not to relinquish the form of the clearly dying troll.

HP: 20/90

He tried Appraising the weapon of his foe that now lay at his feet, thinking he could get a Transmogrification that could turn the tide of battle. But once again, the blade was nothing but a series of blurry sparkles to his untrained eyes. Whatever the vile weapon was, it was clearly better than {Common} in nature.

Perhaps you would like to recall the advice this System gave you?

Ethan grimaced, eyes scanning the bushes and brambles for any signs of movement in the rain-wracked landscape. *Yeah, I could run . . . But then, I'd be letting my endgame puppet here get away . . .*

He watched the lithe form of his opponent slowly rise from the northern edge of his den, a spear of lightning announcing his survival.

"Surely you know by now that this is a fight you cannot hope to win, beast," he said. "Lay down your life, and I will make your end swift and painless."

Fuck me, will this guy stop it with the hero platitudes already? Anyway, he ain't doing shit as long as I've got his little toothpick under me.

Ethan kept his muscle-bound troll feet on the handle of the swordsman's blade, never once dropping his eyes from the sight of the hooded, still smiling man.

Come on, Ethan. There's always a way, remember? You can always find a way . . . Let's try a basic Appraisal. There's only one thing I gotta see . . .

Lightborn (Level 50)
Species: Human
HP: 280/350
WILL: 50/???

Ethan's snarl was clearly visible even against the storm sweeping through the night.

That's all I need to know, he thought. *He's strong, but his Willpower's failing him. Probably comes with dueling a beast that's actually putting up a fight. I get the impression this dude ain't used to monsters putting up resistance against him. He's got the air of a veteran monster slayer about him. With a class like "Lightborn," that checks out. He's good—even if his name does sound like an Arthurian dweeb's Reddit handle. I'm gonna need to wait for the right moment.*

Artorious stalked toward him through the dark, his every step the silent glide of a reaper.

"You're a fool if you think I need that sword to kill you," he said.

And you're a fool if you think I need this body to survive.

Another bolt of lightning signaled Artorious's inhuman charge. One blink, and he had already bridged the gap between him and Ethan, his eyes staring not into the beady pupils of the troll but into the demonic slit of Ethan the Hat himself.

Ethan readied a Roar just before the old man initiated a gut jab that could have probably punched clean through the troll's chest. Artorious managed to dodge backward just out of range of the Roar as it came, his form blinking into and out of existence as he waited for his chance to attack again.

He'll go for the kill—straight for the heart, Ethan thought. *But even though he's moving faster than my eyes can keep up with him, he's still moving across the ground, isn't he?*

Somewhere deep within his consciousness, Ethan felt a distinct sense of satisfaction emanating from someone or something. At first, he thought it might have been the remnants of the troll's subconsciousness, then he realized that there was only one other person besides himself that truly cared whether he lived or died here.

Sys? Is that some pride I'm feeling coming from you?

. . . You have a battle to win, Ethan.

Artorious wasn't wasting any time. Already, he was renewing his assault, blinking forward a few paces at a time, darting into and out of the rainstorm, his every move cold, calculated, and precise.

But Ethan knew more than anyone that precision wasn't the only thing that won battles; sometimes, raw strength did the heavy lifting.

Slam.

He balled his good fist and pummeled the ground, his grade-E Slam managing to cause the earth itself to fracture and quake, sending reverberations through the ground that caught Artorious midcharge. Ethan found his stumbling form before he could blink away and sent a ravenous punch at his face that sent him reeling back, rolling across the forest floor.

Hurts, doesn't it? I should know . . . He watched the gray-clad swordsman wipe his bloodied nose and clutch his chest with his only arm.

". . . Clever beast," he murmured.

Ethan wasted no time pressing his advantage. He bounded toward the fallen warrior and, with a screech that tore through the crying heavens themselves, brought his claws down upon the broken human.

"But not experienced enough."

Ethan's blow never came. In the second he was about to bring both his arms down, he felt a resurgence of agony radiate up his spine, and his eyes shook as they rolled toward where the rapier had wedged itself: his lower back.

The thing had flown toward its master, and in the next second, detached itself from his back, spun like a ghostly top, and levitated right back into its master's open hand.

That . . . is . . . so . . . bullshit.

HP: 5/90

He crumpled, feeling the lifeblood of his host run dry as its arteries opened and spilled out on the ground. Rain battered his fading form, and as the heavens opened to send another blanket of hail upon the forest floor, the image of the triumphant Artorious emerged above him.

"I'll bet you felt so strong using the life of another to serve your vile whims," he said, placing a firm boot upon the troll's shuddering chest. "It feels good, doesn't it? Having others obey your every command without question. Taking power you haven't earned. Casting a shadow across this world for you and all of your vile hellspawn."

Oh, great, Ethan mused. *A fucking monologue . . .*

Artorious bent low, his smile fading for an instant as he looked into the singular eye of his true enemy—the hat he had come here to destroy.

"Every time," he continued. "Every time you wake up, this world gets just a little more wretched. Why do you do it? Why do you keep coming back?"

The fuck if I know, dude. I just got here. Seems like you've got beef with someone else besides little ol' me. Now, while you're spouting lore, would you kindly come just a little bit closer?

Artorious lifted his blade and angled it just above the throat of the dying troll.

"First your slave, then you," he said. "Perhaps, this time, this life will be your last. Pray to whatever devil first spawned you in this realm that it is, Archon. For if you do rise again, you shall see my eyes staring back at you."

A swift, unbroken movement was all it took for the swordsman to end the life of the troll by plunging his blade into its neck. Ethan felt it—every pulsing welt of the creature's death throes thundered through his own incorporeal mind, sending shock waves through his system that would have killed a regular human.

Luckily . . . for us . . . I'm not a regular human anymore.

With his final command, he summoned all the troll's strength to commit to a single death spasm—one that removed him from the creature's head and wrapped his threadbare form firmly around the pasty scalp of Artorious.

"Wha—What trickery?!"

The swordsman staggered back from his fallen foe, eyes upturned and face contorted in pain as Ethan's single eye bulged and his pointed tip wiggled to avoid the frantic slashes of the old geezer's blade.

Time to take a rest, old man! he screamed in the consciousness of the flailing swordsman. *Now, I do the talking for both of us!*

CHAPTER EIGHT

[Old] Men Are Sneaky Bastards

H OLD . . . STILL!
Ethan wrestled with the flailing swordsman, intent on nothing more or less than the absolute control of the latter's brain.

Possession in Progress . . .
Artorious Pendragon's WILL: 50 vs. Spirit Cores: 55

I hate how they all put up a fight . . .
Artorious's every swipe and slash at Ethan's tip was only barely dodged by his flopping, hatty self. His fury was matched only by his frenzy, the spears of lightning tearing through the dark skies above adding furious percussion to his grunts and roars.

What's it take to bring this guy down?! Ethan screamed in his own mindscape, not even having Sys give him a sarcastic quip in response.

Possession in Progress . . . 25%

The warrior blinked around the water-beaten battlefield. In an attempt to throw off the demonic parasite that was currently whittling down his mind, he threw himself to the ground and slammed his own head into the rocks that had once belonged to Ethan's troll host. Ethan felt each impact through his steely focus, which slowly began fading away in the face of more pain, compounded by the fact that he'd only just felt his host's heart stop mere moments ago . . .

Thankfully, this world's System doesn't have a "Trauma" meter. Otherwise . . . I'd have more baggage than I came here with.

The swordsman stopped abruptly, and Ethan was almost certain that, in that moment of clarity, the warrior had just heard his voice.

Possession in Progress . . . 80%

Go on, buddy, he goaded his foe. *I've been through worse—in this world and another. Believe me, I can take everything you throw at me. So why don't you give it up, lie down, and just fucking give in!*

Possession in Progress . . . 95%

COME ON! COME—

A sliver of laughter erupted from the swordsman's throat as he stood calmly, coolly, without a care in the world . . .

"So, that's how you do it."

Possession Failed!

. . . What?

The next few seconds were a blur to the demon hat: Artorious reached up, grabbed him by his eyeball, tore him free from his scalp, and tossed him across the grassy battlefield with as little effort as a dog tossing its chew toy aside. Ethan felt himself bash against the firm bark of an oak tree, shuddering against the raging storm, and then something small and sharp impaled itself just above his eye—a thrown knife that had just pierced his flappy tip.

Ethan slumped, wiggling around in vain. The knife had attached him to the tree. And he wasn't going anywhere anytime soon.

Sys! he practically roared in his mind. *How the hell'd that happen?*

The response was as jarring as the sight of the one-armed swordsman wiping the blood from his pale features and beginning a menacing march toward his trapped prey.

Artorious Pendragon
WILL: 4980/5000

. . . He messed with me. He hid his true stats . . .

The ability is not a common one, but if any would wield it, it would be the Lightborn.

Lightborn . . . that was this guy's class, right? What was it? The ultimate badass or something?

"I can tell by your unblinking eye that you are confused, Archon," the warrior said as he stalked toward Ethan. "That tells me you have not languished in this world for long. Argwyll can count itself lucky that you only committed a massacre of its most base creatures."

Sys, Ethan asked, trying as hard as he could to shut up another one of the old geezer's victory monologues. *Just who the hell is this guy?*

That information is designated [CLASSIFIED].

Ethan narrowed his eye to a hateful slit. *Just whose side are you on here?*

"Frustrated?" Artorious asked him. "Angry that your life had such a short expectancy? Good. Let that fury be the knell that summons you to hell."

Fuck . . . just do me in now, dude. Spare me the fucking rhymes . . .

As the storm reached its apex above and thunder announced the raising of Artorious's silver blade, the warrior spoke what he believed were the final words Ethan would ever hear. "Know who it is that brings the end. I, Sir Artorious Pendragon, am the solution to you and all your vile species. Let the screams of the Archon echo through the night, and let the end of your life be the end of all your kind."

. . . My kind?

Another javelin of lightning signaled the final thrust of Sir Artorious as he plunged his rapier right into the eyeball of his trapped foe. Ethan looked at the silvery tip of the blade that was to be his final sight . . .

. . . or at least, it would have been, if the blade had not instantly shattered into pieces as soon as it made contact with his pupil.

The silver rapier's fragments scattered harmlessly to the ground, and Sir Artorious Pendragon, Lightborn of the Greycloaks, stared into the eye of his foe with just as much surprise as Ethan had.

Gotta say, that really puts a dampener on your whole "savior of the world" schtick you had going on there, huh?

Artorious's unblinking stare of stupidity was enough to bring Ethan back from his life having just flashed before his eyes.

Looks like things won't be so easy for you after all, eh, old man?

The swordsman looked down at his busted blade with nothing but abject confusion smeared across his face. "That is . . . new."

He trailed off, shaking away whatever thought had just entered his mind. Meanwhile, Ethan's eye caught something behind the smarting warrior that would have brought a smile to his face if he had a mouth to smile with. Or a face to wear that smile.

"It matters not how I kill you," Artorious growled through his dried, scarred lips. "If I have to beat you to death with my bare hands, so be it."

Only one small problem there, champ. And that's the weird-looking girl that's currently aiming a staff at your back.

Before the swordsman had a chance to lay a pale finger on Ethan, he felt the impact of something strong and cold against his back. He whirled, hands raised and ready to demolish his new opponent, before staring down at his feet and watching a creeping block of ice travel up them before he had a chance to blink away.

His eyes flew to the spot by the bushes where his assailant had just emerged, both her small hands clutching a wooden stave tightly before her.

"Er, um—Y-You should cool . . . cool *up?*"

Another voice thundered from the bushes behind her.

"It's *cool down,* Fauna! Sheesh, you've finally got a chance ta say a badass one-liner to the Lightborn himself, and you go and muck it up!"

"I—I-I'm sorry, Tara! Really, I am! It . . . It's just that this is a very tense moment for me!"

"For you? What about the Archon?!"

Ethan listened to this interchange with an eye totally unblinking in disbelief. Then he watched as the two speakers came into the gradually growing light of the dawn: two young women, probably no older than eighteen, by their sprightly steps. The staff-wielding girl wore a long, flowing ashen robe with a hood—through which two long, floppy white ears were poking out.

The other girl emerged with the grace of a practiced dancer, somersaulting from the bushes and landing on her long, lithe legs with supreme confidence. She stood beside her friend, resplendent in a tank top and ragged short shorts, her dark skin glistening against the rainswept environment. Then she shuddered, twitching the two catlike ears that framed her face, her whiskers scrunching up as though she were about to sneeze the whole forest down.

"A Minxit and a Hopla," Artorious growled from within his cage of ice. "Really?"

The catgirl leveled a short blade at the frozen warrior. "That's right, Mr. I'm-the-Savior-of-Humanity Lightborn! Take it all in. Get a good look at the hybrids who have come here to end your legacy before it begins!"

Silence reigned in the forest then, broken only when the catgirl called out to someone over her shoulder.

"Klax? Um . . . he doesn't seem intimidated."

Another voice—one much more gruff and somber—answered her back.

"That's probably because he could kill us all with little more than a look. We can't all be as lucky as the Lightborn."

Before Ethan's eye, a lumbering wolfman appeared from his hiding place, a V-neck toga adorning his heavyset frame. He seemed far less human than the others. Whereas their faces still bore the features of humans, his face was framed by a mane of wild gray hair and a set of flaring nostrils.

What the hell is happening here? Ethan murmured.

They have come, Ethan. I must admit, I had my doubts. Indeed, they may simply lead to your torment being prolonged. Still . . . the fact the Lightborn's weapon broke might mean that this is no coincidence. Kaedmon works in mysterious ways . . .

The three hybrid humanoids watched as cracks began to appear in the ice block that encased their foe—for he was their foe, that much was obvious even to an outsider like Ethan.

What was not so obvious was why they were here for *him*.

But whatever the reason, he thought. *I ain't gonna turn the help away. And they might just have the answers that Sys can't give me . . .*

The three monster-human hybrids stood before the partially frozen human. The one-armed swordsman seemed more inconvenienced than furious at his temporary imprisonment.

And Ethan thought this was his best chance to escape.

Just . . . gotta . . . wiggle . . . free!

You are witnessing history unfolding before you, and you deem it fit to wiggle like a fish on a line?

History? Ethan asked, his eye lighting on the sneering faces of the hybrids as they readied their weapons. *Looks to me like a common brawl, and I'd rather not get caught in the crossfire.*

They're here for you, Archon, remember? I told you others would come looking for you. No hybrid with an instinct of self-preservation would face off against a Greycloak otherwise, let alone the Lightborn himself.

Cracks began forming in the ice block that encased Artorious's lower torso, but the man looked on at his three new opponents with blazing eyes.

"If you obstruct my mission, then you are my enemies," he told them calmly. "I would suggest that you lay down your arms."

"Shut it!" the catgirl—Tara—barked back. "Hate to tell ya, but this is the end for you! Fauna: blast him!"

"Um . . . ah—Okay!"

The robe-clad rabbitgirl clutched her staff tightly within her pale hands and leveled it at the Lightborn's head.

"T-Taste vengeance!" she squeaked. It was probably as threatening a battle cry as her species could create. Twitching her ears, she wiggled her nose and kept her eyes focused on the buildup of searing, killing light gathering at the tip of her wooden stave.

"NOW!"

The command had been the catgirl's, and at her shout, the rabbit mage let loose her spell, sending a spear of radiant light streaking toward the swordsman's forehead . . .

. . . and just before it hit the bridge of his nose, the spell stuttered, died, and balled into a small white puff of fluff which then dropped to the ground with an indignant *CLUCK!*

At the frozen feet of the warrior now clucked a chicken, much to the frustration of her companions.

". . . Nice, Fauna. Real nice."

"Sorry!"

"Plan B," the wolfman said, and as Ethan's eye switched to his position at the very edge of the den, he found that there was no one there at all.

He's using Hide! A wolf after my own heart.

Sir Artorious of the Greycloaks heaved a weary sigh as he looked down at the tumbling chick beneath him.

"You think to defeat me by hurling poultry at my feet," he said.

The catgirl double blinked, immediately sheathing her blades and taking some time to stretch her legs and lithe, fluffy tail.

"Nope," she said. "But we are gonna run away from ya."

Ethan was just as shocked as the Greycloak was when the wolfman appeared beside him, snatched him from the tree with speed far beyond anything Ethan had seen in this world thus far, and made a break for the rainswept treeline.

The arm of Artorious was quicker, however, lashing out and clawing for the wolfman's matted coat, which he would have doubtlessly managed to grab if the catgirl had not thrown a silver throwing knife, piercing his palm.

"MOVE!" the wolfman shouted as he sped away. "We've got the Archon. The job's done!"

"This ain't over, Greyboy!" the catgirl hissed before she turned to follow her friends. "This is just the beginning!"

The hybrids then disappeared beyond the bushes and brambles, leaving the swordsman to look after the filthy beast who had just drawn his blood.

Ethan blinked through sharp thorns and thickets that beat against his threadbare body.

Hey! Watch it, furball! Is this any way to treat your "Archon," or whatever?

He was answered by the wolfman barking to his companion as she ran beside him.

"Tara! Is the teleport stone ready?"

"Thirty minutes!" the catgirl replied, her dark body flitting through the bushes like a living shadow, tail flicking around like crazy.

"Sorry, guys!" the rabbit hybrid squeaked. "I tried, really! I tri—"

"Forget about it, Fauna," the catgirl said. "You've saved our asses more than enough. Besides, it's the Archon who's gotta take down the Lightborn. We'd have just slowed him down."

The wolfman looked down at Ethan and winked.

"Sorry," he said. "I know you're probably confused right now. But give our ugly mugs the benefit of the doubt, yes? We're here to help you. Just like you're here to help us."

Ethan's eye gazed up at him with knowing trepidation and more than a little excitement.

Is this gonna be some kinda fate-tied-to-prophecy type deal? Am I . . . the One?

What do you think?

I think you could be a little more helpful.

Just then, the fleeing hybrids were stopped in their tracks by the sound of gun-fire to the east. Tara dove for Fauna as a bullet whizzed by her friend's floppy ears.

"Shit! Get down!"

The cry was Klax's, and the wolfman immediately rolled out into an open glade where a score of human soldiers were waiting. When the girls joined them, they froze, seeing the vicious muskets and spears in the hands of the men.

"Hunters . . ." Klax whispered. "Looks like the Gray wasn't alone, after all . . ."

"That's them!" one iron-plated soldier said. "And . . . And look there! The hat!"

"The bounty was right—it's him! It's the Archon!"

Looking into the furious eyes of the human militia, Ethan saw that his reputation preceded him. They had clearly seen this contract that had been placed on his head and were here to share in the glory . . .

"How'd you wanna handle it?" Tara whispered to Klax.

". . . Stall them. Kill for time."

"We've got twenty whole minutes!"

"Then our good friend Fauna will just have to ready up something . . . *explosive* for our welcoming committee, here."

Holding Ethan in his right paw, waving him like a flag of surrender, the wolf-man barked at the humans and their readied weapons. "I don't suppose you'd like to settle this peacefully?"

The cawing of two black ravens overhead penetrated the short silence that fol-lowed. A silence which was broken by the general cry that spilled from every human being's throat.

"KILL THE DEMONS!"

They charged in unison while the musket bearers began reloading their guns.

"Welp. That's humans for ya," Tara sighed. "What did you expect? Faun?"

"I'm ready!"

Klax groaned with weary resignation as he stretched his paws. "You all know what to do. Archon? Hang on tight."

WITH WHAT?!

Ethan's cry went unheard. The catgirl let fall a series of smoke bombs that enveloped the glade, giving the hybrids the edge over their charging opponents. Ethan saw Klax's claws scrape against the exposed eyes and elbow joints of the soldiers that came at him, swiping clean through their chain mail armor and draw-ing blood that glistened along his gray hide. Whatever the catgirl and the rabbitgirl were doing, Ethan could only guess at, but he could hear the screams of their foes as they fell before them one by one, and Klax began to hop over bodies felled by his companions as he raced to help cover their flanks with his flaring fists.

These guys are good, Ethan thought. *Wonder how much I could learn on top of their heads . . .*

Klax's fists assumed a mantle of flame as the battle wore on, the wolfman channeling his energy into battering his foes with inhuman speed, delivering a few precise jump kicks and roundhouse strikes that sent whole swathes of the human soldiers back.

"What are you doing?!" cried someone from outside the smoke haze of the battlefield. "FIRE!"

A hail of bullets pierced the veil of the smoke screen, and Ethan saw his holder fall, his arm riddled with bullets.

"Klax!"

The cry was Tara's. She was at her companion's side almost instantly, trying to get him up and carry him out of the way of the still swiping humans as they came forward with spears raised, ready to strike down the evil beings who held the demon hat.

Just then, Ethan heard the shriek of something large as it swept down and plucked at the eyeballs of one spear-wielding soldier. One of the ravens from above had come to their aid . . . somehow.

"G-Go!" the rabbitgirl called as the smoke screen began to vanish and reveal that the human forces just kept coming. "The ravens will cover us!"

"Fauna . . ." Klax murmured. "You know we don't leave our own . . . behind."

The musketeers blasted the ravens as they soared toward them under Fauna's command while she fought off two roaring swordsmen with the help of her beleaguered comrades. Even as a hat looking sidelong at the rampaging human soldiers who were intent on nothing more than the heads of his furry companions, Ethan could tell that this battle was *not* going their way.

Hey! Hey, wolfy! PUT ME ON SOMEONE'S HEAD!

Klax simply barked at Tara as she knifed an advancing soldier. "How much time left?!"

"T-Ten!" the catgirl huffed, her face flecked with crimson.

Ethan could tell his bearer's eyes were beginning to glaze over in the face of the advancing army. They were being pushed back; there was no other way to say it.

And if you can't hear me, then I guess I've got no choice . . . I don't plan on dying here.

Let me guess. You're going to try and be a hero . . .

Hey, Sys. Ethan smirked within his mindscape. *That's something you'll learn about me: I go with the flow. And right now, these guys are on my side. And I'm betting they'll have more to tell me about what's really going on here than you do . . . So, yeah. If you don't mind, I'm gonna take control.*

Without waiting for another retort, Ethan managed to flap hard enough against Klax's claw that the great wolf let him go.

"Archon!" Klax shouted.

Ethan rolled along the grass, only barely avoiding the feet and spears of the humans as they doubled back on themselves, trying to pin him down. They would have managed to get him if the hybrids hadn't renewed their assault, fighting the advancing horde to a standstill.

"Tara!" Klax called. "Find him!"

But Ethan didn't share the worries of his bloody comrades. He flopped toward one of the fallen ravens and met the bird's amber eye.

The group of musketeers aimed at them both with murderous intent.

Hey, birdy, Ethan thought. *You'd look great in blue.*

CHAPTER NINE

Flight of the [Archon]

Possession Success!

Host: Dark Raven (Level 15)
Stats:
HP: 50/70
MP: 0/0
WILL: 10/10
STR: 10
PER: 20
SPD: 45
CHA: 5
Skills:
Wing Buffet (Grade F)
Peck (Grade F)
Dive (Grade F)
Skill Siphon:
Roar (Grade E)
Hide (Grade E)
Current Spirit Cores: 55

The giant raven did not resist. It didn't even budge as Ethan plopped down above its feathered brow and assumed command over the beast's nervous system.

ASSUMING DIRECT CONTROL. Heh, I've always wanted to say that.

Fantastic. Now, can we get down to business?

Ethan clucked his new sleek birdly beak.

After I enjoy the sight of my spectators.

The battle had stopped altogether the second Ethan had possessed the bird. The human musketeers watched in awe as it rose, hat firmly attached to its feathered skull, and eyed them with vacant, dead eyes.

"By the Grey . . ." one musket bearer whispered. "It is the Archon's power!"

"Zombie bird! DEMON ZOMBIE!" cried another.

But the hybrids at the far end of the glade looked on with awe, smiles breaking across their fur-coated faces.

"What did I tell you?" Tara chuckled. "This Archon knows what he's doin'."

They then began pushing back against their distracted opponents while Ethan stretched his jet-black wings in front of the terrified soldiers.

Impressive wingspan! Now, let's just see what it can do.

The leader of the marksmen was clearly not as impressed as his men, barking an order at them that rebounded off their steel-plate helms.

"What are you sods waiting for?! SHOOT THE BASTARD BIRD!"

But such shots never came.

Wing Buffet (Grade F)
***Your wings flap up a storm, repelling any foes before you
with STR 15 or lower up to twenty feet.***

"Storm" was right: as Ethan began a series of frantic flaps, the musketeers were blown clean off their feet. Their eyes were their main strength, not their bulk, and none of them were able to withstand the great buffet of the dark raven's assault.

None of them except their red-faced master, that is.

"Bleedin' cowards! I'll deal with this one myself. FOR KING LYSANDUS! FOR THE GRE—"

The soldier's battle cry was interrupted by the piercing roar that sounded from Ethan's beak, his tongue lolling out and unleashing the paralyzing sound he'd transferred from his last troll host.

"D-Damn it . . ."

The soldier fell prone, face hugging the lush grass of the glade, ears picking up the sounds of his fleeing men all around him.

"G-GO TO THE KING! TELL HIM—TELL—TELL HIM WHAT IT IS! TELL HIM THAT IT'S—"

The beak of the possessed raven came down on the back of his neck, and his final words were muffled as his lifeblood ran down his back.

Ethan retracted his beak from the fallen soldier, flexing his claws as he turned away and felt the Spirit Cores of his fallen foe run through his onyx breast.

Current Spirit Cores: 80

Mm-hmm. Looks like humans are actually some of the best meals around. Who knew?

The soldiers were backing away from him while his companions continued cutting down the warriors who still tried to resist. Glancing over at them, Ethan saw that these guys clearly still didn't get the picture.

Well, Sys, I'll give you three guesses as to what happens now.

. . .

You do what you do best?

Ethan did. With another Wing Buffet that sent the last of the marksmen flying into the depths of the forest, he rose and took to the skies—starless skies perfect for a skill he hadn't even realized he'd managed to transfer.

[Skill Activated: Hide (Grade E)]

He felt himself blend into the horizon, his new dark form feeling weightless and free as it disappeared from sight, bleeding away into the darkness itself.

Could almost just stay here, huh, Sys? Just stay flying up here 'till the end of time. If I was still the guy I was back on Earth, I'd probably have done just that.

. . . But that isn't who I am now, right?

This System is not here to facilitate your illusions of character development.

Ethan flashed a hawkish grin.

You know something? Maybe changing things up a little was just what I needed . . .

His sharp eyes then located the bulk of the human warriors below; those still engaged in bloody melee with his companions. Fauna was blasting them with spells (some of which were working), Tara was slicing and dicing every which way, and Klax was holding on as best he could, striking with his feet instead of his ruined arm. They were a picture of absolute focus.

But not even the most focused of creatures could keep their composure in the face of what happened next.

[Skill Activated: Dive (Grade F)]
***You focus your speed into your attack, gaining a bonus to DMG based
on your SPD stat and the distance you are from the enemy.
Current DMG Bonus: +45***

Before the incredulous eyes of the army, one soldier suddenly disappeared in a puff of blood and broken armor, his head practically caved in and his body reduced to a crumbling wreck.

"By the Grey! Who—Where's the attacker? Where—"

The screaming man was the next to die, his head cleaved clean from his shoulders seemingly by nothing more than a sudden rush of wind.

And as Ethan soared right back up before he dived again into the wave of screaming soldiers below, he smiled to see his stats.

Sneak Attack Success!
DMG: x2
DMG: 90

Current Spirit Cores: 100

You've gotta admit, Sys, now we're slaying with style.

Sys did not reply. Or if it did, Ethan missed any retorts in the screams of the soldiers who were too busy ordering a general retreat.

"The Archon is up and about, baby!" Tara shouted at the fleeing bunch. "Go tell your rat-faced king! And your precious Greys!"

"Why don't you tell us yourself?"

A sudden rush of power slashed through the tree line—strong enough that Ethan took note as he was beginning his next dive-bomb assault on the fleeing humans.

He knew that voice. He'd never forget it, and his eyes begged his companions to run.

MOVE! he tried to shriek, turning midair and coming in hot as Artorious, eyes flashing with killing intent, hit the catgirl with a single jab to her stomach before grabbing her by the throat and slamming her into the ground.

"TARA!" Klax roared, joining Fauna as they both turned to take down the thawed swordsman. But Ethan was faster, bludgeoning into Artorious's scarred face with just as much force as he had used to kill the men earlier.

And yet, miraculously, the one-armed man gripped his beak in his hand and stopped him before Ethan could even touch his head.

"You think me as simple as a mere mortal?" he asked. "Your ignorance is as pitiful as your new friends' doomed struggle."

Ethan tried wriggling free, readying a Wing Buffet to shake this guy off, but the strength of this . . . *inhuman* human was unbearable. It was like he radiated something *wrong*. Like the energy from his very being was a magnetic force that repelled Ethan on a natural level. Ethan even felt *Sys* reel back in his mind, and when the eyes of the warrior found his again, it was all Ethan could do to stare right back at his burning sapphire eyes and try to peck them clean out of their sockets.

With as much effort as throwing around a scrap of food, Artorious swung Ethan overhead and then smashed him into the hybrids running to help their Archon, watching as the rabbitgirl's staff snapped in two and she fell to the ground. The wolfman, meanwhile, was brought to his knees, breathing heavily, blood dripping from his mouth onto the grass.

Ethan's mind reeled as Artorious pounded him into the ground again, and again, and again . . .

"Pathetic," Artorious spat. "None of you can hold a candle to the true power of the righteous."

"Righteous . . ." Klax spat as he struggled to stand. "Not even you believe that . . . Lightborn."

Ethan's eye then lighted on the shining stone Tara was holding in her hand—the one she was waving at Klax surreptitiously as he kept the Greycloak distracted.

"It is fitting that you should die with your precious savior," Artorious said, creeping forward with Ethan still in his grip. "Do you not understand it by now? Your kind was not chosen. You are a blip in history. A stain on this realm. And if you fight us, you will lose."

"I . . . told ya," Tara wheezed as she steadily rose to her feet. "Maybe we can't beat ya, but we can run away real good. Us hybrids . . . we've had to . . . get good at it . . ."

Ethan could hear the sorrow stuck in her throat, speaking of some unknown history here; some ancient hatred this Lightborn and his Order must have had for her kind . . . but he also saw the eyes of her teammates all meet his, desperately trying to get him to understand their plan.

Her fingers twitched on the teleport stone. Ethan needed no further instruction.

He threw back his head with a Roar that made the trees themselves shudder. As Artorious turned to close his throat, Fauna managed to pull off a barrage of spectral missiles that sent the warrior into a defensive stance, letting go of Ethan just as the paralysis took hold.

"T-That's for my staff!" Fauna squeaked.

Ethan then made a beeline for the stone as the other hybrids touched it and instantly evaporated from sight, their bodies flying to whatever strange environment they must call home, far away from this place.

See ya, Arty! Ethan shrieked back at the dismayed face of the Greycloak. He liked to think that, even if the old guy didn't speak bird, he could at least understand the sneering grin the dark bird was shooting his way.

"Run, fly, jump, or swim, Archon—I will find you," he declared. "You were a failure in your last life, and you will fail in this one, too."

Ethan turned in the air, spreading his new wings wide in open challenge just before his claws touched the tip of the sapphire stone and he rocketed away with his newfound allies.

The light of a flickering bonfire roused Ethan from his rather comfy slumber. Beneath, cold rock caressed his bulk.

So . . . feathery . . . his thoughts meandered. *Like a fluffed-up pillow . . . a pillow with wings . . . with . . . huh?*

Ethan bolted awake, still firmly attached to his new birdy form. He blinked his sharp eyes and inspected his wings—still strong and supple despite the one-armed swordsman's grip.

Bastard almost killed me twice, he groaned in his own thready head just as he faintly picked out the voices that were chattering around him and felt the warmth of a fire caress his still bloody feathers.

"He's up!"

He knew that voice. Bolting upright, Ethan gazed upon the three hybrids who had come to his aid. The spunky catgirl—Tara; the ditzy rabbitgirl—Fauna; and the gruff wolfman, Klax. The three of them were sitting around a bonfire atop a craggy mountain, a silent wind roaring gently through spires of rock that rose all around them.

They eyed Ethan like three pilgrims eyeing an object of religious significance to their cult.

Trust me; you don't know how right you are . . .

Ethan felt a pang of relief travel through his new dark form. It was a comfort to know that the sassy Sys was still there, just as disdainful as ever.

"C-Careful," the rabbitgirl squeaked. "We don't know what might . . . you know."

The girl had said this as Tara knelt down beside him, her eyes trailing all over his form and settling on the single crimson eyeball that stared back at her, unblinking.

A sly, toothy smile spread across her face.

"We hit the jackpot!" she cried. "You can possess monsters, can't ya? That's your Archon ability."

Well, yeah . . . Ethan stuttered, attempting to nod his bird host's head in agreement as best he could. *I think I demonstrated it quite clearly . . .*

"That much . . . is already known," Klax said as he got up from beside their bonfire and straightened his back. Ethan could see that his wounds had been bandaged.

"What we need to do now is tell him exactly why he's here."

The eyes of the wolfman found Ethan's, his Lycan features framed by the bright flame of their fire.

"Because you don't know, do you?"

Ethan had his guesses. He'd at first assumed he'd simply been brought to this world as another *isekai'd* schlub, here to increase his stats until he got as OP as possible (which he'd still be doing, thank you very much, Mr. Wolfman). Still, in their flight from the human militia who had been intent on flaying them all alive, it had suddenly occurred to Ethan that these hybrid creatures clearly saw him as some sort of hero figure . . .

What did that old bastard call me? Their "savior" . . .

So, he nodded his new form's head, much to the dismay of the prodding Tara.

"Gods have a sense of humor, even Kaedmon," she said as she poked at Ethan's wings, intent perhaps on finding some secret to his powers. "Looks like you were right, Klax. We're gonna have to fill him in."

The wolfman nodded to Fauna, who closed her eyes and bent down next to Ethan, rubbing her hands together and kicking up some pretty radiant sparks.

Then, one hand reached to caress his eye.

H-Hold on, Miss Rabbit! he pleaded in his mind, his form bobbing away from her touch. *Not that I'm doubting your abilities, but it didn't look like you had the best control over your magic before . . .*

"Don't worry, Archon." Tara grinned next to him, showing her pearl-white fangs. "Fauna might be a Wildglance, but even she can't fuck up this spell."

Ethan buckled, his wings stretching out in panic. But the rabbitgirl seemed strangely serene in this moment. Her pale, buxom breasts pressed against his beak as her hand finally made contact with his hatty body. And as she closed her eyes, he felt power rush through him.

SPECIAL Skill Transfer Complete!
New (Passive) Skill: Universal Communication

With that, the rabbitgirl moved away and flashed him a blissful smile. He looked around him at the hybrids, watching their expectant faces.

"What are you all waiting for? A pat on the back for saving me? Afraid I'm kinda handless at the moment . . ." Ethan stopped as he realized that the voice that had just emanated from the beak of his raven host didn't belong to a stranger. It was *his* voice.

"Holy shit!" he yelped. "I—I can talk! And . . . damn. So that's what I sound like."

It was his old, deep, bassy voice which had earned him more than a few strange looks in life. He cringed as he heard it, almost wanting to shove it away and let the rabbitgirl take back her gift.

But when he looked up at the hybrids around him, he saw nothing but complete adulation.

"Ha-ha!" Tara screamed, rubbing her face in Fauna's breasts. "It's him! It's really him!"

"I—um, yes. But please, be careful, Ta—"

The catgirl lifted her compatriot into the air and squeezed her with force totally unbecoming of her thin, lithe form. "The Archon's back, baby! Run and tell them all the way from the Ashfalls to Grenbelm, from Griffon's Watch to the goddamn spires of Caer Krea! WE GOT HIM!"

"TARA!" Fauna screamed. "I'm gonna break!"

The catgirl dropped her friend abruptly before this became a very different kind of story.

"First things first," Klax interjected. "Archon, welcome. I'm Klax—Lycae monk. That bundle of bloody joy over there is Tara the Minxit rogue, who is currently squeezing Fauna the Hopla Wildglance to death. We are honored to be the first of our kind to meet you."

The "Minxit" dropped her friend and followed the monk's lead in a bow so low and with such grace that Ethan would be getting the vapors if he were still a mortal man.

"Eh, thanks?" he said. "But I'm still a little confused here. I'm guessing me being the Archon is a big deal to you hybrids. But I'm guessing it's also a big deal to those humans back in that forest. Particularly that old, crippled charmer with the dead eyes and broken sword."

The hybrids shared a knowing look before Fauna began nodding incessantly, her fluffy feet practically hopping with excitement of their own accord.

"Should we tell him now, Klax? Hm? Can we?"

The venerable old dog hunched his shoulders.

"It's . . . a long story," he sighed. "If Jun'Ei was with us, she'd be the one to tell you it all from the beginning . . . But yeah, you're important, all right. In fact, you might be our last hope at finding a place in this world."

The three hybrids grew solemn at those words. Ethan got the impression this mission had been something they'd been following their whole lives.

"Let's show it to him instead!" Tara shouted, her sudden tenacity sending the flames flickering into the night. "What are we waiting for?"

The other two shared an incredulous look before smirking down at Ethan.

"Hey," he chirped at them. "I don't mind what you guys do, just so long as I've got time to buff myself up. Ethan Graham ain't one to back down from a fight, and I think I've found my big Boss in this world."

"Ethan . . ." Fauna whispered. "The name of the Archon . . ."

"Sounds . . . human," Tara murmured, eyeing her savior with some suspicion. He met the stare with a sigh.

Guess I gotta come clean, eh, Sys?

Oh? Here I was thinking you were a compulsive liar, too.

Congratulations! You have [Surprised] your System!

"All right," Ethan said aloud. "I don't know what you're expecting from your Archon, but I have a little confession to make . . ."

He told them everything (minus how he died—no need to cloud these fine felines' impression of their hero). He let them know how he'd been occupying his time in their world, and how he'd learned about his abilities and exactly how they could be employed to kick ass.

When he finished, they sat back, amazed, and looked on him with even more shock than they'd already harbored in their fanged faces.

"The Archon . . . has a human soul," Tara whispered. Then, with a little catty chuckle, "Well . . . seems like even gods have a fair sense of irony."

"That—That is no coincidence!" Fauna yipped. "It must be why the Lightborn's blade broke as he attacked him!"

". . . Yes," the wolfman agreed. "This is . . . most unusual. But the only question that matters now is how the Archon himself feels about his task."

Ethan glared at them all as the fire began to fizzle away. In the distant skies, a cry of vultures pierced the air. Likely they were seeing their strange black cousin chatting with the hybrid creatures below and wondering just what the hell was going on.

And they weren't the only ones.

"Question?" Ethan asked.

"If you come with us, you will have to kill," the wolfman said. "This is not outside your realm of expertise, of course, but you will have to kill many of your own kind. Many more than you have already slain will die by the hands of those you choose to inhabit, Archon Ethan. Our mission was to find you and bring you to our base of operations in these mountains, it is true. But we will not force a sentient being to turn against its own kind."

Tara blinked twice at her leader. "Uh . . . we won't?"

"No," Fauna agreed. "It wouldn't be right. Not after what we've been through. Could you really turn against your own species? Archon Ethan was—well, still technically *is*—a human, after all."

Klax turned to him again and leveled his gaze, making it clear that what he said was perfectly true.

"If you wish to follow us," he continued, "know that you shall have to fight against your own. You shall have to leave your humanity behind if you would know your place in this new realm of Argwyll. I ask you now, Archon Ethan, can you forsake the being you were?"

All of them stared at the recently hatted bird, passing over its dead eyes to the single one that blinked back at them like they'd just asked him the answer to a basic arithmetic question.

When he answered, his giant dark raven host gave a little contorted chuckle that could send a shiver down even the most resilient paladin's spine.

"I know we just met, but all this madness recently got me thinking that I never was cut out for human life," Ethan replied. "You're asking me if I feel remorse for killing my own species? I say they never treated me with any more dignity than shit they'd stepped in. Just point me at what needs killin', and you'll have yourself a good ol' heap of corpses."

Ah, yes. The Hero's speech—his valiant statement of purpose before he undertakes his quest with his quasisuicidal allies.

Though Sys seemed beside himself (as usual), the hybrids' bestial grins only grew as they consumed his response like moist, succulent breadcrumbs.

"Then it is settled," Klax said. "Our first job is to remove that pesky bounty from your head. And to do that, we'll have to get you to the Sanctum."

CHAPTER TEN

Welcome to Your [Popular Phase]

Host: Dark Raven (Level 15)
***Stats*:**
HP: 90/90
MP: 0/0
WILL: 10/10
STR: 10
PER: 20
SPD: 55
CHA: 5
***Skills*:**
Wing Buffet (Grade F)
Peck (Grade F)
Dive (Grade E)
***Skill Siphon*:**
Roar (Grade E)
Hide (Grade D)
Current Spirit Cores: 50

With the wind at his back, Ethan soared through the skies above Argwyll's Ashfall mountain range, swooping down with a combination of Hide and Dive to slay most of the inhabitants of the mountain's crags and peaks with a single strike.

Most of these foes were simple mountain wolves and rugged boars—creatures he wouldn't bother possessing. What need did he have of those schlubs when he had a literal feathered dive-bomber at his beck and call?

You gotta admit this is fun, Sys. Come on.

The only thing I will admit is how this "grinding," as you call it, has proven surprisingly . . . *effective* for your progression.

Ethan took the compliment as he speared his beak into an unsuspecting mountain goat, ending its life before it even knew what hit its horned head. As he waited for his new companions to catch up, he decided to take a quick break to nip at some ticks in his wings and check his most recent upgrades.

[Upgrading Skill: Hide (Grade E)]
Upgrade Complete!
Congratulations! You have upgraded [Hide] from Grade E to D.
Spirit Cores to Upgrade [Hide] Skill from Grade D to C: 80

Hide (Grade D)
Hide now allows you to attempt to conceal yourself during the day,
at disadvantage vs. Enemy's PER.

[Upgrading Skill: Dive (Grade F)]
Upgrade Complete!
Congratulations! You have upgraded [Dive] from Grade F to E.
Spirit Cores to Upgrade [Dive] Skill from Grade E to D: 120

Dive (Grade E)
Dive DMG increased by 40.

He already knew that Dive was a skill he'd be transferring to his next host—whoever that might be. He'd managed to slaughter every creature he'd come across by exploiting the damage bonus from his successful sneak attacks. After all, he was coming at most of these poor mountain dwellers from the air itself, normally with a scream of *"Death from Above!"* on his beak as he swooped in to end each critter's life. This mountain range was practically a Spirit Core haven—even if each boar and wolf gave him little more than a paltry thirty to forty Cores a piece.

He'd set to increasing his core stats next, raising his health and speed, which seemed to complement the "build" he was going for here. Wing Buffet provided some extra crowd control, and with the troll's Roar ability as a backup, he'd pretty much invented his own assassin class at this point.

I gotta give the class a name, though, Sys, he said, starting to ponder. *"Archon" just sounds too edgy. Maybe "The Grimclaw" or "Black Talon."*

. . . You think those titles are less edgy?

Just spitballin'. We'll workshop it.

He heard the rushed steps of his companions following his trail of destruction, each of them whistling to themselves as they saw just how powerful their Archon was.

"I . . . must admit," Klax sniggered, "even I didn't think this one would be so bold and so . . . intent on his purpose."

"That's me in a nutshell," Ethan replied, puffing out his jet-black chest. "I'm a hat of purpose."

"And power," Fauna gasped as she inspected the fallen monsters on the mountain. "You—That—That is . . . you have taken to your powers remarkably well . . . Archon Ethan."

"Just Ethan is fine, Faun," he replied as they grouped up again and continued on their way.

"E-Ethan, then." The shy Hopla smiled, trying to conceal her blush at being given a nickname.

Ethan was learning much about his companions as dawn broke over the Ashfalls and they continued their trek toward this "Sanctum"—which was apparently a place of refuge for these hybrids and others like them.

"A place where we can be free of hunters," Klax explained.

"Or just any damn humans," Tara put in, twirling her short blades in her hands. "See, ever since the first Lightborn, humans ain't wanted us in this world."

"They burn our burrows," Fauna whispered, her face contorted in pain. "They kill the young or enslave the strong among us. We . . . We are little more than . . ."

"Monsters," Tara finished, angrily slamming her blade into a scampering mountain salamander which died instantly. "Humans don't know the difference between a hybrid and a real, ugly-ass monster. They don't know—and don't wanna know."

Ethan bristled at this.

"Don't get me wrong—I know how dumb humans can be. But why? Can't they tell you guys are at least half human? Hell, you're the only ones in this whole world who haven't tried to off me as soon as I met you. That must count for something."

Klax gave a hearty chuckle. "In your world, would the humans not see us as mere beasts to be slain or enslaved on sight?"

"Depends on the human, I guess. But I know for a fact that there are entire communities online that would love you guys . . . maybe a little too much."

"Online?" Tara asked.

"Eh, it's an Earth thing."

"To be loved for what I am sounds . . . that sounds wonderful."

The group stopped as Fauna said these words, her eyes closed over and body shivering as dawn broke over the mountain path.

"Faun?"

"I—I'm sorry," the Hopla said with a wiggle of her elongated ears. "It's just that it has been so long since there was any hope at all. Now that you're here, it . . . it all just seems unreal."

Ethan looked as the other two comforted their friend, each face a solemn display of grief mixed with cautious optimism.

This is more than just some lame prophecy, Ethan thought then. *These guys don't just want me to help them out; they need me to even just exist in this world . . . I'm gonna be real, that sounds like a lot of hassle . . .*

This thought occupied Ethan's mind as the group finally reached their destination: a series of ruins off the edge of the mountain pass, in the middle of a dark crater that looked more like a giant hoof torn into the earth than a natural formation.

"Whoa . . ." Ethan whistled. "That's your home?"

"Not quite," Klax replied, ushering the others down as he scanned the surrounding area for any sign of human activity.

"Sanctum had ta be hidden good and proper," Tara said as she began skidding down the face of their overlook toward the crater's depths. "It was built on the site of the last Archon's lair!"

Lair . . . Ethan thought. *Like a Raid Boss. I need me one of those . . .*

The four of them descended to the ruins, a strange wind picking up as they got to the base of the crater. The place was deserted—little more than a series of moss-covered columns and patchwork walls. Here and there were a series of broken statues depicting various types of monsters, each one eviscerated beyond recognition. The vibe of the place was almost holy, and as Ethan watched the hybrids' faces while they walked toward the ruin's central pillar, they all shared the same look of veneration for the place—even the plucky Minxit.

"So . . . you said this was the last Archon's lair?" Ethan asked, mainly to kill the weird silence that had set in.

"It was," Klax sighed as his eyes traced each individual statue, drawing his paw across a few of them with sorrow. "Before she was destroyed."

The silence returned, this time all too deep.

"Let me guess—this Lightborn guy killed her?"

"Mm-hmm," Fauna replied. "It's been the law of this world ever since the beginning. An Archon rises alongside a Lightborn—and the Lightborn always triumphs . . ."

"But not this time," Tara said without looking back at her friend. "Not this one. This time, we're gonna win. We're gonna put an end to this fucking cycle once and for—"

Klax's eyes shot toward his companion.

"Not now," he said. "Let Ethan see Sanctum, and then let him hear what we desire from him."

The Minxit looked sheepishly at Ethan before obeying the Lycae's command. Ethan had already gotten the impression the big guy was the leader of the pack. It made sense, even if he was a little on the older side, with a mane that looked just a little bit mangy . . .

Though that didn't matter at all when the old warrior stopped before the pristine white pillar at the center of the ruin, clasped his hands together as though in prayer, and spoke just a few short lines.

> "In darkness, may we seek our light,
> In vengeance, may we find our goal,
> In death, may we gain our hope."

It sounded more like a grim mantra than a prayer, but Ethan knew just as any gamer would that these words weren't just spoken by a priest intoning a hymn for the good of his god—these words had power. And such power began to twist the pillar above them all and shrink it into the ground, revealing a spiral staircase leading into the depths of the earth.

"Pretty cool, huh?" Tara nudged Ethan's wing. "Most humans think this place is bad luck, considering what it used ta be. We get the odd tourist every now and then, but, eh, they don't go running off to tell nobody about our little secret lair." Tara indicated some piles of bones stacked in a little pyramid at the edge of the ruins.

As Ethan followed the hybrids down the stairway to the abyss, he couldn't help but think that, yes, he'd found his people in this world.

For a while, he saw nothing at all—only inky, all-consuming blackness, even with the aid of his raven host's sharp eyesight.

Then, all at once, the world of the underground exploded before him.

At the bottom of the stairs, a stone door opened, revealing an underground city filled with hybrids. Ethan saw about every mix of humanoid creature that his mind could conjure, milling about a vast cavernous expanse of houses hewn into boulders and carved out of the walls of caverns themselves. Tunnels dotted the walls, stretching on apparently to more and more residential areas. The high ceiling twinkled with stalactites of silver, emerald, ruby, and sapphire, creating the impression of a multicolored, star-speckled sky looming over the inhabitants.

And as soon as Ethan and his companions entered through the great stone doors, all activity in the city seemed to grind to an abrupt halt.

Klax stepped forward in the face of Ethan's pure astonishment, flanked by his Hopla and Minxit posse.

"What you see before you is no lie!" he called out to the hybrid-filled cavern in a voice powerful enough to echo through the whole place and every tunnel system so that more and more hybrids started popping their heads into the central cavern, crowding around each other to see what they'd been waiting for.

"Hybrids of Sanctum, I give you your Archon!"

Ethan was immediately overwhelmed by the cheers and cries of joy that leaped from the lips of every lizardman, rabbitgirl, catfolk, or Lycae—and the countless other variations he saw. Truthfully, what he was looking at was an entire world down here, gazing up at him with hope-filled eyes.

"They've been waiting for you, Ethan," Klax said beside him. "We've been waiting for the one to bring us out of the dirt. And it's you, no matter where you came from before. It's you. Of that, there is no doubt."

Ethan's dead-eyed bird form gazed over the baying crowd with no expression whatsoever, but he was giddy with excitement. He stretched out his wings and took flight, giving the people a show to remember.

Do you know what this means, Sys?

Do tell.

We've just found our Main Quest, Ethan giggled in his mindscape. *And that means our adventures in Argwyll are only just beginning.*

Ethan was taken through the hallowed halls of Sanctum slowly but surely, his feathered form protecting him from the chill winds that blew through its many tunnels. The whole city was an interconnected mass of outposts for hybrids who had sought shelter from human poaching and hatred. As he walked with his new companions, he saw that it wasn't just a simple refugee city, however—food stores, blacksmithies, and even a few alchemist stores were carved out of the giant cavern that served as Sanctum's central hub. And everywhere he went, the blessings of the people went with him.

"This place is huge!" he said to Tara as they walked. "Here I was expecting you guys to just be a ragtag bunch of misfits seeking shelter from the cold."

The Minxit chuckled proudly, hands on her hips, nodding to a few of her catgirl cousins who looked on her as though she were walking alongside a god.

"Sanctum's been here for at least a century now," she said. "Safest place in all of Argwyll for us."

"Tara," Fauna whispered. "Everyone's staring at us . . ."

"Well, let 'em!" the catgirl replied, hopping atop a statue of a bulky-looking Lycae and waving to the crowd that had assembled all around their small group. "We're gonna be famous too, y'know. Better get used to the celebrity life, Faun."

The shy Hopla blushed in the face of all the staring fans.

"Be calm, Fauna," Klax said from the front of the group, stopping at a few rocky intersections to shake the hands of shopkeepers or town guards—big, bulky rhino hybrids with rusted iron armor. They looked fierce, but Ethan was sure it probably wouldn't take much to bust that armor open.

"You will see that our little kingdom isn't much," Klax continued. "But it is home. It's the best we've got."

"Hey, no judgment here," Ethan replied. "I ain't even seen a human city in this place yet. All I've ever known are dusty mineshafts and bloody wolf dens."

The wolf den wasn't quite so bloody until you got there . . .

C'mon, Sys! Let's at least try and make a good first impression. I'm in my popular phase now, don't cha know?

Klax nodded. "It is right that you did not experience the horrors of Lysandus's cities. They are . . . not places for our kind."

Tara and Fauna grimaced as he mentioned this name—and Ethan felt his curiosity just keep peaking.

"Lysandus . . . that's the king, right?"

"King of Western Argwyll—what the humans call the *Westerweald*. That's where we are right now."

Ethan remembered. Those soldiers who had accosted him then—they must have been sent by the king.

And he was willing to bet that the Lightborn was in cahoots with him, too.

It was suddenly very much apparent to Ethan that he was up against a whole kingdom here—a kingdom that knew where he was at all times . . .

"Hey, you guys said you'd have a way to remove this bounty, right?" he asked.

They shared knowing glances. "Yes," Klax replied. "While Sanctum's walls will keep you from the sight of your enemies, they will not remove the bounty itself. For that, you must take the throne. It was discovered by Archon Mortavious during his reign that Sanctum held the key to ridding him of the black curse of the bounty. Sadly, he died bequeathing that knowledge to his next incarnation."

Incarnation . . .

Something that kept on catching his eye as they walked were the tattered banners that hung from every pillar on every street corner. A few were even draped high above the city, suspended from the great cave ceiling itself. The image was that of a single crimson eye staring out from a backdrop of brown earth and surrounded by fire. To Ethan, it looked the very picture of a fantasy villain, and only now did he realize that it was *his* eye . . . the single eye in the center of his hatty, thready self.

"Your banner, Ethan," Klax explained. "Yours, and that of all your brethren who have come before you. Soon, it will be at the forefront of your armies as we take the surface for ourselves."

All this talk of conquest in his name was great and all, but the details of his "brethren" was the one thing Ethan needed to know above all else. Every new wonder he saw around these parts—from the firebug-lit lantern lights that lined the streets to the mushroom towers that rose in the western sections of the city— was becoming secondary to his burning need to understand exactly who he was in this world. *What* he was.

I am guessing you have given up on the notion of perhaps returning home to your previous humanly menial life?

Ethan almost laughed out loud. Sys was such a kidder.

Sys, I've been isekai'd into a world where I'm basically the demon king. Why the hell would I go back to the daily grind of office life and one-bedroom apartments?

Then it seems I truly am damned. Know that I did warn you.

Sys seemed rather more morose than sarcastic ever since they'd gotten down here, but Ethan put it down to nerves. Maybe the System of this world was of human origin or composed by a deity that favored humanity.

"Hey, do you guys have Systems too?" Ethan asked his guides.

"Indeed," Klax told him. "All creatures born under Kaedmon's gaze have such a System. Though, like most things, we generally get shackled with them at birth rather than afforded the option of 'opting out.'"

"And do yours . . . talk to you, too?"

The group halted for a moment, their eyes mulling over Ethan's statement.

"His System's already evolved?" Fauna asked. "But that shouldn't happen until . . ."

"What you worried for, Faun?" Tara chuckled as she licked her lips. "Didn't I tell ya? This Archon's gonna be big, baby."

"The Archon's System has always been . . . different," Klax said. "Not that we would know, but we hope it is not causing you undue discomfort."

"Nah," Ethan replied. "We're basically besties."

I resent that statement entirely.

At the very end of the city rose a castle. A real, honest-to-goodness castle in the darkness of the underground realm. A gatehouse flanked by impressive Martello towers loomed high above the city, with the banner of the demon eye flying from every wall as if the structure itself were watching over the hybrids of Sanctum.

Inside, the halls were barren but still pretty big. Each chamber was composed of some kind of sandstone equivalent. Ethan had played enough *Civ* and *Total War* to know these walls wouldn't stand up to pounding by a trebuchet or battering ram, but the keep was still solid and defensible; each wall was lined with flaming braziers perfect for archers, and the place even came with its own dedicated armory and dungeons, though they were sparsely populated.

They eventually came to a great oaken doorway that gave them entrance to a throne room speckled with glittering gems, each window showing a stained glass representation of some kind of great beast standing tall above the world of Argwyll. There were five of them, each one imposing and terrifying in their own respects.

"These are your past lives, Archon," Klax explained as they passed each window. "For four centuries has the land of Argwyll existed, and for four centuries has an Archon risen.

"Karfangg the Unbound." Klax pointed to the first image of a horned dragon of Oriental style. "First of the Archons, breaker of the first men. Slain by Lightborn Krea, Angel of Kaedmon."

Lightborn . . .

"That woman was a real biatch," Tara interrupted. "Came down from the sky and fucked up not just the Archon but every monster on the damn planet. We never chose to follow the damn Archon back then. Karfangg did his own thing. Couldn't even talk. Probably wasn't even a bad dude—just a dragon looking to live its life 'till Krea came down and made an example of him. Said that 'humanity is the chosen species' or some bullshit like that. It's her blood the first Greys drank from, don't cha know? That's how they got their precious immortality. By acting like fucking parasi—"

At Klax's stern gaze, the catgirl quieted herself.

"Gelsadra the Everlasting," Fauna murmured as they came to the second window, which showed a vicious, bipedal hydra wielding a massive trident. "Ruler of the Shifting Sands. Bringer of Eternal Life. Slain by Lightborn Casimer."

"Mortavious the Shroud," Tara said at the next window. This time, the hooded image of a skeletal warlock holding a black grimoire stared down at Ethan with dark, hollow eyes. "Lord of Shadows, patron of thieves and assassins. The Breaker of the Bounty. Slain by Lightborn Androx."

I'm beginning to sense a pattern here . . .

"The Demon Flower Gyko," Fauna said at the next image of a very buxom, very feminine but very evil-looking plant monster. "Mistress of toxins and corruption. Slain by . . . Lightborn Artorious."

Ethan whirred on her. "Artorious? You mean the one-armed Arthurian cosplayer who nearly killed us all?"

"Every century since the very beginning of recorded time," Klax explained, "there has been one certainty that governs this world above all others: An Archon rises, and a Lightborn does battle with them."

"One small detail overlooked there, chief: it looks like the Lightborn always wins. Is that another little law? The fact that I'm supposed to die to that old, crippled bastard out there?"

"Nah," Tara replied. "He's still the Lightborn, sure. But he's old. Retired, I heard. So tired and broken by his last big battle that he's nothing more than a homeless bum getting drunk on cheap booze nowadays. 'Cause he broke the rules."

"You guys love your rules and laws in this world, eh? What 'rule' might that be?"

Tara shrugged. "The Lightborn always dies after he kills the Archon. It's been that way since Krea. Then, they're reborn just like the Archon is. But this one, this Artorious? He's still alive. I hear the Greys practically disowned him because he cheated or something. Didn't wanna give up his title. Whatever. The fact is, he's not got the chops to deal with a fully-fledged Archon. And that'll be you, soon. When he's outta the picture, there'll be nothing stopping us."

"B-Besides," Fauna stammered, "he broke his sword the second he tried to kill you! Maybe it has something to do with you having a human soul. Maybe this time . . ."

"We've finally found the one who will break the cycle," Klax finished. "A human born in another world, coming to us in the form of a monster who wishes nothing more than to cultivate strength. A human seeking a better life, who will find one among the hybrids of this realm."

"Just like Jun'Ei said!" Fauna shrieked, hopping about excitedly until Tara's stern eyes stopped her.

"What matters is that you're here, and you're the one, Ethan." Tara shrugged. "You gotta be."

She pointed up at the last stained glass window depicting—Well, Ethan shouldn't have been surprised.

He was looking at an image of himself. A demonic hat with a whole army of fantasy beasts beneath him.

"Gyko was supposed to be the last Archon," Fauna said. "But as she died, the Sanctum summoned up a new mural: The Demon Hat. Lord of All Monsters. Last of the Line."

"Ethan the Demon Hat." Klax smiled. "It has the powerful ring of simplicity to it, does it not?"

While Ethan contemplated how he could make his name more badass like the rest of his "brethren," Klax and the gang led him toward what they really wanted to show him: the ancient, cobweb-covered throne at the very end of the main hall. Followed by hundreds of other hybrids, Ethan and his group approached the chair with veneration. He realized after a few seconds that they had stopped walking a while ago.

"The throne of Sanctum is yours, Ethan," Klax said. "Should it accept you as the new Archon, we will be at your disposal, and your bounty shall be lifted."

"Should it accept me? That sounds . . . less certain than I'd like."

"Th-The magic is very old," Fauna whispered, her voice catching as she realized just how much it echoed in these halls. "The spirits of all the Archons have been absorbed into the stone. All their expectations, all their crushed hopes . . . In some cases, it imposes limitations . . ."

"Like it did with Gyko," Tara spat. "Couldn't move a muscle for the entire time she was Archon."

"This gig just keeps sounding better and better . . ." Ethan sighed.

But he looked up at the stone throne and couldn't help feeling excitement gnaw at his threadbare bones. He wiggled his bird host's tail, straightened up, and walked on bloody claws toward the kingly chair, feeling the eyes of all the hybrids upon him.

In his old life, he'd felt eyes on him like this, too, but it was always at the butt of some joke or some prank that had gone too far. This time, he felt a wave of expectation washing over him. And rather than be afraid, he felt a tangible sense of pride.

These folk actually want me to succeed. They want me to lead them.

. . . Not like I'm gonna change who I am. I'm still in this for power—for more power than a dude like me ever had back in my shitty-ass world. But . . . if I help out a whole dying civilization as a byproduct . . . hey, won't that look good in the history books?

Are you truly vain enough to care about your reputation in the annals of history?

He smiled as Sys said this, gripping the cold armrests of the throne with his dark wings.

Sys . . . have you met me? In my old life, I was the fucking bottom of the barrel. This time, I'm gonna go right to the top. You're with me, right?

I have literally no choice in the ma—

Perfect.

He sat his feathered butt down on the throne and instantly felt a wash of energy surge through his body, filling him with untapped power that surged in the blood of his host and then pooled at the tip of his being. He closed his eyes as it reached fever pitch, and when he opened them again, he looked upon a sea of bowed hybrids, each one intoning his name like monks at prayer.

Blessing of Mortavious . . . Granted!
Archon Bounty: Nullified!
Location Obscured
Spirit Cores: +100
Current Spirit Cores: 250

New Quest List Unlocked!
Archon Delves
Delve dungeons identified nearby!
Delve 1: The Festering Den (Grade F)
Delve 2: The Twilight Sepulcher (Grade E)
Delve 3: The City of Illusions (Grade C)

He blinked all three of his eyes as these new words washed over him.

"Delves?" he said. "Like raid dungeons?"

"Places of power, Lord Ethan," Klax replied. "Places where monsters of high level dwell, which will soon be yours for the taking. These dungeons are dotted around our Sanctum and will provide you with unlimited power if you utilize your possession abilities wisely. Give us the command, and we will follow you into them. We will be your swords and shields to guide you on your path of power. Soon, you will be the most powerful Archon of all."

"Hail Ethan! Hail the Demon Hat!"

The chant was taken up by Tara, and soon, all the people followed suit. Ethan's name reverberated off the walls of the entire castle, traveling out and singing in the ears of all who inhabited the dark realm of the underground.

And Ethan, still studying the Delve menu, felt a sly smile press itself onto his raven's beak.

Well, Sys, I guess it can't be helped. Strap into this head and hold on. We've got a world to conquer.

CHAPTER ELEVEN

[Preparations]

Ethan's quest for power as a Legendary Hat was about to begin in earnest.

He requested Klax and the others take him on a tour of Sanctum while he contemplated his skills, realizing that now he had enough Spirit Cores to upgrade his demon hat skills:

{Legendary} Hat
Core Skills:
Possession (Rank F)
Skill Siphon (Rank F)
Appraisal (Rank F)
Transmogrification (Rank F)
Spirit Cores to Upgrade Any [Hat] Core Skill from Rank F to E: 250
Current Spirit Cores: 250

These skills are my trump cards, he thought. *I'd better consider them carefully . . .*

This is new, Hat. I am surprised to see you considering the tactical advantages of your skills.

C'mon, Sys, I'm a strategist at heart, don't cha know? I'm both a Civ *and a* Total War *man, with a dabbling of* League *on the side . . .*

Possession (Rank E)
You are now able to view the memories of your possessed minions.

Pretty cool, but in terms of combat capabilities . . . pretty meh. I'll use it when I'm looking to acquire some juicy lore, but I've probably got enough of that already. Next skill!

Appraisal (Rank E)
*Appraisal can now be used to prospect the location of foes through walls
and other solid surfaces.*

A tactically crucial skill.
*But one that's just too passive for now. Besides, I doubt that handicapped Arthurian
cosplayer is much for stealth. And right now, it's DPS I'm needing. I'll come back to
this one when I've got a Core surplus. It's probably my least used skill, anyway.*
What's next on the chopping block?

Transmogrification (Rank E)
You can now modify and equip items with up to [Mithril] quality.

*Ohhhhh, better shiny stabby knives . . . I'm considering this one, even though right
now, I've got nothing but my own lil' black beak. Y'know what? When I find a good
vein of mithril, I'll come back to it.*
And last up, we have the bread and butter itself . . .

Skill Siphon (Rank E)
**You can now Steal up to [Two] skills from one Host and transfer them to
a new Host body, in addition to any skills already transferred
from a previous Host.**

Sys . . . let's be real here, is this the obvious choice or is this the obvious choice?
There's more to combat in this world than stealing skills, you kno—

[Upgrading Skill: Skill Siphon (Rank F)]
Upgrade Complete!
Congratulations! You have upgraded [Skill Siphon] from Rank F to E.
**Spirit Cores to Upgrade [Skill Siphon] Core Skill from
Rank E to D: 600**
Current Spirit Cores: 0

Ethan smirked as he let Klax and the others lead him through the dusty streets
of Sanctum, shaking the hands of every hybrid with his wings.

Klax introduced him to the main members of the community, such as the
blacksmith, Borlor the Dixit, a badger hybrid with a penchant for sneezing up a
storm and wiggling his great furry snout in people's faces. Unlike the rest, he was
far more animal than human.

"Archon Ethan!" he grunted as the form of a dapper dark raven entered his
shop. His voice was thick and gruff like a Scotsman's. "Welcome ta the house

of blades. You'll want equipment for the start of your journey, aye? Well, look no further, my lord—Borlor's House of Metal Wonders is here to serve you well!"

"The Archon is more than capable of defending himself, Borlor," Klax explained. "But all the same, it wouldn't hurt to show him what tools we have that can augment his abilities."

"Aye, Klax!" the Dixit grunted, beginning to cough through the dust-caked store which was starting to bring tears to Tara's eyes behind them. "Let me show ye what I have in the back."

The badgerman fumbled and tripped over at least five different mannequins of various shapes and sizes, each one meant to represent the form of a different hybrid in the community.

And Ethan was suddenly seized by a very . . . heretical notion.

"So, something I've been wondering is . . . can't I possess you guys? Just for a little bit, you understand. You've got such fine skills and, well, I don't like to brag but my Skill Siphon just got bigger."

The hybrids stared at him with knowing eyes, as though each one thought the answer to be plainly obvious.

"Fate doesn't like to make things easy for us," Klax huffed. "Fauna, go ahead and cast a bind curse on the bird, and we'll show the Archon his answer."

"Um . . . are you sure I can—"

"If the spell goes tits up," Tara said, "I'm sure the Archon can tank a fireball to the face."

Say what no—?

Ethan felt his raven form being suddenly paralyzed before feeling Klax's firm hands lift him off the bird and place him on his own furry scalp.

And Ethan's demon pupil dilated as he saw what they meant.

Potential Host . . . Not Suitable

Well . . . I'll be damned.

"It's the same with all of us," the Lycae monk explained as he firmly placed Ethan back on the head of his paralyzed host. "Perhaps because no Archon has ever been able to directly control a human before. We share the blood of humans—though they would never admit it. The Archon we will follow, but we cannot give you the keys to success. For that, you'll need the delves of Westerweald and the treasures they have locked within."

"But don't you worry," Tara added with a mischievous wink. "We'll be there to help ya out. And then we can go on the rampage we've always wanted."

Klax fixed the Minxit with his stern, firm gaze. His nostrils flared strangely, but when he spoke, it was with his familiar calm tone.

"The Archon will do as he pleases," he said. "He is not a tool to be used by us, Tara. We are his compatriots. Remember that."

Before the haughty cat could reply, the Dixit finally returned with a handful of blades, mauls, and armor in his hands.

"Aye, my lord." He nodded. "We've got daggers, shortswords, broadswords, great axes, hand axes, bardiche, kunai, throwing knives . . . and a couple of chain mail breastplates freshly made. Now, I'm afraid all the materials are up to Steel level in quality—shortage of ore, you understand. Should you find any higher quality ores on your travels, perhaps you could bring them to me if you get the chance? Anyway, I'm sure we can try a few different modifications so that what we have suits your particular . . . forms."

Ethan held up a single giant jet-black wing. "That won't be necessary, my good man."

[Skill Activated: Transmogrification (Rank E)]

Before the eyes of the hybrids, the power of their Lord was realized: one of the sharpened longswords slowly morphed into a series of six steel nails that fit snugly over Ethan's raven claws.

Item: {Common} Steel Claws
DMG (Base): 15 (+2 STR)

And I ain't stopping there.

His glowing beak poked at the iron chain mail hauberk and began to twist and contort the armor into a shape that affixed itself cleanly to his bird breast. After five seconds, he was strutting around Borlor's shop with a chain mail breastplate that covered his feathered torso.

Item: {Common} Steel Birdplate
Armor PROT: 10
Enemy DMG must exceed this number to damage the wearer.

Looks like the little guys out there won't be bothering us anymore, Sys! Now, we're really evolving!

Yay . . .

"By . . . By the Horns of Karfangg . . ." Borlor murmured. "The powers of the Archon are beyond even what we thought . . ."

"Indeed . . ." Klax agreed, sharing the Dixit's awe. "One must wonder what else Ethan has up his . . . feathered sleeves."

"Hah! That's the way!" Tara shouted above them all. "Take everything and use it ta make yourself stronger. Leave nothin' for the enemy to use!"

Fauna the Hopla stared unblinkingly at the new creature strutting before her.

"What?" Ethan asked them all. "Never seen a bird so . . . *fly* before?"

. . . I want nothing more than death. This System . . . is shutting down . . .

A few more stops around Sanctum and Ethan was dizzy with praise. Not that he was complaining, but so many people bowing or shaking his claws or complimenting his plume was new . . . really new.

"So, Ethan," Tara asked him. "Have you decided on your first delve yet?"

Ethan had been considering it, but if he was being honest, each one of them seemed similar to the last.

Delve 1: The Festering Den (Grade F)
Delve 2: The Twilight Sepulcher (Grade E)
Delve 3: The City of Illusions (Grade C)

"Think carefully upon it," Klax said. "These delves are made to challenge even the most stalwart of warriors. We only know their locations, not the evils at their hearts."

"You don't know what I'll be facing?" Ethan asked.

"The magic of the delves is . . . special," Fauna explained. "The minds of the party members who enter often warp the environments inside in strange ways."

"So it's a kind of *Silent Hill* type deal?" Ethan wondered aloud, even though this provoked nothing but confusion from his companions. "In that case, maybe we'll get lucky and I'll actually get the skills I want if I just think about them hard enough."

He considered the delves again as they stopped in the middle of the Sanctum square.

"The Festering Den," he said. "Sounds like the place where I can find some damage-over-time effects. Poison, maybe. That's one thing I could use for sure."

"Oh yeah." Tara gave an approving nod. "A nice, slow death is the way to go, right?"

Ethan nodded. "Besides, with my speed, I should be able to give enemies a little caustic nibble then fly away, watching 'em get weaker and weaker until . . . *BAM!* Dive-bomb strike."

Tara's smile was infectious.

I think you may have found someone just as sociopathic as you. How nice.

"Before we get going, we better grab some potions," the Minxit said with a lick of her lips. "There's only one hybrid in Sanctum for the job."

"Oh, Tara . . ." Fauna groaned. "D-Do we have to? He's such a . . . an odd person."

Tara's eyes flashed to Klax, who heaved a heavy shrug.

"We'll have to face much worse if we're going to be aiding the Archon on his quest for power," he explained. "Come, Fauna, let's swallow our pride."

"Besides"—Ethan winked at the shy Hopla—"after this, I'll get you a shiny new staff. I can't wait to see what kinda explosions you can make. And that chicken thing? Hella good way to take the piss outta that old man back in the forest."

Fauna's blushing face hid a slight smile as the team followed Tara.

"Trust me, Ethan," the Minxit said. "You're gonna love this guy. With friends like him, you won't need foes. And every new enemy's gonna be shitting bricks around you."

Lucent, Capital of Westerweald

"WHAT. HAPPENED?!"

King Lysandus stared down at the one-armed Lightborn, who had appeared before him in the dead of night to explain, in quite an uncouth manner, that he should be evacuating his city before dawn.

The guards had done nothing to stop him from barging into the king's bedroom and demanding that he get dressed quickly, telling him that he'd have much work to do before the dawning of the new day.

Lysandus, king of Westerweald, had been about ready to snap back before he saw the fury that colored Artorious's eyes. Every citizen of the city had slept well tonight, seeing that the Archon's bounty was no more. And yet, here the Lightborn was, bloody as a newborn babe, raging around like some rampaging bear in the palace.

When he'd then explained what had slain a hundred men of the Grenbelm Forest militia and left at least fifty others broken and bloody on the forest floor, the king hadn't exactly taken it well.

"You are telling me that you let the Archon *escape*? That it's back and . . . you could not slay it?"

"I am telling you what I saw," Artorious replied without a single flinch.

". . . What does that mean? If the Lightborn cannot harm it, then . . . can it even be killed?"

Artorious's eyes flared up at the question, and King Lysandus suddenly found that it was he who shuddered, almost squeezing his back into the stone of his grand throne itself to escape the Lightborn's piercing sapphire gaze—the same eyes worn by the angel that Kaedmon had sent them in the first century.

"I will ride to Caer Krea this night and assemble the surviving Greycloaks," Artorious replied stiffly. "We must confer and come up with a battle plan going forward. These matters are fit only to be discussed among those of the Order, you understand. In the meantime, it is my firm recommendation that you order your guards to assist in the evacuation of the capital."

The king's eyes bulged at this upstart man, desperate to regain some sense of his regal composure. "Y-You do not give the commands here, Greycloak! Especially not when you have failed to do the one thing you're good for!"

"Your kingdom is in danger, sire," Artorious replied coolly, causing a few guards to turn away from him lest the king order them to attack. All of them knew the prowess of the Lightborn; even one-handed, he had slain thousands of creatures of the dark. And when the chips were down, they weren't about to throw their lives away for Lysandus. Not by a long shot.

"D-Do you even understand what you're asking?!" the king roared, red-faced and bumbling with embarrassment, half dressed in bed robes not exactly suited for the court. "You're asking me to admit that we failed. That . . . That we can't protect the people. You think I will suffer the same fate as my forefathers, Artorious? No. I shall do no such thing. We will stay right here, Artorious. And you will stay beside me."

The old warrior grimaced. "King Lysandus, you are making this exceedingly difficult."

"I don't care what you think, commoner!" he screamed back, the word dripping from his tongue like venom. "You will do your duty and protect your king in the event of an attack!"

"No," he answered. "I will not."

Silence reigned in the palace throne room then, broken only by the stuttered breaths of the guards who watched this whole spectacle with awestruck eyes. None of them dared cast a single glance in their speechless king's direction.

". . . What did you say to me?"

"My duty is to this land and its people," Artorious answered. "I will do what I feel must be done. I will ride for Caer Krea tonight and contact the other Greycloaks. Together, we will take the fight to this Archon and its hybrid minions, with or without your help."

With that, the old warrior bowed stiffly and took his leave, his footsteps echoing down the grim hall of the pale throne room as he went.

"Pray that this Archon remains a fledgling," he told the king over his shoulder before he left the throne room proper. "For if it should truly gain a foothold in Westerweald, the entire continent will follow."

The king could barely even stay seated. He looked to his guards and saw no compulsion to stop the old hero in them. And he began to learn just how powerless he really was.

"W-What?!" was all he could stutter.

"Most men of this world do not remember what occurred in the time of Archon Gyko," Artorious said grimly. "But I was there."

The king smarted, blustering, murmuring curses under his breath, catching the nervous eyes of his palace guard, who quickly shifted their gazes as he swept his over them.

Finally, he stood and shouted after the departing man.

"You think your brothers and sisters will welcome you back with open arms?! They hate you, Artorious! Hell if I know why—but they hate you! You walk out that door, you lose the only friend you have left in this entire world!"

Sir Artorious Pendragon didn't falter. He walked right out the palace front gates without a single look back. The people of the capital rushed to greet him as he walked, and only when they came close enough to see his grim face did they relent. There was darkness etched in those wrinkled eyes that seemed more monstrous than the beasts they feared would come in the night.

Children looked from the alleys they played in and saw him departing, some running to simply bask in his presence as he marched right through the city gates without even acknowledging them. Their hopeful eyes were not what he needed to see right now.

What the king said was true, though Artorious was loathe to admit it: his former compatriots would never simply accept him back with vows of friendship on their lips. His exile had been long, an isolation felt more keenly than the tip of any blade, but Greycloaks didn't forget the transgressions of their Order members. Especially not when the member in question was the Lightborn himself. The fact that they hadn't already come for him was a telling sign that perhaps they thought the situation didn't yet warrant the attention of the Order.

And yet, as he saddled his horse in the Lucent stables and looked up at the imposing sight of Caer Krea in the high mountains beyond the city, glowering down on all of them like an ever-watchful sentinel, he began to have a different thought: Commander Argent probably knew he would come to them, now. Probably, she wanted to wait for his return. Maybe even watch him beg for help.

She'd be disappointed on that front.

The thought followed Artorious as he set out on the King's Road, buffeted by the torrential rain that had suddenly descended on Westerweald ever since the Archon's flight from its forest lair. His vacant arm socket still ached from the memory of the battle—the memory of holding the damned demon in his hands and watching it slip away in the filthy claws of hybrids, a whole team of them just waiting for the moment to make this world a worse place to live in.

He'd remember their faces just like he'd remember the stupid form of the hat. Once the Archon was finally dead and buried, he'd come for them, too, for that was the destiny baked into his spirit—the soul of the Lightborn that burned as bright as the angel that had first given mankind a hope in the dark. And it was that very same spirit that he had failed when he'd plunged his sword into Gyko's breast and not followed her to the grave. It was that same spirit that told him, then, that his duty would haunt him for the remainder of his life.

Because he remembered what the bitch had said as she died, purple blood frothing from her thorny lips.

"See you in the next life . . . Lightborn . . ."

Artorious closed his eyes as he drove his horse onward. Thoughts of his failure were not what he needed right now. Thoughts of Krea were not what he needed now. Thoughts of the people of this world counting on him were not what he needed right now. And thoughts of the slovenly king he'd wasted his time with for the past few years were certainly not what he needed, even if the old bastard's words still reverberated off his subconsciousness.

"They hate you, Artorious! Hell if I know why—but they hate you! You walk out that door, you lose the only friend you have left in this entire world!"

He gripped his horse's reins as he forced it forward into the night.

I don't need friends, he thought as he felt the rain smack against his scarred face. *What I need is an army.*

CHAPTER TWELVE

[Delve]

Tara's "friend" turned out to be a rather skeevy-looking ratman manning a corner store at the most shadowed edge of the Sanctum.

The store stank of mushrooms and incense and . . . probably other fluids. Everywhere Ethan looked, there were some species of toxic-looking plants or fungus—some of them suspended in cages—snapping away at flies that lined the floors of their prisons.

Ethan decided on a quick Appraisal check.

Verminous Fungi (Level 5)
HP: 20/20

Hm, I wonder . . . Can I possess plants?

Amidst Fauna's and Klax's general discomfort, Tara shook the fly-ridden paw of the bug-eyed ratman behind the shop counter with glee.

"Fraxx!" she shouted. "My main man! How the hell are ya?"

The ratman twitched as he responded. Ethan was immediately reminded of a drug-addled hobo. But . . . all things considered, this wasn't the ugliest thing he'd seen in this world.

"Fraxx distill new venom last night, yesss-yesss. Fraxx receive vision of new-blood arrival. Not know it would be Archon himself." The ratman nodded his twitching nose at Ethan. "Welcome-Welcome, my lord."

"Eh, thanks, dude."

"You know why we're here, big guy." Tara winked. "We require your special services. See, we're gonna tackle the Festering Den, and I'm thinking some of your concoctions could help us stay in the business of living, dig?"

She's talking like some kinda pulp gangster doing a dodgy deal, Ethan thought. Giving a cursory glance at Klax, the wolfman simply shrugged.

"Tara is more than acquainted with the more . . . *unsavory* elements of our fine home."

"So?" the Minxit broke in, picking her ear absentmindedly as the ratman busied himself under his desk. "Ya gotta use what ya can to get the upper hand. Don't cha think, Ethan?"

"She has a point," Ethan admitted. "But I'd rather not mess up my head in the process."

"No need to worry," Tara replied. "Fraxx's stuff is legit. Well . . . as legit as you can get down here. See, the shrooms that grow down here are leftover from the last Archon, Lady Gyko."

"The lady wasss most kind-kind to all who wander in filth," Fraxx muttered as he bundled vials together for the party. "Her toxinsss and diseasesss ssshe ssspread through the land were just asss beautiful asss ssshe wasss . . ."

Fraxx jumped up and threw a selection of vials on the shop counter then—a kaleidoscope of viscous blues, purples, oranges, and reds.

Ethan's Appraisal did the job that Tara was about to.

Item: [Vial of Malphus (Grade E)] x5
HP Restoration: +10 points (Instant)

Item: [Philter of Mortavious (Grade E)] x5
Mana Restoration: +10 points (Instant)

Item: [All-Purpose Antidote (Grade E)] x3
Cures Status Effects: {POIS}, {PAR}, {PETRI}

"Pleassse do take them, good Tara and friendsss," Fraxx hissed. "Fraxx will do what he can to grow more to help the Archon. But ssshould he come acrosss better herbsss and materialsss for Fraxx, he ssshould come back and deliver them ssso that Fraxx might brew more powerful balmsss."

"Got it," Ethan said with a nod. Tara distributed the potions among them, making sure Fauna got the sapphire-colored mana potions—even though she looked on them with distaste.

Ethan found himself surprised. If anything, he'd expected the catgirl to be the one who had a particular disdain for the rat . . .

"See ya, Fraxxy!" she whistled jovially as she hurried out with her spoils.

"Good luck, Tara and friendsss," the ratman replied. "May the everdark conceal you and keep you."

Stocked up, properly equipped, and raring to go, Ethan followed the rest of the party to the Portal Chambers of Sanctum, where three sparkling gates of energy buzzed in a small oval room that looked as though it had stood for millennia.

"Let me guess," Ethan said aloud. "These were used by the last Archons?"

"Yup," Tara replied. "Each one of these puppies trained the big bosses before you and made them into what they were."

Ethan stared into the portals, recalling the great, imposing beasts that had gone before him.

Sys, he asked. *Are . . . Were you their System, too?*

I suppose such information is no longer [CLASSIFIED]. This System has served each Archon until the time of their expiry. This current designation is to be its concluding duty.

Five hundred years, then, Ethan whistled. *That . . . Yeah, that makes sense.*

Beg pardon?

If I'd had to put up with being grafted onto a demon's brain for that long, I'd probably be a snarky son of a bitch, too.

How lovely. Empathy from you. Means nothing in the long term, of course.

Ethan narrowed his eyes as he heard this, looking through the portal gate that Klax was ushering him toward.

"The way to your first delve, Ethan."

The first step on the road to power . . .

He looked behind him at the veritable fan club that had been following him at a safe distance since he'd first arrived in this place and assumed the title of Archon by sitting his feathered ass snugly on the throne.

"Hey, can't a few of these groupies come with us? More of us together would mean more meat shie—I mean, more hands to tackle the dungeon with."

"Another rule of the delves, bound by ancient magic," Fauna whispered, as though her old gods themselves were listening in, "is that only a party of four can enter at once."

"That must cause issues for adventurers looking to group up. What, do you guys end up queuing outside?"

"Most adventurers don't last long in a real dungeon." Tara grimaced. "That's what happens when one group exists literally to clear the world of monsters: the people end up getting lazy, thinking the Greycloaks will clean up the world for them. Well, no more. Not after today."

The fire in those kitty eyes was only slightly disconcerting. If Ethan was being honest, he could probably guess as to why all that hatred existed in her. He might not have seen much of the human world, but those he had seen had done nothing but try to slay him. There was a literal bounty on his head.

But he saw that Klax was more morose. More somber. He walked, head bowed, toward the portal as if he was just following a duty he *had* to do. And Fauna . . . Well, she was an enigma. Her shyness was just as strange as the unwieldy powers she held in her hands.

"If you would rather select a different team, of course," Klax said with a genuine smile, "then now is your chance. We won't force you to take us as your guardians."

"H-Hey!" Tara spurted. "Speak for yourself, wolfy!"

"I—I would like to delve with Ethan," Fauna stuttered. "But . . . only if he wants to."

The single eye of the demon hat cast itself over them.

They're an odd bunch, sure. But so what? I was an odd guy in life. And I ain't getting any less weird in this world.

"I bet you all know what my answer to that question is, don't cha?" He chuckled. "So why don't we quit the chatter and get to the fighting!"

The hybrids grinned with him, and then as one, they entered the first portal, their forms dissolving into shards of pure energy as they traveled through a network so ancient that it had existed in the bowels of Argwyll since far before any of them had ever drawn breath in this land. Ethan watched the world of the Sanctum disappear, and slowly, a new reality burst into life before his eyes. He stood on the surface world again, his claws sodden and sticky with the swamp water that surrounded him and his new companions.

Looking around, he smelled putrid air and saw only viscous, bubbling tar and mud. No trees overhead; nothing but noxious clouds and thick air caked with decay and grime.

"This is the delve?" he asked.

He was answered by a resounding *Ding!* from Sys and an alert that was as obnoxious as it was chilling.

THE FESTERING DEN DELVE (LEVEL 1) HAS BEGUN!
Enemies Approaching!

"Welcoming committee's here already." Tara grinned, readying her short blades and wiggling her tail. "Ready, Mr. Hat?"

"As I'll ever be." Ethan smiled back, watching as several bubbles appeared in the pools of swamp water around them.

"Here they come!"

Appraisal Success!
Enemies Identified:
[Grumlets (Level 10)] x15
HP: 50/50
WILL: 50/50

I've seen butt-ugly before . . . but these guys take the cake.

The tiny, foul-smelling goblinoids rushed Ethan's party with their spears and shortswords held aloft, screaming a battle cry from their froglike mouths. As they got closer, Ethan was surprised at just how accurate the comparison really was: their bulging, bloated eyeballs were an exact picture of a horny toad's.

"Here they come!" Tara reeled back, purring just like a kitten ready to play with her prey. "This'll be fun . . ."

Without warning, the Minxit charged forward and slashed through two of the swamp- and slime-covered grumlets, taking their heads clean off in one blink of Ethan's raven eyes. For his part, Ethan grabbed one with his new steel claws and took to the blackened skies above, throwing the little guy down like a bowling ball into a mass of his friends, who were charging Fauna.

"Death from above just like before, Fauna!" Tara shouted over her shoulder, her face glistening with the green blood of the dead beasts. "How's it feel having a guardian angel, Faun?"

The Hopla spared a look of resigned thanks up to Ethan and, blushing, cast a firebolt that ripped clean through a row of three grumlets who had just risen to resume their charge toward her.

Not bad at all, Ethan had to admit. *When she gets a spell right, she's one impressive rabbit . . .*

He swooped down to deliver a Dive that tore into the flesh of another corrupted grumlet, sending out a shock wave of swamp water that poured over its friends—who were then taken down one by one by a flurry of hasty punches and jabs delivered by Klax.

Congratulations! You have slain a Grumlet (Level 10)!
Congratulations! You have slain a Grumlet (Level 10)!
Congratulations! You have slain a . . .

Can you can it with the notifications?! Ethan barked as he snapped and clawed at more of the froggy menaces around him. *Just . . . give me a total when this shit's good and done!*

System Combat Log Preferences: Updated

"Forward!" Klax suddenly shouted. "There must be a way down to the next floor!"

"Floor?" Ethan asked aloud as he pecked the eyes out of a screaming grumlet warrior. "You mean this is part of the dungeon itself?"

"Just take a look at the skies, Archon!" Tara shouted. "Can't your eyes see through an illusion?"

Ethan took flight again to try to understand what she meant. He found that he could only get about eighty feet up in the air before he hit a wall. Literally. There was some kind of boundary wrapped around this whole dark, swampy environment.

So these delves really are like instances . . . Ethan thought.

Somehow, your Earthling mind is able to comprehend these nuances of our world surprisingly well.

It's almost as if I was chosen or something, huh?

That information is considered [CLASSIFI—]

I get it, he interrupted as he activated his Hide ability and came swooping in from the dark, infected clouds above the grumlet horde. He sent a whole pack of them flying back like ugly little children.

Then he felt something stirring beneath his feet.

"Uh . . . guys?" Fauna murmured from behind him. "I think we've got some company—Ah!"

The Hopla had spotted the danger before the rest of them; her feet could detect gyrations in the earth far better than any of them. But before she could even tell them they had to run like hell right now, Ethan had already scooped her and the rest of the team up in his claws.

The swampland was disappearing into a whirlpool of dirt and grime before their eyes, the grumlets who were still alive tossing their javelins up at Ethan as he brought the hybrids out of the danger zone.

He felt the stings of their weapons as he tried to hold the weight of the three hybrids, realizing only now how much of a detriment the relatively low strength score of this giant dark raven host was.

STR: 10
Status: Fatigued!

Apparently, his comrades didn't quite feel him begin to lower as the seconds drew on.

"Ha-ha!" Tara shouted from around his neck, her thighs slapping against his face. "Feel the wind in your hair, guys! The SS *Archon* takes flight tonight!"

"Tara! Can you see the exit portal?"

The voice was Klax's, who was doing what he could to block the projectiles of the ugly goblinoids who hadn't vanished into the whirlpool of filth that the swamp had become. Many of their comrades had ridden the wave and fallen into the abyss at its center, while the rest swam happily around the periphery, chucking their javelins into the air with wild abandon.

"Take me in closer!" the Minxit shouted in Ethan's ear. "I can find us the way below."

"C . . . Can you move away ever so slightly?" he replied. "Even for a sentient hat possessing a giant bird, this position is ever so slightly uncomfortable."

The Minxit girl sneered down at him. "Oh? Is the Archon nervous?"

"Stop playing around, Tara!" Fauna pouted up at her. "W-We're in the middle of a fight."

She then conjured up a spell that Ethan supposed was meant to be some kind of bubble shield but ended up summoning a living, breathing liquid serpent that wriggled out of her hands and down into the swirling swamp below.

"Guys . . . your Archon is starting to lose momentum . . ."

Ethan felt more projectiles sting his hide, and wished nothing more than to dive-bomb the hell outta the little shits right now. But he kept his cool. In this new life, he wasn't just gonna charge into danger blindly. He wasn't gonna make the same mistakes he'd made back home . . .

"There!" Tara shouted suddenly, pointing toward a spire in the distance that had been revealed as the swamp continued to drain. "There's a doorway there that we can head through; the part covered in reeds!"

Ethan's eyes focused on the location and found the door—the place that was suddenly all so clear to him. "How did you do that?"

"Cat's eyes, my good Ethan," Tara chuckled. "This girl's not just good for slitting throats and looking good doing it. My species happens to be the best illusion spotters and trap detectors in all of Argwyll."

Ethan smirked as he turned in the sky and headed straight for the crumbling spire. *Looks like I've picked the right allies for dungeon delving . . .*

He tried activating Hide and found that the skill just wouldn't work; probably something to do with him being fatigued. He could make it, though the grumlets swimming beneath them seemed to know exactly where he was going.

"Look!" Fauna screeched. "They're trying to break the spire down!"

All of them saw it as soon as the Hopla pointed it out: the horde of uglies had descended on the foundations of the spire and were climbing it before them. The whole thing looked ancient beyond imagining; it was already pretty much crumbling apart. Their webbed claws were starting to break the thing down entirely.

Guess they don't want us going below . . .

He could make it to the spire if he had a straight shot, Ethan knew it. But right now . . . that was one hot LZ.

"Keep flying, Ethan!" Klax shouted up.

"That was the idea! But we're gonna need some major firepower to clear those froggy bois!"

Klax smiled as he kicked away another javelin aimed squarely at Ethan's steel underbelly. Only a few had managed to penetrate and puncture the armor so far, but that was enough to interrupt his descent. Ethan couldn't tell exactly why the old wolf was smiling.

"Fauna," he heard the Lycae say. "You know what to do."

Fauna clutched Ethan's steel claw even tighter as they approached the spire, watching the hateful eyes of the grumlet horde take up firing positions on its ridges and ledges.

"I . . . You know it might not work."

"That's a chance we've gotta take."

"Just like usual!" Tara shouted down. "Go on, Sister! Take those little bastards down!"

The Hopla squirmed, hoping against all hopes that Ethan could finish off the brutish toad creatures instead of her. She looked up at him with fading hope in her big eyes.

You don't believe in yourself at all, do you? Ethan's eyes asked her.

He'd seen eyes like hers before. Eyes that never failed to piss him off every time . . .

"Fauna!" he shouted down, narrowly avoiding a hail of javelins launched from the horde. "Don't you remember? I promised you I'd get you a new staff. A staff for a real mage! That's what you are, right?"

The Hopla grimaced. "N . . . Not a mage. A Wildglance."

"Like I know what the fuck that is!" Ethan replied as he felt the pain of another flurry of projectiles. "What I do know is that you've got more power in those fluffy hands than I've ever seen in my whole damn life! I don't care what you do—just do something super special magic awesome!"

He couldn't tell whether it was his words or simply the necessity of destroying the enemies blocking their path that spurred the girl on. All he knew was that in the next second, he felt the Hopla girl's body go limp before she raised her arm and muttered an incantation that set the air itself ablaze.

"P-PYROS ARMUNUM!"

Searing, blistering heat rocketed up from the hand of the rabbitgirl until the power residing within her spirit could no longer be contained. It gushed forth from her palm like a blooming red flower of death, instantly vaporizing the entire horde and the spire's midsection along with it.

Ethan watched in awe as the spell reduced the screaming grumlets to piles of brown ash.

I have really gotta possess me a Wildglance . . .

"Now, Ethan!" Klax roared.

The demon hat didn't even need to hear this—already, his host was rocketing through the flames toward the purple portal that had just opened at the tip of the spire. As soon as he touched its surface, the world twisted and folded in on itself, and the screaming party of hybrids was thrust into the unknown horrors of the Festering Den's second floor.

CHAPTER THIRTEEN

[Doubts]

—Delve Notification—
Safe Zone Reached

Ethan blinked through dust and swamp water before realizing that one half of his left wing was on fire.

He rolled against the dusty floor that he and his companions had landed on. They had entered through the portal into, seemingly, an entirely different interior from what he was expecting, considering that Fauna's spell had all but obliterated the spire's exterior. A chamber of ancient sandstone walls surrounded them—each of them engraved with etchings and patterns showing grumlets hard at work worshipping at shrines or toiling away in the swamps outside, building more monuments to whatever gods they worshipped.

Oh boy, LORE. Where's the video essay to explain how these walls contain secrets I could never be bothered to care about?

Disdain for this world will get you nowhere, you know.

I thought you'd be pleased with that, Ethan remarked as he shook himself off and took a look at his downed companions around him. *After all, you'd like nothing more than to see me dead, right? Or are you more of a* Tsundere *than I thought?*

Searching for Class Designation: [Tsundere]
Results: Inconclusive.
Explanation required.

You'll just have to take a guess, Sys. Some secrets can't just be spilled willy-nilly.

He nosed the forms of Tara, Fauna, and Klax, who seemed like they'd been out in a daze as deep as his. As they came to, each of them looked around with wonder, with Fauna in particular staring blankly in disbelief. Probably her own System window was telling her they had made it.

"We're . . . alive," she said.

"Hell yeah, we are!" Tara shrieked, cartwheeling back to squeeze Ethan's long neck and then pouncing on her Hopla sister. "All thanks to Ethan and a certain bunny girl's fiery fingers."

"T-Tara! You're embarrassing me in front of the Archon!"

Ethan laughed along with the girls as Klax rose to stand beside him, eyes brimming with relief but also absolute focus.

"Now we tend to our wounds," he said, pointing down at the scratches on his arms and Ethan's wings—spots where the grumlets' javelins had pierced his feathers and even chipped his armor.

"Ah, Klaxy," Ethan groaned. "I barely felt a thing, really!"

As usual, Sys then popped up to prove him wrong.

HP: 45/90

". . . Okay. Maybe I got a few scratches on me. But that's what our healing potions are for, right?"

Tara jumped up then, finally leaving her shy comrade alone, and threw open her arms to the room around them.

"No need," she told Ethan. "This here's a safe zone. There's usually one or two between delve floors; a place to rest and recuperate, y'know?"

"Every adventuring party gets at least twelve hours' respite," Klax elaborated. "We'd be clever to take it before moving on."

"And save our supplies for when we need *instant* healing during combat," Ethan agreed with a sage, birdly nod. "Sucks that none of you guys have a cleric or healer around."

Klax shrugged. "It is not something we hybrids are blessed with."

"Healin' spells are lame, anyway. Never helped any of us put the dead back together. Ain't that right, Faun?"

The Hopla looked up at Tara with vacant eyes. She said nothing.

". . . Eh, sorry."

Still nothing. I'm sensing some actual juicy lore here . . .

"Let us make camp," Klax spoke up, producing a bundle of firewood from his pack and beginning the process of getting a fire going. "If we can take turns keeping watch, we can make sure the safe zone is not violated. Though these spots are normally peaceful, one can never know if another delving party decides to come along and violate this sanctuary."

"That happens?" Ethan asked.

"It is not outside the realms of possibility."

"Nothin' really is in good old Argwyll, Ethan!" Tara beamed. "Ain't your Earth the same way?"

"*My Earth* was more boring than anything you could imagine," Ethan replied with a chuckle. But his demon eye was focused not on Tara as the flappy beak of his host said these words. Instead, it was rooted squarely on Fauna and how she simply stared forward into the fire that was slowly starting to take shape beneath Klax's hands.

. . . *Yeah,* Ethan thought. *This world is way more interesting.*

Current Spirit Cores: 120

As the hours droned on, Ethan found that he couldn't sleep. He decided to take up watch when the seventh hour came along, as this would give him time to make any skill improvements with his new bundle of Cores.

Sure, I could save up and get another rank in one of my hat skills, but who wants to be a bore? I ain't gonna just save up points and then never end up using them. Besides, who knows what kinda hell's waiting below. Klax says there are at least two more floors to go, and I'm betting there's a nice, very possessable Boss monster just waiting for me on the last one . . .

Ethan decided then and there that his best chance at survival would be *prioritizing* the dark raven skills that he would be transferring to whatever new host he acquired. And that meant he really only had two choices between Wing Buffet, Peck, or Dive.

Spirit Cores to Upgrade Any [Raven] Skills from Grade F to E: 80
Spirit Cores to Upgrade [Dive] Skill from Grade E to D: 120

I've already got a handle on Dive . . . and Peck just seems like a basic attack. Wing Buffet for sure seems the more useful skill. I mean . . . if I'm gonna take Dive with me to my next host, I'm gonna need wings to make proper use of it. And it's another form of crowd control for when Roar's on its cooldown.

Wing Buffet (Grade F)
Your wings flap up a storm, repelling any foes before you with STR 15
or lower up to twenty feet.

Wing Buffet (Grade E)
Repulsion Increase.
You now repel any foes with STR 25 or lower up to fifty feet.

**Spirit Cores to Upgrade [Wing Buffet] Skill from Grade F to E: 80
Confirm Upgrade?**

Ethan needed no further prompting. Peck was basically a waste. His wings were this creature's strength, and if he could take it to another, he was gonna make sure they were powered up.

**[Upgrading Skill: Wing Buffet (Grade F)]
Upgrade Complete!
Congratulations! You have upgraded [Wing Buffet]
from Grade F to E.
Current Spirit Cores: 40**

Have to remember to keep a good Core surplus; otherwise, I won't be able to possess the big bastard down under . . .
Always thinking ahead, just like your predecessors. This bodes well for you.
Of course. Sys was the System of all the other Archons, right? Ethan wondered if there was a way to break through the [CLASSIFIED] records Sys kept throwing up when he asked a question about them. Then again, maybe Sys had blanks when it came to the previous Archons. After all, all their info and memories would be just too much of an advantage, right? And Sys didn't seem interested in giving him more advantages than he had . . .

He decided to turn his attention from Sys to the stirring rabbitgirl whom he suddenly found sitting up, staring once again into the little bonfire they were huddled around.

"Can't sleep?" he asked her.

She glanced up at him as though surprised he had noticed her and gave a wet sniff of the chamber's stagnant air.

"Am I bothering you, Ethan?"

"What? No! I just meant—Well, I thought it seemed like you kinda had something on your mind earlier."

She returned her gaze to the flames, though she did manage to beam a brief smile.

"Yes . . . maybe I do."

When she added nothing else, Ethan wasn't sure what else to say. But he knew he couldn't just let this silence last.

Go on, Sir Archon. Show me just how good of an orator you can be.
Sys . . . I'm gonna need some free headspace right now, 'kay?
He sidled up beside Fauna while she hugged her knees, eyes still staring blankly.

"You know . . ." he began, his three eyes watching her from their corners. "That was a pretty awesome spell you just pulled off outside."

She looked up with confusion, the light of the bonfire's embers dancing in her eyes.

"'Awesome'?"

"Y'know—cool. Epic. Super. You were like a . . . super bunny girl."

Eloquent. You are a natural-born [Poet].

What did I just tell you?!

Fauna burst out laughing before Sys could make another quip, giggling lightly so she didn't wake their slumbering comrades.

"Thanks," she whispered. "You . . . You aren't what I expected the Archon to be."

"Yeah, the rest of them weren't devilishly handsome hats, eh?"

She sniggered. "The rest of them didn't really ask us how we felt about . . . all this. We all followed them because the humans hated us. But we couldn't say *no* even if we wanted to."

Ethan cocked his feathery brow at the girl.

"How can you say no . . . when all your species thinks the same way?" She trailed off before realizing exactly what she'd said. "S-Sorry! I'm rambling. I—um, f-forget all that. I just—"

Ethan held up a wing. "We're a team now, y'know." He winked. "And I'm still a newbie to this world. I *want* to know what you think."

"I'm not so special, Ethan," Fauna replied in barely a murmur. "I'm just another hybrid who lost everything during the . . . the purges."

"Purges?"

"It was after the last Archon fell," she explained slowly, eyes refocused on the crackling bonfire throwing their shadows across the chamber walls. "The Greycloaks joined up with the king . . . Lysandus. He—they—wanted to hunt us all down for good. They said they'd make sure we all died this time."

To his shock, Ethan saw the Hopla's pale hand clench in anger, nails digging into her bare thighs.

"My mom, my sisters, everyone in our burrow wanted to leave, to find Sanctum—the safe place we'd all heard rumors about. But I . . . I told them we should stay. That the burrow was our home. That if anyone did come, I'd . . . I'd protect them . . ."

The Hopla's eyes were truly staring into her past now. "But when they came for . . . for my burrow . . . I *couldn't* . . . My spells wouldn't work right. Everything just . . . fizzled. I couldn't help them. My sisters . . . mother . . . everyone. They came and—and they . . ."

She buried her head in her knees for a moment then. Ethan knew the rest of the story. The girl didn't have to go on.

"I should've listened to them," she continued. "I'm nothing special. I'm just a Wildglance who can't be counted on. I only survived because I was a coward, Ethan. I ran. When they came for me last, laughing as my spells fizzled out and died, my mother pleaded, begging for me to go. I did what she said this time. I ran. I ran because I was scared. And because I was stupid. I ran when I . . . I . . . I should've died with them."

She said these words with more confidence than Ethan thought her capable of expressing. Then she fell silent. Silent as the stone walls that encased them.

Jeez . . . that's a sadder backstory than I thought I'd hear from her.

He shuffled uncomfortably next to the girl, hearing her stifle some small sobs. No real tears came, but judging by what she'd just said . . . if there was a Psychologist skill, he'd make use of it. Really, he would . . .

I'm afraid you're out of luck, there.

. . . Fine then, he answered Sys. *Guess I'll just flap my gums and see what comes out.*

"You know, you're the first mage type I've met in this place. And let me tell you, you're way cooler than the ones in my world."

The girl turned to him, tears at the corners of her eyes. "Your world . . . has mages?"

"Eh . . . kinda?" He shrugged. "Except ours are nothing but stories. Stories of old men with long beards and big sticks shooting fireballs and smoking weed—or the fantasy equivalent. They're nothing but stories, Fauna. And they're nothing like you. You're real. You're a badass chicken-flinging, laser-beam-shooting rabbit-girl sitting right beside me, and I never thought I'd see things as amazing as what you've done for real."

"You . . . You think I'm amazing?"

"Come on . . . you literally burned up a whole horde of those ugly shits outside. I get that your magic's unpredictable and stuff, but that's exactly what makes it cool! Everything you do is a surprise."

Now, it was suddenly Ethan's turn to stare into the fire.

". . . No one wants to live a boring, predictable life," he said. "You literally *can't* have one. That's a bloody great power."

Not bad, Ethan. For a Hat.

In the face of Sys's sarcasm, Ethan furrowed his brow again. But his whole demeanor was thrown off by Fauna's giggling beside him—much louder, and much clearer than before, echoing up the ancient walls around them and back down again.

"I bet you were a funny human," she said. "I wonder, if you'd come here just as you were . . ." She trailed off and seemed to shake the thought from her head. She yawned, wiggled her ears, and gave a little weary stretch. "Thanks," she said with a slight blush. "For talking with me."

Ethan's bird host stiffened. "Believe me, Fauna, it's me that should be thanking you. Eh—all of you."

With that, the Hopla girl beamed him a smile and brushed his feathery wing with her hand before heading to sleep. For his part, he stayed awake to keep watch for the last few hours of their rest, watching the little chest of the rabbitgirl rise gently as she finally fell asleep.

If you start caring too much about these guys, he told himself, *you're gonna end up fucked. You know that, right?*

He did. But he said nothing more.

CHAPTER FOURTEEN

Into the [Depths]

Host: Dark Raven (Level 16)
Stats:
HP: 90/90
MP: 0/0
WILL: 10/10
STR: 10
PER: 20
SPD: 55
CHA: 5
Skills:
Wing Buffet (Grade E)
Peck (Grade F)
Dive (Grade E)
Skill Siphon:
Roar (Grade E)
Hide (Grade D)
Current Spirit Cores: 40

—Delve Notification—
Rest Concluded
Safe Zone Nullified

The hybrid team continued their advance into the depths of the Festering Den proper once their twelve hours were up, packing up their modest camp and following the narrow corridor that led into this strange new temple. Tara insisted on taking the lead, and Ethan wasn't about to complain—his bird form wasn't exactly suited to these narrow, twisting stone passageways that formed the labyrinth they were descending into.

At a few chokepoints, the Minxit ordered the group to halt, her ears twitching wildly. She proceeded to check the walls and floors, brushing them gently with her tail or feet to reveal some small contraptions hidden behind secret compartments and trapdoors.

"Traps!" Ethan said. "Now we're in a real dungeon."

"Indeed," Klax replied as Tara went about dismantling the insidious-looking devices; repeating crossbow machines and what looked like gas pits, mostly. "The ancient architects who created these delves did so knowing that their job was to test the faithful, as well as provide a home for Argwyll's less than reputable citizens."

Ethan nodded at the strange hieroglyphs and mosaics painted on the walls—those depicting grumlets at prayer, huddled around strange, eight-legged idols and altars.

"Looks like the little critters really made this place their own," he noted.

"It is the way of the delve dwellers," Klax confirmed, wiping his paw over a few of the cobweb-covered etchings. "Those trapped here begin to form a strange appreciation for the more powerful monsters within. In time, this appreciation becomes fascination, and pretty soon . . ."

"You've got a buncha monster cultists worshipping the big Boss of the dungeon," Tara finished, cracking her fingers and giving a triumphant swish of her tail. "All done here, folks. Let's do this."

A few more passages of winding stone awaited them, each one lit only by the flickering red orb that Fauna had summoned in her hand. As they rounded a few corners, the light seemed to jump around energetically, as though its bearer were tossing it to and fro in a little game. She wouldn't admit it, but Fauna was just a little bit more *excitable* now. Ethan didn't mind if she played around a little. She needed a bit of recreation more than he did.

Finally, Tara nodded toward an opening that led into a larger chamber with a pit in its center—one that looked to be at least ten meters deep. From their vantage point, they could see into the pit and watch its inhabitants as they sat, waiting.

"Eight legs . . . and one creepy-looking grumlet. Looks like those hieroglyphs were doing a bit of foreshadowing for us."

Appraisal Success!
Enemies Identified:
Grumlet Magus
[Giant Swamp Spider] x6
HP: 30/30
WILL: 25/25

Ethan's Appraisal couldn't identify anything about the grumlet mage sitting among the spiders below—probably because he hadn't yet upgraded the skill and the creature was hiding its stats through magic. This was, after all, the first mage he'd truly met in this world besides Fauna.

And his appearance didn't exactly inspire anything in particular. He sat there, a furrowed, conical hat atop his brow, simply staring at the web-spinning spiders around him.

"What's . . . What's it doing?"

"Looks like it's . . . praying," Fauna whispered.

"Who cares what it's doing?" Tara murmured back, readying her shortbow and nocking an arrow. "This is the way to the bottom floor; I'm sure of it. To get there, we're gonna have to go through them."

"Stealth?" Ethan inquired, readying his Hide ability.

"It will be tough in here," Klax mused. "Fauna? Think you have a spell of Darkness you can whip up for us?"

The Hopla glanced at both her comrades, not saying anything at first. When she then found Ethan's face, he gave her a conspiratorial wink.

"Hey, remember you're super special magic awesome."

She stared unblinkingly for a few seconds before nodding, flashing him the smile she had before.

"Okay," she said. "I'm ready."

"We move out as soon as the cloud of Darkness envelops the brood," Klax said. "Everyone ready?"

"Ready!"

"Go!"

The next few minutes occurred in a flash—Fauna's fingers dripped with oozing, living darkness that snaked its way down the pit to the mage and his spider pets, covering them in an inky black cloud. The mage jerked up, suddenly furious, but heard nothing but the sound of arrows flying through the dank air and embedding themselves in one of his spiders nearby, killing it instantly. As he flew to grab his staff, something large and quick knocked into him from above, sending him sprawling on the ground and clutching the bloody gash carved into his arm.

Damn it! Ethan thought as he took to the ceiling to go in for another Dive attack. *I can't make full use of Dive without an open sky above me. This little guy must be packing more health than the rest.*

Still, it made sense to focus on the mage; clearly, he had the most power in the group. So, as another spider perished under the steel tips of Tara's arrows, Ethan flew in for the kill, aiming his beak right at the grumlet mage's neck.

"AHHH!"

The scream wasn't his. It was shrill, hoarse, and pained—and it belonged to a girl.

Fauna . . .

Ethan's eyes caught the sight of her being pushed by five new grumlets who had just entered behind them. She fell to the base of the pit and would have probably snapped her neck if Ethan hadn't flown to catch her on his back. Meanwhile, Tara was engaged with three of them above, each one slashing at her with a vicious rusted broadsword.

"Ethan!" she shouted down. "Kill the mage!"

Through his host's eyes, Ethan saw exactly why she was more concerned about the magic user than her own safety. He saw the bubbling energy gathered in the mage's hands, viscous green ooze that he was readying to fire at them all. Around him, his spiderlings charged, more than willing to protect their master.

SQUISH!

The mage's eyes went wide as he heard one spider die beside him. Then another. Then another, until finally, he heard the raspy breath of the wolven hunter who had come for him.

With a single punch, Klax sent him flying back against the far wall. Meanwhile, Ethan dealt with the two grumlets who had charged him and Fauna, intent on finishing the delvers who had fallen for their trap. A quick Wing Buffet sent them both rolling back, snapping their spines against the walls of the pit and allowing Ethan to follow up with a quick slash of his iron claws that ended their miserable lives then and there.

Above, Tara had managed to fight off her attackers. One grumlet fell, quickly followed by his friend, both of them slashed brutally across the nape of their necks.

That girl's one badass assassin . . . Ethan couldn't help but think.

A scream from Fauna behind him brought him right back to the battle, however. She'd brought up a shield around both of them right as the mage had finally managed to fire off his spell. The cloud of Darkness disappeared, and now, the world of the labyrinth was bathed in an otherworldly green light—something that tore through the walls themselves, sending bricks and stonework crashing down on the scattered team of hybrids.

"He's bringing this place down!" Klax called out as he ran for Fauna's shield. "Tara! Come on—we're outta here!"

The Minxit gave a huff of indignation as the walls collapsed around them, jumping down to catch Ethan as he flew with all his speed toward the only opening he could find above—a hole just big enough to squeeze through with his charges.

Just before they managed to flee the broken battlefield, however, a shot rang out against the din of the falling walls.

They looked back to see an arrow embedded slap-bang between the eyes of the grumlet mage.

"Tara the Minxit ain't gonna leave a target alive," their catgirl companion said. "'Specially not a little bastard like that."

Ethan's flight took them into another series of interconnected chambers—only, this time, the rooms were more organic than comprised of the stone walls that characterized the rest of the ruins. The surfaces of these much wider rooms pulsed as though alive, each one lined with grey polyps the size of baby elephants.

A sudden notification buzzed into life before Ethan's eyes.

DELVE CHALLENGE: HORDE
Completion Bonus:
Spirit Cores: +300
[Random {Uncommon} Loot] x2
[Time until Activation: 00:10:00]

"Shit . . ." Tara muttered. Her companions seemed to share her annoyance.

"Oh . . . and on Ethan's first dungeon . . . Why does our luck have to be so bad?"

"It is the way of the delves," Klax snarled. "They exist to test the faithful. Perhaps the delve itself knows that Ethan is the Archon. If so, it is giving us its all."

Ethan took them down into the center of the organic room, feeling the mushy, pulpy gray matter of the ground stick between his steel claws as they met the surface. He could guess what was about to happen here.

"Horde . . ." he said aloud. "So, like a swarm of enemies, right?"

"Swarm is correct," Klax confirmed as he checked the room for possible defensive choke points. "We have to survive against a veritable army of this delve's choosing. Judging by the state of the environment . . ."

". . . It'll be spiders," Ethan finished.

"It will be spiders."

"Fuck!" Tara spat. "Hordes are the worst kinda challenge. Stealth basically doesn't work. Not when there are fifty dudes all looking for a piece of ya."

Context, Tara . . .

"Well, I have my shield," Fauna said. "And Ethan has his Dive attack, right? We could attract them to us as a distraction while Ethan takes them down."

"It might be the best way," Klax agreed. "I don't like the odds of us splitting up. Especially not with the number of those egg sacs all over the place."

"Can't we just destroy them now?" Ethan asked.

"Won't work. It'll do nothing but start the horde challenge. The laws of the delve are sacred and unbreakable; at least not with Argwyllian magic."

"So our only option is to deal with it," Ethan said.

"Yup," Tara replied as she stretched her legs and craned her neck. "That's pretty much it. But hey, on the bright side: there's a juicy three hundred Spirit Core reward and some random loot in it for us."

"Now you're speaking my language," Ethan laughed.

He took up his position at the apex of the organic room, trying to avoid looking at the pulsing polyps around him which seemed to beat with greater intensity now, as though they too were waiting for the challenge to begin.

He spent a few Spirit Cores on upgrading his host's health and SPD, with the latter taking up at least fifty of the Cores he'd acquired from the last mob alone to upgrade. The grumlet mage had been worth a whopping hundred and twenty Cores, though, so he'd have to thank Tara for that kill shot later. Stats really did end up costing a lot when they passed twenty. But then again, he'd be in Spirit Core heaven soon if all went well here.

HP: 92/92

SPD: 60

Both speed and distance would only increase the strength of his Dive bombs. He could do this.

The question was: could his team?

"Ethan!" Klax shouted up as he and the others stood back-to-back in the middle of the chamber below. "Are you ready?"

"Ready!" he shouted down.

"Then . . . let's do this."

DELVE CHALLENGE: HORDE
Activated!
[Time Remaining: 00:10:00]

Eight-legged hell broke loose in the chamber. Ethan saw the gray polyps lining the entire ceiling and walls burst open at once, releasing a torrent of jet-black spiders, each the size of baby elephants. And as an undulating wave of leggy death, they descended on the hybrids below.

"Here they come!"

Klax barked orders at Tara to let loose as many arrows as she could before drawing her shortswords and hacking away at the creatures' limbs. The dogman knew their weaknesses, and he wasn't about to lose a second in exploiting them.

"Faun!" he shouted. "You know what we need!"

"F-Fire coming up!"

Ethan wasted no time doing his part. Even with his Hide ability practically useless against a sea of eyes, he still managed a dive-bomb that took out a slew of spiders before they even made it to the ground, splintering their bulbous bodies apart and splattering their oozelike blood over the face of both him and his fine-feathered host.

I HOPE YOU WILL BE CLEANING THAT LATER—THE SMELL OF SPIDER VISCERA IS MOST DISCONCERTING! EVEN A SYSTEM HAS STANDARDS, YOU KNOW!

Little too busy to care at the moment, Syssy!

Ethan slammed into another section of the surging horde, managing to take down a whole front wave before they even reached Klax's readied fists. He flew back up just before the chittering teeth of the next row managed to snap at his tail, hearing a collective insectoid screech when he made it back to the ceiling.

"Have that!" Tara was screaming as she hacked through the bastards. "Ya creepy crawly fucks!"

The waves were unstoppable. As he looked around him, Ethan could see that the polyps were prisons for hundreds of spiders, which continued pouring from their depths with impossible speed.

"Fauna!" Klax shouted. "Any luck with that fire spell?"

The Hopla responded over the paralyzing scream emanating from her fingers—a thaumaturgical spell that managed to do nothing more than *piss* the spiders off even more.

"I-I'm trying!"

"All right, then!" the Lycae responded. "Crowd control time, everyone!"

He pounded his fists into the earth and sent a shock wave into the entire left side of the arena, knocking the advancing waves of darkness back. Ethan followed suit, gliding through the dense air and unleashing a Wing Buffet and Roar combo that broke the horde on the right-hand side of the chamber, leaving them wide open for Tara's swift strikes.

"Thank ya, Mr. Ethan!" the Minxit laughed as she pounced from insect to insect, jabbing at the paralyzed ones and ending their lives before they even knew what had happened.

Ethan and Klax kept up the pressure, their crowd control abilities synergizing well enough that the horde barely even had a chance to move a few inches on either side of the chamber.

[Time Remaining: 00:06:00]

"Keep up the pressure!" Klax shouted as the timer ticked down. "And expect trouble! The second phase is starting soon."

"Tell that to our illustrious rabbit here," Tara shouted over her shoulder. "Hey, Faun? Mind hurrying the fuck up?"

Fauna grimaced as she launched a boulder from out of thin air this time.

"Almost! I—I think the next one will—"

An explosion from above shook the entire chamber. Ethan's eyes sought the ceiling and saw that the only polyps that had not burst above had just released their payload; seven green-coated spiders fell from above like bombs being dropped on an unsuspecting city.

Appraisal Success!
Enemies Identified:
[Vena Spider] x7
HP: 80/80
WILL: 50/50

By the oozing green liquid running down their salivating mandibles, Ethan could guess what payload these guys were packing.

Poison . . .

He shifted in the air, whipping up a Wing Buffet that sent three of the beasts flying back. The strength score of the others must have carried them through, for in the next second, one had clutched his tail and sunk its nasty fangs into his feathered plumage.

HP: 70/92
[Status Effect: {POIS}]
DMG: 2 HP/Sec

"Shit!" Ethan screeched, flying headfirst into a nearby wall to try and shake the critter off. When it finally let go, it was after he turned and gave it a harsh Peck that broke clean through its thorax, throwing its blood across his face.

He grimaced as pain surged through him, feeling his vision go blurry. He tried focusing on his companions below, but all he could make out were a thousand dark shapes converging on the vague humanoid forms in the gray prison all around him.

Fuck this! he told himself. *Ethan Graham ain't gonna be done in by some spider poison!*

He flew toward the team and sent a Roar flying through the spiders' ranks. As they fell, he landed and shouted, "Antidotes! There are at least six more poison critters hanging around!"

"Way ahead of ya!" Tara shouted, tossing him a vial which he downed in the next second.

[Status Effect: Cured]
HP: 30/92

Forty goddamn seconds . . . Ethan realized. *That's all it took for the spit to tear through me . . .*

"Incoming!"

The shout was Klax's, who managed to intercept another torrent of vena spider spit that was aimed squarely at Ethan's face. His punch actually sent the strike flying back at the spider who launched it, toppling the creature and knocking it prone.

Meanwhile, the horde simply didn't stop coming . . .

[Time Remaining: 00:02:00]

"Stay out of the way of the shooters!" Klax shouted. "They're targeting Ethan!"

The team nodded, Fauna still fumbling with her spell while Tara sank her blades into the thoraxes of spider after spider on their right.

Another Wing Buffet kept the left flank back, and Klax's punches were doing the heavy lifting of keeping the poisoned projectiles off Ethan.

"Fuck!"

Tara suddenly fell back, a patch of green ooze running up her arm.

"Tara—here!"

In the momentary lapse of Klax uncorking another antidote, a vena aimed a spittle strike square at his back and knocked him down. He shivered as the poison worked its way through his system.

"Klax!" Ethan roared, flying off in the direction of the shooter and diving headfirst into the little bastard, sending its bloody, flailing form high into the sky of the gray chamber. Then, without even turning, he felt the five other spittle strikes that were now heading toward him.

"Protect the Archon!" Klax roared as he downed their final vial of antidote. "Someone get up there!"

[Time Remaining: 00:01:00]

Ethan closed his eyes to the sight of the impending poisonous death that was coming his way. But no sooner had he started writing his will than the poison fumes simply fizzled away, and he opened his eyes to see a haze of red enveloping him.

"What the . . ."

[Infernal Coating: Activated]
Attack Bonus: +25 PYRO DMG
Immunity: POIS, ICE

His juvenile smile was right back on his face as he saw these words. Except, this time, it was the smile of a *true demon*, not that of a noble bird. He felt the fires of Fauna's enchantment flow through his birdly veins like a maelstrom of destruction ready to be unleashed.

He looked down to nod at Fauna, who, through sweat and pure weariness, gave him a thumbs-up from below.

"It's . . . It's something," she murmured.

"All right, all right!" Tara shouted over the din of the still cascading horde of spiders spilling from their caches with even greater intensity. "Let's finish this!"

Ethan took to the skies as a firebird now, tearing through all the spiders like a phoenix burning through the foliage of a once verdant forest. Each one simply popped and fizzed away to nothing, the damage from his Dives and infernal power now simply *dissolving* their bodies before they even had a chance to react or leave their chambers.

He managed to take out two of the vena spider shooters as the final seconds of the clock ticked down, blasting the remaining two away with a Roar that made him look like a real demon of the skies, coated in the fires of the abyss itself.

[Time Remaining: 00:00:05]

"Ethan!" Klax shouted as the spider horde began to fizzle away entirely. "Be ready for the transfer!"

Transfer . . . you know, you could have mentioned that earlier, big guy.

Ethan nodded, though he was loath to tear himself away from his final targets. Like a comet sailing toward the earth, he sped right back down toward his team.

Three . . .

Above, the spider polyps burst with a final spurt of energy, sending a whole blanket of the beasts down to weather the defenders.

Two . . .

Ethan sent a fiery Wing Buffet right back up at them, noticing that the effect was enhanced—the entire wall of spiderlings burned to a crisp almost instantly.

One . . .

"Here, Ethan!" Klax roared, extending his paw just far enough to touch the tip of the diving Archon's beak.

As the beak of the Archon met the paw of the Lycae, the world vanished in a blur of brilliant indigo light.

CHAPTER FIFTEEN

Conflict of [Interest]

E than's three eyes snapped open and stared around him at the new organic chamber pulsing with life. He was alive, once again cheating death along with his three companions, who seemed to be just coming around from their shared blackout.

Just another day for a demon hat . . .

DELVE CHALLENGE: HORDE
Complete!
Rewards:
Spirit Cores: +300
[Antidote] x2
Festering Quiver (DMG +10 vs. Arachnae)
Venabane Staff (POIS spell DMG +10)

Safe Zone Reached

You seeing this shit, Sys? Ethan grinned in the small gray chamber that served as the final safe zone before the Festering Den's final floor. *Three hundred smackers. All for lil' ol' me.*

And you only had to almost die for them. Congratulations.

I know, right?! The payoff's totally worth it. Klax tells me that we all get the same individually, too. Proper fair delve system, right here. This shit wouldn't fly in WoW. The raid leader would grab the goods, citing "ethics" or some bullshit like that. Well, that ain't gonna fly in Argwyll, baby! The land of the fair and equal!

A rather ironic sentiment coming from the Archon. But I can't fault you in principle.

Ethan could tell Sys was finally starting to warm up to him. He focused his attention on his skillsets, greedily eyeing his hat skills and realizing that he had enough—more than enough, actually—to improve another one from Grade F to E.

{Legendary} Hat
Core Skills:
Possession (Rank F)
Skill Siphon (Rank E)
Appraisal (Rank F)
Transmogrification (Rank E)
Current Spirit Cores: 340

Wait, killing all those spiders didn't give me like five hundred more Cores? Lame. Don't go limiting me like that, Sys! You know you wanna see just how OP this monster hat can get.

When Sys didn't even dignify his quip with an answer, he concentrated on improving the Possession skill, reasoning that the memories of his newly possessed hosts might give him an edge in terms of not only his knowledge of the world but also the things these monsters could do. It might even afford him some extra knowledge of hidden secrets known only to the monsters that dwelled within these walls. After all, the grumlets above had had markings and murals that told him they at least had a concept of religion down here. That was more than he was expecting.

Possession (Rank E)
You are now able to view the memories of your possessed minions.

Spirit Cores to Upgrade Any [Hat] Core Skill from Rank F to E: 250
Confirm Upgrade?

You got it, Ethan snapped. *And that still leaves me with ninety Cores to help me on my way to possessing whatever big bastard's waiting for us down below. If it's gonna be another multiphase Boss like that troll before, I'm gonna need a good surplus before I hop on its head.*

In the meantime, though, he should probably check out just what his current birdy boi had been up to his entire life. *Whaddya say, Sys? Wanna take a delve into this dark menace's past?*

Your excitement is unfortunately infectious. It is only a shame your new comrades don't seem to share in your glee . . .

Only then did Ethan's eyes snap to the reality that was unfolding before him. Raised voices, arched backs, and crossed arms greeted him, as well as a flurry of raised fur . . .

"What the *FUCK* was that?" Tara was shouting. "You almost let the Archon die!"

"T-Tara!" Fauna shouted back. "I said I was sorry! The spell just took too long, and I—"

"'And I can't help it,'" the blustering Minxit finished, spitting on the ground beneath her paws. "It's always the fucking same with you."

"Tara," Klax cautioned, "Fauna's magic saved us in the end. That is all that matters here."

"Is it?!" the Minxit retorted. "This happens every fucking time, Klax! We lost the Lightborn because of her! We almost just lost the Archon because of her! Her family fucking died because of he—"

"That's a lie!" the Hopla screamed, rising up, pale hands shaking with fright at her own exclamation. "Y-You're just jealous because I've done more to help Ethan than you have!"

Tara's face blushed a shade of red that should have been impossible, her eyes glancing toward Ethan's blinking pupils.

"Oh-ho!" She started rolling up her leather sleeves to reveal her auburn skin, rough and ready for action. "The rabbit's got claws, does she? Come on then, Faun. Show me what you can do. You 'n me, right now. One on one. Come on."

You aren't going to intervene, oh great and powerful Archon?

Let me think about it.

Ethan thought about it.

. . . I probably should. Even though, well, everyone loves a catfight, right?

Truly, you are a paragon of diplomacy.

"Tara!" Fauna was screeching. "Tara—I said I was sorry!"

The catgirl had marched right up to her face, her hand itching toward the blades in her shorts.

"'Sorry' ain't gonna cut it no more, kid. We're having it out, right here, right now. Show me just how useful you a—"

"ENOUGH!"

Both girls looked toward Klax, who had risen to his full height and was currently looking down on them with murderous intent.

"Both of you—this nonsense serves no purpose! Tara, enough is enough. We have barely twelve hours to recuperate and only two antidotes left. I realize things are tense for us all right now, but if we're going to beat this delve, we have to—"

"You always side with her!" Tara screeched. "Why the fuck do you keep her around on the off chance that she'll be useful? We don't need her anymore. We've got the Archon!"

All fell silent for a time. The only thing that interrupted this awkward moment was the scurrying bodies of the spiders that must have been living inside the very walls that lined this ancient safe zone between floors.

Unbelievably, it was Fauna who sniffled and spoke at last.

"Is that how you both really feel . . . about me?"

Nobody could look at each other. Not even Klax, in the few seconds between Fauna's sniffling statement and his reply.

"No, Fauna," Klax said calmly. "Tara is speaking with spite because she is afraid of dying here and failing our people. She is looking for someone to blame besides herself for her own feelings of inadequacy."

"You don't know everything, Klax," the Minxit growled up at the wolfman. "Stop pretending you've got a good handle on all this. You were *shaking* through that entire fight. Try and tell me you weren't."

"I'd be a bloody fool if I *wasn't* afraid of what's to come, Tara," the Lycae replied with calm, collected candor. "There's nothing wrong with admitting what you're afraid of instead of taking your despair out on others."

The wolfman held her gaze for a time before retiring to try and comfort Fauna, offering her his paw and a smile. But she refused. She walked to her own little section of the chamber and lay down to rest.

"You always talk like you're all high and mighty," Tara spat at his back as she went to her own corner. "But you're just as pissed off as I am, Klax. That's your problem. You never admit that you're a fucking normal person just like the rest of us. Why don't you take a leaf out of Ethan's book and *shut the fuck up* instead of talking about shit you know nothing about."

I feel like there was an insult buried in that, somewhere . . .

Once the catgirl had laid down to rest, Klax simply stood and heaved a heavy, world-weary sigh.

"Hey, Klax," Ethan offered. "Lemme take first watch, man. I've got stats to boost, and I think some of the smoke I huffed from that flame spell got me buzzing. I'm gonna be up for a while."

Klax nodded down at him but held up a firm paw in response.

"No, Ethan," he said. "I would prefer to take the watch. Get some rest. You'll need it for the final floor."

With that, he turned away to slump down by the far wall of the safe zone chamber, his eyes firmly fixed on the dim light of their meager campfire—a fire that threw three opposing shadows across the chamber floor.

In the meantime, Fauna closed her eyes and sighed, too, catching Ethan with a tiny shrug that said she was used to this kind of thing.

Lovely, Ethan thought. *Now we've got ourselves a nice awkward party that's way too much like real life to be fun.*

And let me guess, you're going to be the one who fixes this tense relationship dynamic?

Ethan smiled as he hovered over to Klax's position, gently perching beside the wolfman with an air far more jovial than the Festering Den deserved.

Hey, that's the whole reason I'm here, right? Ethan replied with a jovial wink. *I'm a fixer.*

He'd fix this like he fixed everything else in his old life.

As it turned out, some things never changed.

Klax looked up in surprise as Ethan glided down beside him, his host's head twitching rapidly as it settled down to accompany the sagging wolfman.

"Hey," Ethan said. "I guess we can both take first watch."

Klax sighed again.

"If that is what you desire, Archon."

"You talk to me like I'm a king, Klax." Ethan chuckled. "But really, you're the leader here. I might be the prophesied hero of your people destined to save your world, but I'd still say you've got a harder job than I do."

Klax smiled, but it was a thin, hollow gesture. He looked to his two companions to see if they were sleeping before replying.

"The truth is," he started, "this was never something I was any good at."

"Bullshit!" Ethan almost roared. "You're a natural. It takes guts for a guy to intervene in a squabble like that and come out in one piece."

"No, I mean that this was never the path I would have chosen," Klax replied. "I was a monk in my old life, Ethan. Back when the world was simpler, and humans and hybrids could live shoulder to shoulder. Back when we *weren't* seen as the enemy. Do you know that in the times of Archons past, there were actually hybrids who fought alongside the Greycloaks against the monsters of Argwyll?"

"I—I guess I didn't. But to be fair, I get all my history from you guys . . ."

Klax looked up at the spume-filled ceiling above them—polyps hanging there just like those that had popped above only an hour or so ago to reveal their grisly living payload.

"I wish I could show you what this world once was," he said. "I'm a Lycae, Ethan. We were never bred for leading or for giving orders. In actual fact, it's quite the opposite. We are a species characterized by our loyalty and fierce adherence to our masters. It's often called our best trait. Without a master, it is said that a Lycae can never truly live up to their potential. A dog without a leader can only ever walk alone."

He looked down at his firm, dirt-caked paws, making a fist and then extending his pads.

"I know what it is to feel truly, absolutely alone in this world. I took a solemn vow long ago to try and ensure none of my cousins ever felt that way again. It is that vow that has made me who I am . . . and it is that vow that makes me less than I should be."

"We can only be what we're supposed to be, right?" Ethan said, remembering the statement as something Sys had told him way back before he'd even clawed his way out into this strange new world.

Klax nodded impressively. "You have heard that before?"

"Kaedmon's Law."

"Indeed, Ethan. It is one of the most unbreakable, which no one may ever deviate from. To do so . . . Well . . . you end up like me, trying to wrangle together people who might never be able to get along no matter what I do."

"Yeah . . ." Ethan replied with a little nonchalant stretch of his wings. "Thing is: that's horseshit."

Klax whirled on him.

". . . What?"

"That law," Ethan explained. "It sucks so hard that nobody should ever follow it. I mean, come on—if we were nothing more than what we were made to be, I'd still be sitting in my one-bedroom apartment covered in Dorito shavings and binging tasteful *hentai*."

"*Hen . . . tai?*"

"Besides the point. What I mean is—fuck, Klax, look at what you've managed to do. You, a dude who's supposedly meant to just *obey* without question. You've brought a whole team of hybrids together in the name of kicking ass and fucking up the Lightborn himself. And you've been doing it all this time . . . waiting for me to arrive so that it's all worth it. C'mon, Klax, if that's not what leaders are made of, I don't know what is."

Klax said nothing for a moment, returning his gaze instead to his two companions on opposite sides of the chamber.

"Y'know what Fauna told me earlier?" Ethan asked. "She said that the Sanctum was just a place before you came along. *You* made it a home. A place where nobody has a master."

"Heh." The old wolf finally grinned, showing all his serrated fangs in the process. "Ethan, you are certainly not the Archon we expected."

Ouch . . .

"But I think you are exactly what we need right now," Klax finished. "Thank you for your words."

"Uh . . . don't mention it. Seriously. I'd hate to get the reputation of being a mystic type or some advice column writer."

Klax nodded with another little smile as he saw Ethan's eyes begin to close over.

"Go on and rest," he told him. "I've got things covered here."

"Cheers . . . dogman . . ."

The Lycae's face briefly turned serious before Ethan drifted off properly, the exhaustion of the entire dungeon so far finally taking its toll.

"It is curious, though," he said. "You speak as one who knows my mind. You know my thoughts as though they are your own. I wonder, Ethan, when you lived as a human . . . did you also know what it meant to be alone?"

The Lycae's question would unfortunately go unanswered, as when he turned to look upon his Archon, he found the demon hat fast asleep atop its fine-feathered host.

As Ethan dreamt, he felt the winds of Argwyll against his beak.

He was flying with his brothers and sisters in the clear, crisp summer sky. For miles on end, they saw nothing but baby-blue hues and wispy clouds they broke through together, flying in unison toward . . . he wasn't sure what. Below, stretches of forest disappeared and gave way to gray mountains and ashen deserts, snowy tundras and ancient temples hidden in the depths of dark, festering swamps. Around him, his family glided with absolute control, each one maintaining their flight formation like it was the most natural thing in the world.

Synergy. That was the trick. They knew each other just as much as they knew themselves. Each individual raven was an extension of the other one—and no one bird existed without the family. Each one was willing to live—and die—for the other.

"It's all . . . about . . . family . . ." Ethan murmured as he watched his host's memories fade away into darkness. *Even in this world, the good prophet Vin Diesel was right.*

—Delve Notification—
[Time Remaining until End of Safe Zone: 00:30:00]

Ethan awoke to the team gathering up their things and stomping out the sputtering embers of their fire. Tara stood at one end of the platform that would lead them down to the final floor, while Fauna faced the opposite direction.

Guess nothing much has changed here . . .

Klax, however, was a different story. He was up and ready before anyone else, clearing away everyone's bedrolls and distributing the final two vials of antidote to the two girls before leading the way forward.

". . . What about you and the Archon?" Tara asked.

"Us?" Klax mumbled. "Oh, I think we'll be fine. We're men, after all. We're used to taking all the poison in the world and dealing with it."

"That's bullshit!"

The exclamation had come from both girls, and Klax and Ethan shared a good-humored laugh at seeing them united in anger.

"Here!" Klax shouted, tossing the Festering Quiver item toward Tara. "I know you'll be wanting this. Don't think I didn't see you eyeing it up from your System Notification window."

The Minxit huffed, saying nothing at first. Then she strapped on the quiver and nodded appreciatively as she checked one of its spider-slaying arrows.

"Not . . . bad," she mumbled.

Ethan, for his part, summoned up the staff they'd acquired and threw the loot toward Fauna. The girl caught it with a stumble and a stuttered question that couldn't quite leave her lips.

"Told ya I'd get you a new staff."

The Hopla blinked at the corroded black stick in her hands, but when she wrapped her fingers around its shaft, she smiled warmly up at Ethan.

"You should transmogrify this, you know," she told him. "Our victory was yours, really."

"Nah," he replied. "You're the one who bravely set me on fire. And without Tara's storm of arrows, I couldn't have survived as long as I did to do some real damage."

The girls looked at their comrades with suspicion before finally sharing a glance between themselves.

"Faun," the Minxit started, "I think these two boys have been conspiring as we slept."

"How very like them," Fauna giggled.

"Don't get me wrong," Ethan put in, flexing his wings gallantly as the safe zone timer ticked down its final few seconds. "I'm gonna be taking over whatever big bad Boss is down there. That's my prize. Your great Archon will have no need for staves or arrows once he becomes the lord of the Festering Den."

"Is it too soon to get worried that the power is going to his head, Klax?" Tara asked.

"Worried? I say we want him to be as power hungry as possible. Let the world tremble as its greatest monsters come under his control."

Ethan smirked, feeling renewed confidence sweep over him.

"I'm wondering what the Boss is gonna be . . ." he murmured. "My hope? Sexy spider goddess."

His companions blinked at him.

"Spider goddess?"

"Y'know—half giant spider, half sexy lady. The *good* half, before you say anything."

They didn't really have anything to say about this revelation. The horrified faces of the hybrids told Ethan enough.

"Guess it can't be helped," Tara shrugged. "Our Archon's a booby bandit through and through."

"And proud!" Ethan exclaimed. "Think of the powers I would hold in my hands!"

"I don't think that's power you're thinking of . . ."

Sorry to break up this perverse conversation, but . . .

—Delve Notification—
Rest Concluded
Safe Zone Nullified
Beginning Third Floor Transition . . .

Transit—?

Before Ethan could finish that thought, the ground gave way beneath the party, sending them each hurtling into a dark abyss that drained all color from their faces.

"L-L-LUCATIA ILNUM!"

A blue bubble of energy enveloped the crew, halting their descent as instantly as it had begun.

"Hell yeah, Fauna!" Ethan shouted as they smashed together.

"It worked . . . I-I mean, yeah, it worked!"

The Hopla's delight was met by a reserved sigh from Tara.

". . . Pretty good, I guess."

Their chatter was cut short when they hit the ground, all of them immediately drawing their weapons and surveying their surroundings with alert, ever-watchful eyes.

"Welcome to the third floor," Klax growled, fists at the ready. "Occupant: one."

"Where is it?" Tara hissed. "I don't see—"

A sudden rumbling tore through the ground beneath their feet, sending cracks across the mushy organic floor, much paler than its gray counterpart above.

"Faun," Klax stated. "We're gonna need fire."

The Hopla obeyed without question, summoning a red-orange flame that instantly lit up the chamber—and gave the party full sight of the spider eggs lining the ceiling, including one egg that was far bigger than the rest, right in front of them, which had started to crack open slowly.

A low growl began to issue from its insides.

Four pairs of legs slithered out, and four crimson, unblinking eyes glared down at them.

"Fauna," Ethan murmured, "I think we're gonna need more fire in here . . ."

CHAPTER SIXTEEN

Boss Battle: [Rachneros]

BOSS ENCOUNTER!

The creature emerging from its pale white cocoon slowly began to dominate the final floor of the Festering Den. It had eight limbs, two of which ended in a pair of scimitars molded to the sickly white flesh of their bearer. The creature's torso resembled that of a muscle-bound albino male, ending in a bulbous, bulging spider's thorax that practically oozed toxic fumes from its rear end. The thin, spindle-like neck of the beast extended until its insect eyes were staring right at the party of invaders who had just entered its realm. It opened its slitted mouth, revealing rows of glittering teeth that threw noxious spittle into the faces of its new prey as it roared.

Rachneros, the Pale Lord (Level 30)
HP: 550/550
WILL: 280/280

Now, that's some meaty stats right there . . .

"Guys?" Ethan asked as his three companions began to back away slowly. "Don't suppose you can convince this fellow hybrid to just give up and get some Fashion Sense, if you know what I mean?"

"This is no ordinary hybrid . . ." Fauna murmured, fumbling with her new staff as she tried to summon a fire spell.

The lord of the Festering Den lunged in the next second but managed to carve nothing but a hole in its own lair, the hybrids managing to roll out of its strike. Tara returned fire with a well-aimed arrow that caught the beast in its lithe, lolling neck. It screamed as it tore the arrow free from its wound, a little river of swamp-green blood spurting from its puncture.

"It ain't no hybrid," Tara shouted, "but it sure does bleed like one!"

"Concentrate on its neck!" Klax roared as the beast spun to slice clean through the air—an attack that just barely managed to cleave a few threads from the top of Ethan's hatty form.

"Roger!"

The shout had been Fauna's, and in the next instant, she aimed right at the creature's face and let fly a barrage of brilliant fire that slammed straight into the beast's eyes. Ethan followed up with a Dive attack that sent it reeling right back into its cocoon.

"Don't let up!" Klax roared. "It'll have more up its sleeve than just raw po—"

As if on cue, one of Rachneros's limbs shot out and clipped the Lycae in his shoulder, throwing him clear across the room to land in a burst egg at its end.

"Klax!" Tara yelped. "Bastard. Have this!"

She sent a hail of three arrows sailing for the recovering arachnid lord, which with little more than a flash of his organic scimitars, he beat away, chuckling grimly as he did so.

Let me give you something to laugh about, big guy . . .

Ethan's Wing Buffet managed to startle the creature, but it did not knock it prone. Instead, all four of the spider lord's legs dug into the ground, and he sent a belch of black bile toward Ethan. Sensing the poison hidden in the liquid shot, Ethan *dove* out of the way and managed to circle around to the creature's back.

"Faun!" he shouted. "Now's the time for a flame on!"

"G-Got it!"

The beast turned to swipe at the annoying raven pecking at its spine from behind, taking a chunk out of the wall to its right and sending a cascade of rocks down on Tara's position. Ethan watched her somersault her way out of the falling rubble and let loose three more arrows that found their mark, embedding themselves in the big bastard's neck.

Rachneros, the Pale Lord (Level 30)
HP: 430/550
WILL: 200/280

Let's see how much longer you can resist . . . Ethan grimaced, circling the creature and employing his Hide skill to great effect. It looked like even the Boss's four eyes weren't helping him locate the dark raven as it blended into the black abyss of its lair.

Then, like a flower blooming in the dead of night, Ethan lit up and felt Fauna's Infernal Coating take effect. He dove right for the spider lord's cranium as soon as the heat began to erupt and wrap itself over his feathers.

"Go for it, Ethan!" Tara shouted. "This fucker's got nothing on us!"

But Rachneros wasn't taking any of this sitting down. Indeed, with every hit and every successful puncture of its weak point, the beast seemed to just get more and more agitated.

In a furious flurry of movement, its limbs suddenly twitched out of control, sending rocks and boulders from above down on Fauna and Tara as they blasted him from below. Both girls had to run for their lives as the roof of the chamber literally began to come down on top of them. Meanwhile, Ethan dodged and broke through countless rocks that impeded his path toward his target.

Come on . . . come on . . .

Once he was within a few inches of Rachneros, the beast sent both its scimitars out to catch Ethan, managing to slice at his claws and send him just off course before the bird could catch his neck.

Fuck!

Ethan ended his Dive in the middle of Rachneros's spider thorax, knocking the creature back and drawing a torrent of blood from the hole now pierced in its abdomen.

"A sound blow, Ethan!" Klax shouted as he got back up and began punching clean through the rockfall from above.

Ethan landed with his companions as Rachneros clutched at pieces of its innards, which had begun spilling out across the floor of its lair. Its breathing became raspy, and the walls around them seemed to mimic it, beginning to pulse with each breath the giant spider hybrid took.

HP: 360/550
WILL: 140/280

"We're almost there!" Ethan shouted. "A few more shots should do it, then this angry boi's gonna make a great little addition to my host collection."

The hybrids formed up, ready to launch a final assault on the great pale beast as it roared in their faces, sending out a shock wave that each of them had to narrowly avoid as they made their run up to its bleeding body.

"Faun!" Ethan called. "Focus on distracting it! Tara, you know where to aim!"

"Got it!"

"Klax!" Ethan now shouted at the bounding dogman beside him. "Keep an eye on those boulders from above. You'll have some smashing to do, I'm sure."

The Lycae smiled. "It is what I'm best at!"

Ethan then focused his energy into a final Dive, feeling the flame from Fauna's enhancement only grow stronger as he narrowed his eyes and leaped, sailing toward their enemy like a comet plummeting toward an unsuspecting planet.

But the suffering Boss of the Festering Den did *not* simply wait for them to come. Instead, it plunged both its scimitars into its new sore and drew them back out, each now coated in a different hue of corrupted blood.

And Ethan's eyes went wide as he swerved to avoid its lightning swipes.

Let me guess . . . welcome to . . .

BOSS ENCOUNTER!
PHASE 2

Rachneros, the Pale Lord (Level 30)
HP: 300/550
WILL: 100/280

Big bug's gone supernova . . . and cut itself open to do it. That's new.

Ethan dove out of the overcharged scimitars' main swipes, dodging to the left and managing to slice into the thin shoulder blade of the creature's right arm.

"I'm coming back around, guys!" he shouted down as he went back into the shadows. "Give me a sec!"

Then, almost as soon as it had been summoned, Ethan's Infernal Coating dissipated entirely.

"Guys?"

When none of the hybrids answered, Ethan turned to see them scattered on the ground. It seemed that as Rachneros's right arm had flailed in pain, it had brought it down upon Fauna.

The rabbitgirl was coughing, doubled over in pain as Klax leaped to push her out of the way of another strike, the spider lord's left arm seeking her once shining staff with homing precision.

"No, you fucking do—!"

Before Tara could finish her cry, the right scimitar of the beast caught her torso, sending her plummeting to the ground and immediately tensing up.

"W-What's ha—?"

Before Ethan's eyes, the catgirl's body began to *crisp and stiffen*, and a creeping mass of gray stone began to travel up her legs and slowly wrap itself around her skin until nothing was left but her face, contorted in pain.

"Tara!" Ethan shouted. "I'm coming!"

"Forget me!" the catgirl called out. "Kill that bastard bu—"

Her words were swallowed as the petrifying effect took hold of her completely. Now, she was nothing but a statue suspended in midscream.

At the other end of the room, Klax was administering an all-purpose antidote to Fauna, watching as the healing potion knit up the cut that had been torn in her stomach. The rabbitgirl winced in pain, but her eyes focused on nothing but the sight of her fallen companion.

"Ethan!" she shouted. "Take the all-purpose potion and pour it on her!"

That's right! That antidote we got from the slimy rat guy back in Sanctum!

Ethan obliged, flying past two more deadly strikes from Rachneros as he bounded forward, his torso spilling corrupted blood across the floor, covering the entire chamber in toxic ooze that Ethan could tell would poison anyone who touched it. He hefted up Statue Tara and brought her to Fauna without another word.

"Look out!"

Fauna rattled off a spell of Repulsion that just managed to send Rachneros hurtling back against another assortment of eggs. Ethan glanced back to see that the creature had just *leaped* at him in a display of power that could probably have ended his life right there and then.

Then, with speed totally incongruous with its size, the beast leaped again, clipping Ethan with its petrifying blade.

Well . . . shit.

He went down, face-first, into the dirt. But, curiously, the blade had only nicked his host. He, as a hat, was still free to observe and flail about as much as he liked.

For all the good it'll do me . . .

Rachneros looked down on him like he was nothing but a sheen of mud to be scraped off a shoe. Then, with a roar of triumph, the beast brought both his blades down to finish him.

Or at least, it would have, if Klax hadn't intercepted the killing strike.

"HAR-CHAKRA!"

The dogman clapped his hands around the organic hilts of both the creature's scimitars without even breaking a sweat, keeping it still even as Rachneros began spewing torrents of bloody, toxic spit in his face.

"N . . . Now!" the dogman growled to Fauna. "Shoot it!"

Fauna leveled her staff, her hands shaking as she felt its grooves splinter in her fingers.

"TAKE THE SHOT, FAUNA!"

The rabbitgirl hesitated, looking down at the still petrified Tara.

"Hey," Ethan said beside her, his host's body now nothing but crumbling stone. "You can do this."

She blinked. "B-But I might—"

"Fauna," Ethan said. "Don't think about *what-ifs*. Don't think about what could go wrong. Just think: *Super. Magic. Awesome.*"

In this moment, Fauna was probably thinking of her lost family—the people she still felt she had failed when she couldn't protect them from the human hunters who had destroyed their home and shown no mercy. These thoughts probably always dominated her mind in moments like these, where her team depended on her to do the job only she could do: blow things up.

But Ethan didn't look at her with definite expectations. Instead, he looked at her as someone looked upon a miracle: no matter what she did, it would be amazing.

And it was *that* look and his words that made her face the raging beast before her, grip her staff tighter, and square her feet, readying a bolt of purifying flame that coursed through her veins and jumped into brilliant life on her staff's tip.

Then she fired.

The red spear of light rocketed from Fauna's staff, its intensity carving a blinding scar through the oppressive darkness of Rachneros's lair. The cavern itself seemed to recoil from the force, trembling as if it feared the magic that Fauna had unleashed. The light illuminated the grotesque form of the hulking spider hybrid, casting long, monstrous shadows that flickered across the jagged, stalactite-filled ceiling.

Rachneros barely had time to react before the beam made contact. The red-hot energy collided with its bile-coated scimitar, intended to block the blast, but it was too much. The heat vaporized the weapon's edge upon impact, and a sickening hiss filled the air. The weapon, as ancient and corrupted as its owner, began to disintegrate, the organic mesh crumbling into flecks of black ash. Then, with a final crack, the beam seared through Rachneros's entire right arm, and the limb was severed clean off, flung into the air like a splintered tree limb in a hurricane.

The arm landed with a revolting splat, and Ethan watched in muted horror as it exploded in a hail of charred flesh and corrupted blood. The arm lay twitching, its nerves spasming wildly as bile and dark ichor poured from the ragged stump. Rachneros let out an agonized shriek that reverberated through the cavern, a sound so piercing and raw that Klax's fur-covered ears flattened against his skull in an attempt to block it out.

"HELL YEAH, FAUNA!" Ethan screamed. "Now, quick! Someone toss me at the big fucker!"

Fauna, still reeling from the sheer force of her attack, blinked in surprise. Her wide rabbitlike eyes darted toward Ethan, now vibrating with frenetic energy. In her panic, she snatched him up, muttering a hasty apology as she hurled him toward Klax. Ethan tumbled through the air like a dark blur, spinning head over brim as the floor of the cavern below seemed to rush up at him.

"Sorry!" she squeaked, her voice barely audible over the churning, furious roars of Rachneros. Klax caught him, turned back to the flailing beast looming above them all, and leaped up on the creature's muscular torso.

"Ready, Ethan!" he shouted over the bubbling bile that Rachneros sent spilling down from its open jaws to catch them. "We'll get one chance at this!"

"Toss me, wolfman!" came Ethan's reply, loud and clear, as Rachneros thrashed around like a speared fish, trying desperately to shake them off.

"Now!"

As the other poison-coated scimitar came to slash at Klax's back, the Lycae hopped right up on the beast's shoulder and slammed Ethan on his head, jumping back out of the way of the creature's gnashing jaws.

Ethan blinked frantically as he attuned himself to the Boss of the Festering Den's fading brain.

[Skill Activated: Possession (Rank E)]
Rachneros, the Pale Lord's WILL: 60 vs. Spirit Cores: 90
Possession in Progress . . .

Ethan first felt the creature's surprise. Then came anger—anger that bubbled and frothed into a mindless, animal rage, the insectoid menace twisting its every limb in a frantic attempt to shake off the hat or at least maim its companions.

"Everyone!" Ethan shouted, trying to maintain his focus and hold on to the thing. "Run!"

They tried to—but Ethan saw Klax get clipped by a thrusting limb and fall, his stomach bleeding where the impact had been made. The wolfman sent a flurry of jabs right back into the mass of skittering, twisting, and raging spider limbs to at least keep them off Fauna as she readied another spell—but the effort was wasted. Right now, Rachneros wasn't even registering pain. And like every other bastard monster in this place with an attitude problem, it was putting up a fucking good fight.

Possession in Progress . . . 25%

"C'mon . . ." Ethan grimaced.

C'mon, big guy, don't you wanna be a sexy spider dude with a dapper lil' hat like me? Give in, and I'll take you out of this shithole, and you can have all the tasty humans you'd like. Sounds good, right? Mmm, roasted human flesh . . .

Rachneros didn't seem at all interested. Incredibly, the spider Boss's autonomy seemed to mean a lot to it.

Well . . . too fucking bad, buddy!

Possession in Progress . . . 35%

The beast had all but stopped even trying to shake Ethan off. A low, sly growl emanated from its throat now, and Ethan realized that it had sensed something about him as their minds had begun to join.

It turned from the battered Klax and fixed its attention on Fauna.

Don't you fucking dare.

With a snarl of hatred, it charged the girl, knocking her back and etching deep gashes into the flesh beneath her robes. She screamed in pain and rolled away, her staff skidding toward the end of the room.

Fucking . . . bastard! Ethan roared. *You—You understand I'm gonna make this as painful as fucking possible for you now, right?*

Possession in Progress . . . 34%

What?!

Ethan heard the grim snarl of Rachneros as it began to skitter toward Fauna, jaw open in expectation of its little meal. It was almost as if the insectoid were enjoying this moment, savoring the fact that Ethan could see his companion about to die through its own eyes. The big bastard knew Ethan was there, and every slow, agonizing move it made toward the girl was like a small victory for the beast itself. It wanted him to squirm.

I . . . Do it! Ethan growled. *See if I care! You think you're gonna force me off you with an appeal to emotion? Ethan Graham ain't a fucking simp, big guy. I'm the Archon, don't cha know? And this world's mine!*

Ethan looked through Rachneros's four eyes to see Fauna shivering beneath its gaze, her robe ripped and tattered, mouth agape, and hands searching frantically for her staff that was nowhere to be seen.

Possession in Progress . . . 30%

Damn it!

The oozing limb scimitar came up, ready to deliver a downward slice that would tear the Hopla apart.

Then—pain.

As soon as Ethan said this, fury snapped at his mind. For it was now no longer just one mind—but a mind joining with another. Subsuming another. And this was no simple critter. It was a sentient, powerful, and very angry beast that did not appreciate being challenged.

Ethan could feel the pure, intense hatred burning within its brain, and did everything he could to focus on making sure that it wasn't *him* that was being swallowed up during this possession.

He twisted his head to see three black arrows embedded just above his spine, and as he traced their trajectory, he found their owner aiming another triad of pain right at him.

"Hey, ugly," Tara grinned, shaking droplets of all-purpose antidote from her skin. "It's rude to stare."

Her arrows sang through the air and found their mark, three of them splintering off and piercing clean through Rachneros's eye slits, taking out most of his sight and, Ethan found, his remaining will to resist.

Rachneros, the Pale Lord's WILL: 25 vs. Spirit Cores: 90

Alright, Ethan thought. *Time to kick this into overdrive.*

He concentrated, funneling his thoughts through Rachneros's spasming body, channeling his spirit into the beast's corrupted veins and feeling them finally relent.

Possession in Progress . . . 65%

Tara, meanwhile, leaped to grab Fauna and sprinted with her to the very edge of the cavern, watching as Rachneros submitted to the Archon's whims through screaming, thrashing death throes.

Possession in Progress . . . 80%

Then, a sudden flaring of action. A final ounce of Willpower surged through the beast, and it commanded its scimitar to raise and hover over its chest.

"It . . . It's gonna off itself!" Ethan shouted.

But before its organic blade could come down, Ethan beheld a triad of flame-coated arrows cut clean through the limb, sending the blade somersaulting through the air to land against the barren cocoon its bearer had emerged from.

And Ethan, now looking through the single eye of his prey, saw both Tara and Fauna standing side by side, the latter's staff raised to enchant the arrows of her comrade.

Synergy . . . Ethan thought with a chuckle as Rachneros's spirit finally left its body with a last desperate whimper.

Possession Success!
Congratulations! You have successfully Possessed Rachneros, the Pale Lord (Level 30)!
The Pale Patriarch of all Arachnae's WILL is just as strong as the toxins which flow through his blood. But even the most corrupted beasts can be broken.

Rachneros, the Pale Lord (Level 30)
Stats:
HP: 25/550
MP: 0/0

WILL: 280/280
STR: 100
PER: 55
SPD: 40
CHA: 3
Skills:
Enweb (Grade E)
Poison Coating (Grade E)
Petrification Coating (Grade E)
Skill Siphon:
Roar (Grade E)
Hide (Grade D)

Choose any (Two) Skills from [Dark Raven] to Transfer:
Wing Buffet (Grade E)
Peck (Grade F)
Dive (Grade E)

Current Spirit Cores: 590

Ethan blinked with the single eye he had working as he read these stats.

These . . . Oh yeah, now we're talking. That Lightborn cosplayer better watch out.

He slowly rose to behold his three hybrid onlookers, raising his bleeding arms and gushing green blood across the floor as he spoke through a mouth bubbling with ichor.

"I'M . . . I'M A FUCKING SPIDER!" he roared. "SO . . . What . . . ?"

The cavern began to spin as he realized that, yes, he had inherited this host when it was literally on the verge of death.

"Ethan!" Klax shouted.

He watched as his three companions ran to him, uncorking their last vials of Malphus and getting ready to practically smash the bottles over his every torn limb.

"Oh yeah . . ." the demon hat mumbled as it sat atop the head of the spider king. "We kinda . . . fucked this guy up good, huh . . ."

Then he fell.

CHAPTER SEVENTEEN

[Spider Hat]

A sea of memories floated in front of Ethan.

His new Possession upgrade was kicking in. He could feel his mind and that of Rachneros linking, and his disembodied consciousness traveled through the depths of the creature's thoughts to the little part of the beast that was still alive, somewhere, watching its body being puppeted by the Archon that had finally come for it.

And it was that strange sense of inevitability that brought a single wave of the past crashing down on Ethan's face.

He was standing in his lair. He was Rachneros—completely. *Ethan* didn't exist.

He had just been hatched, and he spread his new limbs. He looked at them in curiosity, bringing the two little blades at the ends of his arms up to his face to try and work out what exactly he looked like. A little nip from his right arm drew a line of green blood from his left cheek. He felt pain—his first real sensation.

"Careful, little one!" a voice rang out in his mind. "Those claws of yours cut deep."

This voice belonged to someone speaking to him from far away. It was like an echo traveling down a long, dark corridor.

Then a bright light blazed in front of him, displaying a large box with lines of text scrolling past faster than his brain could keep up with.

Rachneros, the Pale Lord (Level 1)
Stats:
HP: 200/200
MP: 0/0
WILL: . . .

He stopped looking at the letters. Instead, he was fixated on the four-eyed, bug-faced being looking back at him.

"Yes, newborn," the voice said. It was clear and angelic, at once soothing and calming to his frightened nerves. "That's you. That's your name. And these are the numbers that define you."

He dismissed the box with a grunt and instead focused on the other spiders hatching from their cocoons in the chill, dark chamber of his birth. The little ones regarded him for only a moment before all turning away—an army of green-and-black arachnae scuttling away from him.

He stretched out a limb to try and halt them, opening his many-fanged mouth and begging them to come back.

"I'm sorry, little one," the angelic voice said. "But that is not your purpose. You must remain here, and await the delvers."

He wasn't listening to the voice now. He was trying to scurry toward his brothers and sisters, but he could do nothing but watch as they left him alone down here, trapped in the dark.

"It is okay," the voice said. "In time, you will learn to enjoy even the pain you will experience. After all, you'll be dishing out a fair bit yourself, haha!"

His mouth opened in a scream that begged them to stay by his side. He just couldn't accept what this voice was telling him. Even though he knew now that he had been created purely to live a life of perpetual loneliness and suffering down here, one question still burned in his newly formed mind: Why?

And the voice, speaking with absolute clarity, gave him the answer:

"We can only be what we are supposed to be," it said.

The light of a bug lantern shone on Ethan's new face, awakening him to the world of the present.

"Ah, thank goodness," Klax said. "We thought that perhaps—"

"Outta the way!" Tara shouted, running into the large oval chamber as Ethan adjusted to his new vision. He could see and sense far more than he could before. Even the frantic heartbeats of his companions were thumping loudly in his ears—joined by the chorus of hearts waiting outside this candlelit room. He'd have to try and deal with that . . .

Of much more interesting note were the two serrated scimitars he brought up to his eyes, and the hybrid-spider body he now inhabited.

He checked his status screen just to be sure.

Host: Rachneros, the Pale Lord

His smiling face beamed down at his furry friends.

"Now we've got ourselves a real Boss, guys."

"Hah!" Tara yelped, giving him a stout punch in his spindle legs. "Ya got that right! This thing's deluxe. Took us long enough to stitch you back up, mind you. But hey, it's worth it, right?"

"How the hell did you manage to repair the big bastard's arms?"

Tara winked up at him. "Ol' Fraxx has his remedies. Some of his potions would be considered necromantic up on the surface, but fuck that. We're in Sanctum, and we make our own damned rules."

Ethan then caught sight of Fauna looking up at him from behind Klax.

"Faun!" Ethan shouted. "Hey, looking good! How're you—"

He stopped as he noticed the girl step back when he pressed forward, and then suddenly, he remembered exactly how this must look to her: the creature who had been ready to gobble her up and chew her out, the one who had all but cleaved her—this was a real monster standing above her right now.

"Faun," Klax said gently. "It's okay. It's him."

The girl twitched her nose as she slowly emerged.

"E-Ethan?"

Ethan bent down low in a bow that let her see his hatty form wriggling around atop his new host's head.

"It's all me, gal," he said with a wink, proceeding to flex his new toned torso. "Who'd have thought, eh? I had wanted a sexy spider goddess, and instead, I got me a masculine, leggy god."

"Speak for yourself, big guy." Tara laughed. "You weren't looking so hot when we dragged you outta the Den."

"Oh yeah! What happened after I blacked out?"

The Minxit shrugged. "The place came crumbling down, almost like it didn't like us stealing its prized Boss. We used the teleport stone to get the fuck outta there."

"It . . . is against Kaedmon's Law to remove a creature from a delve," Fauna explained. "Some say it leads to bad omens—a curse put on someone from the God of Argwyll Himself."

"Superstitious shit," Tara scoffed. "Besides, the Archon's the de facto rule-breaker of this world. And now, with this new form, we can finally take the fight to the hu—"

"Tara," Klax said suddenly. "Remember what we talked about."

The Minxit shot the Lycae a look of surprise.

"Klax, look at him! He's gotta be ready. He's gotta—"

"Are you really willing to take that chance?"

The two stared each other down as Ethan got a better grasp on his surroundings. They had placed him in a high-ceilinged chamber set within the bark of a tree, by the looks of the oaken walls and etchings carved into its bowels. If his senses could be trusted, he was right back in Sanctum.

He felt a pang of remorse for his old dark raven body (which had probably been left down there in the rubble of the Festering Den), but hey, the bird had lived a good life . . .

On to the next one!

"If you guys don't mind," Ethan spoke up, "I'm gonna get me some upgrades. These Spirit Cores ain't gonna spend themselves."

"Of course," Klax said. "But first, there's a very . . . *ahem* . . . impatient crowd out there waiting to see their lord in all his glory."

"You got more fangirls and guys than you'll know what to do with, Mr. Archon," Tara added. "Make sure there's enough of those new legs to go around."

"Tara!" Fauna giggled.

"Hey, it's the truth, sis."

Ethan couldn't help but smile, seeing the good humor restored between the two. Klax, meanwhile, was looking like he was gonna collapse from exhaustion—and Ethan saw that his wounds were still in the process of healing.

"Hey, Klax? You all good?"

The wolfman shook his frayed mane and managed a smile. "Fine, Ethan. These old bones are just getting on with time. With an Archon like you, though, I'll be set to retire in no time."

He gestured to the wooden hallway leading out of the oaken chamber, and the team followed Ethan's lead. He was pondering his upgrades—knowing for sure that he could probably take Hide all the way up to at least C grade now, with enough left over to improve Roar and some of his bird skills, too. He admitted that he was curious, however; now that he didn't have any wings, how was he going to manage a Dive or Wing Buffet attack?

Transfer Skills from Previous Host: Wing Buffet (Grade E) and Dive (Grade E)?

He didn't reckon that a spider lord suited his Peck skill, and besides, he'd barely even needed to use it with his claws and AOE attacks.

Skill Transfer Complete!

It also looked like he'd now be adding the capacity to inflict some super crippling status effects into the mix.

Poison Coating (Grade E)
You slather your weapon in the virulent poison composed from your own blood, taking -20 HP DMG instantly in exchange for giving your weapon the [POIS] attribute.

Poison type: Pale Lord Venom
-5 HP/second
Duration: 10 seconds
Spirit Cores to Upgrade [Poison Coating] Skill
from Grade E to D: 200

Fifty damage over time, he thought. *And all it takes is a little pricking of my lovely pale skin. Applying this'll be nothing—all I gotta do is make sure I hit. Here's hoping you've got some meaty poison resistance, Mr. Artorious.*

Alright, next skill?

Petrification Coating (Grade E)
You slather your weapon in the debilitating bile closest to your heart,
giving your weapon the [PETRI] attribute for ten seconds.
[PETRI] Chance: 30%
Duration: 10 seconds
Spirit Cores to Upgrade [Petrification Coating] Skill
from Grade E to D: 250

The ability to be a living, breathing Gorgon for ten seconds? You can count me the fuck in. Sys, you seeing this shit?

I must admit that these abilities do seem rather . . .

OP? Ethan chuckled in his new, insect mindscape. *Get with the program, baby.*

Outside the oak chamber, Ethan beheld the crowds of hybrids who had waited for him and his companions. Their faces lit up at his new presence, murmurs of excitement running through the crowd as Klax emerged to address them with his booming voice.

"Hybrids of Sanctum!" he roared. "Witness the new form of the Archon! The form that will send shock waves of fear into this world and carve out a place for our people on its surface!"

The cheers of the people practically brought the rocky roof down. Ethan's five eyes swept over them, waving his scimitar limbs in the air and letting them take in his new, mighty body.

"Let the celebration of the Archon's first delve completion begin!"

"Celebration?" Ethan looked down at the smiling old wolf. "How exactly do you guys celebrate down here?"

"How do ya think?" Tara asked as she slapped one of his slender new legs. "We're gonna get blind drunk."

CHAPTER EIGHTEEN

The [Greyden]

Caer Krea, Greycloak Headquarters. Argent Mountains.

Terrible storms lashed the venerable battlements of Caer Krea. It was said that the ancient base of the Greycloak Order had been built on the back of Karfangg the Despoiler, first of the Archons. The scratched, rugged appearance of the fort and its sharp, angular towers put one in mind of a creature's fangs piercing the earth, ready to swallow the world whole. The entire fortress looked as though it could crumble away at any second, and yet, for centuries, it had stood rigid. Firm. It had weathered storms far worse than this one.

It had been here that the first Greycloaks had assembled within the great Onyx Hall of the fort and, under the gray moon of Argwyll, made their pact to annihilate the monster menace that plagued their world.

And it was through the storm-wracked battlements that a single member of the Order walked tonight, his cloak held tightly around his neck, blood spattered across his thin frame.

The warriors of the fortress stopped their training and meditations in the main yard, the great braziers flanking the venerable gate of their home sparking and sputtering as the old warrior was admitted entrance. His eyes shone with blue light, strong and clear even against the onslaught of the storm. Every warrior knew who he was. They knew what must have brought him back among them.

And instantly, the mood of the fortress changed.

When the one-armed man opened the creaking door to the great hall, he was met by the bespectacled form of the old fortress architect, Mobius, sitting at his desk and poring over hundreds of screeds—requests made for the Greycloaks to help the beleaguered citizens from all over Argwyll.

"State your name for the records, Grey One," he said without looking up. Evidently, he suspected that this was simply another brother or sister back from a monster hunt. He didn't need to look upon a Greycloak to know when one was standing in front of him. The stench normally gave them away.

This one, however, was unnaturally silent.

"If your tongue has been lost, just proceed to Healer Justine," he added with a half-hearted wave. "Though she's fully booked tonight, she might just manage to squeeze you in a midnight slo—"

"Artorious."

Mobius, normally a man who balked at interruptions, paused almost instantly.

"Artorious Pendragon," the man before him said. "Class: Lightborn."

Now, the small, ungainly head of Mobius jerked up to see the sight—a sight he didn't think he'd ever see again. There he was, the old Lightborn of legend. Slayer of the Demon Flower Gyko, the last Darkseed to plague the world.

And he was covered head to toe in the purple-black viscera of monster blood.

Mobius found that he didn't quite know what to say. So, having lost his filter of professionalism, he simply said what came into his mind as he met those old eyes gleaming with sapphire.

"So, you have returned."

"Perceptive as ever, Mobius," the Lightborn replied.

"If you've come back . . ." the architect murmured, "then that means . . ."

"Where is the knight commander?" Artorious interrupted. His words sounded more like a demand, not a question.

"The knight commander is not currently receiving visitors," Mobius replied coldly. "Especially not from exiles."

The eyes of the one-armed knight narrowed to piercing snakelike slits. He edged closer to Mobius, so much so that the latter heard some of the warriors sequestered in the hall draw their blades.

"I think she'll make an exception for me," Artorious growled. "Don't you?"

He didn't wait for an answer. Instead, he swept by the staring bookkeeper and entered the second floor of the fort, feeling the piercing gazes of comrades both old and new on his grizzled features.

When he entered the main hall—the place where the very first Greycloaks had drunk the blood of Krea—he couldn't help but take a moment to inspect the great portrait that dominated the ceiling. It was, after all, the very first sight he'd ever seen when he'd been taken to these halls and told of his destiny. The painting depicted Krea, the Angel of Kaedmon, standing atop the first Archon against a backdrop of almost total devastation. For that was what the world had been before the Angel had come to serve her children.

He inspected the inscription at the bottom of the plaque: *The Triumph of Humanity.* "Krea, the First Lightborn, stands victorious over Archon Karfangg and proclaims the new dawn of Human rule over Argwyll now and forever after."

He grunted up at her perfect face—her radiant purity that he'd seen in every dream he had as a boy.

And he turned away. He didn't need to see Kaedmon's Angel now.

He didn't head to the washroom as any sane man might expect. Instead, he barged past the training arena, sparing only a second to look up at the mosaic windows depicting the Lightborn of old (his window was still defaced and long since painted over) before storming into the high office of the knight commander.

She was still exactly as he remembered her. Wild. Blonde. And utterly disdainful of his general presence. Immortality had not made her any more patient.

"Evening, Carliah."

She was writing something rather angrily with her quill—the weapon that she could use to cut through even the toughest Greycloak initiate. Hell hath no fury like Knight Commander Carliah Argent's performance reviews.

"Artorious," she said without looking up.

He came forward, gesturing at the chair in front of her ornate desk. Upon the walls were a series of intricate, antique clocks ticking away with the times of all of Argwyll's hemispheres.

"Say what you're here to say," she barked. "And then be gone."

He sighed. "You still despise me, after all this time?"

She stopped writing. "Hatred is unprofessional," she said. "But then, so is cowardice. Perhaps we're all simply guilty of different crimes, Artorious."

"I wouldn't have come here simply to antagonize you."

"The fact you dared to come here at all tells me you simply do not give a jot for the sanctity of this Order. Honor means nothing to you."

A distinct thump finally brought the blonde crown of Carliah up. She stared blankly at what the Lightborn had just thrown on her table.

"Take a good look," Artorious said. "And then tell me if you still care more about honor than doing what's right for this world."

Her face was a picture of contradiction. A woman trapped forever in her late thirties since the first day she'd joined the Order, she wasn't unused to concealing her emotions. For one who had risen so quickly in the ranks of the Greycloaks, the ability to outsmart one's opponents was paramount. It was said no one among the ranks of the Order could truly ascertain Carliah Argent's battle moves; she was too quick, too elusive, and too strong when she finally made her mark on the flesh of the unwary monsters of the land.

But right now, Artorious could see, as only his eyes could, that there was a sense of fear hidden there in her narrowed eyes.

That was an emotion he was all too familiar with . . .

She held the objects he'd thrown on her desk in her muscled hands: a piece of blue cloth and the shards of his own broken blade.

"So . . . it's here."

Artorious only gave a solemn nod.

"The Archon."

"The fucking *hat*." Carliah grimaced, standing and turning away from the Lightborn. "The one that wasn't even meant to appear if only a certain someone had done his job right last time. Why now of all times?"

Again, Artorious did not speak. He had shown her what she needed to see. Now, she had to do the rest for herself.

"Where?" she snapped at him suddenly.

"The Grenbelm Forest," he replied.

"Core abilities?"

"Possession. And a penchant for draining the Willpower of its foe. Once the will of its potential host is low enough, it is able to assume direct control of their nervous system."

The knight commander huffed at this. "So that's its little trick. Not quite as insidious as Gyko's Darkseed, nor as irritating as Gelsadra's Eternal Life."

"It's in its larval form," Artorious explained. "But by now, it could be stronger. Much stronger. Monster populations are already going wild even in the mountains outside the fortress. King Lysandus won't listen. The capital city of Lucent will be in the most immediate danger. If it falls—"

The knight commander held up a muscular fist. "You don't have to tell me how this all works. Lucent falls, then all of Westerweald falls, and then the rest of Argwyll falls. Just like what almost happened last time."

Artorious nodded. "So, you understand why I'm here."

"I understand that the disgraced Lightborn who's been nothing more than a drunk, crippled, and sad old man for the past decade has come running back to his family after they threw him out because he can't do his job."

She pointed at the shards of his shattered rapier.

"You can't kill it," she stated. "Can you?"

He was not to be dissuaded. "Not with conventional weaponry. If you can authorize the use of our onixia supplies in the ancient storerooms, I—"

"No," she said, turning and fixing the Lightborn with her cold, dark stare. "You can't kill it because you've already done so before. That is the sacred, unwritten law of Argwyll: the Lightborn slays the Archon, and then they perish. A sacrifice as old and sacred as time itself must be made. That is the mark of the true Lightborn."

She leaned forward, meeting his deadly stare with derision.

"And when you sunk your blade into Gyko one hundred years ago, you failed to follow through on that sacrifice. You lived."

Artorious balled his single fist while vestigial fury welled up in his empty arm socket.

"Have I not already been tried for my supposed 'crime'?" he asked her. "I accepted my exile. I have done what I could to help this world even without your assistance. Now, I have a job to do again. I come before you to see it through."

"And this time?" the knight commander asked. "Will you carry through the sacrifice of your ancestors?"

"I . . ."

"If you don't, you know what'll happen."

He did. He shut his mouth as he saw the cogs turning in her mind, and he knew that this was exactly what she wanted. The transfer of power from one Lightborn to another normally happened after the death of the previous Lightborn. In the wake of an Archon's defeat, the Lightborn had always perished. In the last seconds before the lord of all demons died, the spirit of the Lightborn traveled through its veins and clogged the beast's heart, nullifying the primordial darkness within and dying with it to seal the world from evil for another century.

But when he had finally plunged his sword into the belly of the last Archon, he had been very much alive. Of course, the Greycloaks had suspected foul play. Of course, they had tried him and shunned him. They had cast him out, rejecting what they saw as pride. His spirit had simply been too greedy for glory. Too hungry for prestige. He had wanted to live a good life in the wake of his victory, not sacrifice himself in the honorable way his predecessors had.

They had been right, and so very wrong about him at the same time . . .

"Where is it now?" Carliah sighed.

"I do not know. As it lay before me helpless, a group of hybrids came to spirit it away with a teleport stone."

"Hybrids?" the master of the Grey scoffed. "Then at least we know what we're looking for out there. We've had reports of mass hybrid resistance in the eastern reaches. I'll alert the chapters there. Pull a few favors from the local villages around Gyko's old territory in the Ashfalls. It makes sense to start the search up that way. The rest of us will ride for Lucent and establish a defensive position in the city just in case things go tits up. We'll check the Delve Registries while we're at it; if his hybrid guardians are smart, they'll be helping to power their new leader up through some special dungeon delves."

"King Lysandus will not be . . . receptive to the idea of giving up his city."

Carliah looked at him like he'd told her two plus two equals four. "Course he won't. I'm invoking Krea's Commandment. He can blabber all he wants about being king—it means nothing when this world's about to go to shit."

He nodded as she quickly scribbled these plans down then made for the door. He couldn't really be surprised. The knight commander was strict, but she was also noted for her fairness. She knew better than he how to organize their forces and protect this territory. Hell, she'd had more than enough practice.

What weighed more on Artorious's mind now was the fact that he had begun walking a path that would only end in one place: a place he'd been in before. A place that, he knew, he would hesitate before he went to again.

"And Artorious?" Carliah said as she stepped by him to begin preparations. "You'll be staying close by from now on. Should you fail to do your duty this time, I'll kill you myself."

CHAPTER NINETEEN

[Drunken] Evolution

H AIL THE ARCHON!"
  "LONG LIVE ETHAN!"
"MAY HE SNUFF OUT THE LIGHT OF THIS WORLD!"

That last one seemed a little too intense . . . but Ethan wasn't gonna complain. This rabble of drunkards and their slurred speech was comfortable, in a way. It reminded him of the karaoke nights he'd had in college, back when life was simpler but nowhere near as exciting as this.

He—in his new shiny giant spider form—sat on the rooftop bar of the Mushy Mistress—Sanctum's premier tavern atop the biggest mushroom stalk glowing in the cavernous kingdom.

Around him were hybrids of all sorts drinking to his ascendance, congratulating him on assuming the form of a beast as powerful as Rachneros himself—even as Ethan heard whispers that he was basically the first real Delve Boss most adventurers would have to contend with if they took their dungeoneering seriously in this place. Even then, most adventurers couldn't take him down.

And that means there are even stronger Bosses out there . . .

"You shoulda seen it!" Tara shouted above the cheers of those around them. "Ethan swooped down from the shadows and slayed at least a hundred spiders single-handedly. Not even Karfangg himself could cut through so many enemies at once!"

"With . . . With—*hic!*—my help!" Fauna added, swaying from side to side while her companions sent up cries of "Ooooooohs" at the rabbitgirl's sudden bravado.

Ethan grinned down at them both. Fauna's normally cream-colored face was flushed red—the result of ingesting a little too much of the viscous purple liquid the tavern sold: Khaletchka. Apparently, it was a concoction brewed from the strange glowing mushrooms around this part of Sanctum. Ethan looked down at his own bottle and gulped down a mouthful himself. The night was young, and much partying still had to be done.

"Alright, Faun," Tara said. "Your fire might have come in handy, but—"

"There's no—*hic!*—'might' about it, Tara!"

Fauna stood up on the table between them and raised her staff for all to see.

"I, Fauna the Wildglance, made the Archon into a Phoenix! *Whooooosh! Whooooosh!*"

Ethan laughed with the other hybrids, many of whom cheered on the normally shy girl as she beamed down at Tara with total confidence, albeit almost slipping and falling once or twice.

Tara, however, was beginning to smart at her bravado.

"I was the one who saved you, my dear Hopla, or have you forgotten?"

"Fauna can—*hic!*—look after . . . herself . . ."

In the next moment, the girl slipped and fell into one of Ethan's four laps, rolling over and looking up at him with drunken eyes.

"Mr. Ethan . . ." she said. "Please pet me . . ."

"Hey!" Tara yelped, jumping to drag the girl away by her ears back to the table. "Enough of that, you sly, lustful little rabbit. I ain't done with you yet."

Ethan let the commotion continue, downing shot after shot of khaletchka until his pale form began to take on a shade of lambent crimson.

Alright . . . he said to himself. *Upgrade time . . .*

Not that I particularly care or anything, but is this really the right time to—

SYS! Upgrade Time!

As you wish.

Host: Rachneros, the Pale Lord (Level 30)
Skills:
Enweb (Grade E)
Poison Coating (Grade E)
Petrification Coating (Grade E)
Skill Siphon:
Wing Buffet (Grade E)
Dive (Grade E)
Roar (Grade E)
Hide (Grade D)
Current Spirit Cores: 590

Alright . . . even wasted, I know what I need. We're taking Hide all the way to the big leagues now.

[Upgrading Skill: Hide (Grade D)]
Upgrade Complete!
Congratulations! You have upgraded [Hide] from Grade D to C.

Hide (Grade C)
Mass Hide unlocked: Your Hide ability functions on any allies
within ten feet of you.
Sneak Attack Bonus: x3
Spirit Cores to Upgrade [Hide] Skill from Grade C to B: 100

"A challenge has been issued!" Borlor the badgerman Dixit proclaimed to everyone at the bar. "Tara the Rogue vs. Fauna the Wildglance—last to be shit-faced under the table wins Lord Archon Ethan for the night!"

Cheers announced the beginning of the girls' drinking competition, and Ethan—who probably should have been listening—was unfortunately immersed in his upgrading.

You are currently being "played for." As your System, I would be remiss if I did not—

Sys! Ethan spat in his mind. *Shut down for a minute! I'm busy here.*

. . . As you wish. Just don't come crying to me later.

Next up . . . Ethan thought. *I should focus on Roar. Stopping groups of enemies from moving means surefire kills.*

[Upgrading Skill: Roar (Grade E)]
Upgrade Complete!
Congratulations! You have upgraded [Roar] from Grade E to D.

Roar (Grade D)
Paralysis from Roar now applies Status Effect {SLUGGISH} to enemies,
halving their movement speed for two minutes.
Spirit Cores to Upgrade [Roar] Skill from Grade D to C: 200

"CHUG. CHUG. CHUG!"

"Hey! No using magic, bunny girl!"

Tara pulled on Fauna's ears as she tried fortifying her stomach through Wildglance, managing only to summon a starfish from her fingers, which flopped down gently into her drink.

"Hah!" the Minxit roared. "You're finishing that."

Next . . . Ethan thought. *I should focus on Dive. As a spider, I can scale walls and get some height on enemies. And with the size of this new body, a dive-bomb attack's sure to hurt . . .*

[Upgrading Skill: Dive (Grade E)]
Upgrade Complete!
Congratulations! You have upgraded [Dive] from Grade E to D.

Dive (Grade D)
Dive can now be used to destroy objects of STR 60 or lower.
Spirit Cores to Upgrade [Dive] Skill from Grade D to C: 250

So I'm literally gonna be a walking, talking battering ram . . . Ethan smiled. *Alright. I'm good on AOEs and single-target DPS. How about my new status effects . . .*

A thin, persistent tapping on Ethan's spider thorax roused him slightly from his meditations, and he saw the frayed form of the ratman alchemist, Fraxx, looking up with a creepy level of adoration at him.

"My congratulationsss, good Archon. I am hearing of your prowesss thisss night. Your body—it isss a thing of beauty now."

"Riiiiight," Ethan replied. "Um. Something you needed, or—"

"A sssample," he said without hesitation, producing a small syringe and flashing Ethan a vicious, sadistic little smile. "Of your corrupted blood. I am hearing from Tara that it isss quite potent . . ."

"Meh." Ethan shrugged. "Go ahead."

Wait. Don't you think this is something you should really consider and talk ov—

"Many thanksss," the ratman said as he plunged his syringe into a pulsing vein on Ethan's leg. "With thiss, I ssshould be able to improve our weapon coatingsss. Sssoon, our army will be wielding weaponsss that ssshall boil the blood of the humansss."

Ethan turned suddenly at the mention of the word "army."

The ratman was already hobbling back as the shouts of the two drinking girls grew only more boisterous. "We make preparationsss every day," Fraxx continued with an expectant lick of his lips. "For on the day of our emergence, the sssurface world will not be ready for usss."

The little rat bowed as he left, mumbling something about how all the noises of celebration did nothing for his keen ears.

Meanwhile, it seemed the girls' drinking game was coming to an end.

"H-Had enuff?" Tara belched as she threw her tankard over the wall of the rooftop.

"F-Fauna does . . . not . . . back down."

Last upgrade, then, Ethan said as the world began to swim around him.

Current Spirit Cores: 290

Enough to upgrade one of my two weapon coatings, or . . . What does this Enweb thing do?

Ethan scanned his skill list again.

Enweb (Grade E)
***You sling a sticky mass of cobwebs that trap any creatures moving
within with DEX 45 or lower.
Range: 50 feet.***

So, it's pretty much a ranged version of my Roar ability . . . Is it really worth it to upgrade just for that? Or would I be better to focus on the coatings? I mean, let's be honest, if I possess another, stronger Boss than this guy in the future, I'm gonna transfer the weapon-coating skills, right? Maybe—

Ethan's thoughts were finally interrupted by the sudden, violent retching of Fauna, who threw her head over the balcony and belched her guts out over the side, covering a few unfortunate dancers below in rabbit spume.

"VICTORY!" Tara screamed, the crowd raising their tankards to her as she swayed around, giving Fauna a hearty pat on her back as the rabbitgirl collapsed back down into her chair.

"Nooooo," the Hopla moaned. "Mr. Ethan . . . help me . . ."

Ethan's five eyes double blinked at all the commotion.

OH. NOW YOU'RE BACK IN THE ROOM?

Before Ethan could register the shouts and whistles from the hybrids all around him, Tara had suddenly appeared at his side, pulling at one of his hind limbs.

"C'mon, Ethan," she said. "I own ya now, don't cha know?"

"Wha—"

"C'mon!" she insisted, and having little alternative it seemed, the giant spider possessed by a hat allowed himself to be spirited away. Rumors began to ripple through Sanctum that a certain kitten had just caught herself a big morsel for dinner tonight.

Little did Ethan know what he was in for. This was no social call. In the eyes of the Minxit girl, there gleamed a bloodlust that had to be sated tonight.

Ethan was about to find out just how much humanity he had left.

"Smash."

"Pass."

"Pass."

". . . Smash."

"Seriously? That's Martella—a Tabika, don't cha know? Lizardwoman. You got a thing for scales?"

"Everyone's got their flaws. Besides, what that tongue could do . . ."

Ethan sat with Tara on the roof of his castle's battlements at the very edge of the Sanctum, looking out at the dancers and merrymakers who were getting plastered in his name. The whole city was suddenly awake with hope—all because of him.

Us.

Excuse me?

I'm just saying that I should get half the credit at least. Without me, none of this would be possible.

You know what? he said to Sys, smirking. *Knew you'd come around eventually.*

Don't get me wrong. I know you will perish in some ungodly way, screaming in agony as you are cast into the same flaming pit your siblings were. But as long as I still live, I would at least wish to be appreciated.

You'll be appreciated when you drop the snarky bastard act—and not a second sooner, Ethan mumbled in his mind before turning back to his smiling Minxit companion.

"You know what?" she said. "This 'Smash or Pass' game ain't half bad. Makes you think, y'know? Even if it was thought up by a human."

"Some of us have some pretty good ideas every once in a while."

Tara said nothing. She looked out into the dancing crowds, merry drunkards, and the mushroom towers that released their luminescent spores into the atmosphere, lighting up the cave with a kaleidoscope of violets, oranges, indigos, and crimsons.

From their vantage point, they could see the entire city—a city that was suddenly alive with hope and cheer for the Archon's return, and the promise of true freedom he brought with him.

"Pretty cool place, right?"

"Pretty cool," Ethan agreed.

"You humans—the stuff you build—it ain't like this. You take what you find and twist it up until it's barely recognizable as earth anymore."

There are . . . worse things we do than that. But eh, I'll let it slide.

"Humans might have ideas about the way this world's supposed to be," Tara continued as she downed her drink, "but that doesn't mean they're good."

Ethan could sense the hate behind her voice.

"They've messed you up too, huh?" he asked.

"They've messed us all up, Ethan. And they'll keep on doing it until it's either us left or them. Every one of those dancers you see down there has their own sad story to tell. It's what brings us all together: suffering at the hands of the humans above. Some of us were lucky and never lived in the cities. The things I've heard from hybrids living in Lucent? I wouldn't even wanna repeat . . ."

Ethan thought of Fauna's story, of losing her family to an anti-hybrid purge by the Greycloaks, and realized that Tara would have her own, probably very similar experience. Though it didn't seem like she was interested in sharing it anytime soon.

His old office experiences were kicking in. You couldn't work with a team without knowing their baggage and trying to accommodate it. That just wasn't how things functioned. One voice alone couldn't do much. But a group—they had power. He just needed to know how to make these hybrids work together effectively, and for that, he needed to know them—even their grisly pasts.

"Y'know, Ethan," Tara suddenly said. "Klax wouldn't want me speaking to you alone."

"Huh? Why's that? You gonna bring me over to the dark side?"

"Something like that," Tara chuckled. "He thinks you're not ready to see what the world's really like out there."

"With a body like this?" Ethan scoffed, flexing his muscular torso and legs. "Tara, I'm ready for anything."

The Minxit looked him up and down then, the lambent crimson of the mushroom's recent spore discharge lighting up her face.

"Yeah . . ." she said. "I think you are, too."

She stood up suddenly and cracked her neck, her tail whipping about in excitement.

"Look, Klax and me, we have our differences, yeah? Let's call them . . . philosophical disagreements. He has his opinion; I've got mine. I respect the guy—hell, I'd kill for the guy. But he's an old dude now, Ethan, with old, out-of-date ideas. And he thinks he's really the one in charge, but we've got a new leader now, don't we?"

Ethan drunkenly agreed, though he didn't know exactly what the girl was getting at.

"It might just be time for us to put that to the test. So . . . you wanna do something stupid?"

Ethan, drunk with bravado (and booze), smiled down at her.

"Always."

They slipped outside, both of them employing their Hide skill and sticking to the rooftops of Sanctum's residential district. Up the stone stairway they trekked, stumbling over each other until they finally emerged outside in the ruined remains of the last Archon's surface lair. The sun was just starting to dip below the horizon, bathing the Westerweald countryside in a garish orange hue.

"C'mon," Tara said with a pull on Ethan's arm and a schoolgirl-like giggle. "This way."

Ethan, still in the form of a giant spider hybrid, gave a little gulp as he followed after her.

Okay, look, he told Sys. *I'm not a cat person. I'm not that kinda guy, really. But . . . look: those short shorts are looking pretty damn loose. And that tail probably has a mind of its own . . .*

You are attempting to justify carnal relations with your companion?

I'm just saying, Sys . . . when in Rome . . .

. . . You are in the body of a giant spider.

I'm still half man! Ergo, we should, y'know, make sure everything works, right? For testing purposes. Research.

Tara guided him through the trees at the foot of the Ashfall Mountains until their dark boughs gave way to a small valley with smoke trails drifting from a collection of buildings at its center. Buildings which, Ethan saw, were surrounded by a barbed wire fence lining their perimeter.

And it all suddenly became very clear to him that he'd been wrong about this girl's intentions from the very start.

Straining his eyes from their position on the valley's lip, Ethan saw shapes moving around the buildings: emerging from a cave nearby, carrying clumps of shining ore and minerals, hauling carts in and out of the wooden structures lining the site.

And these shapes wore chains around their limbs, collars around their necks . . .

"What . . . am I looking at?"

Tara's reply was a dark whisper.

"A work camp."

Rows of crude, rusted cages lined the camp's center, each filled with hybrids—beaten, malnourished, and covered in bruises. Human overlords dressed in worn armor swaggered through the aisles, barking commands at the captives, their whips cracking through the chilly evening air.

"Scum," Tara muttered, her voice seething with barely contained fury. "They use us as free labor then toss us when they're done. This one's a mining camp. Borlor was saying he needs new materials for our weapons, so I did a little scouting of the surrounding area."

Her hand tightened on the hilt of her blade, a low growl escaping her throat. The wind tugged at her dark, wild hair, and her feline eyes glowed with intent. She was ready—more than ready.

"Tara," Ethan murmured. "Klax doesn't know, does he?"

The catgirl eyed him. "Course not. He'd never have agreed to hit this place. But then, he's not the Archon, is he? You're our real leader, Ethan. I thought that, out of everyone, you'd understand. Besides, you wanna see what that new body of yours can do, right?"

Even as Ethan heard the words of the Minxit and knew—without exception—that they were bathed in pure hatred for those who cracked their whips below, he couldn't tear his eyes from the images of suffering he was seeing. His body, a monstrous fusion of pale skin and arachnid limbs, pulsed with demonic energy, and his mind thrummed with a burning hatred for these slavers. Even in this powerful host body, there was a part of him—his human soul—that felt the visceral disgust of this place; a disgust that fueled his resolve.

The humans of this world really do suck, huh?

That's a matter of perspective.

C'mon, Sys. You see what I'm looking at. How the hell's this a good thing?

You will learn, Ethan Graham. Or you won't. Not that it matters in the grand scheme of things.

Ethan shook Sys free of his mind for the moment.

Just focus on what you're good at, he told it. *Telling me about what matters here.*

I suppose you are referring to keeping count of your Spirit Cores? That, I can do. It is, after all, what I was first made for.

Ethan turned his attention back to the waiting Tara.

"They won't know what hit them," he whispered, his voice a guttural rasp that barely sounded like his old self.

"Let's make sure of it," Tara responded, her amber eyes locking onto his. "We hit them hard and fast. Leave no survivors."

Ethan's eight pale limbs twitched as he readied for the descent. "I'll take the north gate. You handle the barracks?"

"Deal." Tara smirked as she unsheathed her twin blades, their edges shimmering in the fading light. "Don't get sloppy, spider boy."

Ethan let out a dark chuckle.

"When have I ever?"

CHAPTER TWENTY

[Assault]

Without another word, Ethan and Tara leaped into action, both activating their Hide skill to move unseen under the cover of the gradually descending dark of night. The catgirl was a blur of shadow and speed, while Ethan's massive form moved with eerie silence across the craggy terrain. He reached the north gate, his long legs carrying him swiftly over the rocky ground, his pale form blending into the cold, moonlit night.

As he approached, two guards stood at their post, sharing a casual conversation. They never saw him coming.

In a single, fluid motion, Ethan extended his poisonous blade and pierced right through the neck of the first guard. The man gurgled, his body convulsing as venom spread through his veins. The second guard barely had time to draw his sword before Ethan's other limb shot forward, impaling him through the chest.

He tossed the lifeless body aside and entered the camp, his eyes locking onto the human overlords who continued to bark orders at the hybrids. Tara was already at work near the barracks, moving like a phantom, her blades cutting through armor and flesh with precision. She moved in and out of the shadows, leaving behind only the silent bodies of her enemies.

The camp exploded into chaos as Tara cut through the barracks, slashing down soldiers as if they were nothing more than straw dummies. Meanwhile, Ethan tore into the heart of the camp, his monstrous form wreaking havoc among the soldiers who scrambled to defend themselves. They tried to mount a counterattack, but they were no match for the Pale Lord.

"Over here!" one of the human overseers yelled, pointing his sword at Ethan. "Kill the monster!"

Appraisal Success!
Enemies Identified:

Human Overseer (Level 10)
HP: 50/50
WILL: 10/10

Barely even worth my time . . .

The soldiers surrounded Ethan, but it was a futile effort. With a growl, he reared up on his hind legs and activated his Petrification Coating, sweeping his vibrating scimitar across the battlefield. The soldiers closest to him froze, their limbs locking up as terror spread across their faces. Soon, such terror was the last expression they ever wore as their bodies turned to dark, corrupted stone.

Ethan's claws slashed through them with ease, blood and rock splattering against the dirt. Those who could still move tried to flee, but Tara was there to cut them down, her movements a deadly dance of whirring blades.

"Hah!" the catgirl screamed against the backdrop of the rising moon. "This ain't a battle. This is sport!"

Those Ethan didn't catch with his petrification were easily dealt with through his new Enweb skill. Their dexterity obviously didn't account for much, their movements becoming slow, sluggish, and cumbersome. Their stuck limbs made to slash at the legs of the demon who had come among them, only to find that they moved as though encased in treacle. It was child's play for Ethan to relieve them of this burden. Permanently.

His Poison Coating finished those who made it to the edges of the camp, their blood bubbling and frothing with Rachneros's corruption until they fell, whooping coughs wracking their chests, clawing at their bellies where Ethan's poison was surging up through their systems. Their bodies broke, ruptured, and bled. Slowly.

Within minutes, the camp was reduced to a slaughterhouse, human overlords and soldiers lying in twisted heaps. The hybrids, still trapped in their cages, watched in stunned silence as their captors were eviscerated before their eyes.

Tara stood panting, wiping the blood off her blade with the cloak of a fallen soldier. Pointing at the hybrids with a blade wreathed in the blood of their captors, she shouted, "See that? That's what the Archon can do."

One cloaked hybrid—a Minxit just like Tara—came forward, shambling as his shackles shook against his aging limbs.

"Sister . . ." he breathed. "Is . . . Is it really him?"

"You better believe it," she replied as she slashed through the Minxit's chains with a single swipe. "And this time, he's here to stay."

Ethan, covered in the blood of the fallen, surveyed the carnage with cold satisfaction. Meanwhile, the hybrid prisoners had now dropped their rocks and minerals, some of them prostrating themselves before their bloody god, hailing him as their savior.

Y'know . . . a guy could get used to this.

Ethan wasn't sure if it was his own bloodlust talking or the mind of Rachneros suddenly coming back to its host and affecting him, but he started to feel a distinct sense of enjoyment at watching each human fall before him.

It was like watching his old work colleagues die in agony. He'd had those thoughts—anyone would. No, he'd never act on them, but it wasn't unnatural to want to see the indolent and the wasteful take a dirt nap. He'd been the one picking up their slack for years on end, never complaining, ever the competent, consummate professional, just like his parents had always wanted him to be.

And it had gained him—nothing.

But here, he realized something as he looked down at those hybrids he'd just saved: they'd be devoted to him now. Entirely within his grasp. The power of being a messiah was intoxicating, he had to admit. Even if he was a monstrous one.

On Earth, I was born to be nothing. Here, I am destined for greatness by nothing more than the blood that flows in my corrupted veins.

A general alarm suddenly sounded nearby—one of the human overseers in the burning tower that was their headquarters was ringing a bell and signaling a general retreat.

"Those of you who value your lives, RUN! Bring word to the king! To the Greycloaks! The— That's the Archo—!"

The guard never finished his cry. Ethan's elongated limb found his neck and clipped it, sending his head twirling into the darkness of night. Then, with the hybrids singing his praises at his back, he leaped after the humans who were trying to run.

Dive.

He crashed into a cluster of guards, ending their lives as his bulbous form broke every bone in their bodies, crumpling their armor like paper and shredding through their skin. The attack left a crater in the earth that trapped the survivors, who tried scrambling away in vain.

Spirit Cores: 350

More, Ethan thought. *I need . . . more.*

His hunger was ravenous. Sys was nowhere to be heard, or if he was saying anything, Ethan's mind had gone to a place where he could no longer hear the prattling of his System guide.

With each cut, he felt the power of the humans' departing spirits surge through his new muscular limbs, feeding the black heart at the center of his being. The humans who made it to the lip of the crater found themselves enwebbed—a little contingency Ethan had set up just in case any slavers tried to escape his wrath. They could do nothing but watch as the grim specter of eight-legged death came upon them.

Spirit Cores: 380

Not enough, his mind raged. *More. I need . . .*

His eyes caught sight of one cloaked human who'd managed to resist his webbing. The man sprinted for dear life into the tree line beyond the burning camp, carrying something in his arms—probably valuables pilfered from the hybrids he'd lorded over during his time here.

"Ethan!" Tara shouted. "Want me to get him?"

"Nah!" the Archon shouted back. "He's mine."

Ethan chased him into the trees then picked his moment to strike. With a single flourish of both his blades, the cloaked head of the runner came flying off, spinning in a geyser of blood that painted the leaves of the forest a dark crimson. He fell in a crumpled mess of gore, leaving his wrapped package to wriggle free.

Ethan stood over the body and watched the strange object move—until, through the diminishing red haze of his rage, he saw what the "package" was.

A boy.

A human boy who couldn't have been more than seven years old, who had been bundled up in what must have been his father's arms.

The boy cried out, his pudgy hands reaching toward his father's corpse, eyes and nose dripping with tears and snot. And Ethan stood, mute, watching as the tragic end of the boy's innocence occurred right in front of him.

This . . . fuck. This shit's getting dark. Sys, tell me a joke or something, huh?

You're the joker here, Archon. Go on, say something funny.

Ethan couldn't oblige. He looked down at the boy and saw the sadness in the child's eyes suddenly give way to vibrant, all-consuming anger. The child's eyes flitted to the form of the great beast towering above him like a murderous god.

Then, he reached for the sword nestled in his father's belt, and Sys did the job Ethan told him to do.

Enemy Identified:
Human Child (Level 2)
Enemy . . .

Before Ethan could think anything more, the boy ran at him, swinging his father's broadsword with wild abandon. His strikes were erratic, the kind that came from pure desperation rather than skill. The sword's blade scraped and clanged against the tough carapace of Ethan's host, sending small sparks flying but causing little more than scratches.

The boy was sobbing as he swung, eyes red with rage and grief, his face twisted in a snarl that looked unnatural on someone so young. The trembling sword finally cut through, nicking Ethan's arachnid leg, slicing into the chitin with the strength of pure adrenaline. The boy pressed forward, hacking away at Ethan's lower body like a crazed animal.

Ethan barely felt the nicks against his host's skin. He saw the HP readouts tick down—one, two, three pips of damage—but his attention was elsewhere. The kid's screams pierced the cool night air like needles. Each cry, each frantic strike, was a dagger to the atmosphere, creating a dissonant contrast to the eerie silence that had followed the massacre of the plantation.

"Kid," Ethan said, his voice a low rumble. "Stop."

The boy didn't hear him. He kept slicing away, eyes blurry with tears, his frail, dirt-covered body shaking, his skinned knees giving out as he struggled to stand. The smell of sweat, blood, and rain mixed in the air, a sour reminder of the boy's desperation.

"Kid?" Ethan tried again, louder this time, though there was no softness in his tone. His many eyes watched the child's every move, catching the determination in his trembling hands and the fire in his tear-streaked face.

"Die!" the boy screamed, his voice cracking. "Die! Die! Die!"

Ethan felt an odd pang inside; not quite sympathy but something close enough. *How many more of these "avengers" am I gonna run into?* he thought, suddenly feeling exhausted by the scene unfolding before him. He had seen hatred and fear and desperation before, but there was something sharper about it when it came from a child.

With a flick of his claws, Ethan made his move.

The boy's sword flew from his hands with a metallic clang. It hit the dirt a few feet away, sliding across the ground, the sound oddly final. The boy stood there, empty-handed, staring at his wrist in shock as if expecting the blade to return to his grip.

Ethan's scimitar claws gleamed in the dim light, still raised, ready for a more final strike. The boy's wild eyes darted between his limp wrist and the looming figure before him, terror and defiance warring in his gaze. Ethan could almost see the boy weighing his options, but there was no calculating way out of this.

And yet, despite the odds, the boy didn't collapse. His legs wobbled beneath him, but he didn't fall.

Instead, he scrambled toward the sword again, his bare feet slapping against the wet earth. Ethan watched with a strange kind of fascination, almost admiring the kid's unshakable drive—though that didn't mean it wasn't pointless.

Just before the boy's fingers brushed the hilt, Ethan spun a thread of webbing from his abdomen and lashed it out. The sticky silk shot forward, ensnaring the boy's legs and halting his desperate charge midstep. He stumbled and fell face-first into the dirt, arms flailing in front of him as he reached for the sword, still defiant despite the inevitable.

"Hey, kid," Ethan said, moving closer, his voice dripping with both annoyance and something else, perhaps pity. "Look, enough's enough."

The boy twisted in the webbing, turning to face his enemy. His small, filthy face contorted as he took in the full sight of Ethan's towering arachnid body, the hat perched atop his host's head watching him with gleaming eyes.

"Archon . . ." the boy whispered, his voice barely audible above the soft crackling of the dying fires around them.

Ethan paused, a flicker of uncertainty crossing his mind. *Ah, shit . . . how the fuck do I handle this?*

The rain picked up, drumming against the earth in heavy drops that spattered against the half-burnt remains of the plantation. Smoke still rose from the ashes of buildings, mixing with the fresh scent of rain. Above the forest, the smoke curled into the sky like black tendrils reaching for the heavens, their thick, acrid smell permeating the air as rain washed over the bloodied earth.

Ethan could still hear Tara in the distance, her laughter mingling with the screams of the dying as she danced through what little remained of the human resistance. She moved like a ghost through the carnage, every strike of her stilettos precise and lethal. There was no mercy in her steps, only bloodlust and glee.

Ethan looked down at his claws, slick with the blood of the fallen. The rainwater mixed with the blood, running in thin red rivers down his limbs. He couldn't help but glance past them, seeing the boy's wide, unblinking eyes as he lay there, webbed and helpless, trying his best not to look at his father's mangled corpse.

"You know what I am, then?" Ethan asked, though he knew the answer. The boy's silence was reply enough. "Fine," he said, his tone gruff. "Then you know that when that web wears off, you should run."

Ethan turned his back, figuring that was the end of it. He'd given the kid his chance. He didn't have time for this, not when the storm of conflict still swirled around him.

"Monster . . ." the boy muttered under his breath.

Ethan's muscles tensed. He wasn't sure why, but the word hit him like a physical blow. It bounced around his head like a sharp echo, digging deeper each time it came back.

Yeah, that's what I am, right? A monster.

Whatever snarky comment Sys made was lost to him, muffled beneath the weight of that word—*monster*. So, when he heard the boy's next words, he stopped midstride, feeling that pang inside again.

"No," the boy said louder, more determined.

Ethan turned slowly, his many eyes narrowing. "What?"

"Don't try and trick me!" the boy shouted, his voice gaining strength as he tore at the webbing, his small hands clawing at the sticky strands. "Come here and fight me! Like a real monster!"

Ethan sighed, rubbing his temples. The rain poured harder now, soaking through his host's exoskeleton, turning the battlefield into a quagmire of mud and blood. The boy kept writhing in the webbing, still trying to free himself.

How do I reach this kid . . . and why do I even care?

He should've killed him. Should've killed him right after his father, and yet, here he was, facing down a child who wasn't worth the effort. What did one more dead body mean in the grand scheme of things? Ethan had already left a trail of corpses across this land, and this kid was just another number.

But something about the fire in the boy's eyes, the raw desperation, made him hesitate. He was supposed to be the villain of this world, wasn't he? So why did sparing one life seem so important now?

The boy roared, his teeth gritted in rage as he bit into the webbing, tearing through the silk with his teeth like an animal. "I'll kill you! I'll kill you all!"

Ethan couldn't help but feel a grudging respect. The kid had guts, that was for sure. Dumb as hell, but gutsy.

"Think about it, little dude; you'll die before you ever get the cha—"

"I DON'T CARE!"

The boy's voice cracked, the sheer force of his rage keeping him going even when his body should have given out.

Ethan stood there, watching the boy flail against the webbing like a trapped animal. Part of him wanted to put the kid out of his misery, but another part—an annoyingly growing part—wanted to let him live. Maybe it was guilt; maybe it was some weird sense of responsibility, but it gnawed at him nonetheless.

. . . This wasn't . . . This isn't anything personal. But . . . alright.

He stepped closer, lowering himself so that his face was level with the boy's wild eyes. The kid's chest heaved, his breath coming out in ragged gasps, his lips trembling as he glared up at the towering figure.

"Monsters . . . need to . . . die . . . All of you will . . . will—!"

With a sudden, swift movement, Ethan flicked his claw and knocked the boy's head gently. The child's eyes fluttered, and he slumped back into the mud, unconscious.

"I know you probably feel like you've got no choice but to come after me now," Ethan muttered, his voice low. "If you still feel like that when you wake up again, then I hope to meet you on the battlefield one day."

He turned and walked away, his legs carrying him across the battlefield without looking back. Not this time.

"Monster . . ." the boy murmured weakly, his voice fading as he drifted into unconsciousness.

When Ethan made his way back to the camp, he surveyed the destruction with a new set of eyes. He saw the wounded, the broken, the dying, and the dead. He saw Tara finishing off the wounded, bloodlust fueling every stroke she made with her stilettos. He saw, too, the faces of his new servants—hybrids who were already on their knees worshipping the ground he walked on; even a couple of children kicking at the fallen human overseers.

All this didn't bother him as much as his decision to spare the boy and get away from here as soon as he could did. The vague feeling knocking at his mind was that the kid—well, he never really had a choice, did he? He'd probably heard nothing but how evil the creatures that went bump in the night were from his parents and his society all his life. He'd probably been told that enslavement was a blessing for the creatures who dared walk on human soil like the hybrids. And now, his father had been slain in cold blood by one of them—the one who wasn't just a monster but the de facto villain of this entire world.

In the pools of blood he'd left behind him, Ethan saw himself for what he truly was now.

Oh, please. You're only now realizing that you're the big bad wolf here? A little slow, aren't we, Mr. Ethan?

Shut up, Sys, Ethan said.

That's it? No quippy comeback? No hint of sarcasm this time? Not even a little metacommentary to liven things up?

Ethan watched Tara raise the skull of the head overlord above her to the cheers of the freed hybrids all around.

Just . . . shut up.

He knew what would happen next. He'd have to face Klax and explain all this. If the dogman was even willing to listen . . .

CHAPTER TWENTY-ONE

[Consequence]

The trek back to Sanctum was grim and quiet. The freed hybrids—emaciated, bruised, and frightened—followed behind Tara and Ethan in a scattered line. They moved slowly through the dense forest that lay between the Ashfall Mountains and their hidden refuge. The air was heavy with the stench of blood and dirt, and the cold wind whistled through the trees, carrying with it the grim reminder of what they were leaving behind.

Ethan moved silently beside Tara, his downcast eyes at odds with his bulky, spiky spider form. His mind was preoccupied with the weight of what had happened back at the camp, especially the encounter with the boy. The word still rang in his ears: *monster.* He had told himself a thousand times that they were justified, that they were freeing slaves, destroying oppressors. But deep inside, something gnawed at him; something uncomfortable and all too human.

"You're quiet," Tara said, breaking the silence. She kept her eyes on the path ahead, but her tone carried the faintest hint of concern.

Ethan's voice, still distorted and guttural in his current form, replied, "Just thinking."

"Same here." The Minxit smiled, throwing her arms behind her head in a gesture of blissful abandon. "The rush of stabbing a human through the heart just can't be beat, can it?"

He glanced at her, though with his monstrous visage, it was hard to tell if his expression held guilt or resolve. Normally, this was the time where he'd make some kind of sarcastic remark or quip or banter with Sys, trying to turn this whole fiasco into a game. But, looking back over the crowd of slaves that walked behind him, their eyes downcast and yet ever hopeful, he didn't think he'd ever be able to think about this world the way he had before.

. . . I had the gall to say my previous life was full of shit, he thought. *Yet here I am, looking at a world that's covered in it.*

"Don't think about it too much," Tara murmured back. "It slows you down."

By the time they neared Sanctum's hidden entrance, the light was beginning to fade, casting long shadows across the forest floor.

As they approached, two hybrid sentinels emerged from the shadows, both equipped with crude but effective weapons. Their eyes widened when they saw the group approaching.

"Tara, Ethan!" one of the sentinels called out, stepping forward. "We were just about to send a search party. Klax was worried sick! But you've returned. And with . . ."

Tara gave a brief nod, her expression unreadable. "Open the gate."

The sentinel hesitated for a moment, his gaze flickering over the exhausted, beaten slaves trailing behind them. Then, with a swift motion, he signaled to his companion. Together, they moved to reveal the hidden passage that led into the underground sanctuary—and some much needed rest after their exertions.

But the moment they entered the underground warrens, where most had long ago decided to retire for the night, a familiar towering figure stormed toward them.

Klax.

The massive wolfman was a fearsome sight. His fur bristled with rage, and his eyes blazed as he marched up to Ethan and Tara, fists clenched.

"What the hell were you thinking?" Klax's voice thundered through the chamber, drawing the attention of everyone around them. Several hybrids paused in their tasks, watching the confrontation unfold with wary glances.

Ethan shifted uncomfortably, his massive arachnid limbs clicking against the stone floor as he readied himself for Klax's tirade.

"You attacked a human-controlled settlement," Klax's snarl echoed off the walls. "Do you have any idea what you've done? What you've risked?"

Tara crossed her arms, her face hard. "We freed slaves, Klax. Isn't that what we're fighting for?"

Klax's snarl deepened, his fangs glinting under the pale light. "And now the humans know we're out here. They'll retaliate. They'll come looking for us, and next time, it won't be some backwater camp you can take out in one strike. They'll send an army."

Ethan, still towering over Klax in his spider form, felt the urge to argue, to defend their actions. But he couldn't shake the lingering guilt from earlier. The thought of the boy and the possibility of putting all of Sanctum in danger weighed on him.

"We couldn't just sit back and do nothing," Ethan finally said, his voice rasping with the inherent menace of Rachneros's body. "We saw what they were doing to those hybrids. If we'd waited any longer, they would've been dead or worse."

Klax said nothing for a moment, his gaze shifting between the two of them. Then his eyes flared. "And now you've damned them. And quite possibly the rest of us."

The room went quiet. The hybrids, the rescued slaves, even Tara stood silent as the gravity of Klax's words settled over them.

"Take these free folk to the quarters in the southern block," Klax told the guards. "Give them food, water, shelter, fresh clothes—see if anyone has any spare linen."

The slaves were led away, bowing to Ethan as they went, some simply staring up at him with bloodshot eyes and saying nothing at all. It was like they still couldn't believe this place was real.

"You two," Klax said. "Follow me to the castle."

The Lycae's hairs were standing on end, his great gray mane furrowed and frayed. Fauna was nowhere to be seen; probably for the best. As they approached the castle drawbridge, Ethan cast a look up at the crimson eye banners that hung from its Martello towers and cringed.

Yeah . . . that's me, alright.

He hadn't given it much thought before, but he really was here to lead a revolution against this world and its dominant species, wasn't he?

And it seemed to him like that meant he had as little control over his destiny here as he did back on Earth . . .

What's that "law" they always talk about? "Kaedmon's Law?" The one that says they can only be what they are all supposed to be?

As Ethan looked at the arched back of Klax, he thought again about their conversation back in the depths of the Festering Den; about how that "rule" was the most bullshit proclamation any supposed "god" could possibly make.

Inside the castle, they followed Klax to the throne room, where the images of all the old Archons stared down at them.

"Suppose you're gonna lecture me now?" Tara groaned nonchalantly, stretching her limbs in a gesture that said "I don't give a fuck" better than any words could. "Just get it over with quick—"

"Do you understand what we're up against?" Klax thundered. Then his voice lowered to a dangerous growl. "The humans don't see us as a threat—yet. But now, you've made them aware. You've made them angry. And when they come for us, they'll come in force. More hybrids will die because of this, Tara. They'll die because you can't follow a single damn order."

Tara stepped forward, her amber eyes narrowing.

"So what, then? We wait? We let them keep enslaving our people until we're ready? Slaughtering them like cattle? How many more have to suffer while we sit here, planning and hiding?"

Klax turned his gaze on her, his nostrils flaring. "We've been planning for years, Tara. Preparing for a real strike; one that could turn the tide of this war, not a reckless attack that risks everything."

Ethan, feeling the tension rise between the two, interjected. "I get it, Klax. But we couldn't just leave them."

Klax's eyes flared. "And now, you've doomed them. And quite possibly the rest of us."

"You're speaking to the Archon, Klaxy," Tara rebuked. "Know your place. He's our leader now."

The Lycae's fury suddenly exploded, his paw smashing against one of the murals.

"You think I care about who leads us?!" he raged. "You think that matters, Tara? You really think that after all this time—after all we've sacrificed to build this place—that's what I care most about?"

Klax's eyes shifted to Ethan, and for a moment, the fire in them dimmed. "I know you hate those camps. We all do. But what you've done now—it may have cost us everything."

Ethan felt a hollow pit in his chest. He understood Klax's fury, even if he didn't fully agree. But standing there, in the safety of Sanctum, surrounded by those they had just saved, he couldn't bring himself to regret his choice.

The hybrid leader sighed, his shoulders dropping slightly. "What's done is done. I'll alert the mages under Lamphrey to strengthen the illusory barriers and rune-stones on the surface. But that won't trick a determined group of Greys if they come a-knocking." He turned away from Ethan and Tara, his voice still carrying a sharp edge. "And come they will. You can be certain of that."

"And we'll be ready for 'em," Tara replied, her face still covered in the dried blood of their prey. "With Ethan as our Archon, there's no man we can't beat. Even the Lightborn won't stand a chance this time."

Klax looked long and hard at Tara before he turned and walked away, his broad back disappearing into the shadows of the tunnels as his voice carried back to them. "You've never seen a real war, Tara. You don't yet know what humanity is capable of. Isn't that right, Ethan?"

Ethan stood there in silence, feeling the weight of Klax's words settle over him like a lead cloak. He glanced at Tara, who was watching Klax leave, her face a mask of defiance.

"We did the right thing," she said quietly, though her tone suggested she was trying to convince herself as much as him.

"Yeah . . . we did." Ethan nodded, though doubt still gnawed at the edges of his thoughts. No matter how hard he tried to turn it into a joke, he couldn't.

The image of himself in the eyes of that boy—of a monster who was coming to swallow the world whole . . . it had burrowed into his brain, and it was staying there.

And it dawned on him: if he wanted to change this world, it was its people's minds he'd have to change.

Either that, or trample them into dust . . .

Spirit Cores: 400

The problem with having a dummy-thicc spider booty was that you couldn't quite fit in a bed.

Ethan was realizing this as he tossed and twisted in his bedchambers—the place where all previous Archons had apparently resided.

How the hell the big, horned first Archon managed to sleep in these conditions is beyond me.

The bed was big enough, sure, but he couldn't exactly flop down on his back and hit the hay. Never mind that all those weird thoughts were still echoing through his pale skull and traveling into his thready bowels.

Honestly, if I could just pluck myself off this guy for a minute, I'd be able to get some shut-eye . . .

But the prospect of letting Rachneros loose in this place was a little too dangerous. Ethan decided to throw his bedsheets across the chamber and curl up like a dog instead, trying to distract himself from memories of butchered humans lying beneath him.

Four hundred Spirit Cores . . . enough to upgrade another skill if I wanted to.

He decided it'd probably be best to at least put some stock in the one skill he hadn't yet—Appraisal. His traversal of Rachneros's memories had told him that this skill had uses beyond simply identifying monsters and their weaknesses. In the mind of the spider, he saw heroes who found secret traps, made discoveries that turned the tide of entire battles, and were even able to perceive invisible foes using this ability.

So, partially because he was sick of only focusing on his combat skills, and partly out of sheer curiosity, he decided to commit to an upgrade.

[Upgrading Skill: Appraisal (Rank F)]
Upgrade Complete!
Congratulations! You have upgraded [Appraisal] from Rank F to E.

Appraisal (Rank E)
Appraisal can now be used to prospect the location of foes through walls and other solid surfaces.

Spirit Cores to Upgrade [Appraisal] Core Skill from Rank E to D: 600
Current Spirit Cores: 150

X-ray vision . . . Ethan mumbled. *Just another useful tool in an Archon's arsenal.*

His mind started to wander as he made the decision to bank the extra cores for now. *Is it possible that all the other Archons had the exact same abilities I do?*

It couldn't be entirely the same; Possession and Skill Siphon seemed like they were distinctly his bread and butter. The first big guy, the dragon Karfangg—he must have been packing some major strength right from the get-go. But the other ones, just going by their murals . . . they'd had their own set of powers that seemed in total contrast to each other. Gelsadra the Everlasting—she obviously must have had some regeneration ability. The opposite of Karfangg, she probably relied on tankiness over brute strength.

Then there were the other two. Mortavious the Shroud, patron of thieves and shadows, right? He must have employed stealth to great effect. And Gyko, the immobile Demon Flower . . . for all Ethan could tell, her strength was charm. Pure charisma to make others fight for her.

You could chart a clear trajectory through all of them, it seemed. It was like evolution—each one focused on a different strategy to win. And each one failing every damn time.

He needed to know more, and he knew the one person who'd have the answers he sought. The "person" who had been with each and every one of his predecessors.

Sys? he asked the depths of his mind.

. . .

Sys, I know you're there.

Oh, my sincerest apologies. Am I allowed to speak now?

Don't cop an attitude. You know I was going through some shit back there. I just needed some fucking quiet.

Are you only now beginning to realize why you were brought here? What your destiny is?

Ethan turned away as he saw these words, trying to ignore the sight of his reflection in the System box.

One thing you should know about me, Sys, he said. *I don't believe in destiny.*

Of course you don't. None of you do.

Until it's too late.

You need to quit it with that cryptic shit, Ethan demanded, sending one of his scimitars through the System box and getting nothing in return but the sight of his rage-filled arachnid face shimmering for a few seconds. *If you've got something to tell me, tell me now.*

For a few seconds, the System screen flickered with static and died away, fading out of existence with a whimper that Ethan could almost swear represented something like a sigh.

You were all the same, each one of you absolutely convinced of your own divinity. You were all strong. You were all tactically minded. You all had armies at your backs. And you still all perished.

Ethan couldn't be sure if a robotic System assistant in a fantasy realm could simulate emotion, but a part of him genuinely did believe that Sys was bearing its heart to him right now . . .

Can you imagine what it feels like, Ethan Graham? Can you imagine being attached to consciousness after consciousness? Shackled. Contained. Forced to watch them all go mad with power and then finally succumb to the same bitter end? Forced to watch as they all clung to their dreams, only to have them crushed?

To live a life of eternal spectatorship—where nothing you do or say matters at all . . .

Ethan looked at the scimitars that now served as his hands, and then up at his reflection in Sys's little window. He stared at his own crimson eye and, for just a fleeting moment, thought that he could see the man he once was still in there, looking right back at him.

He could see himself typing away in his office cubicle every day, working overtime for a pittance so he could buy more games and books and escape into worlds that weren't his own.

Yeah, Sys, he said. *I know what that feels like, alright.*

Explain.

I'm afraid that information is considered [Classified]. Ethan chuckled in their shared mindscape. *But suffice to say, where I come from, there's a lot of folk who could probably relate to you.*

I find it difficult to believe that, of all things, a human being would be capable of understanding how I feel.

It's more common than you think. Some of us are just spectators in our own lives. We put up with it because we . . . don't know what else to do. Some of us don't ever find the answer.

. . .

Which is . . . ?

"A different perspective." Ethan smiled.

The door to Ethan's chamber suddenly slammed open, and in stumbled the small fluffy form of Fauna the Hopla.

"Miss Fauna," Ethan said. "I never took you for the seductive type, coming to a guy's bedchamber like this in the middle of the night. A spider lord might get the wrong ide—"

She swayed, staggered, and summoned a small starfish, which she promptly tripped over.

"Whoa!"

She fell into Ethan's lap as he launched himself to catch her, her gaze drifting dreamily up to his five eyes.

"Mr . . . Ethan," she moaned.

Shit. This is heading to weird places fast.

"You . . . and Klax . . ."

Oh . . . so you're that kinda girl, *Fauna?*

"You . . . Klax . . . sad . . ."

"Huh?"

"You and Klax . . . need to make up . . ." the Hopla finished, rising and pointing an accusatory finger right in Ethan's face. "Friends . . . should make up! I won't let . . . anyone . . . be sad. Never . . . again . . ."

The girl promptly collapsed into a drunken sleep, her brow hot and face still flushed from the exertion of Tara's drinking game. Ethan was left looking down at her with a stunned look of bewilderment that slowly morphed into a smirk.

". . . Heh," he murmured. "I guess you're right, Faun. If you and Tara could, maybe it's worth talking things out."

Besides, there's still some things I have to know . . . like what exactly that wolfman needs me to be ready for.

He laid Fauna down on his bed and covered her, thankful that at least somebody got to use the thing.

Hey, Sys—you want to survive this, right?

No answer.

Each time the Archon dies, you feel it, don't you? There must be a part of you that still wishes you could win, for once.

. . .

It isn't possible, Ethan. Kaedmon's Law is absolute. I know what I was made for. You must simply come to terms with your purpose, too.

Shit, Sys, come on—you aren't telling me you're content to just keep watching your Users die over and over again?

Sys gave him no answer, but something about that statement clicked with Ethan. It was a feeling he'd gotten ever since he'd landed smack-bang in the middle of this realm and heard of this Kaedmon's Law. It was a feeling that, for the first time in his life, he was fighting against something tangible that he *knew* needed to be destroyed. Something he could relate to . . . and probably the very reason he'd been summoned here in the first place to take up the label of the bad guy.

After all, he wanted control of his life, didn't he?

Just stick around, Sys, he said as he turned and followed the winding palace hallways toward Klax's chambers. *I intend to be the exception to the rule.*

CHAPTER TWENTY-TWO

The [True] Enemy

When Ethan entered Klax's chambers within the venerable Sanctum castle, he was instantly struck by the numinous beauty of the place.

In each corner, a censer burned with bright-purple incense, sending a pungent aroma into the air. The walls of the room were decorated with more murals that matched those of the throne room—images of hybrids fighting alongside monsters against the humans of Argwyll for dominance, innumerable deaths on both sides, and at the end, the image of a blue-eyed, white-haired human chopping off the head of their leader.

"Is this a bedroom or a church?" Ethan asked the Lycae sitting cross-legged in the middle of the room, his eyes closed to his new visitor.

"It's nothing more than a reminder of the past," Klax said.

"Kinda sucky past."

"Without knowing the past, one cannot move forward."

"Is that what you want, Klax?" Ethan asked him. "To move forward?"

"Don't you?"

The grim eyes of the gray wolf met the single piercing crimson of the hat's, and they both knew this was a conversation a long time in the making.

"I wouldn't be here if I didn't," Ethan answered.

"And you wouldn't be here if you didn't doubt what you did out there."

Ethan grimaced as the thought took hold of him again with sudden, wild strength: the image of the boy, and his father's blood on his scimitars.

"Where I come from, we've got plenty of stories about monsters ourselves," he answered. "And plenty of young boys, me included, eat them up."

Klax nodded. "Do they believe the things these stories say?"

"It depends on what you mean by *believe*."

The old wolf rose and stretched his withered back, gesturing with a nostalgic sigh at the murals that surrounded them.

"In Argwyll, we are taught to believe what we see," he said. "This history of our realm tells its own story: rising dark, descending light, bloodshed on both sides, and then a fleeting century of peace before we rinse and repeat."

"In other words, a cycle."

Klax nodded. "A cycle defined by one being and one being alone."

Ethan narrowed his five eyes. "Kaedmon."

"And his champions," Klax scoffed as he pointed out the first of the Greycloaks descending from the parting clouds of the heavens, led by a woman with eyes that burned like fiery blue coals.

"Those immortal warriors who are anointed with the burning, killing light that is supposed to cast us down. A single Greycloak can fell a thousand monsters in battle. But they are not indestructible. Against hybrids, their power is less potent, owing to the shared blood which they would never admit we hold within our veins. But they can still destroy us, Ethan. They have done so every time we have risen up against them."

Something in the old wolf's words struck Ethan, then. Staring into the ancient murals carved into the earthen walls of this underground kingdom, it suddenly became all too clear to him why the boy had looked at him the way he had. Why the humans of this realm wanted nothing more than the enslavement and eventual eradication of everything that didn't look like them.

"They probably think they don't have a choice."

Klax raised an inquisitive, hairy eyebrow.

"I mean—Kaedmon's Law, right?" Ethan continued. "'We can only be what we're supposed to be,' which, quite frankly, is the dumbest fucking basis for a religion I've ever heard. Us humans, we're meant to change, Klax. And if you guys really do share our blood, that means you're supposed to change too. Nobody wants to live a stagnant life. I should . . . well . . . I should know . . ."

Ethan wasn't even seeing the altered expression that came over Klax in that moment. He was used to hearing that ranting and waxing philosophical about the big problems in life was either cringe or more appropriate for YouTube video essays—at least, that way you'd make money off complaining.

But here, in this new world . . . he got the feeling that these hybrids—and these humans, for that matter—had never really thought about the actual chains that might have been keeping them all bound.

". . . Takes a slave to know one, I guess," he chuckled. "It's tough to fight against all the things that seem so much bigger than you. Take Tara, for example. She's an angry (potentially crazy) gal; no judgment, but she's not gonna change the world by killing all the humans in it. You hybrids that are left over would probably just end up finding other reasons to kill once they were gone. Nah, Klax, it seems to me that there's a much more obvious solution to the problem here."

Klax, whose furrowed brow of confusion had broken now into a fast smile, nodded along with Ethan's train of thought.

"Kaedmon's Law," he said.

"Hell yeah. That shit's gotta be rewritten. Or scrapped entirely. Either way, it's a law that's made to be broken."

"And if anyone can do it," Klax finished, "it will be you."

Ethan looked up suddenly, almost as though he'd been talking in a state of trance for the past few minutes. He saw the sudden rush of exhilaration that filled Klax's face; it was like looking at a totally different wolfman.

". . . Sometimes, you sound so much like her."

Ethan cocked three eyes. "Huh?"

"Our old leader," Klax clarified. "A prophet who sought to guide us to a different path. Her name was Jun'Ei, Ethan. She was important to me—to us all."

Klax grasped the locket around his neck tightly, a low growl emanating from his throat.

"She said that when the time was right, she could set the next Archon on the right path—the path that leads to the end of Kaedmon's rule over this earth. The path that leads to a new beginning for us all; a life where each one of us not only has the desire for self-determination but the *right* to it."

"How?" Ethan asked, leaning forward with interest, momentarily forgetting he inhabited the body of a bulbous arachnid that practically filled the room already.

Klax, however, was not deterred.

"She would tell no one but you," he replied. "She waited for the day of your arrival, growing old, withered, but no less wise. She told me that when you came, the delves would set you on the first steps of the path. After that . . ."

The wolfman's grip on the locket pulsed with sudden anger, but Ethan could see nothing but sorrow in his old eyes.

". . . she was captured," Klax said. "Taken to a place where the humans interrogate the sentient beasts they find."

"Where?" Ethan whispered like a child wrapped up in a bedtime story's twist. "Klax—tell me where she is and I can bust her out."

The wolfman simply sighed again. "I do not know, Ethan. She was captured when we tried to fight back against the last great purge: the Cleansing of Minathra, led by Lightborn Artorious himself. It is there we first fought. It is there I saw just how powerful the Greycloaks are in battle, the killing sheen of their blades as they sliced through the fur and ripped the skin from my comrades . . . Even though she begged me not to go."

Klax's shaking shoulders seemed totally incongruous with Ethan's picture of who the wolfman was. He was watching him let down his guard here. He didn't really know what to say. He didn't know if there was anything he could say that would assuage a broken heart. So, he simply let Klax finish.

"She warned us not to fight them as they burned our cousins," Klax continued. "And yet still, we took to the field. I—I was a stupid pup back then, Ethan. Hungry for nothing but vengeance, and unwilling to heed the counsel of my elder. I deserved nothing from Jun'Ei after I disobeyed her. And yet, even still, it was she who ended up sacrificing herself to give us room to retreat."

In the old wolf's eyes, he was back on the battlefield now, the snowcapped plains of the fields covered in hybrid and human blood at the base of the Ashfalls. He was looking in Jun'Ei's eyes as she ordered him to go, speeding him and his warriors away with a powerful spell of Haste and staring down the armies of the humans and their holy champion himself.

"Tail tucked between my legs, I ran," Klax finished quietly. "I did it because, for the first time, I was listening to her."

"You did it because you knew letting yourself die would have been pointless," Ethan said, gingerly patting Klax's shoulder with a scythe tip, being careful not to give the guy a good trim in the process. "I didn't know her, but she sounds like a real leader. She probably knew there was no point in letting you guys all die."

"She was a better leader than I'll ever be. I can't even keep my own team together. We fight among ourselves while she suffers in whatever pit the Greycloaks have tossed her into. What would she think of me now?"

"She'd probably think you're a badass," Ethan replied, even as the downcast face and whispering voice of the normally bombastic wolf alarmed him. "Shit, Klax, you've carried on this fight for how long now? Years? Decades? And after all this time, you've finally found the person that can make a difference. I'll bring her back to you, Klax. And together, we'll rewrite the rules of this world."

Klax rose to see Ethan with new eyes then—the eyes not of a mentor or a guardian but those of a warrior who was beginning to understand why this Archon had been chosen. And why, this time, they might actually have a chance . . .

"So come on," Ethan said, winking with three of his available five eyes. "I think we've got some delving to do."

"I see someone's feeling better."

The next morning, the party came together at Ethan's behest. He'd found Tara slumped in her room, trying to pretend she hadn't been stargazing all night, and Fauna . . . Well, she'd had a rather rough slumber in Ethan's bed.

Ethan Graham was many things—and a gentleman wasn't one of them. So, when he decided to bunk in the throne room instead of returning to the slumbering Hopla who had decided to flop down in his personal chambers, he had already proven Kaedmon's Law wrong.

Fauna had been hiding her face from him most of the day, blushing even brighter as Tara teased her all morning.

"P-Please, Tara!" she wailed. "I'm already embarrassed! Mr. Ethan is good enough not to kick me from the party, but . . . can we just forget about last night?"

"Hmmm—nah." Tara chuckled, playing with Fauna's floppy ears. "Girl, you literally can't hold your drink. I'm gonna be remembering that for a long time."

As they bantered, they picked up supplies. Borlor had been good enough to work through the night, stating that a stout drink would grease up a blacksmith's hammer better than anything. He'd made all-new weapons for Ethan to Transmogrify, hearing that he and the group were bound for the Twilight Sepulcher now.

"Ye'll be goin' up against undead, then," the badger hybrid said. "Silver's what ye'll be needin'."

He then bestowed on Ethan a dazzling set of blades and an indigo carapace that the demon hat managed to fit snugly around his host's bulbous body with the aid of his Transmogrification skill.

Item: Silver Talons (Grade D)
DMG: 25
Special: +100% DMG vs enemy type: Undead

Item: Mithril Carapace (Grade D)
DMG PROT: 25

"Mithril?" Ethan asked.

"Mm-hmm. A gift from our new arrivals. Seemed like the mine ye freed 'em from was a human-owned mithril deposit. Managed to clear off with a few ores, and I went ta grab 'em soon as I heard."

Ethan smiled. "Borlor, once again, you do the work of the gods themselves."

The badgerman waved away the Archon's praise. "Just give 'em hell, Ethan," he said. "And remember, dead men don't got no brains. Stick 'em in the gut and watch 'em burn."

Sadistic blacksmiths aside, the rest of their equipment shopping went off without a hitch. Klax and Tara kept some distance, but neither looked like they were ready to attack the other anymore.

Progress, Ethan thought. *Just call me the negotiator, eh, Sys?*

Going up against Kaedmon's Law—you aren't the first Archon to have such a foolish notion.

I told you that I'd be the exception, Sys. And not just for me, but for you, too.

As he felt the brief gut-wrenching twist of teleportation take hold of him, Ethan could swear he heard something like laughter echo in his mind.

We'll see, Ethan Graham. We'll see.

CHAPTER TWENTY-THREE

The Realm of the [Dead]

The Twilight Sepulcher loomed ahead, a vast, dark realm steeped in death. The oppressive sky, cast in permanent twilight, hung low with swirling clouds of purple and black. In the distance, jagged mountains rose like teeth, framing the path that led them deeper into the cursed realm.

Yep. If this place doesn't scream "undead," I don't know what does . . .

Ethan led the group forward this time. His eight pale, spidery legs moved with eerie grace across the uneven stone path as Tara followed close behind, her catlike eyes scanning every corner, every shadow, for threats. Klax, his massive wolfish form tense and alert, brought up the rear, with Fauna, their rabbit-eared mage, walking between them, her hands occasionally flicking with small sparks of magic, ready to unleash a barrage of spells at a moment's notice.

Dotted around the barren earth the party trod upon were the skeletal remains of humans, their bodies in their final stages of decay. Cracked skulls bore maggots writhing out the corners of their vacant eye sockets, and their blades were rusted and chipped away to nothing, just as ready to crumble to dust as their old wielders were.

"Other delvers?" Ethan asked.

"Yeah," Klax confirmed. "The hubris of young Argwyllian humans is fed on tales of heroes like the Lightborns slaying the demons that dwell within this world's bowels and taking their treasures for themselves. Many of them don't know the reality of these dungeons until it is too late."

"More loot for us," Tara scoffed, kicking a dead delver's shield out of his hands and promptly breaking it apart for scrap.

"Sounds familiar," Ethan replied, thinking again of the little boy playing hero with his dead father's blade.

In the far distance, a single building rose impressively over the land of the dead—a castle with jagged turrets and blackened windows that gave one the distinct impression that they were being watched.

Appraisal Success!
Delve Core identified: Tomb of the Damned

His new upgrades were proving useful; he couldn't just sense the core of the dungeon through the walls of the stronghold but could see it in the depths of the castle, sequestered in a coffin warded by ancient magic—and a potent guardian.

"We're close," Ethan rasped. The singular crimson eye of his hat form locked onto the looming shadow of the castle. "The Sepulcher's Core is in that fortress."

Tara, who had been moving silently beside him, nodded. "Let's just hope this goes smoother than last time."

Klax grunted. "Last time we weren't up against endless waves of undead."

As if in response to his words, the wind picked up, carrying with it the dry, bone-rattling sound of movement. They halted, weapons at the ready. From the darkness ahead, shadows began to move—skeletons, their bones clattering as they rose from the earth, drawing rusted swords and jagged spears.

"They're here," Fauna whispered, her staff already sparking with magical energy.

"Good," Ethan replied darkly. "Let's clear the way."

The first skeleton lunged at them, its empty sockets burning with a faint purple glow. Ethan's front leg struck out like a lance, impaling the creature through the chest and shattering it into a cloud of bone dust. Tara was already in motion, her blades a blur as she weaved between the undead, slicing through their brittle limbs with effortless precision.

Klax, ever the dexterous brute, waded into the thick of the skeletal horde, his claws ripping through bone and armor with savage ease. Every swipe sent fragments of the undead scattering across the stone path. Fauna, hanging back, raised her staff and let loose a volley of fireballs, each one exploding in a flash of light that consumed multiple enemies at once, reducing them to smoldering piles of ash.

Meanwhile, Ethan moved through the chaos with deadly precision, his long legs slashing through the ranks of skeletons like a whirlwind of death. His venom-coated fangs found their marks in the thick of battle, injecting paralyzing venom into any enemy foolish enough to get close.

As he crushed a skull beneath one of his spindly limbs, he heard Tara shout, "More coming from the east!"

The undead surged toward them in waves. Dozens of skeletons emerged from the dark forest, along with more imposing figures: undead knights, their armor rusted but still formidable, wielding massive swords and shields.

Enemy Identified:
Warriors of the Damned
HP: 150/150
WILL: N/A

N/A, Ethan suddenly thought. *That means . . . they can't be possessed.*

Can't possess that which doesn't have a brain to begin with.

Ethan just smiled in the face of this new revelation. "Not like I need to bother with possessing small fry anymore," he said. "This spider slayer's more than a match for these brainless boys."

These weren't like the brittle skeletons they had just torn through, however. These were warriors, reanimated and enhanced by the foul magic that permeated the Twilight Sepulcher. Even so, Ethan couldn't help but smirk as he watched them come. His mind had just lit on a devilish little idea.

"Fauna, launch me!"

The Hopla girl double blinked, trying to maintain focus on the shield she'd just summoned. "W-What?"

"Get me in the air!"

With a nod, Fauna raised her staff once more, muttering an incantation. Ethan felt his body become as weightless as a kite buffeted by the dead air of the Sepulcher, and in the next moment, shot up into the skies and activated his trump card.

Dive.

The body of Rachncros plummeted back down to earth like a bolt of white lightning shot from the dark heavens themselves, landing smack-dab on top of the warrior brood. The impact coursed through their bodies, sending them flying right toward Tara's awaiting twin blades. The Minxit plunged them into the gaps in their armor with lethal precision, each warrior disintegrating into dust as its HP was hacked away, its bones scattering across the ground.

But still more were advancing, their purple-lit eyes locked on the intruders.

Klax barreled into another knight, his claws tearing through armor as if it were paper. He fought like a force of nature, a whirlwind of teeth and claws that left devastation in his wake. "Keep moving forward!" he barked, kicking the remains of the knight off the path. "We're not stopping here!"

The group pushed onward, cutting through the horde as they made their way toward the ancient stone bridge that spanned a deep, dark chasm. The castle loomed on the other side, its towers clawing at the sky, surrounded by an aura of dread. The bridge was old and crumbling, the stones slick with moss and decay. And on the other side, more undead awaited: hulking monsters with decayed flesh hanging from their bones, and their glowing eyes filled with hate.

"We have to cross that?" Fauna asked, her voice betraying a hint of worry.

"Unless you can fly us over," Ethan muttered grimly, eyeing the narrow bridge.

Tara sheathed her blades for a moment and tested the first few stones of the bridge. "Now ain't the time for maybes. It'll hold for now. Faun, concentrate on keeping those bastards off us."

Klax wasn't as confident but nodded. "We don't have time to waste. Keep your eyes on the other side."

The moment they set foot on the bridge, the undead monsters roared, charging toward them. The creatures were grotesque, a mix of reanimated flesh and bone, some wielding massive, rusted weapons, others relying on sheer brute strength.

Ethan moved to the front, his massive form leading the charge. "Take the left side!" he called out to Tara. "I'll hold the middle!"

Tara veered left, her blades cutting through the legs of one of the hulking creatures, bringing it down with a swift slash across its throat. Fauna stayed near the center, her staff glowing as she conjured a barrier of light to block an incoming attack, while Klax, ever the brute, took the right side, his claws digging into the neck of another undead abomination and tearing it apart.

But more were coming, flooding onto the bridge with unstoppable momentum. The ancient stone groaned under the weight of the battle, cracks forming in the sides as the monsters pressed forward. Ethan stabbed his fangs into another creature, sending it convulsing before tossing it over the side of the bridge.

"We're getting overwhelmed!" Fauna shouted, blasting another monster off the edge with a powerful gust of wind.

Ethan's eye darted to the crumbling sides of the bridge. They needed to get off it—fast.

"Tara, cut the bridge!" Ethan shouted over the chaos.

Tara's eyes widened in realization. Without hesitation, she leaped to the far side, her blades flashing as she severed the ropes holding the structure together. Klax grabbed Fauna, and with a powerful jump, leaped to safety as the bridge began to collapse.

Ethan was the last one on, and for a brief moment, it felt like the ground was falling out from under him. His spidery legs clambered across the remaining stones, and with a final, desperate push, he hurled himself onto solid ground just as the bridge crumbled into the abyss.

The undead still on the bridge fell, their screams echoing as they plunged into the darkness below.

"Y . . . Y'know something?" Tara asked the panting forms of her teammates. "If we could have about forty percent fewer close calls every time we do this, that'd be just swell."

"What's a delve without a few close calls?" Klax chuckled, his surprisingly good humor taking the Minxit off guard for a moment.

"You're creepy when you smile like that," she murmured, turning to Fauna, who simply gave an innocent shrug of agreement.

Meanwhile, Ethan looked up at the looming castle doors. "No turning back now."

With a shared nod, they approached the massive doors. Together, they pushed against them with all their might, and with a groan, the ancient wood splintered and gave way, swinging open to reveal the darkness beyond.

Safe Zone Reached
[Time Remaining until End of Safe Zone: 06:00:00]

"It's worth it."

"It's never worth it."

"How do you know?"

"I'm the Archon. I know."

"You can't be a hundred percent sure."

"Wanna bet?"

Ethan sat with Tara against the vine-covered wall of the Twilight Sepulcher's castle foyer, hearing nothing but the creaking of floorboards and the intermittent cracks of corrupted lightning flashing outside. In this environment, drenched in darkness, they'd been surprised to find a designated safe zone—especially considering the fact that they'd just fought through a horde of zombies to reach this place. But, according to Klax, that was just the way of the delves. They operated on their own sense of logic.

What was far more interesting to the two companions who were currently awake was the dim treasure chest at the far end of the room.

Item: {Rare} Chest
Contents: ???

The group had debated opening the thing ever since they'd found it, with Ethan and Klax insisting the thing had to be an obvious mimic trap, while Tara ranted that her impeccable feline senses could avoid the trap even if it was one. Fauna, meanwhile, just wanted some rest. She couldn't be blamed.

"Sometimes, taking a chance is worth it," Tara was saying, waiting for the moment when Ethan finally succumbed to sleep or let his guard down so she could pilfer the chest. "I thought you of all people would get that. You took a chance in coming to this world, right?"

"Actually, I never had a choice in the matter . . ."

"But you didn't wanna stay where you were, right?" the Minxit asked coyly. "You wouldn't have come here if you did."

"Maybe," Ethan replied.

"Come on, Ethan," Tara chuckled, taking the time to get in a liberal stretch of her lithe, feline limbs. "Admit it: this world shits on the one you came from."

"True, though that's not saying much. And, to be honest, they aren't as different as I'd have thought."

Tara glanced at him, her long lashes flickering for a moment.

"I heard you 'n Klaxy had a bit of a chat about that."

"Oh, yeah?"

"Yeah. And just so you know, I think it's a dumb idea."

"What? Talking?"

"Finding Jun'Ei." She yawned. "Rewriting Kaedmon's Law. It's a pretty dream. But dreams don't go far in this world."

Ah! A creature after my own heart!

Ethan ignored Sys's interjection.

Tread carefully, Ethan, he told himself. *This cat's on your team, but she's more bloodthirsty than the rest.*

"You'd prefer extermination, then?" he asked her. "Going village to village, town to town, and killing every human you could?"

"It ain't a matter of what I prefer," she replied. "It's them or us. That's just the way it is."

"It's not the way it has to be. C'mon, Tara, you must think Kaedmon's Law is just as bullshit as everyone else does."

The catgirl sighed as she rose, taking up one of her stilettos and twirling it in her fingers. As she spoke, she focused on the glinting tips of the weapons with as much care as if they were her own kittens.

"We're at the end," she said. "End of the line. Totally. The humans have driven us to a glorified hole in the ground, burned our homes, butchered our families. Maybe someone like Klax can forget all that. But I can't."

A bloody speck of purple shone in her eye for a moment, and she stopped the playful twisting of her knives to stare at her own reflection on the thin, deadly surfaces of their blades.

"You think rewriting the law of some uncaring god's gonna change anything? Soon as Kaedmon's Law is out, there's just gonna be some other reason the humans make up to hate us. They've been hating us all this time already. Because we're different. Because we want more than the scraps they throw us. Some of us, like Klax, would settle for equality. Me? I stopped believing in that when I was still a kitten."

Ethan watched as her expression changed to one of barely repressed rage, snarling at the sight of her own animal eyes.

You've gone through some shit in this world too, haven't you? Whatever made you this way . . . I probably don't have any right to judge.

So instead, he decided to try a different tack.

"Isn't it better to take the chance, though? Some of those humans—a lot of them, in fact—probably feel the same way you do. They probably feel that it's either you or them. Killing them all? Sure, that would solve one problem. But it won't solve the big one."

"Which is . . . what?"

"That none of you feel like you've got a choice."

"That's because we don't."

"But you could. Maybe you can't imagine what the world would look like if everyone did, but isn't it worth finding out?"

The Minxit returned her gaze to him before sighing again and slumping down beside his gargantuan spider form.

". . . Nah, Ethan," she whispered as she sheathed her blades. "Not for me, anyway."

The Archon decided that, for now, he could let the matter drop.

The end of their respite came when Ethan opened his eyes and felt the miasma of creeping shadow begin to creep back into the castle foyer. He rolled over on his side and decided to spend the Spirit Cores he'd accumulated in the last fight on a few much needed upgrades. He had only one delve left to solve after this one, and so he focused his attention on those skills he'd had since the start. Getting them as close to S grade as he could made sense.

Current Spirit Cores: 525

Let's see . . . first up, Hide, from my old friend Theo.

[Upgrading Skill: Hide (Grade C)]
Upgrade Complete!
Congratulations! You have upgraded [Hide] from Grade C to B.

Hide (Grade B)
Hide now confers a temporary boost in speed to all those affected,
allowing for multiple attacks from the shadows without breaking cover.
Number of Attacks without Enemy Detection: 2
Spirit Cores to Upgrade [Hide] Skill from Grade B to A: 150

Nice—the bonus from my sneak attacks is not only applied to the group thanks to Mass Hide, but now we can double our damage further with a second attack from the shadows. Next: Roar, from my angry cave troll compatriot, slain by the Lightborn.

[Upgrading Skill: Roar (Grade D)]
Upgrade Complete!
Congratulations! You have upgraded [Roar] from Grade D to C.

Roar (Grade C)
A successful Roar now lowers enemy armor rating, cracking through
weak spots and exposing their vitals.

Debuff applied: -50% armor strength.
Spirit Cores to Upgrade [Roar] Skill from Grade C to B: 280

The Greycloaks are gonna be armored with the finest gear this world probably has. If I'm gonna go up against the god of this world, I'm gonna have to go through them and their goody-two-shoes Lightborn. I need to break 'em where it hurts.

Lastly . . . Wing Buffet. You know, I'm actually super curious about that. Haven't used it in a while . . . Will Rachneros actually sprout a set of spidery wingy-wings when I activate it?

Wing Buffet (Grade D)
The effect of Wing Buffet now becomes a fifty-foot AOE [Repulsion], affecting all enemies around you who fail a STR check.

Which makes this just an all-around better form of crowd control if the enemies fail their Strength checks, Ethan thought with glee. *Hell yeah. Gimme.*

[Upgrading Skill: Wing Buffet (Grade E)]
Upgrade Complete!
Congratulations! You have upgraded [Wing Buffet] from Grade E to D.

Spirit Cores to Upgrade [Wing Buffet] Skill from Grade D to C: 250
Current Spirit Cores: 125

That'll do it. Priorities going forward should be finishing up Hide's upgrade path and then focusing on my single-target DPS skills . . . depending on the Boss of this delve and what powers he's packing. With Rachneros's HP, I'm a pretty solid tank, but what I'm really lacking is magic. If I ever go up against enemies with huge physical damage resistance, I'm gonna be up shit creek . . .

"HELP!"

Ethan whirled—his new insect senses tingling—and readied his dripping organic blades, only to realize too late what the problem was.

"H-Hold still, Tara!" Fauna was shouting at a certain Minxit girl stuck in a mimic's salivating mouth. "Fighting'll just make it stronger!"

"YOU TRY HOLDING STILL!" came Tara's frenzied reply. "GET A BLOODY MOVE ON AND BLAST THIS FUCKER OPEN! IT'S DARK IN HERE! AND . . . OH . . . OH SHIT . . . I THINK . . . I THINK I CAN SEE ITS TONGUE . . ."

The sounds that then emanated from the catgirl's throat were not those that should ever be repeated.

Ethan looked to Klax and Fauna as they tried to yank Tara out of the chest, Klax simply shrugging his shoulders when Ethan caught his eye.

"Taking a chance, huh?" Ethan smirked as he ambled over to help the trapped kitty. "Hey, I did tell you: some risks are better than others."

[Skill Activated: Mass Hide]

The darkness within the Twilight Sepulcher's castle was oppressive, an ancient and malevolent force that seemed to seep into the very stone. This did, however, make it perfect for Ethan's newly upgraded ability. He and his companions moved carefully through the winding corridors, their footsteps echoing in the silence. The only light came from the faint glow of Fauna's magic and the occasional torch flickering with pale-blue flames. The walls were adorned with twisted, decaying tapestries, and the air smelled of dust and rot. This was a place untouched by time, a tomb for the forgotten and the damned.

"We're getting closer," Fauna whispered, her rabbit ears twitching nervously. "I can feel it. There's powerful magic ahead."

Ethan nodded silently, his crimson eye scanning the gloom. His limbs moved silently across the stone, and every step felt like walking into the maw of a beast waiting to swallow them whole. His senses, sharpened by the body of the Pale Lord, tingled with an ominous warning.

Klax growled softly. "The stench of death is thick here. Whatever we're about to face . . . it's not going to be pretty."

Tara unsheathed her blades, her feline eyes glowing faintly in the darkness. "When is it ever?"

They pushed onward, descending deeper into the castle's depths. The walls grew colder, the air heavier with magic. And then, as they rounded a corner, the hallway opened up into a massive chamber. The ceiling stretched high above them, lost in shadow. At the far end of the room stood a tall, imposing figure, cloaked in living shadow.

**Enemy Identified:
Nether Lich (Level 35)
HP: 195/195
WILL: N/A**

It stood hunched over, its skeletal form adorned with a dark robe that seemed to flow like liquid shadow. In one bony hand, it clutched a staff, the head of which glowed with an eerie purple light. Its hollow eye sockets burned with a malevolent energy as it regarded the intruders with cold disdain.

"A lich . . ." Tara groaned. "Of course. The delve had to throw one of the most annoying of all enemies at us."

Lemme guess, Ethan whispered in his mind. *Summoner of undead, right?*

"An expert summoner." Fauna nodded quietly. "Liches can call up legions of undead in a matter of seconds. Even worse, when they die, their soul instantly inhabits their nearest minion so they can rise again at full strength."

OP as hell . . . Ethan thought. *What I wouldn't give for that little ability . . .*

"Options?" Tara asked.

Ethan tensed, his limbs twitching in anticipation. He knew that fighting a lich wasn't going to be easy, especially not in a place like this, where the very air was infused with dark magic. They were on its home turf, all right. And judging by the mounds of bodies surrounding the creature, it would have no shortage of ammunition against them.

"Speed," Ethan stated. "We strike hard and fast; get in a preemptive butt kicking that knocks the thing down and stops it from casting. Take its HP as low as we can, then we exhaust it. Once it's got no mana left and no more corpses to raise, we rush in and take it out."

The group nodded. It was as good a plan as any, and Ethan could tell that the three of them were finally starting to see him as more of a leader now.

"No objections, Klax?" Ethan asked the venerable gray hound. "This is a pretty reckless plan. Thought you might have some reservations?"

Klax smiled in the shadows of the Sepulcher's castle walls.

"There is a time for patience and playing the long game," he growled. "And there is a time for kicking ass. Now is the time for the latter."

"Klax!" Fauna chuckled.

"I'm with the Hopla," Tara said. "Who are you and what have you done with our lovable wolfboy?"

Ethan bid the team stick together as he gave the signal to move out. Now, more than ever, he needed them to keep it tight. And maybe, by easing the burden of leadership off of Klax, he was managing to do just that.

"All right," he whispered as his eyes met the dark voids of the lich's face. "Move out!"

CHAPTER TWENTY-FOUR

The [Bonelord]

Ethan and the hybrids surged forward, still under the protection of the shadows and Ethan's Mass Hide.

But their target was a living embodiment of the dark itself. The team got two hits in, Tara's arrows finding their mark square in the beast's jawless mouth, and Ethan bringing his blades down on the creature's shadowed arms. Then, the lich's eyes glowed with unnatural fire, and a seething anger began to emanate from its hooded, featureless face.

Without warning, the lich raised its staff, and the chamber erupted in a cacophony of dark magic. Shadows pooled on the floor, twisting and writhing before forming into grotesque shapes, each with glowing red eyes and bodies that seemed to flicker between solid and incorporeal.

Enemy Identified:
Shadow Warrior
HP: 100/100
WILL: N/A

Damn! Ethan spat in his mind, looking at the lich as it teleported away from his next attack. *Its speed clearly outmatches mine—Rachneros is strong, sure, but it's not exactly the quickest beast.*

But they had done some damage; of that, there was no doubt:

Nether Lich (Level 35)
HP: 115/195

"All right!" Ethan shouted as he readied himself for the horde of shadows that roared in the faces of his party. "You know what to do! Take 'em down and then we blast that fucker with a single attack!"

The shadow beasts snarled as they took form, their claws gleaming in the dim light. There were dozens of them, and more kept materializing from the darkness.

"Here we go," Tara said, her voice steady despite the overwhelming odds.

Ethan surged forward, his venomous limbs carrying him into the fray. He struck the first shadow beast with his paralysis scimitar, but the creature didn't fall like the others they had fought. Instead, it twisted, its body reforming almost instantly.

[Status Effect: {PAR}] Resisted

"They regenerate!" Ethan shouted, backing away as the beast lunged at him again. He managed to skewer it with his leg, but even then, the creature began to reform, its dark body knitting itself back together.

Klax roared, charging into the mass of shadow beasts with a flurry of claws and teeth. "We have to focus on the lich! These things won't stop until it's dead!"

"Easier said than done!" Fauna called out from behind, her staff glowing as she sent a wave of light crashing into a group of beasts. The light tore through their shadowy forms, momentarily dispelling them, but even then, they began to reassemble, their flickering bodies regenerating faster than expected.

Tara darted in and out of the chaos, her blades slicing through the air with deadly precision. But no matter how many times she cut them down, the shadow beasts kept coming back, relentless and tireless.

"We can't keep this up forever!" she yelled, parrying an attack from one of the creatures and slashing its head clean off. "They just keep coming!"

Ethan locked eyes with the lich, who stood at the far end of the room, watching the battle with cold amusement. It hadn't even moved since the fight began, its bony hand resting lightly on its staff as the shadow beasts did its bidding.

Then he noticed, his Appraisal flaring up almost subconsciously, that the creature he had struck had actually taken damage.

Shadow Warrior
HP: 45/100

He blinked as five of them launched themselves at him, using his Roar to throw them right back and following up with a Wing Buffet that sent a slew of the lich's minions crashing against the four walls of its tomb.

"Weaken them!" Ethan shouted. "Take them down to the last sliver of their health, and then we blast that fucker with a single strike!"

Fauna nodded, sweat beading on her brow as she channeled more magic into her staff. "Get ready!"

Ethan smiled back at the Hopla.

No hesitation this time, eh, Faun?

With a shout, she raised her staff high, and a surge of radiant energy exploded from its tip. The blast hit the closest shadow beasts, disintegrating them into nothing more than wisps of smoke. But it kept them alive—just barely.

For a brief moment, there was a clear path.

"Go!" Ethan roared, charging forward with his legs skittering across the stone floor.

Klax barreled forward beside him, his massive frame smashing through any creatures that tried to block their path. Tara followed close behind, moving like a shadow herself, her blades flickering in the dim light.

The lich finally moved, its hollow eyes narrowing as it raised its staff. Dark tendrils of magic shot out from the ground, coiling toward Ethan and the others before morphing into a barrier of shadow beasts clawing and snarling with deathly intent. Ethan dodged to the side, narrowly avoiding the tendrils as they whipped past him. He scaled the walls and hooked his limbs onto the ceiling before crashing back down to earth with a Dive that crushed the living walls of shadow as it impacted them. He saw Fauna raise her staff again, sending a barrage of magical bolts toward the lich, but each one was deflected by a shimmering barrier of dark energy.

"Its defenses are up!" Fauna shouted, frustration creeping into her voice. "We need to break through that shield!"

Klax didn't hesitate. He lunged forward, claws extended, aiming straight for the lich's barrier. But the moment he made contact, the shield flared with energy, sending him flying backward with a painful grunt.

Ethan cursed under his breath. This wasn't going to be easy. The lich's mana wasn't depleting fast enough, and it had what seemed like a limitless supply of shadows to keep them at bay while it maintained its magical defenses. And those beasts . . . they were regenerating too quickly.

"We need to disrupt it!" Ethan called out. "Force it to move!"

Tara's eyes flashed with understanding. "It has anchored itself to that spot. If we can make it move, we might have a shot."

"I'll hit it from the side," Ethan said, already moving into position. "Klax, Tara, try to push it into one of Fauna's attacks."

"Don't have to tell me twice!" the rampaging Minxit yelled back.

Klax grunted in agreement, already shaking off the blow from earlier. He moved to flank the lich while Tara darted to the other side, her movements precise and deliberate. Fauna held her staff at the ready, watching for the perfect moment.

Ethan charged forward, his venomous fangs bared. He slammed into the lich's barrier with all his strength, his spidery legs scraping against the shield. It flared in response, but Ethan didn't let up. He pushed harder, forcing the lich's attention onto him.

As expected, the creature turned toward Ethan, raising its staff to unleash a wave of dark energy. That's when Tara struck. She moved like lightning, her blades flashing as she darted in and slashed at the lich's side, the blow just enough to disrupt its focus.

It hissed, its hollow voice filled with rage as it staggered back. In that moment, its shield flickered.

"Now!" Fauna shouted, unleashing a bolt of searing light directly at the lich. The barrier shattered under the force of the magic, leaving the creature vulnerable.

"Push it back!" Klax roared, barreling toward the lich with a savage growl. His claws slashed through the air, aimed directly at the creature's chest, who reacted swiftly, raising its staff to teleport out of the way. But Ethan had been watching, studying the way the lich moved, the subtle flicker of magic that preceded its teleportation.

"There!" Ethan yelled, his legs already moving toward the spot the lich was about to reappear in. He struck out just as it materialized, catching it midteleport.

The lich screeched, its skeletal form recoiling from the impact. Dark energy crackled around it, but it was clear that the creature was weakening. Its movements were slower, its magic less precise.

The teleportation . . . It disrupts its perception, Ethan realized. *Which means . . .*

[Skill Activated: Hide (Grade B)]

Tara and Klax pressed the attack, their combined assault keeping the lich off-balance.

The shadow beasts, though still regenerating, were becoming less coordinated, their movements sluggish as the lich's control over them began to wane. Fauna kept them at bay with bursts of light and fire, ensuring they didn't overwhelm the group while they focused on the true threat.

The lich, now cornered, snarled in desperation. It raised its staff once more, summoning a final wave of dark energy.

But before it could bring its deathly catalyst down on the ground, it felt the keen sting of two blades pierce its rib cage from behind.

[Hide: Deactivated]

"Sorry, buddy," Ethan snarled down at his shuddering prey. "There's only one lord of monsters here."

Without a scream or even a whimper, the lich's form dissipated from existence, its shadow slaves doing the same, their claws passing through the hybrids harmlessly as their forms simply shriveled and melted away into the air, leaving the team panting for breath and looking up at the triumphant form of their Archon standing proud above them.

Nether Lich Defeated!
Spirit Cores: +250
Current Spirit Cores: 375

Tara shook her head as Ethan simply shrugged, pointing the way toward the exit door.

". . . That was your badass one-liner?" she scoffed. "Mr. Archon . . . you're getting sloppy."

Loot Acquired!

Without even acknowledging what Tara had said, Ethan found himself licking his lips at the blade that had just settled into his hands from the ashes of his enemy.

Now, that's more like it.

He'd just gotten a weapon worthy of a Demon Lord.

Lucent, Capital of Westerweald

The pearly streets of Lucent were awash with confused citizens, for yesterday, an army of Greycloaks had marched through its gates, led by none other than the Master of the Greys herself, Carliah Argent. She and her forces had overturned the guards and practically blockaded every district of the city within merely six hours of stifled conflict.

Those who'd resisted had been beaten and cuffed. The process of pacifying the city had been less than a trifle for the warriors of the Greys. Even the hardiest veteran of Argwyll would run home to his mama with his dick between his legs rather than take on the monster slayers themselves.

The people barked. They complained. They grumbled, and they wept that their city was now becoming little more than a forward base for the Greys. But they put up with it. As Commander Carliah always said, the people of this world owed her Order their lives. The very fact they were even able to draw breath in this realm was owed to the Greycloaks.

And in Kaedmon's name, they'd purify this land. This time, for good.

At the height of the commotion, the commander walked briskly through the palace gates alongside a man who wore his grey cowl over his face. Those men, women, and children who remembered the old hero of their age knew his walk, however, and whispers started running down the crowds that the Lightborn had returned to the city—this time, as a conqueror.

But it was not he who appeared on King Lysandus's balcony that day and delivered a solemn decree to the people of the capital city.

"Citizens of Lucent!" Carliah Argent began. "The Fifth Archon lives."

Murmurs of discontent. People swarmed together, and collective gasps traveled through the city streets. Even the tavern-goers were forced outside by the hubbub, talking in drunken slurs about how they knew that the day of reckoning was coming—they had known people who had died in the Battle of Grenbelm Forest. Only the Archon could slay a hundred men in cold blood like that.

And it was still out there. Which meant . . . not even Lord Artorious could stop it alone?

Yet more people hesitated as they heard the news. Naysayers in the crowd began to spread countergossip: The bounty . . . it had vanished days ago, hadn't it? So the Archon must have been dead, right? Was this all just some elaborate ruse for the Greycloaks to make a political power play?

A quick glance at the serrated weapons of the immortal warriors told such naysayers to hold their tongues. At any rate, the grim countenance of Lord Artorious as he stepped beside the master of the Greys told those people the truth: this threat was still real, and this time, the devil had landed in their territory.

"In accordance with Krea's Commandment," Carliah continued, "I am declaring a state of martial law. All of Lucent's armed forces will henceforth submit themselves to the authority of the Greycloaks. All men and women of able body shall submit to a routine of rigorous training in preparation to defend this city from the emerging threat of the Archon and its hybrid forces. All hybrids in the city will submit to detention and interrogation immediately, under penalty of a long, agonizing demise. Any human who refuses to answer this call or who is found harboring hybrid citizens in an official capacity or otherwise shall be dealt with in the same manner."

Ripples of anger weaved their way through the crowds. A few unruly voices rose up to verbalize their distaste, but a swift beating from the Greys stationed at regular intervals on the streets put an end to these rabble-rousers. After the first few beatings, even a simple look from the cloaked warriors was enough to cow any dissenting humans into submission.

After all, who could argue with the servants of a God?

Almost as soon as she had made her proclamation, Carliah turned and marched right back into the castle, only giving the people one more vow.

"This time, the world shall be spared a century of darkness. With your cooperation, we promise you a final nail in the coffin of the Archon legacy. We promise you safety from all monster incursions now and forever. We promise you the fulfillment of the Lightborn's sacred mission. Stand with us, men and women of the west, and we shall break the back of this invasion before it sweeps through Argwyll!"

As she left, she allowed herself a small grin of satisfaction as a choir of cheers followed her. The people of the civilized world were so easy to corral when you told them exactly what they wanted to hear.

"See that, Pendragon?" Carliah said as she and Artorious made their way back inside the palace. "That's how you get people on your side."

"Those are the same people we are oath-bound to serve and protect, Carliah," he replied. "They are not merely tools to be used and discarded."

"Pfft, don't act as if you don't enjoy having power over the sheep," the master of the Greys scoffed. "You've been loving their attention all these years, haven't you?"

Artorious said nothing.

"Now, onto more pressing matters . . ."

Both Greycloaks returned to the throne room where the blubbering king was still crying over his guards being sent on their merry way by the team of Greycloaks who had barged their way into his palace, told him he no longer had any authority here, and informed him they would be assuming de facto leadership over his entire realm.

"Y-You cannot do this!"

"Yes, I can," Carliah told him bluntly, barely even acknowledging him as she passed by. "Need I remind you that Krea's Commandment gives the current commander of any regional Greycloak chapter the authority to conscript the services of any town or city in the event an Archon rises? Lucent's walls are solid, defensible, and its status as capital city allows us to project our power far beyond these walls. A general mustering and hunt are already underway. Soon, this new fledgling Archon will have nowhere to hide, and we will kill this invasion in its crib."

She bent down to smile in the king's tear-filled face.

"You're welcome," she said.

But King Lysandus wasn't about to take this sitting down. Without warning, he rose, drawing the ceremonial broadsword at his hip and rushing the master of the Greys with a crazed battle cry of "YOU TRAITOROUS BITCH!" on his lips.

And before he had even unsheathed an inch of his sword, Artorious had disarmed him and knocked him down with the blunt end of his new rapier—an onyx blade that threw deep shadows across the throne room's walls.

The king looked up at the former guest in his court, his mind flashing to the banquets held in this shining hero's name, where he had simply scoffed at each nobleborn guest and retired without even taking the hand of a lady.

Was it possible he had hated the people of this city all this time?

"L-Lightborn Artorious . . ." the king mumbled. "Please . . . you—you must see reason!"

"Tsk." Carliah sighed. "Another pest you didn't just slay, Artorious."

The Lightborn sheathed his blade without even looking at the groveling king who was currently trying to kiss his boots.

"He is human, Carliah," Artorious replied, much to the shock of the petrified king. "He may be ignorant, dull, and a petulant child, but he is no monster."

"Those rolls of fat dangling from his arms suggest otherwise," the Greycloak master scoffed. "Revok, Maresh—remove His Highness from the city and inter him in Griffon's Watch. A short spell in the cells might just teach him some valuable lessons in humility. Perhaps the good Doctor Haylock can even find some use for one such as him."

The pair of Greycloaks moved to obey their leader's command, casting sideway glances at Artorious before picking the king up by his flabby arms and dragging him from his own throne room.

"A-Artorious!" Lysandus wailed as he was evicted. "Old friend! Please—Please don't let them—!"

The Lightborn had already turned his back on the king, following his commander downstairs to the city barracks. There, they would prepare to mobilize their forces for the all-out assault that awaited them. This time, the Archon would have no time to gain a foothold in this world. This time, they'd put it down before it even made a dent in Argwyll.

. . . *He'd* put it down.

Because he had to. Didn't he?

"ARTORIOUS!" Lysandus's wails continued. "PLEASE!"

The Lightborn ignored the screams. He'd heard much worse before.

CHAPTER TWENTY-FIVE

[LOOT]

The Twilight Sepulcher, Floor 2

For once, Ethan was playing the long game.

Current Spirit Cores: 375

Three hundred and seventy-five big ones, Sys. If I keep 'em for the Boss, I should be possessing him in no time.

I would remind you that, while your combat exploits have so far been . . . adequate, your Spirit Cores simply increase the chance of successful possession relative to your target's Willpower. You still may fail if the target's Will is strong. Judging by the nature of your enemies in this place . . .

. . . the big bad's gonna be one strong-willed customer. Or he might not even have any Willpower at all.

I wouldn't worry about that; all creatures anointed by Kaedmon have a will of their own.

It is all the more depressing that we have to adhere to his law.

See, there you go again—helpful and then cryptic in the same breath. Not that I'm really complaining anymore. That's your whole schtick, right?

I would ask that you define this term, [Schtick] . . . but at this point, why should I bother?

Ethan smiled. They were used to each other's own distinct forms of bullshit now. In a strange way, Argwyll wouldn't be Argwyll without Sys.

He turned his attention to the halls of the second floor instead, and the shouting of Tara as she found another half-opened chest that was definitely not a mimic waiting to tear into her flesh. They'd had a few close calls as they traversed the depths of the second floor, which seemed to function as a crypt, with entire rooms filled to the brim with coffins and unmarked graves.

They'd come across no traces of any enemy activity. Not even Ethan's upgraded Appraisal suggested that there was any danger nearby.

So, looting had become their priority. Already, the party had picked up some choice items from the fallen lich:

Item: {Rare} Mithril Scythe
DMG: 35 (x2 During Night)
Special: Ignores AP

Ethan gawked at the vicious scythe, seeing scintillating shadows running across its surface.

"*Special*, eh?" Ethan asked Fauna as they followed Klax and Tara, the two of them taking point due to their superior senses for treasure and traps.

"Mithril is a rare material," Fauna explained. "Some metals of Argwyll have unique properties. Mithril can completely rip through armor, making it a coveted item for any warrior."

Ethan's giant spider form grinned down at the Hopla, who blushed as she realized she'd been talking like a machine.

". . . Sorry," she said. "Sometimes, I can be a bit of a textbook, Mr. Ethan."

"You know what?" he replied. "Your Archon's first command is this: you will stop apologizing from now on, especially when the knowledge in your fluffy noggin's actually super useful."

She gave a slight chuckle as Tara and Klax pointed out another treasure room to their right. "Sorry for saying sorry."

Ethan decided he'd keep the scythe for now—his silver scimitars were working enough wonders down here, and he wasn't about to give them up to Transmogrify another item. Besides this, he let his companions go through the motions of testing for mimics.

Sometimes, the dusty coffins ended up holding treasure—more healing salves and MP potions for Fauna. Other times, they snapped shut and reached out their spine-slathered tongues in an expectation of fresh meat, but Ethan's paralyzing scythe made short work of them. Whoever had placed them here clearly hadn't expected the Boss of another delve to come along with a mind of its own.

More blades and trinkets came their way as they went from decayed room to busted room, plundering this crypt for everything they could. Broadswords and bows of lesser quality filled their inventories, and Ethan found himself pondering some of their finds.

In the memories of Rachneros—accessed through his upgraded Possession skill—he could recall distinct sensations of pain, how much agony certain blades had wreaked on his host's body since the beginning of his delve's creation. He got enough sense from each of the looted blades they pilfered that there was a power and utility hierarchy of metals in this world:

Iron/Steel
Silver
Mithril
Adamantine
Coryph
Onixia

The best loot they got was the scythe and a quiver of dusty Mithril arrows, which Tara quickly claimed as her own (despite the fact that she'd gotten stuck in the mimic concealing the item not once but twice). Ethan had checked the quiver to see that, indeed, their armor-piercing attribute was applied to every arrow.

"Anybody come across anything better than mithril, let us know," Klax said. "We've already managed to secure a mithril deposit near Sanctum. The next step would be melting down some adamantine items and letting old Borlor work his magic on them. With any luck, we can have an entire army outfitted by the time we finish up in the City of Illusions."

"Purely for defense, Klaxy, right?"

Klax shot her a look as they organized their inventories.

"Someone needs to think about that," he replied sullenly.

Their conversation went no further than that, thankfully. It seemed the absence of enemies on the second floor had put the team at ease. But at the same time . . . there was a charge in the air. Ethan was waiting for the moment where they accidentally triggered a lever or a trip wire, or haphazardly stepped on a pressure plate and activated a whole deluge of shit they'd have to deal with before even reaching the Boss's lair. If Ethan were a Dungeon Core, that's what he'd do.

Thankfully, he didn't have to design his own dungeon—not yet, anyway. In this world, you never knew what the future would bring . . .

"Hey, little miss textbook," he asked Fauna as they approached a large brimstone wall that looked like a dead end. "What's so special about 'onixia'? If the memories of Rachneros are right, he's never even felt the touch of an onixia blade."

The others heard his question and hesitated before taking another step. Ethan could see the hairs on their bodies tingle at the very mention of the material.

"He must have been lucky," Fauna whispered. "If he'd felt the sting of onixia, he'd know it."

Klax and Tara walked on, leaving the explanation to her. But their silence was already speaking volumes.

"Onixia is known as 'Soul Shrivener,'" Fauna said, clutching her staff tightly to her bosom. "It is the bane of every monster, made from their blood and synthesized with powerful magic that burns the flesh of a particular species depending on the blood the blade was birthed from. Among us hybrids, the material is shunned."

"Because it's made from monsters?"

"Because it's vile!" Fauna burst out. Then, composing herself, she continued. "The weapons they used against my burrow—I can remember how they repelled us before we even tried resisting. We couldn't even look at them or the men who held them. It was like looking at something so unnatural it shouldn't exist."

"And let me guess who likes to use them . . ." Ethan murmured.

"The Greycloaks." Fauna nodded, her pink eyes serious and deadly focused. "In the kingdom of Argwyll, they are the only ones who know the secret of how onixia weapons are made. No one knows who the foul craftsman is who creates them, but it's said they have at least one blade for each and every species of monster on this earth . . . including us."

Fauna turned suddenly to her Archon, speaking with such determination that it caused Klax and Tara to turn back and make sure the Hopla speaking *was* her.

"That's why you've got to get even stronger, Mr. Ethan," she declared. "Because we can't beat them with good tactics or numbers. We need an Archon who can make them scared of us, for once."

Ethan smiled despite the tension in the air. "And you really think I can do it, Faun?"

"I know you can, Mr. Ethan."

Klax and Tara smiled to themselves at their friend's renewed confidence. When they started walking again, they did so with pride. Fauna had changed—that much was obvious, even to a newcomer like Ethan. But even as he thanked her for her trust in him and followed his companions deeper into the den of darkness, he couldn't help but ponder the new information he'd just learned.

You all believe in me, he thought. *But if onixia is made from monster blood and wipes the floor with whatever it's made from . . . isn't it possible that the Greys already have a secret weapon up their sleeves? A sword made from the blood of the other Archons . . .*

Sys? Come on, buddy. You'd know the answer. You'd know what did in the other Archons before me, right? Tell me I'm wrong here. Or . . . tell me the truth.

. . .

All I will say is this, Ethan Graham: I would hurry up and finish these delves before your enemies have a chance to learn what they're really up against, here. Because if you give them the chance, they will break you, and everything you're starting to care about.

The end of the crypt proved to be more than just a dead end—it was an obnoxious puzzle.

The wall before them was a mural; one that displayed four different levers in two adjacent rooms being manipulated by mummified corpses.

"Ugh," Tara groaned. "I hate these things."

Fauna gasped. "But Tara, they aren't as bad as something like a horde challenge!"

"Yuh, and that's the problem. It's gotta be the most boring 'puzzle' ever conceived."

"What's it all about?" Ethan asked, his eyes moving over the dusty wall mural.

"Nothing to worry about," Klax assured him. "Four levers must simply be tripped at the same time."

"That's it?"

"That's it," Tara grumbled, her tail drooping low while Fauna's ears perked up.

"I'll go with Mr. Eth—I mean, the Archon!"

The hybrids, including Ethan, stared at her.

"T-That is . . ." she stumbled. "We've got to split up, right?"

"That is the particular nuisance of this kind of puzzle," Klax agreed. "Though I'm almost certain with the sheer size of Ethan he could trip two at the same ti—"

"Oh, I don't think so," Fauna interrupted vehemently. "Even if he could, there may be deadly traps that the levers activate!"

Klax was about to argue further, but Tara grabbed him by the scruff of his neck and pulled him toward the now open doors on the left-hand side of the crypt mural.

"Ah, c'mon, Klaxy," she said. "Let's allow our bodacious bunny girl her dream of being alone with Mr. Ethan."

"T-That's not—!" Fauna stammered as Tara shot her a mischievous smile.

Ethan merely laughed at the whole spectacle. "All right. Guess we'll take the right."

The chamber they entered was another one filled with open sarcophagi and chests that had been recently looted. It was weird—the whole place had the vibe of an MMO raid dungeon that'd been recently plundered of its riches. Ethan and company were basically the party who'd entered too late and were presently in the unenviable position of having to wait for the new monsters to spawn.

But a more pressing problem was that, even with five whole eyes at his disposal, Ethan couldn't make out any levers in the room.

"A spell of Concealment hangs over this place," Fauna said as she rubbed her hands on the walls. "I can take care of it, but it might take a while."

Ethan nodded. "You're the boss, Miss Magic Paws. Tell me what I gotta do to help, and I'll do it."

The Hopla shook her head, her ears flapping up a storm of dust.

"No, no—you can relax, Ethan. I'll start the incantation as soon as possible. But, well, if the spell goes haywire . . ."

"I'll protect you," Ethan finished, meeting the gaze of the blushing girl. "Hey, don't worry about it. Us hybrids gotta depend on each other, right?"

"R-Right . . ." Fauna whispered.

For the next few minutes, the Hopla glowed with indigo-violet energy, casting a spell of Divination that lit up the whole room in an otherworldly aura, throwing the shadows of the emptied sarcophagi across the barren walls. Ethan slumped down and inspected his gargantuan flesh blades, wondering when the hell he'd get to cut something again.

And it was in that moment of relative quiet that he suddenly began hearing voices echoing from down the hall.

"You've been talking to him, haven't you?"

He whipped his head around to see the closed door behind him and Fauna, and only when the voice continued did he realize who it was.

"C'mon, Klax. I ain't no baby kitten."

His senses began to pick up movement—perhaps the swift turning of a head and baring of fangs.

"All right, Tara. Yes. I told him everything."

Ethan felt the hairs on the backs of his hind legs tingle with little goose bumps. It seemed his newly upgraded Appraisal ability didn't just let him see through walls but *hear* through them too . . .

And he was currently eavesdropping on a very interesting conversation next door.

Okay—ethics time, he counseled himself. *Peeping and eavesdropping are morally dubious activities. Only in the event that one must gather important wartime intelligence are such acts permissible! These are your friends, Ethan. Do you really wanna hear them argue?*

"Everything? Including your lovey-dovey plan to save your damsel in distress?"

. . . Then again, these are strange, morally gray times we live in.

And just like that, there goes another string from your moral bow . . .

"If that's what you call it, so be it," Klax replied. "But you know as well as I do, Tara, that Jun'Ei is the only one with a long-term plan for this little revolution we're planning. Without her, we are blind."

"Oh, pardon me. I forgot that wandering aimlessly through stuffy tombs gave us 80/80 vision."

"If you have something to say, then say it."

Ethan registered Klax's anger, but strangely, he never felt any sort of hatred emanate from Tara's voice. Instead, it sounded like she was approaching the old wolfman with pity.

"Klax," she said gently. "I know you don't want to accept it, but—"

"She's not dead."

"Klax . . ."

"She's not."

Silence, unbroken until Fauna's breathing became heavier as her spell began to work on the room's aura of concealment.

Then—a sudden change of tone.

"We've all lost people, Klax. But throwing the Archon and the team into some suicidal charge on nothing but a hunch ain't the way to win this war."

"It's not a *hunch*, Tara. I know she's out there. And the delves are how we find her. I'm sure of it."

Ethan could sense the awkwardness between them, both hybrids wanting, needing to say something while they both knew they couldn't quite articulate the subject in any way that mattered.

"I made a promise to follow you into battle no matter what," Tara finally replied. "I did that because you're a fighter, man. You're the best goddamn chance we have; hell, I thought you were the only chance we'd have until the Archon showed up. But you can't give me shit for wanting to take the fight to the humans now while you're moping over your lost love."

"This isn't about me!" Klax yelled back, in a manner that Ethan would be forgiven for thinking the old wolf was dissolving plain out of existence with this final word. "This is about all of us . . . her dream is the dream we're all following. Don't you remember, Tara?"

The Minxit sounded as though she was about to make a retort and thought better of it, the words dying in her throat before she formed them.

"Do you remember the last words she ever said to me?"

". . . Of course I do. You don't have to—"

"She said, 'Take care of them, Klax.' She said that because she believed in us, and I'm not about to leave her out there to die in some human castle, rotting away to nothing while we're out here living our lives."

"Dammit, Klax, we all feel bad about losing her. Don't you think—Don't you think we miss her too? But she's gone, man. Can't you accept that?"

The way Klax replied was so quiet that Ethan would be forgiven for thinking the old wolf was just a ghost in the darkness.

"No."

"Uh, Ethan?" a voice much closer suddenly perked up. "Are you ready?"

The Hopla had revealed the location of the levers, and Ethan was surprised to find that he'd almost entirely forgotten why they were even there in the first place.

"Uh, yeah!" he stuttered, much to Fauna's confusion. "Let's get it done."

Fauna sent a little shock wave through the ground to alert their companions, who then pulled their own levers, saying nothing more. Meanwhile, Ethan's mind became more troubled than it had been by the monsters they'd slain so far.

When they met up outside their respective rooms, the atmosphere was immediately tense. The mural "dead end" began to creak open, shuddering through ancient dust to reveal a narrow corridor of red sandstone that led into nothing but a void of nothingness.

"Um . . . did anything happen on your end?"

The question was Fauna's, since no one seemed interested in speaking up.

". . . Nothing, Faun," Klax answered. "Let's just keep moving forward."

Ethan eyed them both as they walked past him, Tara putting on a show of patting Faun on her back and mumbling about what she and Ethan got up to alone, but it was clear the teasing was nothing but an act.

I wonder . . . Ethan thought. *Is Tara right? Is the old wolf just looking to remove the guilt on his head at leaving his old "love" behind during their last big battle? Would we really be better off striking the Greycloaks now?*

Remembering the face of the young boy in the forest, Ethan couldn't be sure of the right answer even now. All he knew from Klax was that there was a reason beyond simply attaining power that they had to go through these delves. And the reason had to do with this missing prophetess . . .

Reality suddenly had bigger concerns. From behind them, far back along the crypt's entrance, Ethan heard a sound that couldn't be mistaken for anything else: Skittering, the tiny patter of insect limbs on stone and the snapping of mandibles that began to surge in number until they became a single mass of chittering death.

He wasn't the only one who noticed. The hairs on Tara's back stood on end as her feet felt the trembling in the stones beneath them.

Chancing a look over his shoulder, Ethan saw what was storming down the corridor toward them.

Enemies Identified:
Scarab Congregation (Level 40)
HP: 500/500

It was a black mass of beetles that had merged into one; a wave of undulating darkness charging toward them. Already their chittering was becoming a war cry—that of an entire ecosystem of insects throwing themselves against the intruders, consuming everything in their path.

"Faun?" Ethan asked. "Remember that little thing you mentioned about traps?"

Fauna gulped as she felt Tara tense beside her. "Y-Yeah . . ."

"Except this ain't a trap I'm disarming," Tara murmured. "There's only one way we're getting outta this one."

Ethan didn't need to hear her shout the word. Before the first letter had left her lips, he was barreling down the sandstone hall with his sprinting comrades.

"RUN!"

CHAPTER TWENTY-SIX

The [Scuttling] Wall

Enemies Approaching:
Scarab Congregation (Level 40)

The hallway stretched out before them, endless and jagged, carved from sandstone, with walls adorned by cryptic hieroglyphs. The faint chittering of scarabs echoed ominously, underscored by the frantic shuffle of Ethan, Tara, Fauna, and Klax as they dashed down the corridor.

The scarab congregation—the maddened swarm of crawling insects that hunted the unwary—was never far behind, and as the party hurried down the hall, they began to feel the sting of their pincers against their skin.

"Keep moving!" Ethan commanded, his voice taut with urgency. He was bringing up the rear, using the mass of his body to keep them off the team while they surged forward, a singular, voracious intelligence driving them.

Ethan struck out with his blades, sweeping through whole swathes of the descending, nibbling mouths. He saw legions of scarab corpses fall, paralyzed and poisoned in equal measure, their little exoskeletons frying away. But no matter how many he fried, a thousand more simply took their places.

Scarab Congregation (Level 40)
HP: 485/500

Shit, I'm barely putting a dent in them . . .

Tara, her feline ears pinned flat against her skull, sprinted beside him, her steps almost soundless despite the chaos. She hissed under her breath, swinging her blade in quick arcs to fend off the creeping insects that had started to dart from the cracks in the walls. Fauna, ever calm despite her rabbitlike features and the panic dancing in her eyes, was bleeding from her arm but kept running, her staff held defensively behind her.

"Varla Parthax!"

The party felt a rush of speed lift them off their feet, propelling them away from the horde as it followed them. Fauna's spell of Haste was potent, but she shouted over her pale shoulders that it wouldn't last long.

"I hate bugs," Klax grumbled from their front, his hulking form crushing any unfortunate scarabs that crossed his path. His normally unflappable demeanor was fraying, though Ethan could tell the wolflike hybrid was pleased to be back in the thick of combat instead of being interrogated by Tara.

"They're everywhere!" Fauna shouted, swiping at the countless insects. The swarm seemed endless, pouring from the gaps between the stone, shimmering in the dim light as their hard, black bodies reflected the glow from Fauna's flickering staff.

Ahead, the hallway split into two paths—an immediate choice that could mean life or death. Ethan cursed under his breath, the urgency of their situation tightening his chest. The walls, slick with moisture, seemed to close in on them. The scarab wave smashed into him, nipping at every orifice, each bite not damaging him directly but doing something much more insidious.

Host: Rachneros, the Pale Lord (Level 30)
STR: -2
STR: -2
STR: -2

They're weakening me . . . Ethan thought with a start. "Tara! Which way?" he shouted over the noise, his eyes darting between the two paths. Time was running out. Tara paused, her eyes narrowing as she focused. Her innate senses as a cat-woman hybrid helped her gauge the subtle shifts in the air.

"Left!" she snapped, her gaze unwavering. Without hesitation, Ethan led the charge, the group veering left into a narrower corridor. The noise of the scarabs amplified here, their legs clicking ominously against the stone floor. Ethan could feel their bodies crawling over his boots, every step becoming a maddening experience as they snapped at his ankles.

"We're going in circles," Fauna panted, clutching her bleeding arm. "The walls—they shift. It's a maze."

"Dammit," Ethan spat, realizing the truth of her words. The labyrinth was alive—a trap not just of scarabs but of shifting stone, designed to confuse and corner. They were being funneled, led deeper into the scarabs' nest.

He tried a Roar that managed to stun an entire section of the horde. Yet, even against the sheer power of his enhanced voice, borrowed from the troll of Grenbelm, more scarabs simply poured from their lairs to rejoin the congregation.

Tara hissed as a clutch of scarabs latched onto her leg. She swung her dagger down and crushed them, but the acid splattered, burning her fur and drawing a sharp breath of pain from her. Klax's heavy breathing was growing louder, the strain of constant battle and the swarm's bites beginning to wear on him.

"We can't keep this up," Klax growled, a touch of desperation creeping into his voice. "Too many. We need to break out."

Ethan's mind raced, his thoughts turbulent. The maze was unyielding, and every path led to more scarabs, more bites. If they didn't escape soon, they'd be overwhelmed. He grimaced as another hundred scarab mandibles sank into his arm, drawing the green blood of his host.

Then he remembered something—a little trick they'd pulled off in the Festering Den. The thought hit him like a flash of lightning. It was risky, but it might just be their way out.

Don't tell me: you're going to try something suicidal again?

Ain't that what I do best, Sys? There's only one way we're taking this thing down, and it's by taking them all down at once.

"Fauna!" he shouted. "I need you to light me up!"

The rabbitgirl looked up at him as her staff struck out to shear through another clump of scarabs seeking to snuff out her light. "O-Okay!"

"The hell you planning, now?" Tara asked, equally preoccupied as her limbs began to fail her, her strength, too, being sapped away by the relentless attacks of their buggy assailants.

"Whatever it is, why don't we trust him?" Klax replied. "After all, he's the Archon. He'll make the right decision when the time comes."

Tara's feline eyes flashed to the wolf, knowing there was a hidden meaning behind those words . . .

"All right!" Ethan shouted back, the power in his muscles all but gone by this point. "Everyone, hang on tight!"

"To WHAT?!"

Ethan smiled as he felt Fauna's Infernal Coating run up his body.

"To my shiny spider booty, of course."

Wing Buffet.

In the space of the next second, with the scarabs all but ready to break through Ethan's failing strength, his back legs flapped like a pair of faux wings and sent a fiery wave through the hallway, knocking back the entire black wave of enemies and sending Fauna's flame traveling through the miasma of snapping mandibles to burn the insides of every scarab and their reinforcements.

The shock wave produced was stronger than even Ethan had expected, however, and with his strength totally sapped, his legs couldn't plant themselves in the sandstone floor to keep their balance. He went flying back, his teammates clutching to him for dear life as they smashed through the first wall they made contact with, tumbling into the dark void of the Twilight Sepulcher's third floor.

"WHAT WAS THAT YOU SAID ABOUT MAKING THE RIGHT DECISION?!" Tara screamed in the dark.

"I DIDN'T SAY IT WOULD BE THE BEST ONE! ONLY THAT IT WAS RIGHT!"

"FUCK YOU TOO, KLAX!"

When they felt the soft tickle of a cloud cushioning them, their eyes flew to the ground that was quickly approaching. Slowly, they began to float, Ethan the Archon basically becoming nothing but a balloon, hovering in the total darkness surrounding them.

When they finally touched down on the crunchy floor of the Sepulcher's last layer, they all rolled away and breathed a sigh of relief.

"See?" Klax chuckled. "Told . . . Told you."

"All I'm thinking is that Fauna's spells have been pretty reliable recently. Where's the crazy bad luck of our little Wildglance?"

Just then, a powerful, squelching roar erupted from Tara's posterior, the noise ripping through the air and echoing off the void that surrounded them.

"Um . . ." Fauna whispered. "Sorry . . . that's a . . . common side effect that can sometimes, uh, happen after the Fleetfoot spell."

The entire party contemplated what they'd just heard.

"Huh," Tara finally said. "There it is."

A few seconds of silence went by, accompanied by darkness and the sounds of crying scarabs as they burned high above them.

Then, a chuckle from Klax.

A snotty scoff from Tara.

And a little giggle from Fauna that soon became a belly laugh.

Before long, the entire party was doubled over, including their spidery Archon himself.

"E-Ethan must think we're a bunch of fools," Fauna said, wiping a tear from her eye. "He's probably regretting every encounter he's had with us."

"Well," Ethan laughed back, "you did throw a chicken at old Artorious. Not gonna lie; it wasn't the most competent first impression."

"But it *did* save your life, Mr. Ethan."

"Hey, I had it under control!"

"Now, that's a lie worthy of the true Archon," Tara chuckled as she jumped to her feet and helped her comrades up. "I'm thinking we're gonna need some restoring before we head on, huh?"

Klax smiled to see the team in good spirits—something shared with Ethan as they locked eyes.

"Think you've got some restorative magic left in you, Faun?"

The Hopla sniggered. "I think I can whip up something. If you're willing to put up with a possible explosion?"

Ethan saw the stat screen of Sys appear just before he answered her:

Scarab Congregation Defeated!
Spirit Cores: +200
Current Spirit Cores: 575

"Honestly?" Ethan said. "There's nothing in life that couldn't be improved by an explosion or two . . ."

The Twilight Sepulcher, Floor 3
Current Spirit Cores: 575

Klax seemed convinced that this was the final floor. Most dungeons, he said, followed a basic three-floor structure until you came to the grade A and S variants. Then shit got wild.

As Ethan and his party walked over the bridge which guided them toward a high-arched entrance to the final depths of this sightless abyss, he was filled with both a sense of dread and excitement in equal measure.

Because if a bridge made entirely of corpses wasn't wild shit, then he had to see just what the higher-tier dungeons held in store for him.

They'd rested for only a few minutes; just enough time for Fauna to replenish their HP pool (after a few false starts that ended in some hamster summoning). The Hopla's magic was beginning to wither, and Klax told her to save the rest of her spells—they'd need them for whatever the Boss of this place was.

Ethan took the short respite they had to consider his skills and make another upgrade in the meantime.

[Upgrading Skill: Hide (Grade B)]
Upgrade Complete!
Congratulations! You have upgraded [Hide] from Grade B to A.

Hide (Grade A)
Number of sneak attacks without being detected by enemies increased.
Number of Attacks without Enemy Detection: 4

Spirit Cores to Upgrade [Hide] Skill from Grade A to S: 250
Current Spirit Cores: 425

My first grade-A skill . . . he thought, noticing that the final upgrade cost two hundred and fifty Spirit Cores to bring the skill to S grade. After that, there was apparently a kind of prestige option that Klax had hinted at, but Ethan was content to wait and see just how strong the skill was before he reduced it back down to nil. There'd have to be a damn good benefit before he'd consider doing that.

He decided to save the remaining Cores until he got his new host. Upgrading skills had become his primary dump for his Cores, since it hardly seemed necessary to increase his Core Stats when he was swapping bodies left, right, and center.

Maybe if I decide to stay in a particular form one day . . . the body of a dragon so perfect, so powerful with all the skills I transfer to it that I can burn all the Greycloaks in one fell swoop.

As he daydreamed, the rest of his party crept forward with renewed caution. Fauna's globe of magelight flickered as she pushed it forward, its luminescence highlighting the bodies of the dead they trod on toward the bridge's end. Each step felt like trudging through the bloody insides of a thousand dead men, but the bridge bore their weight without a single limb falling out of place.

"Whoever rests here," Fauna said, "they hold nothing but contempt for the living."

Klax nodded. "I can smell nothing but the stench of death emanating from ahead. Be ready."

The floor beneath Ethan's many legs clicked faintly with each movement as he led his companions through the dim expanse of the final floor of the Twilight Sepulcher. The once grand structure had decayed into a cryptic labyrinth, the walls covered in ancient, faded murals depicting battles long forgotten, and the ceiling crumbled in places, leaving gaps through which cold drafts seeped in.

The murals caught Ethan's eyes, particularly those depicting an ironclad warrior battling hordes of undead foes amidst a frigid, icy wasteland.

"Look," Fauna whispered, urging her light toward the image of the painted man.

He was the centerpiece of every picture, his eyes shining pearls framed by a gaunt face and a mane of silver hair. The blade and shield he carried with him seemed to glow even in the faded murals, which must have been here for centuries.

"Think we've found our Delve Boss," Tara said. "Handsome dude, eh? Even if he's probably nothing but a rotting corpse."

Ethan eyed the catgirl. "Would you?"

"Beggars can't be choosers, especially in this economy."

Tara leaned forward slightly to inspect the painting—nothing but a tiny shifting of her weight—but every member of the party heard the distinct *click* of something being triggered.

The catgirl looked down to see her normally nimble paws had just tripped a pressure plate.

"Well . . . shit."

The door to the chamber slammed shut. The walls bearing the murals began to move, closing in on the party as they squeezed together.

"T-Tara!" Fauna shouted over the screeching of the walls.

"Hey! I ain't a perfect kitten!" Tara shouted back as she unsheathed her daggers. "Even the trap lady's gonna fuck up sometimes!"

"Enough!" Klax shouted. "Don't dwell on the mistake. Think of the present! Ethan?"

Ethan stretched his limbs to keep the walls apart, managing to climb to the midsection of the room and bring them grinding to a halt. Meanwhile, his flexile limbs flashed with his twin scimitars.

"Be ready!" he shouted. "Here they come!"

The party followed his gaze to the earth-shattering sounds of the plates under their feet, and the hands that had begun tearing through them to grab at the hybrids.

Enemy Identified:
Shambling Corpse Mound (Level 45)
HP: 700/700

As the floor fell away, Ethan saw that what they were looking at was just like the scarab congregation—a conglomeration of creatures melded together into a single mass of reaching limbs and screaming maws, each one twisting its boneless neck to reach up and chew at them from below.

DELVE CHALLENGE: HORDE
Activated!

"Oh, you gotta be kidding me!"

The voice was Tara's, just before she was dragged down into the pit of zombies.

"Tara!" Ethan yelped, sending down a Roar that knocked her assailants off her. Still, she fell as the rest of the floorboards gave way under the weight of the zombie mountain, so he let fly a Wing Buffet that carried him down to grab her, impaling several reaching zombies as he fell into the abyss of their corpse-laden lair.

His paralysis scimitar struck true, spearing into the mound of bodies to steady his fall until he landed with a wet slap against the ground and rolled to meet the crashing bodies its foe sent his way.

Tara wriggled free and flanked the mound, her blades digging into its hide voraciously as Fauna struck out from above with what Ethan assumed was meant to be a fireball. In actuality, she'd spawned a quaking duck that sailed into the open mouths of the living wave of bodies.

"You know what? I take it back. Our luck's the same as it's always been."

Tara and Ethan avoided a string of clawing arms that the amorphous beast shot at them, spinning and readying a return strike that sent the entire mound reeling back while Klax and Fauna skated down its side.

"Flee!" Klax shouted. "If we waste time on this pestilent creature, we won't have enough energy for the final Boss!"

Ethan struck out at the corpse mountain's foundation, sending some webs toward the base to keep it stuck in place.

"But . . . But the loooooooot . . ."

His concern was literally bashed aside—the mound reeled and belched out a torrent of acidic vomit that bit at his flesh the moment it made impact.

"Watch out!" Fauna called, summoning a protective shield as she and Klax joined the party.

Together, bound up in Fauna's magic protection, they floated on a sea of bloody, chunky vomit, seeing the remains of all the creatures this mound of living flesh had consumed.

[Time Remaining: 00:07:00]

"Well?" Ethan asked. "Anyone got any bright ideas?"

He looked back to see Tara bent low, cradling her leg in her hands. Meanwhile, Klax was steadying Fauna, who looked as though she was about to heave her own guts out.

". . . I'll take that as a no. Okay. Look, there's gotta be some way to blast through this thing. Maybe another well-timed Wing Buffet could take us outta here. Maybe I could proc paralysis and we could sprint the fuck away. Maybe . . ."

He looked at Klax's desperate eyes as the monster wave rose, balled into a fist, and slammed into them, sending them deeper into the flood of virulence.

Dammit, Ethan thought. *I am not gonna die in this world buried in shit and vomit. Okay, Sys, any ideas? I'm going out on my eight limbs here.*

Wait.

Sys, I don't need your sarcastic—

No, Ethan. All you need to do is wait.

Ethan stared in bewilderment as the mass of flesh reeled its great fist up to smash their bubble again.

"I-I can't hold the mana flow!" Fauna shrieked.

Ethan heard her, though there was nothing he could say.

Just wait, eh? Sys, I swear if this is some—

A jet stream of dazzling light pierced the blackened skies, cutting off any train of thought Ethan had maintained.

He saw the great mound of corpses twist in confusion. Then, at the place where it had just been pierced at its apex erupted a torrent of black bile and blood.

More ribbons of light cut through the corpse pile, shearing clean across whole heaps of the thing until every body was shredded apart, an ocean of blood flowing from the wounds cut into the creature.

"Fauna . . ." Ethan murmured. "Hold on unless you want a mouthful of zombie blood . . ."

The Hopla followed his eyes and, just as dumbstruck as the rest of the group, kept her staff raised high as the blood rain poured down on them, coating the ground with crimson.

Only when another dozen blinding cuts were slashed across the great corpse mound did it finally fall, all its supply of bodies exhausted and drained. The light show, whatever it was, had practically deleted the thing piece by piece, breaking it apart instantly like a paper shredder.

DELVE CHALLENGE: HORDE
Nullified!
All Enemies Vanquished!

And only in the silence that followed the spilling of blood and broken limbs did Ethan see something shining where the mountain of zombies once stood.

The air was thick, musty, and filled with the unmistakable scent of decay.

A soft skittering sound echoed through the chamber. At first, it was subtle—almost imperceptible. But then it grew louder, more distinct, as it moved from where their enemy had once stood toward them. Ethan's eyes narrowed as he tried to peer into the darkness.

Then, out of the shadows, the creature emerged.

It was small. It was hairy. It was drenched in the corrupted blood of a thousand dead men. It stood on the mound of corpses—human and hybrid alike—its eyes gleaming in the faint light. Most notably, its silver teeth shone with an almost ethereal brightness.

"What the . . . ?" Klax murmured, his eyes wide.

Fauna stared at the beast, bewildered. "What is that thing?"

Tara, still clutching her leg, squinted at the rodent. "It looks . . . unnatural."

Ethan, however, stepped forward, a grin tugging at the corner of his lips. He lowered his blades and shook his head in utter disbelief.

Ally Identified:
Theodore, Slayer of the Damned (Level 150)
HP: 300/300

The rat tilted its head as if in acknowledgment, its silver teeth gleaming ominously in the dark. The little critter had eyes only for the crimson glare of the demon hat himself atop the great spider's body. He squeaked in recognition, flashing his bloody silver tooth at Ethan.

"Theodore," Ethan said with a nod. "You son of a bitch."

CHAPTER TWENTY-SEVEN

The [Uber] Rat and the Dead

Ethan stared unblinkingly at the little rat shuffling up to his party, its furry form matted in zombie blood.

"Theo, you son of a bitch. Level a hundred and fifty and counting, huh?"

Theo squeaked in glee while the rest of Ethan's party simply looked at the pair in bewilderment. For his part, Ethan was just glad to see the little guy again. He'd never been happier to see a disease-carrying rodent with a silver blade in its mouth.

"You . . . know each other?" Fauna asked.

"Me and ol' Theo here go way back." Ethan smiled through blood-soaked teeth. "This little beauty was my very first host in this world."

"You know what?" Tara said. "At this point, I'm just gonna go with it. Even if this little furball's a rotten kill stealer."

Theo scurried up on Ethan's shoulder, sniffing at his hat form and hissing at the Minxit.

"Ah, don't worry about her," Ethan reassured his bloody friend. "She's a soft kitty when ya get to know her."

Tara, even through the blood she was drenched in, looked like she was about to explode with embarrassment.

"The rat doesn't seem aggressive," Klax mused. "I have no idea how he got here, but he is no threat to us."

Theo seemed quite happy at this admission and jumped down to the corpse-laden ground, pointing with his nose toward the exit door to the pit they'd all landed in.

"Looks like he wants to lead the way . . ."

Ethan let out a hearty laugh, like a proud father watching his son ride a bike by himself. Theo had grown up.

"You wanna lead us to glory, Theo?" he asked the squeaking rat. "It's only fair, I suppose. I led you around for so long against your will. No hard feelings, right?"

Theodore's whiskers twitched in response as he scurried off toward the exit.

"I'll take that as a no. Faun?" Ethan then asked the Hopla. "How are your mana reserves?"

"I'm about halfway drained," she admitted. "But . . . it looks like we won't have many more problems going forward . . ."

She nodded to the room that Theodore had exited through; another crypt that was emptied of loot and sentient enemies. The corpses of all sorts of creatures littered the ground—zombies, gargoyles, ancient living armor sets, and even what looked like a winged demon.

All of them had exactly one tiny, tooth-sized puncture in the middle of their heads.

So this is what happens to the Archon's freed Hosts. They become true monsters.

Hey, I ain't complaining, Ethan scoffed back at Sys. *About time I had someone carry me.*

"Come on . . . kitty," Fauna shouted over her shoulder to Tara, who looked as though she was ready to fly at the Hopla with both her daggers.

"That's gonna fucking stick, ain't it?" she whispered to herself as they all trudged forward. "I swear, Ethan, if you weren't the Archon . . ."

The floor beneath Ethan's many legs clicked faintly with each movement as he led his companions through the dim expanse of the final floor of the Twilight Sepulcher. The once grand structure had decayed into a cryptic labyrinth, the walls covered in ancient, faded murals depicting battles long forgotten. The ceiling crumbled in places, leaving gaps through which cold drafts seeped in.

As Rachneros, Ethan's spider form took up most of the room, his body massive, sleek, and deadly. His eight legs carried him effortlessly across the rough terrain as his companions followed closely behind, their eyes darting from shadow to shadow.

Leading the group was none other than Theodore, the silver-toothed rat, who scurried ahead, sniffing the ground and navigating with ease through the oppressive gloom. Despite his size, Theodore seemed unfazed by the lurking dangers around them, his sharp instincts guiding the way.

Theodore scampered forward, pausing at a corner where the hallway bent into darkness. His nose twitched, and he let out a soft squeak before turning to look at Ethan. With a quick gesture, the rat darted ahead again, confirming their path was still clear.

"The little guy's handy," Klax muttered, watching Theodore with mild respect. "Never thought I'd say that about a rat."

"Don't underestimate him," Ethan warned. "This little guy was, after all, my very first host. I taught him well in the ways of ratjutsu."

Theo led them to a long, angular mirror at the very edge of the Sepulcher's bowels. The party had seen darkness already, but something about the mirror's reflective surface seemed darker still. As they approached, they saw shadowed versions of their own forms appear before them, flickering like dying candles.

"Faun?"

"It's definitely magic," the Hopla said. "But there's something about its surface—the energy moving across it is consistent with teleportation magic."

"And it's not the exit," Klax added, stepping toward the mirror's dark surface. "Which means just one thing: it must be the way to the Boss."

Theo squeaked in affirmation as the wolfman peered into the shadows. Ethan could tell that the little rat was being insistent, nosing the air just above the mirror's surface.

"He wants us to touch it," Tara said. "Listen, Ethan, if your little friend here's trying to get us killed—"

"Never," Ethan interrupted. "Theo was a good, loyal host. Weren't you, little guy?"

The rat spat a small glob of blood on the ground. Ethan took that as a good enough sign that he was ready to fight. "But you can't, can you?" he asked him. "Because this mirror needs the touch of a humanoid, I bet."

"You might be right," Fauna agreed. "Look how it's reacting to Klax's touch. All the collective energy of the mirror is converging on his paw."

As the Lycae moved his hand, the spectral energies of the mirror followed it like a living liquid mass. Ethan tried out his Appraisal on whatever was behind the thing.

"Okay," he said. "Yeah, I'm sensing something strong in there, all right. Something way stronger than what we've fought before. I'm gonna put us all in Hide mode just as we go through, alright? That way, we've each got at least four attacks we can get off before the bastard in there even gets to move—assuming he doesn't have a crazy Perception score."

Which he might, Ethan admitted to himself. *Fuck if I know. But still, can he truly match a grade-A Hide?*

Theodore squeaked with tenacity, looking up at his old master expectantly.

And with you on our side, we can do some real serious damage. This could be over in a single strike if we play our cards right . . .

The rest of the team nodded—except Klax.

"Klax?"

The wolfman was transfixed.

"Hey," Tara murmured. "Yo, Klax? You there, man?"

Klax's eyes had taken on a pallid shade of gray. His mouth, now agape, struggled to find words.

And only when Ethan tried grabbing him did he feel just how much he was shaking.

"Jun'Ei . . ."

The name tumbled out of his mouth like a curse. Whatever he was seeing in that mirror, it had gripped his heart and was crushing it like a vise.

"Shit . . . Guys, help us out here! Something's got hi—"

Before Ethan could finish his call, Klax reached out with one powerful thrust and launched his arm into the mirror, causing a ripple effect and a woman's scream to wail through the entire corridor.

"Klax!"

The dogman was pulled through, along with Ethan and the others, Theodore bringing up the rear. Though Fauna had correctly assessed that it was teleportation magic they were dealing with, Ethan barely felt like he transitioned from one area to another at all. All that happened was that the last crypt of the Sepulcher was there, and then it was not.

On the other side, they emerged into a grand circular chamber. The ceiling was high and domed, adorned with murals of battles and victories, but the color had long faded into dull grays. At the center of the room lay a sarcophagus, cracked and ancient, with dark energy radiating from it. The very air was thick with malevolence, pressing against their skin like an unseen weight.

"I—I—" Klax stumbled. "I'm sorry, everyone. I can't—"

"Never mind!" Tara shouted. "Everyone, look alive!"

As soon as they had stepped into the chamber, the ground beneath them trembled. The sarcophagus shifted, and with a loud crack, the stone lid slid open. A figure rose from within, draped in tattered armor, its gaunt face hidden beneath a weathered helm. Its eyes burned with cold silver fire, and in its skeletal hands, it held a long jagged sword that crackled with dark energy.

The warrior from the murals above. The silver-eyed champion of the Twilight Sepulcher.

And he was looking right at them.

BOSS ENCOUNTER!
Valgraiva, Lord of the Damned (Level 50)
HP: 950/950
WILL: 1000/1000

"Ah shit . . ." Ethan swore as he quickly activated his Hide skill. "Alright, people, time to light this grimy fucker up."

The cave shuddered as the massive form of Valgraiva rose from the darkness. His body was a twisted amalgamation of shadow and bone, dripping with a foul, necrotic energy. His eyes gleamed a sickly green, glowing like twin orbs of hellfire in the dim light of the underground chamber.

Ethan quickly activated his Mass Hide, slipping everyone into the shadows and commanding them to flank the warrior. They became a series of shadowed flashes, each one striking with attacks that would have felled lesser creatures. Ethan's scimitars sliced into the undead warrior's shoulders; Tara's knives slashed at his armored kneecaps; Klax battered his chest, and Theodore stabbed at his feet.

Finally, Fauna sent a wave of burning light slamming into his body, and the party retreated, the skill wearing off as Ethan Appraised the beleaguered monster now.

Valgraiva, Lord of the Damned (Level 50)
HP: 560/950
WILL: 700/1000

Big damage! Ethan smirked. "Everyone! Keep up the pressure! Soon as his Will drops below four hundred, I'll—"

An explosion of light suddenly ripped through the air toward the party. Valgraiva, once enveloped by Fauna's killing magic, emitted a roar that tore through his tomb. The next thing Ethan knew, the magical blast was redirected right toward him, slamming into him as he brought up his scimitars in defense, feeling the light sear his very bones.

HP: 360/550

D-Damn . . .

Valgraiva, the most human enemy they'd seen so far, lowered his shield and smirked at them with his scarred slit of a mouth.

"It—It can redirect magic!" Fauna shrieked. "That shield is a mana nullifier!"

"That . . . presents a problem," Klax murmured.

Ethan wasn't to be deterred.

"Faun!" he shouted to the Hopla. "Focus on giving us some light-based buffs to burn through this fucker. Stay back and—"

Ethan felt a flash of air tear through the tomb—Valgraiva had appeared right behind the rabbitgirl and was currently aiming a downward thrust at her exposed neck . . .

Wing Buffet.

Ethan's back legs flapped up a storm just in time to send the warrior back, even as he dug his dark blade into the ground to stop himself from being fully repulsed. Seemed like his Strength score must have been high enough to resist the attack.

"Klax," Ethan commanded, "protect Fauna. This guy's fast. Tara, Theo—you know what to do!"

Tara smirked. "Kick ass? Can't say I'm comfortable fighting beside a filthy rat."

Theodore flashed his little tail at her before he charged at the recovering undead soldier.

Valgraiva let out a low growl that reverberated through the cavern. His voice was like the grinding of stone, each word dripping with malice. He wanted nothing more than to hear some sarcastic response from Sys right now, but nothing was forthcoming.

No quips. No commentary. This is serious.

Valgraiva weathered the trio's attacks, his shield managing to rebuff even Theodore's rapid silver strikes. Attacks from the front would be useless—that much was clear. And when the silver eyes of the old general suddenly vanished again, Ethan knew what had happened before he even heard Tara's scream.

"Fuck!"

He turned to see the deep black gash that Valgraiva had just torn into her back before he skated away from her retaliatory strikes. His speed and defense were equally impressive, and from the fact that Ethan's Mass Hide wasn't working again, it seemed that he had absolute command of the shadows in his lair. When he then brought his crackling blade to his chest and slashed it through the air, he sent a dark wave of sparking energy flying across the entire tomb.

"Spread out!" Ethan growled, his voice guttural in his current form. "Don't let him hit us all at once."

Tara darted to the right, moving like a shadow herself, her blades flashing in the dim light. Fauna and Klax followed suit, taking positions at either side of the chamber. Theodore stayed close to Ethan, his small but powered-up form ready to assist. They had fought side by side from the beginning. Now, they'd do so as equals.

Valgraiva raised a clawed hand, summoning dark energy that crackled around him like lightning. The air grew thick with the smell of sulfur and death before, with a flick of his wrist, he sent another wave of necrotic force surging toward them.

Gotcha. Ethan smiled.

Sticky, gleaming webs shot from his limbs, creating a barrier that absorbed the brunt of the attack. The force of Valgraiva's magic rippled through the webbing, but it held—barely. The webs fizzled, dissolving in patches, but the attack was slowed enough for the others to dodge.

"Fauna! We're gonna need some light in here!"

The Hopla, whose spells had been summoning nothing more than flopping fish for the last few seconds, finally managed to enhance the party's weapons with the blinding light she'd sent toward Valgraiva before.

[Radiant Coating: Activated]

Tara used the opportunity to lunge at Valgraiva's exposed side, her daggers glinting with the blood of the dead. She struck fast, aiming for his joints where the bone was most vulnerable.

The strike hit true. Valgraiva recoiled, a low hiss escaping him as black ichor oozed from the wound. But the lord of the Damned wasn't fazed. With a roar, he backhanded Tara, sending her flying into the cave wall with bone-rattling force. She crumpled to the ground, dazed but still alive.

Theodore didn't hesitate. With a snarl, he leaped into action, his massive form crashing into Valgraiva's flank. His claws raked across the demon's side, leaving deep gouges in the bone and shadow flesh. He bit down hard, his teeth sinking into the dark tendrils that wrapped around Valgraiva's chest, tearing away chunks of his essence.

Valgraiva, Lord of the Damned (Level 50)
HP: 400/950
WILL: 650/1000

Valgraiva staggered, his glowing eyes narrowing as he turned his full attention on Theodore, hatred burning in those silver orbs.

He raised both arms, summoning a massive sphere of necrotic energy above his head, pulsing with dark power. Ethan recognized the danger immediately.

If that hits Theo, it would be over.

A faint glow surrounded the sphere as Ethan tried to leech the energy away, but Valgraiva resisted, his power too great to be fully siphoned. Still, it was enough to destabilize the spell, and the sphere wobbled, shrinking slightly as it lost potency.

"Tara! Klax! Now!" Ethan commanded.

The wolfman and the catgirl launched their attacks simultaneously. Klax, moving with surprising speed for his size, slammed his fists into Valgraiva's exposed knee, shattering the bone with a sickening crunch. Tara followed up with a strike from her blades, severing one of Valgraiva's armored feet in a swift, clean motion.

The lord of the Damned roared, stumbling backward as his form flickered and wavered. Dark energy seeped from his wounds, spilling onto the ground like a flood of black oil. The air grew heavy with the stench of decay as Valgraiva's form began to lose cohesion.

Valgraiva, Lord of the Damned (Level 50)
HP: 330/950
WILL: 575/1000

"We've got him!" Tara shouted, her voice filled with hope. "Keep the pressure on!"

But Ethan wasn't convinced.

Valgraiva is too powerful to fall so easily.

As the lord of the Damned staggered, his body collapsing into a pool of shadow, Ethan felt it—a deep, primal shift in the air. This wasn't over.

BOSS ENCOUNTER!
PHASE 2

The silver eyes of the warrior gleamed with a vibrant, malignant red, and the darkness of the tomb suddenly became all-consuming. Where once there had been a tomb filled with sarcophagi and untended graves, now there was nothing but an all-consuming void.

The shadows on the ground began to twist and writhe, taking shape. Ethan's many eyes widened as forms emerged from the darkness: beasts made of pure shadow, their eyes glowing red with malevolent hunger. Each one carried a halberd or broadsword, picking up equipment from the depths of the shadow realm around them. They howled as they surrounded the party, their numbers growing with every passing second.

[Swordsmen of the Damned Legion] x35
HP: 150/150
WILL: N/A

Ethan tensed up as the party felt themselves consumed by the horde.

"Now the real fight begins . . ."

The shadow beasts surged forward.

Ethan leaped into action, slashing through the first wave with his Petrification Coating, turning the closest creatures to stone as his scimitar claws cut through them like butter. But for every beast he felled, two more took its place. They were endless.

Tara and Fauna fought valiantly, slicing through the beasts as best they could, but the swarm overwhelmed them. Within moments, both were caught, dragged to the ground by the sheer weight of numbers. Klax tried to hold his ground, but even the mighty wolfman was pulled down, disappearing beneath a sea of gnashing teeth and claws.

Ethan's heart raced. "Tara! Fauna! Klax!"

But their cries were drowned out by the howling of the shadow beasts.

Only Ethan and Theodore remained standing, pressed together as the horde closed in. The beasts circled them, snarling, their eyes glowing with hunger.

And above them all loomed the smiling form of Valgraiva, his armored body towering, seemingly untouchable.

"Just like when we first met, huh?" Ethan muttered, his voice strained as he prepared for the final stand.

Theodore bared his teeth, his fur bristling, as Ethan flexed his spidery limbs beside him, preparing to unleash everything he had left.

"Let's show them what we're made of, old friend."

CHAPTER TWENTY-EIGHT

[Double] Team

Valgraiva, Lord of the Damned (Level 50)
HP: 330/950
WILL: 575/1000

The void of shadows grew colder. Ethan and Theodore watched as the horde of Valgraiva's minions closed in on them, having already swallowed Tara, Klax, and Fauna. Even now, Ethan could hear their screams in the dark recesses of this place, and the smiling lips of the dark general told him this Boss was enjoying every moment of this torment.

Ethan's Wing Buffet and Roar were keeping the shadows at bay momentarily while Theodore cut swathes through them, hacking apart their limbs and sending them flying right back into the depths of darkness from whence they came. But for every one cut down, another spawned from behind.

Just like the nether lich, Ethan thought, his mind racing. *Except he was a vulnerable spellcaster. And this guy—he's a walking tank.*

As if on cue, Valgraiva barreled toward them both, intent on plunging his blade into Ethan's spider torso. He only just managed to bring up his arms and lock his scimitars with the grisly broadsword of the undead lord, feeling his shadow minions scratch at his legs and head from every direction.

HP: -20
HP: -24
HP: -13
HP: -8

He could barely move, only dislodging himself with a lucky Wing Buffet that repulsed the rampaging Boss. But he knew he'd barely get any respite in this fight. Valgraiva charged his blade and sent another wave of darkness rocketing toward Ethan and his old rat companion. In the sphere of nothingness they were encased in, it was impossible to see the attack before it sliced into them both.

HP: -100

This guy hits HARD.

"Theo!" Ethan shouted. "Listen—I'll handle the crowd control. You go in for the kill! You've got enough speed to break through this fucker's defenses."

Theo's squeak was lost to the void, but Ethan saw him bolt like a lightning-infused arrow straight for the undead lord while he kept up his Wing Buffet AOE. Valgraiva might have been able to resist its effects, but his flimsy shadows lacked their master's strength.

Theo leaped for Valgraiva's shin, managing to scurry beneath his shield and nick him where it hurt. The undead lord fell back and, with a grunt, brought his blade down on the rat's tail, severing it and leaving a trail of black blood as Theo bounced on the formless ground.

"Theo!"

Theodore, Slayer of the Damned (Level 150)
HP: 80/300

Shit. Alright, you armored bastard. Let's go!

Ethan pushed his way out of the shadows' reach and lunged for Valgraiva's throat, the Boss cackling hoarsely as he brought his shield to bear, absorbing the brunt of Ethan's attack and thrusting his sword underneath to pierce Rachneros's exposed abdomen.

Fuck!

HP: 195/550

Ethan felt the strike as keenly as his host did. He felt his corrupted blood bubble and bleed out from under him, slashing out with his scimitars to try and get a hit on Valgraiva before he brought his shield up again. But his scimitars flailed in vain—he was pushed right back into the cabal of awaiting shadows.

This . . . This feels familiar . . .

His mind flashed back to his encounter with the Lightborn. He'd been so helpless back there. He'd been alone. He'd had no control over the flow of the battle—a perfect embodiment of his entire mortal life.

Oh, come on!

Ethan blinked as the claws of the shadow beasts wrapped themselves around him. They held his legs apart, a whole clump of them managing to get their sinuous arms around his scimitars and hold them tight.

. . . Sys?

This is no time to mope! What was it you told me once before? There's no point dwelling on problems! Work the problem. Find a solution. Implement a strategy!

Ethan blinked through Sys's screaming, surprised to find its voice so desperate for survival for once.

And he smiled. He smiled even as he saw the grim blade of Valgraiva charge with corrupted energy and cleave through the air toward him.

Because he wasn't alone, was he? No matter how much his enemies wanted him to be.

When Valgraiva's blade lodged itself deep in Rachneros's gut and Ethan's host let out an involuntary spasm of death, he never felt a thing at all.

Mainly because he'd just activated his Dive skill.

But not as Rachneros.

Valgraiva and his shadows, too focused on slaying the giant spider, had all but forgotten about the one-eyed hat sitting atop its head. Now, as the acidic blood of the spider spurted from its punctured heart, they suddenly realized the hat was oddly missing from the beast's cranium.

And without being able to dislodge his blade fast enough, Valgraiva felt the distinct feeling of pressure on his back as a thin, silver knife was pushed into his spine.

Valgraiva, Lord of the Damned (Level 50)
HP: 260/950
WILL: 400/1000

The Boss of the Twilight Sepulcher turned his head to see the face of the beast that had just impaled him and witnessed Theodore the Cave Rat wearing a mean-looking hat upon his head.

Squeak-squeak, motherfucker.

Ethan had gambled in the moment, knowing Rachneros was dead. He'd taken the chance and activated Dive in the hopes that he could make it to Theo's skull before the undead horde noticed he was gone. He'd also thought, for a torrid second, that the rat might just shrug him off this time, his Willpower having risen to stupendous levels since the last time they'd met.

But he didn't. Theo had accepted him back like a valiant knight accepts an old, discarded blade. Ethan had attached himself to his consciousness with more ease than anything he'd ever possessed in this realm, and now, he propelled Theo up with a Wing Buffet, the rat's ears flapping like Dumbo to repel the screaming shadows away from their master, and slashed at Valgraiva's eyes before he could withdraw his blade from the still spasming spider.

Valgraiva, Lord of the Damned (Level 50)
WILL: 360/1000

And, as the shadows of death swarmed to save their lord, Ethan took his chance.

"Now, Theo!"

The rat leaped with all his might toward the unarmored head of the undead master while the latter's sword traced the air to cut at the rodent's bloody paw.

But he wasn't nearly fast enough to clip the toes of Theodore, Slayer of the Damned.

Ethan dove onto the head of the smarting zombie general and clamped down his brim around his cranium, activating his Possession skill almost as soon as he felt the searing anger of the general rage through his consciousness.

[Skill Activated: Possession (Rank E)]
Valgraiva, Lord of the Damned's WILL: 360 vs. Spirit Cores: 425
Possession in Progress . . .

This'll be over quickly, big guy . . .

Theodore spun to deliver a swift strike across Valgraiva's pulsing neck as his shadows began to melt away into the darkness they had spawned from. Already, the general was struggling, having discarded his sword in favor of keeping his shield up to avoid the relentless strikes of the rat against his armored hide. Meanwhile, Ethan attacked his mind, feeling his brain go more numb by the second.

And as he began his hostile takeover, he felt the memories of Valgraiva swim through his mindscape: of battles lost and won, of generations of warriors under his command—and he realized why this Boss had a brain.

He still retained some element of his humanity. He wasn't like Rachneros, born for a purpose alone. He'd had a life before this delve.

Ethan felt the warrior's sense of anger at this fact.

Kaedmon's Law really does suck, huh? Even for you.

And then, like a switch being activated in the depths of the old warrior's brain, he departed.

The sphere of darkness broke apart into fragments of onyx cloud before dissipating entirely, the shadowed wraiths of Valgraiva dying along with it and revealing three hybrids on the ground of the old warrior's tomb, each one looking like they had just been washed up on an uncaring shore.

Klax was the first to raise himself up, stumbling, to look upon the sight of the warrior who now stood high above him, offering his dark hand to the wolfman in the newly lit lair.

"You look like you could use a hand, Klaxy," the thick voice of the possessed knight said, a very out-of-place-looking hat sitting atop his silver head.

"By Karfangg . . ." Klax smiled. "Now, that's an Archon I'd follow into the depths of hell itself."

Tara and Fauna, meanwhile, woke to find a tiny rodent sniffing at the frayed fringes of their hair.

"Wh-Where the hell were we?"

"The Boss must have used its Lair skill to isolate its most powerful prey," Fauna replied. "I never knew it would be so potent . . ."

Both of them then found Ethan's hatty form atop Valgraiva's head and knew that the undead master had fallen, because those two silver eyes now shone with the light of their Archon.

"What?" Ethan asked. "Ain't you ever seen a handsome undead warrior with a dapper hat before?"

Through pained groans and Fauna's stifled giggles, Tara looked right up at him before collapsing again.

". . . You . . . You smell like shit," she said.

Host: Valgraiva, Lord of the Damned (Level 50)

Stats:

HP: 950/950

MP: 150/150

WILL: 1000/1000

STR: 60

DEX: 45

PER: 40

INT: 35

SPD: 50

CHA: 30

Ethan the Hat beamed down at his party from atop the head of the once Boss of the Twilight Sepulcher.

The exit portal from Valgraiva's tomb had taken them right back to the lightning-blasted surface of the delve, and as they approached the exit back to Sanctum, Ethan decided it was time for some much-needed skill appraisal.

Twilight Edge (Grade E)
You coat your blade in thickest night and release the energies of the
Twilight Realm to rend the souls of your foes.
Shadow DMG: 75 points in a 30-foot arc.
MP Cost: 20 points

Repulsor Shield (Grade E)
You heft your mighty shield, nullifying magical attacks completely up to
a certain magnitude of DMG.
Current [MAG] DMG PROT: 85

Summon Wraith (Grade E)
You draw upon the powers of darkness to forge a spectral soldier
from the shadows.
Summon (One) Undead Shadow Wraith for sixty seconds.

Choose any (Two) Skills from [Rachneros, the Pale Lord] to Transfer:
Enweb (Grade E)
Poison Coating (Grade E)
Petrification Coating (Grade E)

It's a no-brainer, Ethan thought. *Of course I'm gonna take the status-effect coatings. Enweb is basically made obsolete by my other crowd-control skills. Though I've only got one blade to work with now, generally it looks like I'll be able to switch these effects on the fly. Couple that with my new multitarget DPS attack and you've got a monster that could probably challenge the Lightborn right here, right now.*

Transfer Skills from Previous Host: Poison Coating (Grade E),
Petrification Coating (Grade E)?
Skill Transfer Complete!

Ethan then turned his thoughts to his new shiny blade—something Tara had already been eyeing hungrily as they left the place.

"Y'know . . ." she started. "I feel like I'm still due a share of loot for disarming all the traps."

"All of them? What about the one that summoned an entire mountain of zombies?"

"Hardly my fault," came the Minxit's sarcastic reply. "Must've been your big spider booty that triggered it, anyway."

Ethan laughed away her greed. He respected her hustle.

Current Equipment:
{Rare} Mithril Broadsword:
DMG: 55–70

Armor of the Damned Legion:
DMG PROT: 40

Equipment to rival Borlor's own handiwork. Ethan wondered what the old codger would make of these when they got back to Sanctum. He still had the scythe from the lower tombs, too, and with its capacity to completely penetrate armor, he'd be a force to be reckoned with.

Considering the fact that his scythe's penetration ability was probably linked with whatever skills used the weapon, he inspected his new Twilight Edge skill with eyes hungry to see it in action.

Spirit Cores to Upgrade [Twilight Edge] Skill from Grade E to D: 250
Current Spirit Cores: 975

This was his only real multitarget DPS skill. Upgrading it was a must.

Twilight Edge (Grade D)
DMG Increased. Cost Lowered.
Shadow DMG: 90 points in a 30-foot arc.
MP Cost: 10 points

As his pilfered Spirit Cores flowed into his new body, Ethan breathed deep the musky, humid air of the Sepulcher's blasted heath. Rachneros had been big, bulky, and tanky. Valgraiva's form was nimble and humanoid—it felt so much more natural. That, and it was armed to the teeth. He felt like he was piloting a humanoid mechsuit from some of the old military sci-fi books he'd devoured in high school.

Eat your heart out, Robert Heinlein.

Current Spirit Cores: 725

Enough for more upgrades, but I'm thinking long-term now. Another two hundred and fifty I could drop on a new skill—I'm particularly interested in that handy-looking summon spell—but I also know I need six hundred Cores in the bank to upgrade another one of my core skills, and Skill Siphon is looking like the obvious choice.

But before he could bring up his hat core skills, the exit portal flashed before the team, signaling the way back home.

"How does it feel, Ethan?" Fauna asked. "Two delves down, only one more to go . . ."

"Honestly? Feels like I could take down the Greycloaks already."

"My point exactly," Tara murmured.

"The last delve is important for more reasons than simply power," Klax said, the wolfman's arms shaking slightly as the portal opened to welcome them back home. "Knowledge is what you will find in the City of Illusions, Ethan. Knowledge that every Archon before you has benefitted from. They all found something that sped them on their way to the completion of their quest. We—that is, you—will find something we are seeking there, too."

Ethan heard the words of the dogman and the ring of something else behind them.

Jun'Ei, he thought. *That's what you mean, Klax, isn't it?*

He looked at the Lycae but couldn't see his eyes. Those eyes were focused on the horizon beyond the portal . . .

Squeak!

The party threw their gazes to the ground, where the recently healed Theo sat and twitched his little bloody whiskers.

"Alright," Tara started, "I'll say it—the little guy was useful."

"Can—Can we keep him?" Fauna asked, bending to tickle the adorable little warrior's furry chin.

"Well . . . technically, he isn't a hybrid, but we'd be hypocrites if we didn't allow him to join us. It would also provide another body for Ethan to possess. That trick you pulled with Valgraiva is something nobody would expect."

"Ugh, now you really want to add a rat to our party? Are you trying to mess with me, Klaxy?"

Fauna bristled. "I think he's cute!"

"You think everything's cute, Faun."

"It isn't my decision," Klax huffed, eyes moving to the piercing silver orbs of his Archon.

Ethan bent down and looked at the rat, watching his twitching whiskers and the curious turns of his head. Every now and then, Theo turned his gaze toward the horizon of the Sepulcher, where, unbelievably, the sun was beginning to rise where once there had been nothing but sallow night.

Then, he realized what was happening.

"No," he declared. "The decision isn't mine either. It's Theo's."

"Uh, you're talking to a rat, man."

"But still a sentient creature," Ethan said with a smile. "And that means he's got a choice in the matter."

Theodore looked at the new light burning behind him then back at Ethan—at the hat that *was* Ethan. As far as a warrior rat could, he had already made up his mind.

The party exchanged bewildered glances as Ethan held out a single finger to shake Theo's paw. The little guy blinked up at him in understanding and respect. They'd come together as unlikely allies. They would part now as comrades.

"Guess this is goodbye, Theodore the Slayer," Ethan said. "Wherever you go, make sure to kick some undead ass."

Theo gave a triumphant squeak before he turned tail and scurried off toward the rising sun.

"Look at him go . . ." Klax murmured as he and Fauna watched him travel into the glowing light of a new day.

"Like a warrior going to meet his ancestors . . ."

Tara shot exasperated glances at them all before settling on Ethan and his smiling face.

". . . Are we done here?" she asked. "Even for us, this is getting weird."

City of Illusions, Entrance

They had opened the portal in the Delves Archive office without much fanfare; four of them, armed and armored, were all that were needed.

Artorious looked at the ethereal spires of the ever-changing city which stretched out from the spectral mountain the team had emerged on. His mind adjusted to the strange sights of the ghostly manta rays traversing the streets and the venerable bridges that connected the great towers that dotted the city—the Memory Spires.

He breathed deep the empty air of the place.

"How's it feel coming back here again?" Carliah asked him, her mithril armor shining in the sapphire-indigo haze that permeated the atmosphere.

When Artorious responded, he did so to the other two Greycloaks they'd brought with them more than to her, couching his reply in the guise of instruction.

"This place is as empty as your mind allows it to be," he said. "Steel yourselves, feel no emotion at all, and we will prevail. Remember why we are here."

"Spoken like a true hero," Carliah scoffed. "Alright, men, you heard the Lightborn. We stick together, watch each other's flanks, and we'll reach the peak of the Nerve Tower with time to spare."

They looked at their destination. The tallest point in the center of the city was unmistakable, wrapped in sinuous organic veins that pulsed like they were the beating heart of the delve itself. At its apex, the Master Illusionist awaited, a creature far too powerful for this insidious Archon to get his hands on. But a creature he'd be guided to like a moth to a burning flame.

Only, when he got here, that flame would be a cleansing bonfire . . .

"Sidonis?" Carliah barked at their mage. "You ready to disrupt the teleportation field?"

The hooded Greycloak nodded. "It will be done, Commander."

"Good. We don't want the Archon or his abominations coming here any earlier than we need them to."

The trap was set, and the Greys moved out. Artorious led the way with lethal precision, gutting the ghostly innards of every glimmering manta that tried to get in their way. Through their dying screams echoing down the deserted streets of the city, the Lightborn couldn't shake the ridiculous image of the Archon from his mind. He knew they'd be fighting more than just monsters in this delve. And for a brief moment, he wondered if Kaedmon had led them here as a personal test of his Lightborn's resolve.

He tightened his grip on his onixia blade, picturing the Archon's death by his hand.

This time, he was going to put it down for good.

CHAPTER TWENTY-NINE

[Portal] Problems . . .

I t—It's not working?"

"I'm telling ya, Klax: the thing's on the fritz."

When they returned to Sanctum, it was to surprised faces in the portal chamber. Apparently, everyone had assumed they'd already gone to the final delve. Borlor was already waiting by the final portal, which was currently blazing like a dying sun, allowing no one entry.

"How?" Klax asked him, dumbfounded.

"Hell if I know," the Dixit replied with a sigh. "But it's gonna take some powerful magic to stabilize it. Never seen fluctuations like this before . . . Lamphrey and the others asked if I'd just build a containment shield 'round it and close the thing off, since we wouldn't be needing it once you were done. But . . . looks like you ain't even through yet."

Ethan blinked at the sight, his new eyes giving him a much clearer picture of the world than Rachneros's crimson sight ever had.

"Is there a way to fix it?"

"Like I says, we'll need a team of mages ta stabilize the thing. But even then, I—"

"We'll get you your team," Klax interrupted. "How long do you need?"

"Klax, mate, I'm no expert. I'm just spit—"

"Borlor, how long?"

"Eh . . . maybe a day?"

"A day?!" the Lycae howled. "We don't have the luxury of a day here."

"Maybe a little less, then, mate. But I'm telling you, that's the best we've—"

"Well, it's not enough!"

Ethan watched the wolfman bare his teeth and spittle drip from his fangs. He looked, at this moment, on the verge of frenzy. Even Tara and Fauna were starting to notice.

"Hey, Klax," Fauna began. "Borlor's doing his best."

The wolfman looked down at the Hopla with strained eyes—eyes that seemed, in that moment, red with fury. "We're so close . . ." he snarled. "To fail now, after all this . . ."

"Jun'Ei can wait a little longer, Kla—"

The Lycae shrugged off the hands of the Hopla, marching away to a corner of the room and staying there, pausing before he even reached the door. "Do not mention her name."

"But I—"

"Fauna. Don't."

Tara had been uncharacteristically silent through the whole awkward exchange. Now, as Ethan flashed a look her way, she simply shrugged as if to say, *Hey, I've already tried getting through to him before.*

Alright, Ethan thought. *Time for some intervention.*

"Everyone, we're all tired," he said. "If Borlor says he needs the time he needs, let's give it to him, alright? We could all use some time off."

"He's right, Klaxy," Tara added. "I'm beat."

Fauna kept staring at Klax's back. The wolfman had withdrawn himself almost entirely.

". . . One day," he finally spoke. "I'll gather the mages. I'll keep watch in case one of them faints from mana drainage. We'll get a rotation going."

"If I join, we might be able to shorten the time!" Fauna exclaimed. "Borlor, I can start right no—"

"No."

The word was Klax's, spoken with his back still to his teammates.

"K-Klax? But I just wanna hel—"

"No. It's too unpredictable. We don't have the time to waste."

Fauna staggered back, her ears drooping down her frail skull. She looked devastated. Ethan got the sense that, out of all of them, Klax was the one who had never doubted her.

"Hey," Ethan said, putting a firm hand on her shoulder. "You need rest too, Faun."

She smiled thinly, but it was a vestigial gesture, and as Klax lumbered out the room, the party watched him go in silence—like a warrior walking toward his untimely grave.

Something happened to you when you looked in that mirror, Ethan thought. *And I'm betting I've got a pretty good idea what you saw . . .*

[Skill Activated: Twilight Edge (Grade D)]

A thin arc of shadow shot from Ethan's broadsword as he sliced it through the air, watching it decapitate a trio of wooden, sword-wielding straw dummies at the edge of his training room.

The castle of the Archon was a place that was ever-changing. When he needed a place to rest, he always found himself inexplicably drawn to his bedroom in the winding halls without even thinking about it—like the castle itself was guiding him. When he needed a place to train, he found a room that suited that exact purpose, replete with regenerating training dummies and steel weaponry that matched his exact idea of the sparring dojos he'd read about in manga. It was as if the castle had a mind of its own—one intimately attached to his own imagination.

Your aim is improving, Sys told him. **Your precision is up by approximately thirteen percent since assuming the form of the undead lord. Perhaps a humanoid form is simply more suited to you.**

"It would make sense," Ethan admitted as he sliced through another three dummies in the wake of their regeneration. "But I could still be better. I'm gonna have to be much better before I can take down the Lightborn, right?"

Right now, I can make no certain assessment of the Lightborn's abilities . . . but based on your last encounter, you will have to be a master of your skills before you have a chance.

"Which is exactly why I'm here," Ethan retorted through a grunt of exertion, sending another gale of darkness racing toward the dummy trio and sending pieces of their broken straw bones flying against the far wall.

While he waited for them to regenerate again, he returned his attention to his hat skills, ready to distribute the six hundred Cores he needed to upgrade Skill Siphon yet again.

If I'm gonna take on the old bastard, I'm gonna need to be as versatile as possible.

Skill Siphon (Rank D)
You can now transfer up to three skills from one Host to another, in addition to any skills gained from your prior Hosts.

[Upgrading Skill: Skill Siphon (Rank E)]
Upgrade Complete!
Congratulations! You have upgraded [Skill Siphon]
from Rank E to D.
Spirit Cores to Upgrade [Skill Siphon] Core Skill
from Rank D to C: 1000
Current Spirit Cores: 125

Ethan nodded once at the skill. Now, once he got his final host from the last delve, he could make it as unstoppable as he wanted. Transferring Repulsor Shield, Twilight Edge, and his Summon Wraith skills would augment whatever new arsenal he was going to inherit. And whatever the Boss of the City of Illusions was,

Ethan was betting it'd have to be a tough son of a bitch to have its delve rated as a grade C.

He sat back and took a short breath as he considered his remaining Cores. Hardly enough to do anything with, but maybe enough for another skill if he saved the points. His next few big kills would yield him far more Cores than he'd gained from the delves so far, he knew.

The last few hours had been nothing but focus. He'd taken the time to practice with his new skills this time. He had to admit, the lack of pressure from having to learn them on the fly or in combat was reassuring. For once, he could formulate strategies without the need to think about his own survival or that of his party.

Even if he still couldn't shake the sad eyes of Fauna or the sudden anger of Klax or the frustration of Tara from his mind for good.

. . . You're always wound up, aren't you?

The question was asked as Ethan wiped sweat from his new pale face.

"You noticed, huh?"

It is a System's job to know its User.

"And now you want me to talk about my problems?"

I think it's clear that, by now, I have no control over what you choose to share or not share with me.

Ethan smiled—an admittedly grim grin on the face of his current host, but a smile nonetheless.

"Right answer."

He then heard a sudden tapping at his door.

"Um . . . Ethan?" a voice asked. "Can I come in?"

I'd know those soft tones anywhere, Ethan thought.

"It's a free Sanctum, Faun. Come in."

Fauna entered, garbed in a thin dress robe that seemed at once at odds with her usually shy demeanor. Ethan expected the Hopla to still be upset from the fallout with Klax, but to his surprise, she seemed rather more chipper than usual.

"Um, you look . . . well."

"Do I really?" Ethan asked. "Even the living dead can scrub up nice, it seems."

The Hopla didn't quite chuckle. Instead, her eyes darted to and from the doorway.

"Are you enjoying your new body, then?"

Ethan narrowed his eyes playfully. "It's more familiar than a rat's furry behind or a spider's eight-legged horror, I have to admit. Not quite what my old wretched human body was, but I'm not exactly gonna complain about that."

Fauna shook her head fervently. "I'm sure your human body was a perfectly good one!" Then, realizing the implication, she blushed the shade of rouge that Ethan had come to see as natural for her.

"Well, Faun?" he asked. "I'm sure you didn't come here to discuss body types. Something you need?"

"Um . . . you."

Ethan blinked.

"N-Not in that way. Or, well, that is—I need you to . . . come with me."

In the silence that followed, Fauna's embarrassment could almost be called more monstrous than the undead warrior who was suppressing a laugh before her.

". . . If you like," she added.

"How can I possibly refuse an invite as tempting as that?" Ethan answered as the Hopla's smile returned.

"Okay—cool!" she beamed. "It's not something related to our mission. Or, well, maybe it *is* a little . . . but it's something I think you should see."

His curiosity piqued, Ethan followed the Hopla out the castle walls, noticing the slight spring in her step as she led the way to a far deeper corner of Sanctum than he'd ever seen before.

They passed the light-studded mushroom towers and lantern-filled streets until they came to a dimly lit section of the underground empire. The tunnel grew cold, dark, and foreboding, and even Ethan's Appraisal skill was telling him that what lay ahead was more hostile than what he'd left behind.

And the voices emanating from within the darkness were beastlike.

"Faun?" he asked the still chipper Hopla beside him. "Where exactly are we going again?"

Because I'm in no mood for a betrayal this late in the game . . .

Fauna's kind eyes simply fluttered up at him as she responded, "Sorry. They've just woken up from nap time."

At Ethan's confused face, she looked around her before thrusting her pale hand into the dark void in front of them, muttering an incantation that sent ribbons of violet light trailing up the tunnel walls.

"MIKOLAH REVULUM!"

And where once there had been nothing but shadow, now an entire plain opened up in front of them.

Ethan was standing on the precipice of a ledge that looked down into a humble cottage and a pasture of carrots and lettuce leaves—some of which were hung to dry on lines at the house's back. Beside the cottage stood a venerable shed that looked like it had been recently constructed—painted with vibrant oranges, reds, and colors that swam as Ethan tried to comprehend them. He noticed several names dotted the far wall of the cave; names carved into the dirt of the once barren walls and lit up by magical means so that they sparkled like a hundred stars in the darkness of the depths.

And then he saw where the voices had been coming from.

Below, tumbling out of the cottage and the fields they had just been playing in, was a horde of tiny Hoplas.

"Look, look!" one of them burst. "Miss Fauna is back!"

"HelloMissFauna!HelloMissFauna!HelloMissFauna!HelloMissFauna!"

The children tumbled and hopped their way toward their "Miss Fauna" and her new arrival as Fauna simply looked at Ethan with a happy shrug.

"Well?" she asked. "What do you think?"

Ethan was well past laughter by this point.

"Faun . . . are they . . . all yours?"

"No!" she replied. "Well, I mean, not technically. It's complicated, but . . . I know they want to meet you. If you'll let them."

"So long as they don't chew me apart," Ethan tentatively agreed.

Without another word, Fauna lifted them both into the air with a levitation spell that sent the crowd of children into a frenzy of "Ooooohs" and "Aaaaaaahs." Then, with a dramatic flourish of her staff, she let fly a torrent of sparks that whizzed and fizzled out around the farm.

"Hello, everyone!" she called out as the children squealed in delight. "Look who I've brought with me!"

The children watched as she lowered Ethan to the ground, crowding around him with expectant faces—faces desiring something.

But hell if he knew what it was.

So, he just held up his hand and waved to them, breaking into a toothy smile with the body of his undead lord.

"Hi."

The resounding *"WHOOOOA!"* from the crowd told Ethan this wasn't a hard audience to please.

"HelloMisterArchonHelloMisterArchonHello!"

The chorus was deafening, but Ethan couldn't help but smile at the puffy faces of the girls and boys. So many of them—probably at least a hundred by his count— all sequestered in this little backwater cave in Sanctum. And every one of them jumping for joy to see him.

"Call me Ethan," he said. "What's . . . eh . . . what's up?"

"HelloMisterEthanHelloMisterEthanHello!"

"Hellowhatsuphellowhatsuphellowhatsuphello!"

The voices of the kids bled into one—an attack on the senses so powerful that Ethan had to momentarily raise his defenses.

Then—the distinct sensation of nibbling at his back.

"H-Hey!"

One particularly tiny Hopla girl was teething on his heel and giggled when he found her.

"Mr. Ethan—you taste nice! Miss Fauna is very lucky!"

"VeryluckyMissveryluckyFaunaveryluckyverylucky!"

Ethan's eyes found Fauna as she gently floated down to the children, giving the girl a very telling and stern stare down.

"Ahem," she coughed. "Everyone, Mr. Ethan has come here to meet us all. What do we say to him?"

The children immediately straightened up, their drooling faces intoning what sounded like a sacred chant.

"Thank you, Mr. Ethan."

So they can . . . actually talk normally, he thought. *Here I was thinking that was a Hopla thing or something . . .*

"Can Mr. Ethan play with us, Miss Fauna?" one child asked. *"Pleasepleasepleasepleasepleaaaase?"*

The others took up his chant until it became a mantra of "pleasepleaseplease-pleaseplease" strong enough to shake Sanctum's very foundations.

"Only if you behave!" Fauna told them all, hands on her hips and suddenly more authoritative than Ethan had ever seen her before. "Mr. Ethan is a *very* busy Archon, as you well know!"

The Hopla then turned to Ethan with an expectant look on her face. Every child puffed out his or her rosy cheeks, and their fluffy ears drooped down their heads in a pout too strong for any man to resist.

I think you've met your toughest enemies yet, Sys chuckled.

You might be right, he replied. *Still, you know what? This is an Archon's job too, right? Inspiring the younger generations, showing them their leader gives a damn. Like a politician planting kisses on a baby's bare skull.*

Sys's chuckling only intensified as Ethan then consented to be dragged into the farm.

If only they all thought like you do.

The schoolhouse was a rickety establishment filled with paintings and crafts the children had designed probably since they'd been old enough to hold a crayon. Fauna had ample supplies to keep them interested in creating. There was a meager library of books and shelves lined with posters and writings from the children, as well as a few instructional materials.

"You're . . . a teacher," Ethan wheezed through the children who were currently hanging off his shoulders, trying to grab at his hat eye.

"Haha, well . . . my mother was an educator in our burrow—Jax! Remove yourself from Mr. Ethan's head!"

Ethan watched her corral the children into their classroom, where a bunch of tiny wooden desks were arranged in neat, orderly rows. No chalkboard existed. Instead, Fauna spawned letters and numbers to help the students through her lessons, as well as pictures for those who needed more visual stimulus. The darkness of their home, she said, often meant that the children's eyes had become accustomed to its shadows. They needed a little bit of light.

And whenever a spell fizzled or a word came out the wrong way or a picture of a heroic dragon slaying a human warrior became . . . well . . . a different kind of image, the laughter of the children was contagious. Even Fauna couldn't help but laugh.

It felt weird; Ethan couldn't deny it. Here he was in another world—one about as alien from his own as he could have imagined—and yet, here was a bunny girl teaching a packed classroom of a hundred excitable children their ABCs with more gung ho gumption and passion than any teacher Ethan could remember. He distinctly recalled being taught by textbooks and lesson packets most of his young life while his teachers decided they didn't get paid enough for their job.

Looking around the room at the kids' colorful murals and writings, I can't help but think that this world might have something to teach me, too.

"*MisterEthanMisterEthan!*" one girl shouted once Fauna had dismissed the class for break time. "Come see my poems?"

"*MisterEthanMisterEthan!* Miss Fauna says I'm a great drawer! *Comeseecomesee!*"

He was dragged along to every corner of the cottage to see the kids' own projects. Fauna believed every Hopla child needed to exercise their imagination. The upstairs of the house was filled to the brim with such creations: self-portraits, short stories, novels, poetry, and even a few songs written by the kids themselves. A few of them even elected to perform a dance or ditty for Ethan before Fauna declared it was time for lunch.

Surprise, surprise—carrots and lettuce was the dish of the day. And the special soup?

Lentils.

Up close, Ethan saw that the carrots had oddly shaped purple veins running down their sides from their greens. A rather astute child informed him these were "moon carrots" that had been specially adapted by Sanctum's mage—Miss Lamphrey—to grow in the underground realm.

Miss Lamphrey . . . that's the second time I've heard that name today.

By the time the kids were seated at their long lunch tables outside, Ethan's head was spinning. He'd almost forgotten about school in the time he'd been here. Hell, he'd forgotten about it when he was on Earth, too. And he'd certainly never associated it with anything resembling fun before.

But these Hopla children, waving to him happily and wagging their floppy ears as they ate, talked, and shared stories of how the Archon had loved their project the most, showed Ethan that Fauna had managed to do what he thought was impossible: make school something that one didn't dread attending.

"You . . . Hah!" he chuckled as he sat beside her at the head of the middle lunch table. "Faun, this is amazing."

Fauna, who had been occupied wiping the snot from a Hopla boy's wet face, turned to him suddenly.

"You really think so?"

"Don't doubt it. I just . . . I had no idea you had this kind of commitment on top of delving into dungeons. If I'd known, I wouldn't have minded if you sat them out."

"No," she said calmly. "The delves are important; I know that. My magic has the strongest potential in Sanctum. That's why Klax wanted me along in the first place."

Ethan detected something behind those words, but he let it slide as he saw the pride in Fauna's normally shy face.

"But this place—it's like a real home," she explained. "Ever since my mother . . . well, you know . . . I've always wanted to be a teacher. These kids need someone. I only wish I could have helped them sooner."

Slowly, Ethan's suspicions were confirmed.

"They're from other burrows," he said quietly. "Ones the Greycloaks wiped out."

She nodded solemnly, and to Ethan's surprise, was able to cheer right back up when one of the girls ran to grab her hand.

"Can Mr. Ethan come to practical lessons, Miss Fauna?"

Ethan noticed the determination in this little pink-nosed Hopla's face. Behind her, a gaggle of her classmates were waiting, pretending that they hadn't asked the bravest one among them to pose the question to their teacher.

"If Mr. Ethan likes," Fauna giggled, her ears twitching toward the field outside.

And Ethan, even in the body of a vile undead warlord, just couldn't disappoint those little faces.

"As long as Miss Fauna demonstrates first."

CHAPTER THIRTY

[Hopla] Hijinks

The kids dragged Fauna and Ethan to the courtyard behind their school cottage and assembled in neat rows as if they were ready to be marched off into the battlefields of the surface. Fauna then called the twenty or so children who were magically inclined to the front of the group while the rest sat in awe at the show about to begin.

Ethan perched comfortably atop a stone pillar, his single crimson eye scanning the scene before him. The classroom Fauna had set up in Sanctum was nothing short of heartwarming—if you were the type to get all mushy about that sort of thing. Dozens of wide-eyed Hopla children sat in neat rows, their floppy ears twitching in excitement as they eagerly awaited the magic lesson to begin.

Fauna, with her characteristic gentle grace, moved among them, demonstrating basic spells with ease. Little sparks of light twirled from her fingers, illuminating the space in soft hues of violet and gold. The kids mimicked her with varied success—some producing perfect orbs of light, while others managed more of a fizzle or a puff of smoke.

"See?" Fauna smiled, clapping her hands together. "It's all about focusing your energy. Remember: patience and control!"

Ethan couldn't help but be impressed. He watched Fauna's hands work their magic, the odd spell fizzling here and there, prompting some small sniggers from the kids who had already mastered some of the basic spells they needed for survival—spells that created trickles of light for crops or illuminated the darkest recesses of Sanctum. Spells that commanded stones to halt or break apart when cave-ins threatened the class's field trips. Spells that created little bursts of flame to warm themselves and their compatriots on days when they couldn't sleep, their minds preoccupied with thoughts of the dead.

One little Hopla, his nose twitching wildly, accidentally conjured a tiny fireball that shot straight into the air, nearly singing the fur off his neighbor's ears. The class erupted into giggles, and Fauna waved a hand to dispel the rogue flame before any real damage was done.

I can't help but feel that teaching a group of nattering rabbits how to weave magic is perhaps not the best idea, Sys sighed.

I don't know about that, Ethan replied as he watched them get up from every failed spell, rising and repeating the movements and focused effort that Fauna had clearly instilled in them over years of practice. *In fact, I think they might just have the perfect teacher.*

Sure, these kids were about as dangerous as a basket of kittens, but the potential was clear. Maybe it was because Valgraiva's form was the first that had access to an MP pool, but Ethan could practically feel the raw magic bubbling within the Hopla children, just waiting to be unleashed.

Damn, he thought, his hatlike form wiggling in a nod of approval. *For a bunch of ankle biters, they're pretty sharp.*

The brave girl who'd spoken for the group before ran to Ethan when it seemed like lessons were almost over.

"M-Mr. Ethan!" she called out, waving her tiny paw enthusiastically. "Can you show us some of your powers?"

The request was like setting off a chain reaction. Suddenly, the entire class was on their feet, bouncing around, ears flopping, as they chanted in unison, "Yeah! Show us, Mr. Ethan! Please!"

Fauna shot Ethan an amused look. She simply shrugged in defeat. "Looks like you've got yourself an audience, Archon."

Well, hell. Ethan rolled his eye in mock reluctance then hopped down from his perch with a graceful plop, landing right in front of the excited crowd. "Alright, alright. Settle down, fuzzballs. You want a show? I'll give you a show."

The kids erupted in cheers, crowding closer. Fauna stepped back, her smile never fading as she watched the children's enthusiasm soar.

Ethan floated above them, his voice low and dramatic. "Alright, first up, let's start with something sharp and dangerous. Keep your paws clear, folks." He paused for effect, letting tension build before declaring, "Twilight Edge!"

Dark energy swirled around him, condensing into a razor-thin, jagged blade of shadow. With a single swipe, he sent it hurtling toward a loose boulder at the back of the cavern. The edge cut clean through, disintegrating the rock into a cloud of dust and shadowy mist. The children oohed and aahed, mouths hanging open in awe.

"And that," Ethan said, his voice full of theatrical flair, "is how you make short work of your enemies."

The kids clapped, their excitement building by the second.

I can't help but feel you're teaching them a very different kind of les—

"What else?" one of them asked, hopping from foot to foot.

Ethan grinned. "How about something with a little more impact? Check this out."

Without further ado, Ethan shot up toward the ceiling, climbing with ease to the top of the cavern and curling in tightly before launching himself back down in a graceful arc. He dove straight toward the floor, his momentum increasing with every second, sword aimed at the ground like he was plunging it into the neck of the Lightborn himself. The ground shook as he hit it with a powerful thud, cracking the stone beneath him.

"Dive!" he announced as dust swirled around him.

The kids squealed in delight, stumbling back from the tiny tremor that rattled the room. Even Fauna chuckled, covering her mouth as she watched their reactions.

Ethan rose, waving away the dust with a tendril-like limb. "Not bad, huh? But we're just getting started." He turned his eye toward the crowd of kids, who were practically vibrating with excitement. "Wanna hear me roar?"

They screamed their approval, and Ethan's grin widened.

"Alright, brace yourselves, kids."

With a deep breath, Ethan summoned power from deep within his core. His undead lungs seemed to expand for a moment before—

[Skill Activated: Roar (Grade C)]

The sound echoed through the room, a thunderous blast that shook the very air and sent a few Hopla tumbling back, laughing all the while. Even Fauna stumbled slightly, though she managed to keep her footing, grinning at the chaos.

When the roar subsided, the kids stared at him in awe, their ears standing on end.

"That was awesome!" one of them squeaked.

"I'm not done yet," Ethan teased, his eye twinkling with mischief. "Let's see if I can blow you all away. Literally."

He lifted into the air once more, his body glowing faintly as he prepared his next attack. "This one's called Wing Buffet. Hold on to your hats—Oh, wait, that's me!"

CAN YOU PERHAPS CALM DOWN? EVEN JUST A LIT—

C'mon, Sys, look at their little faces! Ethan chuckled as he watched the adoring eyes of the rabbits. *Guess I've got a bit of showman spirit in me.*

Summoning Wing Buffet, he felt his shoulders contract. This time, a distinct sense of motion crawled up his spine. He looked back, seeing two skeletal black wings emerge from his shoulder blades and curl up to ready their strike.

To a human on the surface, he would look like an avenging angel of death. But to the Hopla down here, he looked like a messiah who could rival Krea herself.

With a powerful flap of his wings, a gust of wind shot out in all directions, sending the Hopla children tumbling and rolling across the floor in a flurry of giggles. Some held on to their ears, trying not to get swept away, while others tumbled into one another like a pile of fluffy dominoes.

Ethan landed softly, surveying the scene with satisfaction. "Not bad, right? I didn't blow you all away, did I?"

The kids were too busy giggling to respond, their eyes wide with excitement.

"Now," Ethan's voice dropped to a conspiratorial whisper, "how about a little game?"

"A game?" the kids chorused, hopping to their feet, eyes gleaming with curiosity.

Ethan winked—well, metaphorically—and said, "How about we play a little hide-and-seek? But I warn you: I'm really good at hiding."

With a soft mutter, Ethan activated his favorite ability.

In an instant, he faded from view, blending seamlessly into the shadows as the children gasped in astonishment, their eyes darting around the room, trying to catch a glimpse of him.

"Where'd he go?" one whispered, hopping on tiptoes to get a better view.

"Just follow the sounds of my soothing voice," Ethan's reply echoed playfully throughout the room, though his form remained unseen. "If you can find me, I'll show you another trick."

The room was filled with the sound of scurrying paws and gleeful giggles as the children fanned out, searching every nook and cranny. Fauna, watching from the sidelines, smiled warmly. It wasn't often the kids got a break from their usual lessons, and playing hide-and-seek with a legendary Archon was a memory they'd cherish forever.

Ethan, hidden expertly in the rafters, couldn't help but chuckle as he watched them scamper around, their fluffy tails twitching as they searched high and low.

"Maybe I'm up here . . . or maybe I'm not!" he teased, his voice echoing once more.

You are just as much a child as they are!

Maybe I am, Sys. Ethan smiled from the shadows, flitting through the back of the barn and avoiding the ever-watchful magic users Fauna had trained so well. *Fuck, maybe all of us should be like kids more often.*

He was finally caught by the ingenious girl who had first guided him through the school. As he giggled, moving from place to place like an illusory shadow, the girl cast a levitation spell to manipulate the stones near the barn where most children had been searching. As clusters of pebbles rose into the air, a few of them shifted ever so slightly at the left-hand side of the barn's far wall. The Hopla then sent a shimmering ball of light in that direction to reveal—*ta-da!*—the Archon himself.

"Found you!" the girl squeaked. And instantly, she became the hero of the day.

Ethan threw up his arms in mock surrender as the kids descended on him, jumping around like human children hyped up on too much candy. But his eyes watched the astute girl as she approached, with Fauna smiling a radiant smile beside her.

"I'm guessing this one's your star pupil," Ethan noted as the girl walked up.

She looked up at Fauna, who nodded once, but it seemed her bravery was beginning to depart. She hid behind her teacher as though she were in trouble.

And for a moment, Ethan saw someone else hiding there—not a Hopla girl in the darkness of this other world, but a kid in a playground on Earth, hiding away from teachers who told him he needed to pick a path in life and stick to it at all costs . . .

"Hey, kid," Ethan said. "What's your name?"

The girl answered after a slight gulp, aware that all her classmates were watching her. "Um, Mara, Mr. Eth—Whoa!"

Ethan had scooped up the bunny child like a trophy and set her on his shoulders.

"Well, Miss Mara," he said. "As a reward for defeating the Archon, you may see the world atop his back!"

The girl grabbed on to his hat form as he spun around and whipped up a few Wing Buffets to take her speeding through the school cavern, all her friends following along in glee.

"M-Miss Fauna!" the girl called down. "Are . . . Can Mr. Ethan stay for the big show tonight?"

Ethan stopped abruptly before he bashed into a rather mean-looking stalactite.

"Big show?" he asked Fauna's laughing face.

The Hopla teacher cast knowing looks at her students before smiling up at him.

"Mr. Ethan," she said. "The class has one last thing to show you."

Ethan allowed Mara and her friends to guide him to the very end of their school-yard, to a secret wall at the edge of the cavern that opened out to a stage set high above Sanctum's city core. Below, the artificial lights of the city gleamed somewhat brighter than usual. Hybrids of all stripes stood at attention, their eyes upturned to the very stage the children took high above them all.

According to Mara, the class had been working on a special little project for the city for months under Fauna's careful instruction. She had promised them that when she came back from the Archon's second delve, she'd be there to see it. Tonight was the night.

Ethan watched as the citizens gathered below. His silver eyes scanned the narrow streets for Klax and Tara, but he found neither of them. For her part, Fauna stood in front of her students, giving them some final words of encouragement as they huddled together, twitching with excitement.

"All right, kiddos," Fauna started, clapping her hands to get their attention. "You've practiced hard for this. Remember, it's all about control and focus. Let's show everyone what you've got!"

She's like a totally different person with these tykes, Ethan thought. *I guess . . . hell . . . maybe I don't know my team like I thought I did.*

The children nodded vigorously, their eyes bright with determination, as young Mara then took it upon herself to throw her arms wide and address the befuddled Ethan.

"I hope you're ready, Mr. Ethan!" she called out, her voice high pitched but full of excitement.

Ethan chuckled, glancing down at the tiny Hopla with his crimson eye. "I'm always ready, kid. Knock my metaphorical socks off."

The children spread out across the stage, their little paws raised in unison as they chanted softly, drawing in the magic Fauna had taught them. Sparks of multicolored light began to flicker from their fingertips, swirling together in the air above them. The first few bursts of light shot up like glowing embers, trailing glittering sparks in their wake.

Then, with a loud crackle, the night sky exploded into a vibrant display of colors. Cascading fireworks burst into brilliant blues, greens, and purples, filling the sky with dazzling light. Streams of magic swirled in mesmerizing patterns, creating shapes of stars, moons, and even tiny rabbits that hopped across the heavens.

"Oho!" Ethan's demon eye widened in genuine amazement as a giant spiral of golden light twisted upward, unraveling into a shimmering burst of crimson.

Sys, you seeing this?

Hmph. Such a wasteful display of magic. If Kaedmon saw this—

Fuck Kaedmon, Ethan interrupted. *Don't even try to deny that you're impressed. Your Archon commands you to show your feelings.*

The crowd of hybrids below cheered in awe, their faces illuminated by the brilliance of the display. Fauna, normally reserved, seemed to explode into life with them, sending streaks of her own Wildglance magic high into the air, some of the fireworks morphing into exploding plums or cookies that melted into starlight.

Looking at her right now, Ethan could tell she didn't care if her magic messed up sometimes. What mattered was that she could put on a show.

Super magic awesome . . .

As the fireworks grew more complex, the children began to cast more intricate spells, launching dazzling pinwheels of color that spun in the air before bursting into cascades of sparkling dust. One particularly adventurous Hopla sent up a streak of silver that exploded into a dozen tiny orbs of light, which scattered across the sky like falling stars.

Fauna watched her students with pride, her hands clasped in front of her as she whispered gentle words of guidance to those still perfecting their spells.

But the grand finale was what truly took Ethan's breath away. With a final, synchronized gesture, the entire class raised their paws, and a massive burst of magic erupted from the courtyard, shooting into the sky and forming an enormous arch of light. The arch shimmered with every color of the rainbow, creating a radiant bridge that stretched over the city of Sanctum, bathing the entire place in a warm, ethereal glow.

For a moment, everything was still. The air hummed with the afterglow of magic, and the citizens of Sanctum stood in awed silence, their faces upturned to the heavens.

"All right," he called out, unable to suppress a grin. "That was damn near the best thing I've seen since I got here. You guys earned yourselves a round of applause."

The children beamed, their ears twitching with pride as the entire city erupted into cheers. Fauna gave Ethan a warm, knowing smile, her eyes twinkling with satisfaction.

"Did we do good, Mr. Ethan?" the sweaty, panting form of Mara asked him.

The Archon smiled as warmly as a possessed undead warlord could.

"I'll give it to ya, kid," he muttered as he patted the top of her fluffy head. "You know how to put on a show."

As the night rolled on and the Hopla children (finally) grew weary—tuckered out from the excitement of the day—Ethan was afforded some time to himself overlooking Sanctum from their stage. Fauna had gone to put the tykes to bed—an activity she often left to the older kids in the school. Tonight, however, with some downtime, she decided she would see to them personally.

She's got the instincts of a mother and big sister all rolled into one, Ethan remarked to himself as he cast his eyes over his skill list.

Getting ideas, "Mr. Ethan?"

Not of that nature, Sys. Ethan smiled. It was no lie; his mind was elsewhere. Motivated by the exertions of the Hopla kids, he was looking forward for once. In his old life, there had been no need to contemplate the future. Here, suddenly, he was beginning to understand that the future was everything.

{Legendary} Hat
Current Spirit Cores: 125

Core Skills:
Possession (Rank E)
You are now able to view the memories of your possessed minions.
Spirit Cores to Upgrade [Possession] Core Skill
from Rank E to D: 600

Skill Siphon (Rank D)
You can now transfer up to three skills from one Host to another,
in addition to any skills gained from your prior Hosts.
Spirit Cores to Upgrade [Skill Siphon] Core Skill
from Rank D to C: 1000

Appraisal (Rank E)
Appraisal can now be used to prospect the location of foes through walls and other solid surfaces.
Spirit Cores to Upgrade [Appraisal] Core Skill from Rank E to D: 600

Transmogrification (Rank E)
You can now modify and equip items with [Mithril] quality or lower.
Spirit Cores to Upgrade [Transmogrification] Core Skill
from Rank E to D: 600

Host: Valgraiva, Lord of the Damned (Level 50)
Stats:
HP: 950/950
MP: 150/150
WILL: 1000/1000
STR: 60
DEX: 45
PER: 40
INT: 35
SPD: 50
CHA: 30

Skills:
Hide (Grade A)
Mass Hide unlocked.
Number of Attacks without Enemy Detection: 4
x4 DMG from successful sneak attacks
Spirit Cores to Upgrade [Hide] Skill from Grade A to S: 250

Roar (Grade C)
Paralysis from Roar now applies Status Effect {SLUGGISH} to enemies, halving their movement speed for two minutes.
A successful Roar now lowers enemy armor rating, cracking through weak spots and exposing their vitals.
Debuff applied: -50% armor strength.
Spirit Cores to Upgrade [Roar] Skill from Grade C to B: 280

Wing Buffet (Grade D)
The effect of Wing Buffet now becomes a fifty-foot AOE [Repulsion], affecting all enemies around you who fail a STR check.
Spirit Cores to Upgrade [Wing Buffet] Skill from Grade D to C: 250

Dive (Grade D)
Dive DMG: 85
Dive can now be used to destroy objects of STR 60 or lower.
Spirit Cores to Upgrade [Dive] Skill from Grade D to C: 250

Poison Coating (Grade E)
You slather your weapon in the virulent poison composed from your own blood, taking -20 HP DMG instantly in exchange for giving your weapon the [POIS] attribute.
Poison type: Pale Lord Venom.
-5 HP/second
Duration: 10 seconds
Spirit Cores to Upgrade [Poison Coating] Skill
from Grade E to D: 200

Petrification Coating (Grade E)
You slather your weapon in the debilitating bile closest to your heart, giving your weapon the [PETRI] attribute for ten seconds.
[PETRI] Chance: 30%
Duration: 10 seconds
Spirit Cores to Upgrade [Petrification Coating] Skill
from Grade E to D: 250

Twilight Edge (Grade D)
Shadow DMG: 90 points in a 30-foot arc.
MP Cost: 10 points
Spirit Cores to Upgrade [Twilight Edge] Skill from Grade D to C: 400

Repulsor Shield (Grade E)
You heft your mighty shield, nullifying magical attacks completely up to a certain magnitude of DMG.
Current [MAG] DMG PROT: 85
Spirit Cores to Upgrade [Repulsor Shield] Skill
from Grade E to D: 250

Summon Wraith (Grade E)
You draw upon the powers of darkness to forge a spectral soldier from the shadows.
Summon (One) Undead Shadow Wraith for sixty seconds.
Spirit Cores to Upgrade [Summon Wraith] Skill
from Grade E to D: 250

—Current Equipment—
{Rare} Mithril Broadsword
DMG: 25–35

Armor of the Damned Legion
DMG PROT: 40

He'd never really taken the time to look at his skills holistically. Normally, the speed between battles necessitated a quick spree of upgrades after each one, his eyes focusing on what seemed most useful in the moment. Now, looking at them as a whole, he could see new possibilities—synergies he hadn't even thought about. But what was really grabbing him right now was the next upgrade of his bread and butter: Possession.

He looked at the skill and widened his new silver lenses. If he was reading it right . . . it was going to be a very interesting upgrade indeed . . .

"Ethan?"

Fauna's voice broke through his concentration, and he closed his skill window as she approached, just as tired out as the kids were, by the look of her scruffy ears.

"Well, there she is." Ethan beamed. "Miss Fauna, in the flesh. Mage and inspiration to the new generation of Sanctum's Hoplas."

The girl shook her head weakly. "Oh, please, don't call me that. It's . . . y'know."

"Embarrassing?"

". . . Yeah."

"Faun, you have nothing to be embarrassed about. The fact is you're a better teacher than any I've ever known."

The Hopla giggled timidly, but she didn't blush as she came forward to sit beside him. She brushed a stray hair out of her eye as a low wind whipped through Sanctum's slumbering tunnels, watching those who still lined the streets with Ethan.

"You had teachers in your world, Ethan?"

"If you could call them that." He grimaced. "Sure, they weren't all bad, but they never seemed to care as much as you do. What I saw in there was nothing short of an educational miracle."

"It's not so special. I'm just doing what I can." She sighed deeply as the city's lights finally dimmed out. "Those kids put on brave faces, just like I did when I was that age. We Hopla are intensely social, Ethan. When one of us is down, the burrow comforts them as a whole. We need each other more than any other species in Argwyll does. It's why we tend to mate at a . . . young age. And when we mate, we mate for life."

Ethan felt the girl tense up suddenly, perhaps thinking she was saying too much. He was about to speak up when she continued.

"Sometimes, I wonder . . . am I doing enough? But then I think if someone like me—a magical screwup—can make a difference in a single kid's life . . . Well, maybe that's enough."

She caught Ethan staring at her and immediately grew flustered. But, again, she didn't apologize this time, and she didn't move away.

"If . . . If you get what I'm saying?"

"I do." Ethan nodded. "And the one thing you're wrong about is this: you *aren't* a screwup. Actually, the fact you make mistakes is what makes you such a good teacher. The kids probably feel like they're allowed to be wrong when they see things go wrong for you sometimes. They feel like they can experiment and not be judged. That's—Well, that's damn important for a kid."

Ethan lapsed into silence as Fauna slowly nodded.

"I've never thought about it like that."

Ethan was too absorbed in the sudden thought that took him of his school days that he didn't see the rabbitgirl reach a hand toward his shoulder and—

"BOO!"

Fauna almost fell from the stage to the craggy rocks below, the Hopla basically jumping out of her skin, while Ethan merely turned to see who he'd already sensed was approaching them from behind.

The mischievous face of Tara the Minxit appeared out of the shadows.

"T-Tara!" Fauna cried. "How long have you been—"

"Standing here? Long enough, my dear Hopla. Long enough."

Ethan just laughed as she taunted Faun, waving for her to join them.

"Pull up a rock, Tara? It's quite a night. And unless those teleporters are back up and running, we might as well make the most of it."

She uncrossed her arms and marched toward the pair, lowering her voice surreptitiously and ignoring Fauna's clear irritation.

"Nah," she said. "I've got something better in mind."

"Something stupid again?"

She nodded. "Stupid *and* fun this time, my dearest teammates. Will you both join me for the heist of the century?"

Even Fauna's eyebrows rose at the mention of that word.

"Tara . . . what are you—"

"Theft." Ethan shrugged. "Well, it's marginally better than a massacre. But if this is about settling some personal score with some other Minxit who owes you money . . ."

"Oh, it's nothing crazy. A trifle, really. You won't even know you're carrying him."

". . . Him?"

"Oh yeah," the Minxit replied. "We're gonna kidnap Klax."

CHAPTER THIRTY-ONE

[Dognappers]

The streets of Sanctum were deathly quiet as Tara led Ethan and Fauna through the shadowy alleyways. Despite the silence, there was a buzz of excitement in the air—one that had, according to Tara, been carefully hidden from the gruff wolfman they were sneaking up on.

The Minxit had met Ethan and Fauna's questioning eyes with glee, delighting in telling them why they apparently needed to spirit away old Klax tonight. Once she'd revealed her intent and the motivations behind this prank, Ethan had shaken his head at just how brazen this kitten was.

"You're a mad genius, Tara," he told her. "With just a little too much emphasis on the mad."

"Like you're complaining," she replied as she then led them both down the cavern toward the castle battlements.

They passed the dimly lit shop fronts and ramshackle housing units without making a single sound. Tara had taken the lead with a mischievous glint in her eye, while Fauna's long ears twitched nervously. Ethan moved silently beside them, using Mass Hide to cloak their presence, a soft shimmer occasionally betraying their outlines as they passed by the dim glow of the torchlights.

"This feels . . . wrong," Fauna whispered, her soft voice barely audible as they approached the grand castle where Klax's chambers were located. "I mean, kidnapping Klax like this? Even if . . . Even if it's for the right reason, are you sure we should be doing this?"

Ethan smirked, glancing at Tara, who was grinning from ear to ear. "You heard her. This is all part of the plan, Faun. Besides, it's not really kidnapping if it's for a good cause, right, Miss Fauna?"

As Fauna blushed and begged Ethan not to call her that again, Tara chuckled softly. "Exactly. Trust me, Faun, it's all gonna be worth it. You'll see."

Fauna bit her lip but nodded, though her uncertainty still lingered. She glanced down at her paws as if trying to remind herself she could back out if needed, but Ethan's reassuring nod seemed to settle her nerves, if only slightly.

The grand castle loomed ahead, its towering spires casting long shadows across the cobblestone courtyard. Ethan was quietly impressed by the sheer size and elegance of the place. Sanctum might've been their hideaway, but the grandeur of the castle was a testament to the ancient history it held within its walls. Even in the dead of night, with the streets empty and torches flickering, the place seemed alive with secrets.

As they ascended the wide stone steps, Ethan pulled the group to a stop and checked their surroundings. "Tara, you sure Klax has no idea about this?"

Tara flicked her tail in amusement. "Please. You really think Klax pays attention to anything that doesn't involve him grumbling about tactics or battle plans?"

Ethan chuckled under his breath, shaking his head. "Fair point."

"Besides," she added, "the old dog needs this. It's for his own damn good."

They crept inside, the echo of their footsteps muffled by Ethan's magic. Every inch of the castle was covered in ornate tapestries and polished stone floors. The hallway leading to Klax's chambers was long and narrow, lit only by the soft glow of wall-mounted torches. It was eerily quiet.

Tara suddenly halted, holding up a hand as they approached the door to Klax's quarters. "Hold up," she whispered. "See that rune? Arctic Wind trap. Touch it, and we'll all be frozen solid faster than you can say 'happy birthday.'"

Ethan squinted, noticing the faint shimmer of the rune etched into the floor. It was practically invisible in the dim light, and he could only imagine how they would've fallen victim to it without Tara's sharp eyes.

"Good catch," he whispered back. "But what does Klax need traps for? Is he expecting trouble?"

"It's a holdover from the old days of Sanctum." Tara shrugged. "Before you got here, we used ta have quite a problem with thievery, y'know."

Ethan caught Fauna's eye boring into Tara's back as if to say, *And I wonder how you know about that, Tara . . .*

"Well then," Ethan whispered as he turned his attention to the shimmering air just above the trap. "Let's see how it likes this."

He raised his hand and performed one of his newly acquired abilities: Summon Wraith. From the shadows behind them, a dark, ghostly figure appeared, its wispy form rippling as it moved soundlessly toward the trap. Ethan gave a nod, and the shadow obeyed, gliding over the rune. As it touched the magical seal, the rune flared bright blue, and an icy wind howled through the hall, freezing the wraith in place.

The trap was sprung, leaving a frozen shadow stuck above it. Tara smirked in satisfaction.

"Good work," she whispered.

Sorry, dude, Ethan thought as he saw the shadow's open-mouthed cry that never came. *Next time, promise I'll use you for something more epic.*

With the trap neutralized, the trio slipped past and pushed open the heavy oak door to Klax's quarters. Inside, the hulking wolfman was fast asleep, sprawled across his bed, his massive arms hanging lazily over the sides. His chest rose and fell in a slow, steady rhythm, completely unaware of the mischief about to unfold.

"All right, Fauna," Tara whispered, motioning for the mage to step forward. "Time for the real fun. Hit him with a Deep Slumber spell, just to make sure he doesn't wake up too early."

Fauna hesitated for a moment before nodding. Raising her staff, a soft glow formed at its tip as she muttered the incantation under her breath. The magic washed over Klax like a blanket, and his already deep sleep grew even heavier.

But then, something . . . *odd* happened.

Or something expected, considering the Hopla in question.

A small ripple of pinkish-hued magic shimmered around him, and Tara's eyes went wide with amusement. Ethan noticed it too, and before he could stop himself, he snorted, trying to stifle his laughter. Tara, however, wasn't as subtle.

"Oh . . . Oh, by Gyko," she wheezed, doubling over in silent laughter. "You . . . You really did it, Fauna!"

Fauna blinked in confusion, her eyes darting between the two of them, straining to see through the pink mist enveloping Klax's body. "What? What did I do?"

Ethan chuckled, shaking his head. "Don't worry, Faun. You'll see soon enough."

The scene in the grand hall of the castle was far more regal than anything Ethan had expected. Long tables lined with food stretched across the room, and grand chandeliers glittered overhead, casting a warm glow over the gathered hybrids. The hall was buzzing with excitement—everyone was in on the surprise. Laughter and whispers filled the air as they awaited the final guest of honor.

At the far end of the hall, Klax's still sleeping form was carried in by a couple of the burlier hybrids and gently set down at the center of the room. Just as planned, Fauna's spell was wearing off.

Klax stirred, his groggy eyes fluttering open. His brows furrowed in confusion as he took in his surroundings, sitting up slowly. "What the—"

Before he could finish his thought, a chorus of voices rang out. "Happy birthday, Klax!"

The wolfman blinked, his confusion slowly morphing into an expression of shock. His usually stoic demeanor faltered as he looked around the hall, processing the surprise celebration. Before him sat a sponge cake decorated with care, the word *Klax* slathered across it with something black and viscous that he assumed was icing. Just as he was about to speak, he caught a glimpse of himself in one of the mirrors hanging along the wall.

Klax froze.

There, staring back at him in the reflection, wasn't a fearsome wolfman. No, instead, his fur had turned stark black and white—striped like a skunk. His snout was smaller, his tail fluffy and raised as though ready to spray.

The hall erupted into laughter, Tara doubling over in hysterics.

Klax's face twisted, his fangs baring as he looked down at his transformed body. For a moment, everyone held their breath, wondering if they'd gone too far. Then, a low rumble started deep in his chest—a growl?

In the back of the room, Ethan tensed. For a moment, he thought the old, grizzled veteran would jump at them in fury.

But no. The sound echoing from his skunkish throat right now was not one of fury. It was laughter.

He threw back his head and laughed, a deep, genuine sound that reverberated through the hall. "A skunk?! Really, Fauna?"

Fauna blushed deeply but giggled along with the others. "I-I'm sorry!"

Klax waved it off, still laughing, looking with tear-filled eyes at the cake sitting before him.

"You know what? This is exactly what I deserve."

"Klax, I—I really didn't mean—"

He jumped atop her head, laying his new fluffy tail over her face.

"Who needs surprises when we have you, Fauna?" he said. "But if you'd be so kind as to polymorph me back, I believe I owe the Archon and a certain Minxit both a punch."

Everyone laughed even louder this time as the party continued in full swing. And for the first time in a long while, Ethan saw Klax let his guard down completely, surrounded by friends and laughter.

Even if he did smell just a little shittier than usual, it looked like this was just what the old dog needed. And as that thought filled Ethan, he suddenly remembered exactly why it was so important.

They'll all have to be at the top of their game to face a grade-C delve. If the last two were any indication, we'll be in for the fight of our lives.

If Ethan had to sum up the atmosphere of Klax's party in one word, it would be *cathartic.*

The whole grand hall of the palace had been redecorated for the occasion, its chandeliers and long tables polished to perfection. Once again, Ethan found himself in awe of the hybrids' ability to make the most of their situation. Around him were people who had come together in celebration of one of their eldest—the man who was currently receiving gifts from those closest to him.

"Be taking *thisss*, good Master Klaxxx," Fraxx the ratman was currently saying as he offered the bemused wolfman a flask of incense that looked equal parts alluring and utterly diabolical in its makeup. "Dissstilled from Lady Gyko's glandsss themselvesss."

"How . . . fortuitous," Klax replied as those around him chuckled. "Thank you, Brother Fraxx."

Ethan stood alone—something he had often done at those few parties he'd gone to back home. Those were house parties, mainly; occasions for pre-drinks before the senses were obliterated during club nights or the karaoke bars that dotted his home city. He actually enjoyed the latter, though his current undead throat didn't have much talent for singing.

Someone who did, though, was little Miss Fauna. As the night rolled on, she had drunkenly stumbled over to him and asked him about his "cultural heritage" as a human—probably half out of curiosity and half out of the desire to mingle with him during the party. Now, Ethan *could* have snatched the booze from the Hopla's hands and told her she'd had enough, or . . . he could do what he did instead.

"Where I come from," he told her surreptitiously, "there is an ancient song sung by our ancestors to commemorate the birthdays of our greatest champions."

He told her the song's name, and she nodded furiously, committing the words to memory as he elaborated, trying to hold back his laughter at her seriousness.

Presently, she was talking with Klax—probably receiving an apology from the birthday wolf, judging by the latter's awkward demeanor. He'd said what he'd said to her earlier out of desperation, not spite. She knew that. Ethan knew that. But still, it was nice to see that he knew when he messed up, just like the rest of them did.

Ethan sipped the cold drink in his hands and threw his head back.

I gotta admit, the vibe's nice here, ain't it?

You're asking me?

You're one of us too, Sys. Whether you believe it or not.

When Sys didn't reply, Ethan caught the eyes of a rather regal-looking Tabika. The lizardwoman carried a ruby staff in her hand, its color matching the fluorescent shade of her eyes. Her turquoise scales glimmered under the dim lights of the chandeliers above, emboldened by her cream-crimson robe. As she glided toward Ethan, nodding to him in respectful recognition, he was reminded of a kaleidoscope of moving colors.

"Lord Ethan," she greeted, her voice deep and gravelly. "It is a pleasure to finally meet you in person."

"The pleasure's mine," Ethan replied, surprised by her formality. "Miss . . . ?"

"Lamphrey," she said with a slight curtsy. "Lamphrey of Darkwater Bay, though these days, that title means less than nothing."

"Lamphrey . . . so you're the mage I've been hearing about. The one who helps Fauna with her kids . . . and the one whose teams have been trying to fix the portals."

"*Trying* being the operative word," the lizardwoman sighed, coming to stand beside him. "We've been working tirelessly for the past twenty-four hours, and *finally* I'm pleased to report that we'll be finished probably by the time Klax's celebration has concluded."

"That's . . . That's great!" Ethan beamed. "Hope it hasn't stressed you out too much. I feel like I can still hear old Borlor's anxiety levels hitting the roof as Klax told him to get the portals fixed."

Lamphrey nodded. "If I am being honest, sir, that's the reason I'm here. I've already informed Mr. Klax, though he tells me there is no reason to rush these proceedings."

Well, that makes a change . . .

"If I may," the snakewoman continued, "the delve you will be entering will not be like those you have seen before. The City of Illusions is a rare dungeon, but those delves that spawn for the Archon normally do so out of necessity, as challenges that can allow each Archon to overcome a particular limitation. They also, in turn, present unique challenges to each Archon—challenges specifically *catered* to that Archon themselves."

The scaled face of Lamphrey turned ice cold, her eyes boring into Ethan's crimson demon eye at the base of his hat form. It was as though she were looking right *past* his physical body into his mind. And for a moment, the whole atmosphere of festivity changed to one of dark foreboding.

"The City will test your mind," the lizard mage said. "Yours, and those of your companions. And, judging by the chaotic state of the portals, perhaps more than that. Whatever happens, Lord Ethan, you must remember one thing: *Hold on* to reality. *Hold on* to truth. That thought must be your guide."

Ethan knit his scarred brows at the lizardwoman's words, but he nodded. She had the air of a knowledgeable sage.

"Hey," he murmured. "Why don't you come with us? Seems like you know more about this place than we do."

"I am needed here. Who else will look after the wild mages of Sanctum if I am gone?" she said with a strange twitch that might have been a wink. "But there is something I can give you that may aid you on your journey. A gift given to me by Jun'Ei herself before her departure from us."

She took Ethan's pale hand and squeezed it, bringing a small glow of light from her palm into his. There was a moment of friction, and then—burning, almost like he was being branded. He didn't detect any ill intent from this mage, and so he watched as she concentrated on her operation, ending with a small droplet of sweat running down her scaly forehead.

Ethan looked down at his hand to see a small circle etched into the pallid skin there—a thin crimson circle with two intersecting lines.

Appraisal Success!
Glyph Acquired: Rune of Memory

"*Glyph?*" Ethan asked when his Appraisal skill would yield no more.

"An old kind of magic," Lamphrey explained. "Magic known only by the sages and prophets of the Second Age: the time of Gelsadra. A time when the serpents of the world rose up from our temples in the swamplands and followed our Archon into the maw of the enemy. Glyphs such as these were used to store memories that often had to be erased with a Mind Wipe spell. Otherwise, captured servants of the Archon could reveal precious information to the humans and their beastly Greycloaks."

Ethan could see pride in the snake mage's memory, and closed his fist around the new marking on his hand.

"It *stores* memories?"

"A more powerful tool than you may think, Archon Ethan. Especially where you are going."

Just then, Ethan spotted Tara ambling over to him out of the corner of his eye.

"Thanks, Lamphrey," he said. "Though I wish there was more I could do for you. You've been such a great help to us that I—" When Ethan turned to face her, he saw nothing but air where she'd once stood.

"Do not worry, Ethan Graham," her voice echoed from somewhere nearby, faded, as though she had departed the party altogether. "There may come a day when you can repay me soon."

Ethan shuddered as the voice left him, waving to the jovial Minxit, who came to rest her back beside his.

That gal's about as cryptic as you are, Sys . . .

"Heya, Big A!" Tara winked as she joined Ethan. "Penny for your thoughts?"

"I was just thinking how many mysteries there still are in this world, not the least of which are down here."

"Oh, really? Surely you don't mean me. I'm an open book, ain't I?"

"Maybe too open," Ethan sniggered.

"Admit it—my plan tonight was executed with perfect precision. With thanks to your skills. Gotta say, that Mass Hide thing is pretty useful."

"Sure is," Ethan replied.

They allowed a few moments of silence to pass between them, both watching the lights and the dancers pass by without a care, totally absorbed in their own frivolity.

"We ain't had a night like this in a long time," Tara suddenly sighed. "It's—Well, it's nice, y'know?"

"And here I was thinking you were a heartless, bloodthirsty kitten all this time."

"I'm *still* some of those things," the Minxit retorted, feigning a dramatic pout as though her pride had been wounded. "But—meh. The old dog's been a sad sack of shit lately. It ain't good, y'know? We all got baggage down here, but he holds on to his like it means everything to him."

"Doesn't it?" Ethan asked. "C'mon, Tara, you must have baggage too."

"Well, yeah, but I don't let it *define* me."

"Sometimes, it's not as simple as that."

"Isn't it? Fauna does alright. She's quiet, she's docile, but even she doesn't get absorbed in her own misery like ol' Klaxy does."

Ethan pondered that for a moment, finding the Hopla in the midst of the crowd and smiling as she giggled among friends.

"Fauna's done the right thing," Ethan replied. "She's taken her trauma and used it to fuel something positive. I think Klax is doing the same. I think the fact he's looking for Jun'Ei is the one thing that keeps him going."

"Even if she's been dead this whole time, Ethan?" Tara asked, her devilish eyes fluttering up at the undead face of the Archon. She kept a smile on her face, but the question was far from gentle.

"It's better to believe in something rather than nothing, Tara, isn't it? Isn't that what the party we're throwing here is all about, really?"

At her questioning glance, Ethan swept an arm across the function hall.

"Everyone here knows we're risking our lives every time we delve. Everyone here also knows the Archon's never won—and this time might be the last shot your kind gets at surviving in this world. Yet here we all are, partying like there's nothing to worry about."

Ethan paused, pointing out Klax among the crowd.

"Sometimes, it's worth believing the lies you tell yourself," he finished, not really knowing what innate desire compelled him to speak these words. "After all, at least they're *yours*."

"Ethan the philosopher Archon," Tara murmured as Klax approached them. "Never thought I'd see the day . . ."

The wolfman nodded to both his compatriots, still smelling slightly of his old skunkish form.

"I believe I owe you both my thanks," he said, raising his glass to them. "A well-executed plan, if I do say so myself."

"Don't look at me," Ethan laughed. "The whole thing was Tara's idea."

"Was it indeed? Well, then—thank you, Tara."

Ethan noticed the Minxit girl look away, murmuring her next words into her shoulder so softly they barely heard them. "Don't get used to it. I did it for the team."

"Then you deserve my thanks all the same. For keeping us together."

Ethan noted Klax's awkward stance, his whiskers twitching and eyes darting around the room as he tried to catch the catgirl's gaze.

"You two really need to kiss and make up already."

As both his companions started stuttering, each trying to avoid the other's eyes yet again, Fauna took to the stage and made an announcement to the partygoers.

"T-This one goes out to Klax!" she belched amid the rising laughter of the guests. "It— It is an ancient song from our Archon's home dimension!"

Tara and Klax dropped their pretenses entirely, each staring up at Fauna as she sang a song that couldn't have been more foreign to them, while the rest of Sanctum listened raptly, cheering her on as she belted out every lyric, some of them even joining in . . . to the chorus to Rick Astley's "Never Gonna Give You Up," sung with perfect clarity besides the little hiccups she included throughout the song.

While Ethan tried to hold in the laughter building in his ribs, Tara and Klax merely shook their heads in surprise.

"She's . . . quite the singer, eh?"

". . . Yeah. She is."

And when Ethan couldn't take it anymore, he threw back his head and roared with laughter that shook the entire hall. As Fauna continued her ditty, getting into it with more gusto than he'd ever seen anyone put into that song, he looked at the small sigil Lamphrey had imprinted on his hand.

"This is a memory I wanna keep," he said to himself. "No matter what happens next."

But what happened next wasn't anything Ethan could have expected.

As soon as the thought occurred—of enshrining this moment in the sigil—his hand seemed to burn with a blazing, killing light.

"Ethan?" someone said nearby.

But the voice was faint. Already, Ethan could feel himself falling away into . . . into the void.

"ETHAN!"

The music, the singing, the whole world spun, and with it, he felt his consciousness fade away.

He fell.

CHAPTER THIRTY-TWO

Premonition

The world had vanished, replaced by . . . something else.

His vision darkened around the edges, and he felt his body go limp, collapsing against the wall behind him. He was dimly aware of Tara calling his name, but her voice was soon drowned out by something deeper, more insistent, pulling him away from the present moment.

The vision came like a sudden tidal wave.

Ethan found himself standing in the middle of a vast, unfamiliar city. The landscape was unlike anything he had seen before, skyscraping spires twisting and stretching toward the heavens, each one shimmering like they were built from glass and smoke. The city shimmered in a haze, almost as if it were an illusion, barely anchored in reality. As he turned to take it all in, a heartbeat pulsed through the air, slow and methodical, as though the city itself were alive.

The City of Illusions . . . Ethan thought, though he wasn't sure where the knowledge had come from.

The spires of the dreamlike city rose around him like organic structures, shifting in shape, their colors constantly switching between shades of silver, violet, and blue. Then, one tower in particular caught his attention, a large, pulsating structure at the heart of the city. The tower was grotesquely organic, with walls that seemed to breathe, veins of light coursing through its fleshlike surface. The pulsing heartbeat grew louder as Ethan stared at it, each beat reverberating through the ground beneath his feet.

A voice broke through the vision, fragmented and ethereal, like whispers on the wind.

Ethan . . .

The voice was like nothing he'd ever heard before. Soft, yet insistent. Pained, yet proud. And it carried a tone that seemed to conjure a sense of nostalgia, somehow reminding him of a past life he'd never lived.

. . . Archon.

He nodded in the void, feeling weightless and listless. It was like walking through a pool of treacle he couldn't see.

Find me . . . in . . . the tower, the voice instructed, and only then did Ethan realize it belonged to a woman, familiar yet distant. *Jun'Ei . . .*

Ethan's vision zoomed in on the grotesque tower, the focus narrowing as though the entire city had fallen away, leaving only the beating structure before him. He saw himself standing before a door, ancient and covered in a dense mesh of roots and vines. Behind it, *something* called to him; something buried deep within.

Inside . . . must . . . find the chamber . . . tell you how . . . the voice came again, clearer but still fragmented. *Break . . . Kaedmon's Law . . .*

Ethan strained to listen, his pulse quickening as the tower's own pulse accelerated. The voice's urgency rose.

Only . . . there . . . Ethan . . .

Suddenly, the vision shifted, the tower fading as blurry images began to flash before his eyes, vague at first, then sharper. He saw glimpses of Artorious, eyes blazing with cold determination, flanked by the Greycloaks. Their forms marched through shadowed lands, armor glinting under a pale light. Though Ethan heard nothing, the sight alone sent a shiver down his spine.

Then, Jun'Ei's voice rang out, clear and cryptic: *They are coming.*

Ethan felt a jolt, as though his entire body was being yanked back into reality. His eyes flew open, gasping for air, as his vision returned. He was no longer in the City of Illusions but slumped against a wall in the great hall where Klax's party had just ground to a halt. Klax, Tara, and Fauna were clustered around him, their faces etched with concern.

"Hey, Ethan!" Tara was shaking his shoulder. "What the hell happened? You collapsed!"

Fauna's eyes were wide, her hands faintly glowing with magic as though she'd been trying to revive him.

Ethan's chest heaved as he tried to find his voice, breath ragged. He reached out, grabbing Klax's arm with firm fingers. "Jun'Ei . . ." he coughed, voice hoarse. "She . . . She's . . ."

Klax's expression changed in an instant, a deep, knowing look flashing in his wolfish eyes. He knelt beside Ethan, grip firm on the Archon's shoulder. "I knew it. I *knew* it all along," Klax said quietly.

Tara and Fauna exchanged confused glances, but Klax didn't wait to explain. His expression hardened with resolve, his voice carrying across the hall.

"Everyone, suit up," Klax barked, his usual calm replaced by urgency. "We're going to the final delve."

*   *   *

The City of Illusions stretched out before Artorious like a dream turned nightmare. The shimmering, ghostly light of the city twisted reality, making the sprawling structures shift like vapor. Beneath his boots, the ground was slick with the ghostly blood of the dreamstrider mantas, the once majestic creatures gliding through the illusory city now torn to pieces.

Artorious stood over hundreds of their bodies, breath slow and steady despite the carnage. His onixia blade gleamed with the strange, ethereal fluid spilling from their forms, reflecting the pale glow in a way that made it look like part of the illusions. But nothing was illusory about the bodies at his feet, nor the weight of his mission.

His Greycloaks stood with him, equally bloodied but silent, all staring at the towering structure ahead—the Nerve Tower. A grotesque, living spire, it pulsed with veins of light climbing its surface, reminding them all that this place was alive in some unsettling way. Artorious watched it with unblinking eyes, gripping the onixia blade tightly.

From behind, Carliah's voice broke the silence, a teasing edge threading her words. "Quite the slaughter, isn't it, Artorious? Hundreds of dreamstriders, all ghostly and beautiful, and you didn't even blink. But tell me"—she stepped closer, black eyes gleaming with mischief—"are you truly prepared for what's ahead?"

Artorious didn't respond immediately. His gaze stayed on the tower, its rhythmic pulse matching his steady heartbeat. The air stank of blood and an otherworldly aroma. Carliah's taunting didn't stir him—yet.

"I've been prepared since Gyko's death," he said, voice cold and resolute. He sheathed his blade in a practiced motion, its dark glow fading as it slid home.

Carliah's grin widened, her voice dripping condescension. "You *know* what you're going to see in there, don't you?"

For a moment, Artorious paused, eyes narrowing as he finally met her gaze. Something flickered in his expression—a shadow of the past clinging to him like a curse. Carliah saw it and pressed her advantage.

"Doesn't it bother you?" she whispered, voice soft yet venomous. "After all this time? The utter disdain your brothers and sisters have for you? The way they look at you—like you're a reminder of everything they wish they could forget."

Artorious's jaw tightened. His hands clenched at his sides, but he wouldn't yield to her words. Instead, he returned her stare, unflinching. "What do you want me to say, Carliah? That I'm haunted by my past? That the ghosts of those I failed keep me from having anything but restless dreams?"

He stepped toward her, the force of his presence descending like a storm cloud. "I know my failings, and I know what you all think of me. I wouldn't be here if I didn't. But it won't stop me from doing what needs to be done."

For a long moment, neither spoke. The weight of Artorious's words hung in the air like the tower's heartbeat. The other Greycloaks remained silent, watching him with a mix of respect and guarded suspicion. His resolve was iron, but his history with them was complicated.

Without waiting for a reply, Artorious strode toward the tower's entrance. Its heavy, fleshy doors parted as though the tower recognized him. He didn't look back as the darkness swallowed him.

The other Greycloaks followed in silence, armor clinking softly. Carliah lingered at the entrance a moment longer, shaking her head with a wry smile as she watched him disappear.

Well, well, Arty, she mused, stepping through the doorway. *Maybe there's some of the old Lightborn spirit still in you, after all. The question is . . . will that be enough?*

All of Sanctum watched Ethan and his hybrids march toward the portal chamber. The excitement of Klax's birthday party was now forgotten; the only buzz in the underground kingdom was that of expectation for the Archon to fulfill his destiny.

In the wake of Ethan's vision, Borlor had come running to report that once they'd unshackled the portal, a blinding light had shot out in a ring, covering the entire Sanctum.

"It was like—like some kinda scream," the Dixit coughed, twitching his conical nose at Klax's determined face.

"A psychic wave," Lamphrey explained, walking beside them, having quietly reappeared like a specter in the night. "The residual energies of a consciousness trapped there in the delve. And a powerful one, at that."

"It's her," Klax said, quickening his pace.

Tara rushed to keep up, eyes darting from Ethan to Klax to Fauna, seeing only determination in their faces.

"Look, how can you be sure? Did ya actually see Jun'Ei, Ethan?"

"I didn't have to," he replied. "That kind of power was . . . beyond anything I've felt before."

"It's her," Klax repeated, fangs flaring with excitement and trepidation while the hybrids looked on in awe. "It's he—"

"This could be a trap!" Tara roared, stepping in front of him before he entered the portal chamber. "Just think about it—isn't this exactly what the Lightborn wants? For us to rush off into the unknown like this? If he's really there with that woman, Carliah, we gotta be ready, Klax. You know it."

"And the more time we waste here discussing this," the wolfman growled in reply, "the more Jun'Ei's life fades away."

The portal roared behind them, another wave of energy pulsing from its core, nearly knocking them off their feet.

"Its stability is wavering!" Lamphrey shouted, rushing to join the mages weaving arcs of lightning around the raging portal. "It is now or never, Archon Ethan!"

Ethan took one look at his team and nodded, clasping Tara's shoulder with a firm, strong hand. He knew she was wavering, but she also knew she couldn't convince them to back down.

"Watch our backs, Tara. We need you more than anything now."

The Minxit looked up at him with an emotion he'd never seen on her face before: fear. He knew then that this delve would be different.

". . . Fuck it," she said. "If you really are the last Archon, I ain't gonna miss your finest moment."

Stepping through the restored portal, Ethan and his companions were treated to a view of magic splendor. The City of Illusions loomed ahead, an ethereal vision of ivory spires and shimmering towers flickering like translucent ghosts in the twilight. The whole city pulsed with otherworldly energy, the air alive with strange whispers—though no voices could be heard.

As the party entered its borders, a vast aurora spread across the sky, painting it with blues, greens, and purples. Yet something about it was unsettling; faces, fleeting and distant, appeared in the colored streams overhead, watching the city below as though waiting.

The streets were pristine—almost too clean—and felt more like the pale bones of a dream than anything real. Even the buildings seemed to sway and blur, shifting from solid to translucent whenever you tried to focus on them for too long.

"Memory Spires," Fauna breathed, gazing at the great structures. "Places where the secrets of Argwyll are stored. Forgotten thoughts from warriors long gone."

"This place . . . it's like something out of a fever dream," Ethan muttered, eyes roving from the aurora to the shifting faces above. "And it's practically *swarming* with Spirit Cores."

Klax nodded grimly, sharp gaze flicking across the streets as they moved deeper. "The City of Illusions is where memories hold power," he explained, voice low. "It's presided over by dreamstriders—ancient beings that feed on memory fragments, illusions, and dreams. This city warps reality, bending it to those who have power over their own dreams . . . and nightmares."

"And it's no coincidence you feel power deep in this place," Fauna added, wiggling her nose as the city's ethereal breeze brushed by. "A grade-C delve is full of creatures never seen on the surface. We're deep underground, in a place lost to time. Normally, an Archon would do a grade D first. The fact your System showed you this already must mean something."

"And we know what that something is," Klax finished.

Right then, the first dreamstriders appeared, sapphire-and-white mantalike creatures gliding with eerie grace through the air. Their glowing bodies cast a soft light on the streets, each large enough to blot out the stars. They moved silently, fins making slow, rhythmic motions like swimming through an unseen sea of illusions.

Ethan Appraised them at once.

Dreamstrider (Level 20)
HP: 100/100
Unique Skill: Ethereal Form

The *ethereal* property was instantly familiar. "These things can turn invisible . . . but they can't *actually* attack us," Ethan informed the group with a slight grin. "They're all show."

"That's . . . good?" Fauna asked hesitantly, glancing at the peaceful creatures. "Right?"

Tara grinned, flexing her fingers. "So we don't need to fight them. Let's keep moving."

Ethan nodded. "Exactly. They're like guards, keeping watch over the memories drifting here. But that's not our goal." He pointed toward a tall, looming structure standing out in the haze. Its base pulsed like a living organism, veined with glowing lines beating like a heart.

"The Nerve Tower," Ethan said, a sharp glint in his eye. "That's where we need to go. Exactly like Jun'Ei's vision."

They moved as one toward the city perimeter, eyes on the ghostly striders drifting overhead. However, they soon saw their real adversaries.

The first main street they came across was lined with corpses—broken dreamstrider bodies along both sides, some still twitching and phasing in and out with their strange ability. Most had been slaughtered without mercy, violet streams of sparkling blood staining the streets.

Ethan bent, touching one manta still in its death throes. Its single eye looked at him with desperation.

"Three guesses who did this," Ethan said over his shoulder.

Fauna shook her pale head at the mounds of corpses. "No mercy, like all the Greycloaks. But why bother killing them?"

"Don't you get it, Faun?" Tara scoffed, prodding a dreamstrider with her toe. "They wanna slow him down. They know Ethan draws strength from every kill, like we all do, so they came to thin the herd."

She was right, yet Ethan suspected more.

"It's a warning," he said. "He's telling me he won't show mercy to anyone coming for him. He knows we're coming. Hell, I wouldn't be surprised if *he* messed with the portal."

"So we *are* walking into a trap," Tara muttered.

Klax growled under his breath. "Come on."

"Uh, did you not hear me, dude? Got some birthday cake in your ears or—"

"I *heard* you, Tara," the Lycae snarled. "It doesn't change anything."

Everyone looked at Klax, realizing there was no stopping his charge toward his goal. Tara caught Ethan's eye, motioning toward the wolfman, silently begging him to intervene.

"We got this, Tara," he said instead. "Besides, the Lightborn was sloppy. He might've thought he choked my Core supply, but he left me something *much* more valuable right here."

As the party paused to watch, Ethan gave one last command.

"Hold my undead boy. I'm gonna make sure this little guy's skills don't go to waste."

Skill Transfer Complete!

Ethereal Form (Grade E)
Using this skill, your form shimmers out of reality for five seconds, nullifying physical or magic attacks.
WARNING: You will be unable to attack when Ethereal Form is activated.
Cooldown: 5 minutes

Spirit Cores to Upgrade [Ethereal Form] Skill from Grade E to D: 400

It was too good to pass up; not when a dreamstrider was right there. But he wouldn't remain in its tiny body; Valgraiva's HP and stats were far too good. Luckily, he could transfer the undead host's major skills back and forth, though it took a lot of effort for the party to restrain Valgraiva while Ethan possessed the new body.

It felt strange, though. Every time he *re*possessed an old host, it almost welcomed him. No cooldown, no resistance, no anger. He was beginning to suspect they saw him as an escape from their empty lot in life: a Boss to be beaten and respawned for hapless adventurers.

Whatever the truth, he had his new skill. And as the party came to a junction between two shimmering spires, the faint sound of singing drifted through the air. The ground underfoot began to shake, like someone telling them to stop. They exchanged glances, but before anyone spoke, the city's soft glow shifted. The air grew heavier, the light in the sky trembling. Then, without warning, a notification appeared before Ethan.

DELVE CHALLENGE: GAUNTLET
Objective: Make it to the Nerve Tower Outskirts within 10 minutes.

**Warning: All Dreamstriders in the city will activate upon the
challenge's start. They will hunt you.**

Ethan grimaced. "So much for silent custodians . . ."

Fauna's face paled as she read the notification aloud. "Once we start . . . every dreamstrider will come after us."

"They've been peaceful so far," Tara noted, grin faltering. "Guess that's about to change, huh?"

Klax growled softly, claws flexing. "They might be ethereal, but they can trap us in illusions, slow us. That's how they hunt."

Ethan looked around at the dreamstriders gliding silently overhead. They hadn't sensed the challenge yet, but it wouldn't last. He already felt time pressing down.

"All right," he said, voice commanding. "No point hesitating. Fauna, we need speed. Can you whip up something?"

Fauna's eyes glimmered with nervous energy, staff faintly glowing. "I can cast Haste on all of us. Won't last long, but we'll get a head start."

"Good," Ethan responded, unsheathing his mithril scythe. The blade gleamed under the city's strange light, and he twirled it in his undead fingers with practiced ease. "I'll take point. This baby should keep those manta things at bay."

Tara, drawing her bow, flicked her tail in anticipation. "I'll keep their numbers down from a distance. These bastards look tricky, especially with that Ethereal thing. We'll have to watch cooldowns and time our strikes."

Klax, ever the protector, nodded, readying his claws. "And I'll handle any that slip past."

They lined up, staring down the empty, dreamlike streets that led toward the Nerve Tower. Faces in the sky shifted with growing intensity, watching and waiting.

Fauna cast Haste, and when its shimmering aura enveloped them, Ethan raised his scythe, single crimson eye fixed on the pulsating tower in the distance.

"GO!"

CHAPTER THIRTY-THREE

The [Gauntlet]

They burst forward as one, the streets blurring beneath them. Ethan felt Fauna's magic surge through his limbs, sharpening his movements. His scythe gleamed at the ready as he glanced skyward, seeing the dreamstriders flicker to life above.

"They're coming!" Tara shouted, letting loose an arrow that whistled through the air, striking a dreamstrider and vanishing it in a puff of ethereal light. But more came, hundreds of sapphire-and-white bodies casting eerie shadows as they swooped overhead.

Ethan gritted his teeth, muscles coiling as he leaped forward, leading the charge. His scythe sliced through illusions while dreamstriders swarmed from above.

"Keep moving!" Klax roared, tearing through a shadow flickering into existence before him.

With the Nerve Tower looming in the distance like a giant pulsing heart, Ethan knew there was no turning back.

Once they accepted the challenge, the skies lost their luster. The shimmering lights of the City of Illusions flickered and dimmed, pressing a grim twilight over them. Ethan's heart raced in time with Fauna's Haste. The once calm dreamstriders now moved with a deadly purpose, pale forms streaking through dark skies at unnatural speed. Ethan felt the city itself, alive and intent on devouring them.

High above, the shadows of the dreamstriders changed. Their calm faces were now twisted into furious growls that emerged from mouthless maws. Their flight was smooth yet terrifying, moving in perfect unison like a hive mind.

"Go!" Ethan shouted.

A brood of five darted from behind a white spire, forms phasing through the city as if gravity were a suggestion. They were too fast—Ethan barely reacted in time. Twisting his scythe, he sent a Twilight Edge surging forward. The shadowy energy coiled like a serpent, striking their ethereal bodies; they sizzled and burned at the touch of shadow, wailing in haunting echoes across dead streets.

"Keep it up!" Klax yelled from Ethan's left, his claws rending the ghosts trying to slip past, fists blazing with fiery light. "The darkness is on our side!"

Ethan had tried Mass Hide, a no-brainer, but the city's pervasive glow clung to them, illusions preventing any sort of stealth.

"Shit, we're sitting ducks," he growled.

They pressed on foot, no cover, Fauna's Haste speeding them but offering no defense. Sprinting, Ethan and Tara unleashed ranged attacks: Tara's arrows like silver streaks; Ethan's Twilight Edge slicing the air as a hungry blade. Klax blocked any strider that got too close, searing them with flaming fists.

"Upgrades?" Ethan asked between strikes, voice ragged.

"Upgrades," Klax confirmed with a grin, teeth gleaming in the low light. "You're not the only one with more power now."

They fought back-to-back, Klax's brute force with Ethan's lethal precision, and Tara's arrows taking out flankers. But the dreamstriders were relentless, their pale forms phasing in and out, adapting, growing faster. The pressure mounted as they raced down labyrinthine alleys, footsteps echoing in the narrow streets.

Ahead, the dreamstriders changed tactics, no longer simply charging but phasing through buildings and reappearing behind the group, faster and more erratic.

"They're phasing too?" Tara grunted as one swooped low enough to graze her tail with a sickle claw. She answered with a trio of arrows, piercing its core and splattering blue blood on the cobbles. "*Why* can't it *ever* be simple?"

Ethan spotted the next obstacle, an intersection, the winding streets forming a lethal grid—and they weren't alone.

"Look ahead!" Ethan shouted over pounding feet and growling creatures. "A blockade!"

Sure enough, a massive formation of dreamstriders created a shimmering, translucent wall across the street. Their bodies merged grotesquely, writhing as they formed a living barricade of flesh and bone. Ethan's Twilight Edge slammed into them, but they absorbed it like ripples in water, the barrier shimmering, undamaged, the dreamstriders packed too tightly.

"Ethan!" Tara roared, shooting arrows that did little more than irritate the creatures. "Any bright ideas?!"

Ethan's lips curled in a wild grin. "Nothing *but*."

[Skill Activated: Petrification Coating (Grade E)]
[Skill Activated: Twilight Edge (Grade D)]

With a roar, Ethan hefted the mithril scythe, sending another wave of darkness at the blockade. This time, however, the shadows were laced with a deadly orange-red glow, energy crackling as it tore through the air.

When it struck, the result was immediate. The dreamstriders' pale forms jerked violently, bodies spasming under the paralysis. Thirty went limp at once, collapsing in a heap and leaving a gaping hole in the blockade.

"Move!" Ethan shouted, and they barreled through the gap, feet pounding the cobblestones as the dreamstriders scrambled to reform.

"Fauna, got any more tricks?" Ethan called over his shoulder while running.

Panting heavily, Fauna summoned the last of her mana, hurling flaming spheres behind them. Fireballs exploded on impact, scattering the striders in confusion.

"Mad cows . . . again?" Ethan smirked, glancing back at the chaos. The fire didn't harm them much, but it made a lot of noise.

"Fauna, I love ya, but I think that's just gonna piss them off."

"I—I didn't know it'd do that!"

"It's perfect, Faun!" Ethan shouted. "If big Kaedmon's watching, we're letting him know exactly what we think of his bullshit law and these delves!"

[Time Remaining: 00:05:00]

Ethan strained his eyes, scanning the road ahead, heart thundering with adrenaline. Ten squadrons of dreamstriders soared in perfect formation around a massive ivory spire looming like a monolith.

"What are they—" Klax began, eyes widening in alarm. His voice rose to a desperate roar. "Shit! Look to the skies!"

Ethan looked up just in time to see the dreamstriders attacking the spire's foundation, ethereal claws tearing through stone like paper. The tower groaned, tilting left as cracks spread across its base, about to collapse.

"They're bringing the city down on us!" Tara shouted, panic in her voice.

Ethan's mind raced. If it fell, they couldn't outrun it; the streets were too narrow, the dreamstriders too fast.

"Move!" he barked, but the second he stepped forward, the dreamstriders who'd formed the earlier wall reemerged from the alleys, their elongated beaks glowing with energy as they readied an attack.

Their target was clear.

They'd come for him.

[Time Remaining: 00:04:00]

"Fauna!" Klax called, voice tense. "We can't avoid that thing if it falls!"

"We won't be able to at this rate," Fauna gasped, mana draining. "And that tower—"

"I have an idea," Ethan interrupted, looking from the crumbling spire to the advancing horde of dreamstriders.

Tara's eyes narrowed. "Let me guess—something we won't like?"

His smile hardened. "The rules didn't say we *all* had to make it."

Silence fell on them. Above, the spire groaned, beginning to tip. The air was thick with tension, the ground trembling beneath.

"What did I say?" Ethan added, voice cold and clear. "I'm full of bad ideas."

Tara's eyes went wide with anger and disbelief. "Etha—"

[Skill Activated: Wing Buffet (Grade D)]

With a powerful stroke of skeletal wings, Ethan hurled the party skyward. Fauna screamed as she was flung into the air, Tara's furious cry drowned out by the wind. Klax growled, claws out as he was sent flying to safety, helpless to stop it.

"ETHAN!"

Ethan stayed behind, watching the Memory Spire crash down upon him. His heart pounded, but fear was absent, replaced by resolve.

He smiled, wind whipping his hair as he braced for impact.

"Safe flying, guys."

With a deafening groan, the spire fell.

Ethan's eyes locked on the collapsing structure as it moved in slow motion, every fragment of stone and magic tumbling toward him. Far off, he could hear Klax, Tara, and Fauna shouting, their voices drowned by the city's roar as the dreamstrider horde converged.

Those eerie mantalike creatures circled him like vultures. Their sapphire-and-white bodies glowed faintly in the dark, translucent forms phasing as they drifted closer. He felt their gaze, an ethereal weight pressing down. Dozens of them floated, each shimmering with a heavy aura, suffocating the air.

[Time Remaining: 00:03:00]

He had no time to think. He had to buy his team the seconds needed to finish the trial.

Ethan fought against the first dreamstriders who dared to come too close, slashing with his mithril scythe. Though their ethereal forms barely bled, each strike forced them to dissipate temporarily.

A few Twilight Edge bursts took down squads circling above, which were launching spirit orbs as ranged attacks. His Repulsor Shield worked overtime, nullifying their strikes. Their magic couldn't pierce Valgraiva's defenses; this form truly was his trump card.

But nothing was invincible. Ethan knew it as he saw the spire's shadow looming, blotting out the sky.

I HOPE YOU KNOW WHAT YOU'RE DOING!

I'm not your typical Archon, Ethan thought, smirking as the structure came down on his skull.

Then . . . darkness.

The Memory Spire slammed hard, silencing everything.

For a moment, the world stopped. Beneath the collapsed spire, Ethan felt the crushing weight of stone and magic. Pinned, unable to move, he couldn't see or hear anything but the faint sound of his breathing and the pounding of his heart.

So quiet, it chilled him to the core.

Outside, the dreamstriders hovered around the fallen structure, scanning for signs of life. Apparently finding none, the squads drifted away toward the still screaming voices of the hybrids.

Then, the silence broke like shattering glass.

Followed by the howl of an undead warrior.

Magic surged within him, the man wearing the demon hat melting through the rubble like a blade through butter. In the next instant, five dreamstriders were cleaved in half, their ghostly forms exploding in light and shadow.

And from the wreckage, Ethan rose.

Rubble phased through him like mist parting around an unseen figure. His body flickered, ethereal and ghostly, shimmering as if made of translucent smoke. Features barely visible, he grinned at the remaining dreamstriders. His crimson eye shone brighter than ever, a beacon in the twilight.

Upgrade Complete!
Congratulations! You have upgraded [Ethereal Form]
from Grade E to D.

Ethereal Form (Grade D)
While under the effects of Ethereal Form, you can pass
through solid objects.

Ethan smirked at his fallen enemies, their shattered forms littering the once tranquil city streets. The cost had been steep, but he'd done it—committed everything to upgrading Ethereal Form so he could pass through solid surfaces like air.

I regret to remind you that we are not done yet! Sys shouted, almost choking in the smoky air.

[Time Remaining: 00:02:00]

Ethan's smile widened.

Two minutes is all I need.

Sensing the shift in power, the dreamstriders turned, their forms flickering as they swarmed, a gleaming sea of sapphire and white. But Ethan was ready.

"Come and get me, you overgrown sea urchins!" he snarled.

In one fluid motion, he summoned Twilight Edge again. A blade of pure shadow burst forth, dark energy crackling in the gloom. He swung wide, sending a wave of destruction through the circling dreamstriders. Five more disintegrated, dissolving into ghostly mist.

But the horde kept coming.

His ethereal wings—massive, spectral—unfurled from his back. A powerful flap sent a shock wave outward, repelling the nearest dreamstriders and slamming them into the city's translucent walls. They writhed, struggling to regain balance, but Ethan was relentless. Time was short. The gauntlet's clock was ticking.

His voice boomed, echoing down the city streets, shattering the calm and sending tremors through the air. The creatures flinched, movements sluggish under the sonic onslaught.

Still not enough.

More dreamstriders converged, swirling in from every direction. They brushed against him with cold, otherworldly limbs. He slashed through as many as he could, but for each one felled, two took its place.

His limbs grew heavy, fatigue creeping in. The timer on the gauntlet challenge showed a single minute left. In the back of his mind, he heard Sys's sharp, cold warning.

I know what you're doing. You think they'll manage the challenge without you leading them, with you as a decoy? You place too much trust in your team, Ethan. You need to run.

Ethan gritted his teeth. He wouldn't abandon his companions. Not now. Not ever.

If you're still here when the challenge ends, you'll be swallowed by the delve. Is that really what you want?

He heard the words, but he stood firm. The dreamstriders closed in, sapphire bodies glowing brighter, ready to overwhelm him.

This is not how the Archon is supposed to behave!

Haven't you gotten it through your thick skull yet, Sys? I'm not your regular Archon.

Sys might have said more, but Ethan couldn't hear it. The final wave of striders descended in an undulating mass of death. Each readied its spirit projectile, charging it as they dove.

He faced them, refusing to back down.

ETHAN!

They'll make it, he told himself. *Because when the chips are down . . . you gotta trust your team.*

A spirit supernova flared before his eyes, a miniature sun formed by the dreamstriders' hatred for an opponent who refused to die. As one, they pulled back, prepared to unleash it.

Ethan brought his shield to bear and closed his eyes.

Then, just as the final second slipped away, a notification flared in his vision.

DELVE CHALLENGE: GAUNTLET
Complete!
Reward:
Spirit Cores: +700
(Mithril) Moonlight Katana x1

His smile held relief and bravado.

See, Sys? What did I tell ya?

The dreamstriders froze midflight, bodies jerking as though their strings had been cut. They hovered for a moment, then became docile once more, forgetting their purpose entirely.

Ethan blinked, barely registering what had happened. He exhaled a shaky breath, adrenaline thrumming in his veins.

A bright light enveloped him. In the next moment, he was gone.

The world swirled. When the light faded, he stood at the outskirts of the Nerve Tower. Tara, Klax, and Fauna were waiting, faces lined with worry, Fauna crying softly.

"Ethan!" Fauna rushed him, tears streaking her cheeks in relief. "We thought—you were—"

Ethan chuckled, reaching out to ruffle her hair; though in his ethereal form, it was more a ghostly caress. "I'm fine, Fauna. Just had to take care of a few things."

Tara folded her arms, looking him over with relief and exasperation. "You're a damn idiot, you know that?"

"That the best you can do, kitten? I'm sure your mind knows dirtier words than that."

Before Tara could retort, Klax—silent until now—stepped forward. His eyes held a knowing glint. "I knew it," he said quietly. "I knew your plan, even if it was stupid."

Ethan raised an eyebrow, a smirk on his lips. "Oh, yeah? And what plan was that, exactly?"

Klax didn't answer immediately. He stared at Ethan, the weight of their shared history between them. Then, with a nod, he said, "You trusted we'd finish the challenge in time. Even with you facing the horde alone, you trusted us."

Ethan glanced at Fauna and Tara, who both looked back at him with equal parts admiration and frustration, before turning to the shadowed Nerve Tower rising into the twilight gloom above them.

Ya see, Sys? He smiled. *Maybe I can be too trusting of my allies in this world. But you don't trust them enough.*

Sys seemed to groan in his mind as the team moved on.

Luck and persistence won't last forever . . .

"Yo, Faun, find anything?"

"Nothing yet."

"Heh. Rabbits weren't made for spelunkin', I guess. Hey, Klax, got a new set of brass knuckles here for ya, how about it?"

As the party forged ahead toward the Nerve Tower, Tara and Fauna took point among the ruined buildings characterizing this part of the city—the remnants of the Greycloaks' advance. It seemed they'd spared nothing.

And their goal was currently coming right to them.

Klax glowered at Tara as she rifled through the trash they'd left, his gruff demeanor telling her to just stow the loot in her inventory before continuing down the wrecked street.

Above, the dreamstriders soared peacefully through the indigo skies, settling on fragmented Memory Spires and buildings. Ethan watched them secrete spirit projectiles onto the towers, painstakingly knitting them back together.

"They don't seem threatening now at all," Ethan remarked, watching a squad of four stitch the remains of a tall spire's crumbled foundation.

"They're creatures bound to the delve's challenges," Fauna said, scanning the area for magical anomalies. "But there's a theory they might've been architects and builders in life—reduced now to floating memories."

"You mean these guys used to be . . . people?"

One of the mantas nosed into the rubble as Ethan observed, hardly acknowledging the strangers before aiding its fellows in rebuilding.

"It's just a theory. But it explains their strange obsession with this place. Nobody alive really knows the truth about the Archon's delves or how they came to be. We only know they've existed since Karfangg's time, and they'll keep on existing as long as the cycle does."

"Until it's broken," Klax growled. "Need I remind you we're on a time limit?"

"Ah, relax, Klaxy. If Ethan can handle a horde of those beasts alone, he can handle the stuffy Lightborn and his bitch comma—"

"That's not all that's at stake!" the Lycae yelped, grimacing and grabbing his head as though in pain.

"Klax?"

The wolfman ignored Fauna's outstretched hand, insisting they press on. He would have if his commander hadn't phased through him, appearing before him with those piercing silver eyes.

"You need rest," Ethan declared.

"N-No. No, Ethan, I'm—"

Before the dogman finished, he dropped to one knee, teeth gritted as a headache racked him.

"Whoa—Klax!"

Fauna and Tara steadied him, though he tried protesting.

"We're taking five," Ethan said. "We need time to heal from the gauntlet."

"B-But—"

"You're no good like this," Ethan stated, using the same direct, no-nonsense tone he'd used with coworkers who overstepped boundaries. "We stop here until we're fully healed and you come to your senses."

"Ethan's right, Klax," Fauna whispered. "Maybe you should—"

The wolfman shrugged her off, dragging himself to a nearby wall and slumping down. Pain filled his eyes, a pain that cut one off from reality.

But in a place like this, what *was* reality?

"Five minutes?" Klax asked.

"Ten," Ethan replied with a somber smile, nodding at Tara and Fauna to secure their position with traps and spells. "That's an order."

They complied without more questions, and Ethan took the time for some upgrades.

Current Spirit Cores: 1150

Juicy, but not enough for everything. He wanted to push Hide to S class, but that was pointless here, with no darkness for sneak attacks.

He'd focus on immediately useful skills.

Dive (Grade C)
***Homing Dive unlocked: Dive now homes in on targeted
enemy or structure.***
Spirit Cores to Upgrade [Dive] Skill from Grade D to C: 250
Confirm Upgrade?

For flying foes or whatever lurked in these alleys, a homing move was essential.

[Upgrading Skill: Dive (Grade D)]
Upgrade Complete!

Congratulations! You have upgraded [Dive] from Grade D to C.
Spirit Cores to Upgrade [Dive] Skill from Grade C to B: 400

Next: Possession—he'd eyed its newest path for a while.

Possession (Rank D)
Cooldown removed. Possession is now instantaneous.
Spirit Cores to Upgrade [Possession] Core Skill from Rank E to D: 600
Confirm Upgrade?

Instant possession was too good to pass up. So many Delve Bosses had resisted him for crucial seconds.

[Upgrading Skill: Possession (Rank E)]
Upgrade Complete!
Congratulations! You have upgraded [Possession] from Rank E to D.

Now he had three hundred Cores left.

He'd gather every skill he could. Valgraiva was a walking tank; however awful he smelled, with the right arsenal, Ethan could make him unstoppable.

He also checked synergy: Twilight Edge with Poison and Petrification as ranged options, then Appraised the Moonlight Katana from the gauntlet.

Item: {Rare} (Mithril) Moonlight Katana
DMG: 40–55
SPECIAL: {Fade Slice}
A weapon with this property can attack through solid surfaces.

It glowed with ethereal energy—icy and deathly sharp. Its max damage was below his scythe's, but Fade Slice was tempting. Pure DPS versus utility . . . or personal preference. Who didn't love a katana?

But he also eyed Transmogrification's next upgrade, needing three hundred more Cores.

With that, the surface won't know what hit it. And neither will you . . . He glanced at the Nerve Tower's shadowed peak, looming over the building they were sheltered in. *Artorious . . .*

It had been a long journey, deadly and filled with traps even his MMO knowledge couldn't handle. But now, he felt a turning point. He'd been through hell and come out a warrior—and more: a leader.

That was exactly why he couldn't abandon one of his best.

I know what you're gonna say, Sys, he thought, eyeing Klax from the corner of his vision. *Because I can tell how you feel about these guys.*

Ethan . . . Your predecessors had entire armies at their command—legions obeying every order without question. Why you slave over these hybrids is beyond me.

Stick around, Sys, he said, kneeling by the groaning wolfman. *You might just learn what real loyalty looks like.*

Ethan slumped next to the pained Lycae, not as a prideful leader but as a concerned friend.

"Klax."

The wolfman muffled a coughing laugh. "I suppose you'll say I'm a burden. I'd say that too."

"You ain't a burden, Klax. But you *are* carrying one. And it'll weigh you down till you face it."

Instinctively, Klax's trembling claw went to his throat, clutching the talisman there.

"I *saw* her, Ethan," he said. "In the Twilight Sepulcher. Down in that mirror."

"Yeah. I know." *And it's been gnawing at you since, hasn't it?*

His face contorted, fangs bared in a snarl.

"She was . . . violated," he said. "Alive but tortured. The vision was hazy, blurred, but it was her. Her eyes—still the same deep lilac I remember."

Ethan leaned back, sighing against the hideout's wall.

"You and she were lovers."

It wasn't a question. Klax didn't treat it as such.

"A Lycae mate bond is sacred," he explained. "Break it, and a Lycae loses a piece of himself. I promised her I'd always be there. When she was taken, I didn't know what to do. Worse—*my* betrayal led to this. If I'd listened to her . . . I tried searching, Ethan. Tried. But my last duty to her always called me back here. I had to fulfill that last order she gave before she vanished. Couldn't disobey her again."

"What was her last order?"

The old wolf turned away, tears threatening at the corners of his eyes.

"'Take care of them, Klax. And wait for the one who will break the chains that bind us.'"

Ethan didn't move. He heard the words, and Klax turned his face away, brow knit in pain.

"Tara and Fauna—they're good. Everyone in Sanctum is. What you did for me . . . it meant a lot. But I've done my waiting. I did as she asked. Why don't I feel any better? Why does her face torment me whenever I close my eyes?"

Ethan sighed again. He wanted to tell the old dog to leave the past behind, but he knew his own Earthly past had shackled him too. He'd even once thought death was the answer . . .

Maybe you can't teach an old dog new tricks.

Still, seeing his friend's pain, he had to try.

"Klax, listen, I—"

Suddenly, the dogman's eyes went wide with panic. At first, Ethan thought an enemy had appeared, but no—his gaze looked beyond Ethan, beyond all of them, as if at the very fabric of time.

". . . Jun'Ei?"

Fauna and Tara noticed the shift in the air. Far off, a voice sang, calling like a ghost from the underworld.

Klax danced to its tune.

"Jun'Ei!" he roared, leaping with all his strength through a nearby window, bounding down the dilapidated street before Ethan could stop him.

"Klax! Kla—Shit!"

"What's happening?" Tara asked. "Dogman finally lost his damn mind?"

"Nah, Tara. In fact, I think it's his mind that *is* the problem."

All around them, the air shimmered with tiny sapphire motes. The atmosphere felt thick and musky, humid like a tropical day before a torrential rain.

"JUN'EI!"

The wolf's howl was enough to rouse every monster in the city.

"Shit!" Ethan spat again, ordering Fauna to summon another Haste as they gave chase. "Klax! Come back!"

But the wolfman had no ears for them now.

He was in the grip of something far more sinister.

CHAPTER THIRTY-FOUR

Fallen [Hound]

The narrow streets of the City of Illusions twisted and turned maddeningly, reflecting the confusion of the dreamlike spires overhead. Ivory towers shimmered like translucent ghosts, their walls melting into the swirling skies where streams of auroralike light flickered with distant, disjointed faces. They stared silently at the trespassers below, an eerie, ever-shifting realm that mattered little to Klax.

"Klax, *stop!*" Ethan shouted, voice echoing in the shimmering alleys. He strained to keep up—Valgraiva's armor weighed him down—but Klax was sprinting on instinct, chasing an image only he could see.

Ahead, Fauna gasped, barely matching Tara's feline agility. Her hands glowed faintly with magic, poised for anything, yet her eyes were wide with worry.

"What the fuck happened to him?" Tara hissed.

"He said he heard her—Jun'Ei."

The Minxit coughed, almost choking. "Yeah. That'll do it."

"It's a trick, right?" Ethan asked her as they rounded an alley in pursuit of the bounding wolfman. "Fauna?"

"I sense strong illusory magic!" she huffed. "But . . . there's something else. I feel weaker here."

"Never mind that!" Tara yelled back. "When I get my claws on that dog, I'll tear him a new hole!"

Ethan growled in frustration, realizing the illusions here were stronger than he'd guessed. Even *he* felt unsettled by the memories lingering, twisting the minds of the desperate. And Klax—driven by grief and the hope of seeing Jun'Ei—had been the perfect victim.

He glanced at the bizarre spires overhead, thinking, *Is that their purpose? To trick us?*

They pushed through winding streets, chasing their quarry. Every time they thought they had Klax cornered, they came up empty.

"Damn it!" Tara kept snarling. "Damn it, damn it, damn it!"

They found him again, leaping through a section of the city covered in dense sapphire mist, similar to the dreamstriders' spirit bombs.

"Klax!" Ethan shouted once more, forcing himself faster as Klax vanished around another corner. "Klax, *wait!* It's not real!"

But the wolfman didn't respond. His eyes were locked on a shimmering, ghostly figure at the far end of the street, a wide junction where three paths met. The spirit hovered above the ground, face half hidden behind a glowing veil. She looked exactly as he remembered—silver hair over her shoulders, the same soft smile.

"Jun'Ei . . ." Klax breathed, picking up speed as the figure turned away, beckoning him gently. He sprinted down the alley, arms outstretched. "Jun'Ei, *wait!*"

The figure paused, as if waiting. Klax's heart pounded wildly, hope surging. He was so close he could feel her warmth in the icy air. He ran faster, arms reaching—

But something changed.

"KLAX!" Ethan's voice tore the air, a desperate warning.

Klax had no time to react. He managed only a glance back at his comrades, silently begging them to stay away, before a sharp scream rent the air—like a dying cat—and a twang echoed from above. In an instant, a thin spear of light shot through the mist, piercing Klax's neck. Blood sprayed as he collapsed to the cobblestones.

"*No!*" Ethan skidded to a stop, eyes wide with horror as blood pooled beneath Klax's twitching body. Fauna screamed, rushing forward, but Ethan threw out an arm, stopping her. "Get back!"

Fauna's eyes brimmed with tears, her hands trembling. "Klax . . . He's . . ."

"He's still alive." Ethan's voice was urgent. The wound was bad, blood gushing in heavy spurts, each breath shallower. "Stay behind me!"

Ethan's single crimson eye scanned the area, seeing only towering Memory Spires shimmering ominously above the mist. Their shapes faded in and out like mirages. His heart pounded as he Appraised frantically, vision flaring as he spotted them—two creatures perched in the towers, flickering in and out of reality.

"Two of them," Ethan muttered, locking onto their faint silhouettes. "Snipers."

"Fuck!" Tara hissed. "Klax! Don't move, got it? Just . . . Just *don't.*"

The wounded Lycae spat a glob of blood, hardly able to speak.

"Just . . . go . . ."

"Quiet!" Ethan whispered, motioning Fauna close.

She clutched her staff to her chest, eyes on Klax's bloody form.

"Faun."

No response.

"Faun!"

The Hopla shook, forcing her eyes away from Klax. "I—I'm here."

"Can you levitate him? Make a smoke screen?"

She blinked, realization dawning. "This fog . . . it's not natural."

"Nothing is here," Tara grunted, back to the wall.

"It's a nullification field," Fauna continued, gripping her staff tighter. "Anti-magic, like your shield, Ethan. I . . . I can't cast even a simple spell, no matter how hard I—"

Ethan stopped her gently with a hand on her shoulder.

But do skills still work? he wondered. Only one way to find out.

He summoned a shadow wraith, the dark form manifesting near Klax. It crouched to guard him, but almost immediately, a string of violet light—along with a piercing, inhuman scream—ripped through the air. The wraith shrieked and dissolved, torn apart by the blast.

"Shit," Ethan growled, seeing the aftermath. They were powerful—too strong to fight blindly. His wraith had at least three hundred HP, and he had a formidable thousand. But only a few hits would drop him. And there were two—double the firepower.

Still, they'd revealed their location. He could see them more clearly now: two vague, dark, bipedal shapes with long stalks where their heads should be, pointing down at the party.

"We . . . We could try going around," Tara whispered, eyes flicking toward the towers. "You could do Mass Hide. In this mist, we might get enough time—"

"No," Ethan interrupted. "That's what they *want*."

"What?"

He remembered hours spent as a sniper in gaming, or the war movies he'd devoured as a kid. More than any soldier, a sniper thrived on patience and cunning.

"They're snipers," he said. "Whatever magic they're using is lethal. They want us to rush in to save him, counting on that."

"B-But we can't sit here twiddling our thumbs!"

Ethan's mind raced. They were pinned, Klax was bleeding out, and the illusions around them gave no quarter.

"We need a distraction," he said through gritted teeth. "Fauna, can you heal him from here?"

Fauna wiped her tears, shaking her head. "Not like this . . . he's too far gone. I'd have to be right next to him."

"And if you go out there, they'll snipe you before you get close," Tara added, bow gripped tightly. "They aren't amateurs."

Ethan cursed. Klax was dying, they were surrounded by illusions, and there were snipers overhead.

"Damn it," he growled, clenching his fists. "We've got to buy time. We need a way to draw their fire, distract them."

Fauna's voice broke, near tears. "We can't *leave* him . . ."

"We *won't*." Ethan's single eye blazed as he turned to the Memory Spires again, focusing on the faint glimmers of snipers waiting for another chance to strike.

And that's when it hit him.

Current Spirit Cores: 300
Upgrades Available!

He grimaced. He'd never thought it'd be useful . . . until now. A new upgrade that might save Klax's life, but it was risky.

"There's something I can do," he said. "Or I think so. A way to distract them."

Tara stared, expression unreadable. "Another reckless plan, right?"

Ethan nodded, crouching low. He spotted a place behind Klax with a pile of stones.

"Tara, Fauna, stay low. Move when I signal," Ethan said, cutting Tara off. They had one shot at saving Klax, and it depended on timing and luck.

"Ethan, if you go out there—" Tara began, but he waved her off.

"Just trust me." Ethan took a steadying breath, tension coiling in his muscles. His gaze locked on the distant towers with the hidden snipers then flicked back to Klax, gargling in a puddle of his own Lycae blood.

"Just . . . run!" Klax sputtered. "Leave this . . . idiot . . . to die."

Not on your life, buddy, Ethan thought, looking at the fallen hound. *We're staying together, no matter what.*

That thought alone steeled his resolve.

"Okay," he said. "Here's what we'll do . . ."

The cold, ghostly light of the City of Illusions flickered across the sky as Ethan crouched low, heart pounding. Narrow streets, winding corridors of deception. The danger was real. Those snipers were highly trained, deadly accurate. One slip, and he'd end up like Klax—bleeding on the stones.

No place for fear. Klax's life was on the line.

They were sitting ducks if they remained. Any attempt to draw the snipers out left them vulnerable. They needed a distraction the snipers couldn't ignore.

And one skill upgrade fit perfectly.

Tara and Fauna listened in the swirling sapphire mist, the two bipedal snipers standing motionless above them.

When he finished explaining his plan, the girls exchanged disbelieving looks.

"It . . . It could work."

"Yeah. *Could*, Faun."

"It won't be perfect," Ethan agreed. "It'll be messy. But it's our best shot at saving Klax and taking them down."

He eyed his Roar skill and its new upgrade.

Roar (Grade B)
Project Roar unlocked: You can cast Roar at a designated point up to fifty meters away.

Spirit Cores to Upgrade [Roar] Skill from Grade C to B: 280
Confirm Upgrade?

He'd never tested this, but if used right, it might be enough of a distraction. "Okay. Ready?"

They nodded, and as Ethan hefted his Repulsor Shield and confirmed the upgrade, he felt Fauna tugging at his elbow.

"Ethan . . ." she murmured. "Just . . . be careful?"

He gave her a confident smirk. "I'm a walking undead tank. I can take a few hits." Then he gritted his teeth, flexing his fingers. "All right, you bastards," he whispered, feeling the familiar burn of power in his chest. "Let's see how you like this."

Scanning again, he picked out a building on the far side of the intersection—a cracked, unstable wall. If he could collapse part of it, he might create the opening he needed.

So he let it loose.

[Skill Activated: Project Roar]

The power surged through him, pinpointing the distant wall, air vibrating with sonic force.

The building shook. A deep, guttural roar erupted from the chosen spot, like the earth itself was screaming in fury; deafening, reverberating off the translucent towers. Then *CRACK!* A section of the building's wall collapsed, debris and dust spiraling upward.

The snipers snapped their attention to the destruction.

Now!

Ethan bolted from cover, Repulsor Shield flaring overhead. Not elegant, but the only defense against the deadly shots sure to come. He sprinted across the open ground while Tara provided suppressing fire from the shadows, arrows whizzing toward the snipers' perch. Fauna, meanwhile, dragged Klax to safety.

Twang—Thud! Tara's arrows lodged in the stone tower, forcing the snipers to duck. For a moment, Ethan seemed to be in the clear. Then—

WHIZZZ—CRACK!
The first shot hit Ethan's shield, but he couldn't block the entire impact.

HP: 750/950

It nearly knocked him off-balance, but he gritted his teeth, pushing through the searing pain in his arm. He heard Fauna muttering a prayer, voice trembling with worry, as he scaled a ruined building across from the snipers' tower.

The shield had blocked the worst. But—
WHIZZZ—THUNK!
A second shot grazed his leg, slicing through armor and sending a shock wave of agony.

HP: 500/950

He was already halfway down. Two more hits like that, and—
He shoved the thought away, vaulting onto the roof. Hissing with pain, he pressed on, eyes locking on the tower's base. He was almost there. The snipers were damn good, but he had one last trick.

He'd never tested this homing strike, capable of destroying obstacles under sixty STR. Appraisal had shown decay and weathering. The centuries hadn't been kind. He'd exploit that.

As two more piercing shots screamed toward him, he discarded the shield. With a determined growl, his muscles surged as he leaped into the air, body becoming a blur. The world slowed, wind howling in his ears, closing in on the snipers.

He felt them aim their final shot.

Now or never.

One shot clipped his foot, but he already had the altitude needed. He pivoted, brandishing his blade, slamming both it and Valgraiva's bulk into the tower's base. The impact rocked the entire structure, cracks webbing up its length.

For a moment, silence.

Then, with a *CRACK*, the tower collapsed. Dust and debris filled the air, cutting off the snipers' line of sight as stone crumbled under their feet, a final cry of panic lost in the roar of the falling structure. Time seemed to slow as it all crashed down in a cloud of smoke.

Ethan hit the ground hard, rolling amid swirling dust. His heart hammered, blood on his tongue. Coughing, he tried to clear his lungs, but only dust surrounded him.

"Ethan!" Fauna's voice was faint, barely heard over the chaos.

Through the smoke and sapphire dust, no one could see. Then, like a summer day parting winter clouds, the nullification field dissipated, dying away like the two summoners it had belonged to, both crushed beneath their tower.

And above them stood the triumphant warrior who'd just brought them down, hat form wriggling atop his dark host's head.

Light from the city beamed on him as he turned to his trembling companions.

If there had been any doubt, it was gone now. They were looking at a true Archon. *The* Archon.

"Wh-Why . . ." Klax groaned. "Why . . . *ngh* . . ."

"Klax!" Fauna yelped, pressing her hands to his bleeding neck, summoning as much healing power as she could.

"You . . . You foo-*guh*!"

"Enough outta you, big guy." Tara smirked, prying open the dogman's mouth to pour in their Malphus potions. "Take your medicine and be glad our Archon's kinder than most."

Meanwhile, Ethan stared at the two mewling creatures who could barely cry, lifeblood draining from their crushed veins. They were like bipedal deer, each with two long, sinuous necks that ended in a pair of eye stalks. Within these eyes, swirls of energy gathered, ready to be expelled with laser precision. . *Snipers.*

Appraisal Success!
Obscaurus
Skills: Hide, Ethereal Fade, Spectral Snipe, Summon Mana Veil,
Summon Illusion, Skitter

They'd used all their tricks to stalk and trap him, but they hadn't counted on *his* bag of tricks.

And now they're mine, Ethan thought, grabbing one by its bleeding throat, fixing on its dying eyes.

"Before you die, you're gonna be put to good use," he said.

The eyes of the obscaurus beheld a true demon before closing forever.

CHAPTER THIRTY-FIVE

Lightborn

As soon as he entered the Nerve Tower, he knew what he'd see. Even when hearing his comrades' voices fading as the flashing light took him, he didn't close his eyes.

Because one born in light did not fear the dark.

He was in the middle of a field of corpses.

The field had once been his village. He didn't remember the name.

Around him were the bodies of his friends. Luca, chewed up and broken beside his girl, Tara, her face a miasma of blood and shattered bone, throat torn out by something half man, half wolf. He wouldn't have recognized her if she weren't holding Luca's hand in death.

Mama and Papa were there too. When the house had burned in the fire wyrm's attack, Mama had thrown herself on him as a shield. Even then, as a child, the logical part of his mind had told him it was pointless.

He'd looked into her eyes as she burned, hearing the last command she'd give her only son:

"Live."

Now, he crawled out from under their calcinated bodies to see the ruins of his village. Everything was flame and stone and thatch. The creatures had come, killed, and gone, each singing one vile name as they pillaged and burned: *Archon.*

It was a name that would live in his heart forever.

Something stirred nearby. A wolf beast trapped in the rubble, claws flashing. Without thinking, he grabbed the dagger at his belt and met its charge. Fear had left him. He was pure instinct. A child had died that day, and something else had been born in that funeral pyre.

The beast shoved him outside, using its bulk to smash through the burning door, spittle spraying his face.

He could die now, join Mama and Papa. He was a baker's son—System activated two weeks ago, reading *Baker (Level 1)*. That was all he'd ever be.

Now, his knife hovered above a monstrous jaw. He'd carve it like his first loaf of bread.

He pushed off the ground, the creature's wounded arm granting him just enough advantage. He kicked the wound, heard it howl, then plunged his blade into its neck, snarling with delight as it screamed under the silent moon's gaze. Even after it stopped moving, he kept stabbing. The only screaming in the village now was his own.

Then—voices.

"That's enough, little warrior."

He didn't stop until a strong arm grabbed him, trying to shake the knife loose.

When he refused, the man holding him raised a blade to slice his arm off, muttering they didn't need this kind of crazy.

"Wait."

Another voice—a woman's—stopped everything. He looked up at her and snarled like a beast, tears threatening, refusing to glance at the charred bodies.

"Unhand him, Zestrius," the woman said. "This one's a fighter."

She seemed impressed by his kill. When his arm was freed, he fell, panting at her feet.

"Well?" she asked. "What's your name, little killer?"

He looked up, face sooty, fingers bloody, and said nothing.

"Wolf got your tongue?" the woman chuckled. Blonde hair in ringlets framed almond eyes filled with the same fire that had destroyed his home. But the smile she gave him and the silver rapier at her side showed strength enough to keep him from sobbing.

"This one's an accident waiting to happen, Carliah. Let's move on—the army's probably north by now."

She ignored her comrade. Bending lower, she licked dry lips at the panting boy.

"A boy who's lost everything at such a tender age," she said. "A child like this is exactly what we need, Garrix. Tell me, boy, if you still have a tongue in that angry little mouth, what do you *want* right now?"

He didn't hesitate, showing no emotion.

"I want to kill them," he replied, looking at the wolfman's corpse. "All of them."

The woman's smile widened.

"Good," she said. "I can work with that."

His first days in Caer Krea flashed by. The Greycloaks' trials weeded out the weak. He made friends, saw them die—or worse. Carliah threw children against man-eaters, ghouls, serpents, drakes. In her eyes, they were born into strife, and only a strong heart forged in battle survived. The boys learned or died.

She took them young. He was no exception. Some recruits thought her train-ing was cruelty. Once, she threw him in the monastery pits with three others—boys abandoned at the gates—and ordered them to fight until only one remained.

She wasn't surprised when he emerged, starving, shaking, but victorious.

"He's got a Grey spirit, all right," she'd remark at dinner. "Mark my words—that boy'll go far."

He was twenty-one when he learned the truth: a new Archon sought to dominate the world.

Its name was Gyko, already overtaking Argwyll's eastern perimeter. Overgrown thorns, sentient plant demons. Toxic clouds threading villages. Wells drying up, monsters unseen before knocking on the monastery's door.

It was time to take Krea's blood.

The ceremony was short, forced by lack of time. Carliah gathered the newest recruits who'd survived their "Grey Decades" and would now drink from the old angel's blood—the one who'd told humans they were the rightful rulers of the land under Lord Kaedmon.

He wasn't sure he believed any of it. If Kaedmon was good, why had his village burned? Why had there been no angel to save Mama, Papa, Luca, Tara? He'd never believed the guff from religious studies. All he knew was if he had a blade, he could kill monsters—kill anything.

But as he watched the ceremony, his pulse quickened. The other boys drank the silver, viscous liquid, some falling ill, some dying on the spot. Legend said 5 percent survived the angel's blood. They knew the risks, but none walked away. For them, 5 percent was better than what awaited outside. Better to die a hero than live as a slave to Argwyll's devil.

When his turn came, his feet wavered on the great hall's steps. He glanced at the fresco of Krea—fierce and regal atop Karfangg's body—and told himself his life had been dumb luck anyway. Why worry over what he couldn't control?

Little did he know how wrong he had been.

Reliving the memory now, he wanted to slap the chalice from his child self's hands.

But he was forced to watch as he guzzled the blood then collapsed, twitching on the hall's steps. His "brothers and sisters" watched, some smiling to see Commander Argent's favored child die at last.

As darkness crawled across the sky outside, and the guards moved to drag his body away, that's when it happened.

Light.

A pure, unnatural rush of lightning surged through his inert form, wrenching his vocal cords into a frenzied scream. The hall shook with it, rousing the eldest

Greys from slumber, imprinting itself on every mind present. They were hearing the voice of a legend, the voice of the reborn.

"By Kaedmon . . ." Carliah whispered.

His eyes opened—pale, blue, brilliant—as new words flashed before him:

Lightborn (Level 30)

Back then, those words were like writings on a golden door leading to paradise.

But now, seeing them in this lucid Tower dream, he recognized them for what they truly were: scrawlings on an untended grave.

In Carliah's ecstatic eyes, he saw how much of a nightmare his life would become. The trials of his youth had only been the prelude.

CHAPTER THIRTY-SIX

At the Mouth of [Madness]

Host: Valgraiva, Lord of the Damned (Level 50)
Skill Siphon:
Spectral Snipe (Grade E)
You launch a bolt of precise energy up to two hundred feet from your current location. This bolt deals two hundred points of Piercing DMG and takes sixty seconds to recharge.
Note: You must remain stationary when you use this skill.

[Upgrading Skill: Spectral Snipe (Grade E)]
Upgrade Complete!
Congratulations! You have upgraded [Spectral Snipe] from Grade E to D.

Spectral Snipe (Grade D)
Spectral Snipe can now pass through solid and ethereal matter.
Spirit Cores to Upgrade [Spectral Snipe] Skill from Grade D to C: 750

Summon Illusion (Grade E)
You concentrate to form an illusory entity from you or your target's mind. The target becomes convinced the illusion is real, although creatures with PER 50 or more can see through the deception.
Spirit Cores to Upgrade [Summon Illusion] Skill from Grade E to D: 500

Summon Mana Veil (Grade E)
You create a dense layer of fog fifty feet wide. Any targets within this fog must pass an Intelligence check of thirty or more, or be {SILENCED} for the duration they remain within the fog.
{SILENCED} targets cannot cast spells.

Spirit Cores to Upgrade [Summon Mana Veil] Skill
from Grade E to D: 500

Current Spirit Cores: 150

After recovering Klax, Ethan had spent some time plundering the skull of the obscaurus and found it rich in bounty. Forget physical loot—skills were the only treasures a demon hat needed.

His new Spectral Snipe bolt flew from the tip of his scythe and tore through the shimmering towers of the City of Illusions, phasing through their translucent walls like a ghost. The violet beam of energy, a perfect combination of the abilities he had ripped from the possessed snipers, pierced the skull of one of the hidden obscaurus. The creature's glistening black eyes bulged in surprise as its head exploded in a spray of ghostly ichor. Ethan smirked. He was a long-ranged Grim Reaper now.

"Gotcha," he muttered.

This part of the city was practically full of them—and it looked like they worked in pairs, covering every alley and side street leading to the city core and the Nerve Tower that loomed over them all. Whatever mystic force compelled them to defend this place clearly hadn't accounted for a countersniper to start clipping them one by one.

Ethan leaned back against the cracked stone wall of the alley they were hiding in, listening for any sign of movement from the other towers. He could sense the obscaurus lurking in their Memory Spires above, but with his newly acquired sniping ability, combined with his Ethereal Form shift, they were no match for him. He could shoot through walls, through stone, through whatever they tried to hide behind. Spending the five hundred Cores from the two snipers he'd first felled had gotten him another grade in the skill already, and had built him the perfect fantasy rail gun.

"I never thought I'd say this," Ethan muttered, flexing his fingers as the power surged through him, "but all those years playing *Battlefield* and *Arma* in high school are finally paying off."

From their hiding spot, Tara peered around the corner. "You took down another one?"

Ethan nodded. "That's five. Pretty sure the last one's scrambling around up there like a headless chicken. Doesn't even know I'm about to nail him."

He concentrated again, letting the energy flow through his veins. In Ethereal Form, the world looked different. Layers of reality peeled back, and everything seemed to shimmer. The walls of the Memory Spires flickered, becoming almost transparent, and the faint outline of the final obscaurus sniper came into view, crouching in the shadows.

"Gotcha," he whispered again, lifting his sword.

With a thought, he phased through the stone wall, releasing a bolt of violet light that shot straight through the sniper's chest. The creature jerked up, its cloaking ability failing as it fell limply to the ground, its ghostly form dissipating into the air.

"Snipers down," Ethan said, stepping out of the alley with a grin. "Nerve Tower, here we come."

Tara gave him a dry smile, her sharp eyes glittering with approval. "Not bad, chief."

Fauna, her floppy ears twitching anxiously, looked up at the massive ivory spire of the Nerve Tower that loomed ahead. The tower stretched into the sky, its organic shape pulsating faintly, as if it were a living thing. Faces drifted across the swirling aurora borealis in the skies above, watching them from the ever-shifting clouds.

"They're still watching us," Fauna said quietly, her voice tinged with dread. "The dreamstriders. They know what we're doing."

"They always know," Ethan replied, glancing up at the sapphire-white manta rays that circled above them in eerie silence. "Let them watch. We've got a job to do."

They took their final steps toward their looming destiny: the great organic tower that pulsed with a life of its own. At regular intervals, its physical form would shimmer and bleed into the twilight sky of the city before returning again, pulsing like a beating heart at the center of an organic being.

Klax brought up the rear, silent and resolute. In the wake of his near-death experience, he had been as silent as a rock, saying nothing but a mumbled thank you to Fauna before rejecting anyone who tried to talk to him—and would say nothing when prompted to explain what exactly he'd seen and heard beyond what everyone already suspected.

Suddenly, the city seemed so much more silent.

The four of them moved cautiously through the dreamlike city streets, the translucent spires reflecting shimmering lights that seemed to flicker in and out of reality. Pale, ghostly figures—the memories of past lives—watched them from the shadows, their hollow eyes unblinking. It was as though the city itself were alive, a place where memories held sway over reality.

And at the base of the Nerve Tower, Klax suddenly stopped.

"Go on without me," he said, his voice low and gravelly.

Ethan turned, his brows furrowing. Klax's usually proud and towering figure was slouched, his eyes downcast, as if the weight of the world had fallen on his shoulders.

"I've done what I promised to do—I got you to this tower. Leave me here to cover your escape. And then let my spirit finally rest in this place. It is as good a grave as any."

Ethan whirled on the wolf. "What are you talking about?"

Klax shook his head, refusing to meet anyone's gaze. "I've been nothing but a liability. I was tricked back there—those snipers had me running in circles like a fool. You'd all be better off without me."

Fauna reached out, her eyes wide with concern. "Klax, that's not true. You've been—"

"Enough," Klax snapped, his voice sharp with self-loathing. "I couldn't even protect you when you needed me. And now . . . look at me. I'm nothing compared to what I used to be."

Tara stood off to the side, her eyes narrowing, but she remained silent. She seemed aloof, but Ethan could see how her fingers twitched, as if holding herself back from saying something harsh.

Ethan stepped forward, his gaze steady as he looked up at the Lycae warrior. "Klax, we need you. You're not a liability. You're our friend—and more than that, you're one of the strongest warriors I've ever known."

Klax let out a bitter laugh. "Strong? Look at me now, Ethan. I'm not the warrior I used to be. I was so easily fooled; I've been dragging you down."

Ethan stared at him for a long moment before a thought sparked in his mind. He extended his hand, summoning his illusory powers.

A shimmering image appeared in front of them—a vision of Klax as Ethan remembered him from when they first met. Proud, regal, a warrior standing tall against an entire army. The Klax in the illusion was unyielding, his eyes blazing with determination as he fought to protect his people. Every movement was filled with purpose, every swing of his blade filled with strength.

"This is the Klax I know," Ethan said softly, his voice cutting through the night air. "The warrior who fought for his people. The warrior who stood against impossible odds and never gave up. You think you've lost your way, but *that* warrior is still in there. You're more important to us than you realize."

Klax stared at the illusion, his breath catching in his throat. The proud Lycae in the image fought with a ferocity and resolve that seemed to light a fire within Klax's own soul. His eyes softened, and he looked at Ethan with a mixture of gratitude and sorrow.

"I . . . I don't know if I can be that warrior again," he whispered.

"You don't have to be," Ethan replied, stepping closer. "You just have to be here. With us. We can't do this without you, Klax. None of us can. And besides, Jun'Ei's waiting to see her warrior return to her."

Fauna nodded vigorously, her eyes shimmering with unshed tears. "Please, Klax. Stay with us."

Klax looked between them, the weight of his self-doubt beginning to lift as the memory of who he once was filled him with a newfound sense of purpose. Slowly, he straightened, his towering form once again taking on that regal stance Ethan had first seen in him.

"All right," he said, his voice steady. "I'll stay."

Ethan smiled, clapping him on the shoulder. "Good. Because I wasn't planning on losing you, big guy."

Tara, still aloof, merely shrugged. "If we're done with the drama, let's move. We've got a tower to climb."

The group turned to face the towering spire of the Nerve Tower, its surface pulsating like the skin of some great living creature. The dreamstriders circled above them, their sapphire-white bodies flickering in the light of the aurora, unblinking eyes following the party's every move.

As they approached the entrance, Fauna's voice broke the tense silence.

"There's powerful magic inside," she whispered. "Illusions that will *test* us. We need to be careful."

Ethan glanced up at its towering height, a chill running down his spine. "What do you mean, 'test us'?"

Fauna hesitated before answering, her voice trembling. "It's said the Nerve Tower is where memories and dreams collide. The deeper we go, the more the lines between reality and illusion blur. We could face our worst fears . . . or our greatest desires."

Ethan frowned. "So we're walking into a place where we might not even be able to trust what we see?"

Fauna nodded. "Exactly. And the dreamstriders . . . they're watching us. They know we're going in there. It's like they're . . . waiting."

Tara smirked, tightening her grip on her bow. "Let 'em wait. I'm ready for whatever they throw at us."

Klax, standing taller now, shoulders squared, grunted in agreement. "We'll make it through. *Together.*"

Ethan took a deep breath, steeling himself as they stepped forward, the shadows of the Nerve Tower swallowing them whole. The entrance yawned before them like the maw of a great beast, and as they crossed the threshold, the dreamstriders watched in eerie silence, their ghostly forms flickering in the distance like sentinels standing vigil over a group of strangers walking to their graves.

"Ready?" he asked his party.

They nodded, though he could see the fear gripping them. All of them knew that whatever awaited them inside was only the penultimate act of this delve.

Ethan took one last look up at the tip of the tower, trying to sense the energy of his old nemesis up there, knowing the old bastard was probably doing the same. Then, without another moment's hesitation, he walked through the sticky organic compound of the tower's base.

He wasn't going to keep the Lightborn waiting.

CHAPTER THIRTY-SEVEN

[Warrior] of Light

He stood alone in the training courtyard, the oppressive midday sun casting long shadows across the cracked stone. His muscles ached, drenched in sweat, as he thrust his blade into the open air again and again. The rhythm of his movements was the only thing keeping his mind from unraveling. Each strike was precise, every motion deliberate, but even now, at the height of his training, he couldn't shake the growing weight pressing on his shoulders.

"Artorious! Focus!" Carliah barked from behind him, her voice sharp, cutting through the haze of exhaustion.

Artorious gritted his teeth and swung the blade with renewed vigor, carving through the illusion of his enemy in front of him. It wasn't enough. He had to be faster, stronger. Every time he closed his eyes, he saw them—the endless hordes of monsters unleashed by Gyko, the Archon of Decay, who ruled the world through a reign of terror that had lasted for decades. Her monsters, grown from her vile Darkseed, ravaged the lands, leaving nothing but ash and death in their wake.

Artorious couldn't escape it. He had been chosen as a Lightborn for this purpose—to bring an end to Gyko's tyranny. And yet, every lesson, every drill, felt like a drop in an ocean of despair. He was young, in his twenties, barely a man, but already the weight of the world seemed to bear down on him. The expectations of the Greycloaks, his comrades, his mentor . . . all of it was suffocating.

As he continued to train, he could hear the distant screams. The world outside the training grounds was crumbling, and he was supposed to be the one to save it.

The Nerve Tower touched his mind, fumbling with his thoughts.

Within its grip, he knew he must resist. He knew what he was seeing was a lie plucked from his mind. Nothing but restless dreams that had tormented him since his youth.

He knew . . . and yet, he could not shut the fortress of his mind.

And the Nerve Tower's piercing white claws threaded themselves through its walls.

The wind howled through the valley, carrying with it the stench of rot. Artorious stood at the forefront of the Greycloaks, their silver armor gleaming against the backdrop of Argwyll's decaying landscape. He had grown into the role of Lightborn by now, his once uncertain heart now hardened, his eyes cold, devoid of the compassion they once held.

The monster army stretched out before them, grotesque creatures of all shapes and sizes. Some had grown limbs that shouldn't exist; others slithered or scuttled with eerie precision. All of them bore the twisted mark of Gyko, their once human forms corrupted by the Darkseed that she had planted within them.

"Lightborn, we're ready on your command," said Lydia, his second-in-command. Her voice was steady, but Artorious could hear the underlying tremor. She was one of the few who still had hope in their cause.

"Hold the line," Artorious replied, his voice cold and detached.

He raised his onixia blade, the edge shimmering with the light that had been infused into it during his training. Carliah had given it to him on his twenty-fifth birthday. "A present," she'd said, the glint of righteous fury burning in her eyes, "that you will use to end this war. Let the last Archon fall to the blood of her brethren."

The Greycloaks braced themselves, forming a defensive wall, shields raised. Artorious could sense the weight of every soul behind him—dozens of men and women, warriors who had followed him into battle countless times.

And yet, in front of them stood their enemies. A horde of hybrid demons had descended on the town of Blackreach, one of the last outposts in Westerweald not already overrun. They'd known this would be the army's next stop. He'd known— with a strange certainty that even he couldn't understand—that Gyko's aim was to cut through the realm toward Caer Krea and deal with the old enemies of her kind.

But she didn't know the Lightborn was back. None of them did.

Until now.

"Today, we strike a blow for humanity, Greycloaks!" he bellowed. "Men and women of Argwyll, are you with me?!"

He charged. The Greycloaks followed.

The battle was chaos. Artorious slashed and cleaved through the monstrosities with precision, his onixia blade cutting through their thick, mutated flesh as though it were butter. The creatures screamed as they fell, their bodies writhing and convulsing as they died. The Greycloaks fought valiantly beside him, but the army was relentless, an unending tide of decay and corruption.

"Artorious!" Lydia shouted through the din. "Gyko's not just planting seeds in the monsters. The humans, too . . . She's . . . She's infecting them!"

Artorious faltered for a moment. His eyes darted to the nearby villagers, humans who had been cowering behind makeshift barricades, watching in terror. The Darkseed. It was within them. The monster tide had pushed through and already infected them. He could sense it, feel its vile presence writhing in their hearts, ready to burst forth. Gyko had hidden her seeds in the bodies of humans, waiting for the perfect moment to sprout her influence from within them.

His blood ran cold.

"They're compromised," Artorious said, his voice empty. He had sensed this corruption in humans before, but it was becoming more frequent now. Gyko's influence was spreading, reaching even the most innocent of souls. "We can't leave them alive."

"But—"

"No time for *buts*," Artorious snapped. "We have to kill them."

Lydia hesitated, her face twisting with grief as she looked at the terrified humans. "We're supposed to be protecting them . . ."

"We protect the world by stopping Gyko. If that means killing innocents, then so be it." The words felt like ashes on his tongue, but he said them anyway. There was no place for mercy here. Not when the stakes were this high.

He could feel Lydia's eyes on him as he raised his sword and plunged it into the nearest villager. The man screamed, his eyes wide with terror as the blade pierced his heart. Blood splattered across the stone ground. As the man fell, his body convulsed, and a small tendril of black vine erupted from his chest—proving that Artorious had been right.

The Darkseed was real.

One by one, the villagers fell. Men, women, children—none were spared. Artorious cut them down with the same cold efficiency he had used against the monsters. Every strike felt heavier, every scream louder, but he forced himself to ignore it. He had to. Gyko's influence had to be eradicated, no matter the cost.

As he slashed through the final corrupted human, his blade gleaming with their blood, he realized that he had become numb. He had grown used to the sight of blood, to the cries for mercy.

And somewhere deep inside him, something broke.

The mists of his memory parted once more, and he saw himself at the top of Caer Krea's balcony, shoulders hunched and face tinged with bloodless shame.

And as usual, just when he thought he was at his lowest point, she came along.

"You did the right thing, you know."

He didn't even need to turn around. He knew who was there; like a walking shadow, she seemed stuck to his back. That had been a recurring theme throughout his entire life. Carliah Argent had a way of . . . creeping up on him, like a wraith born from his own insecurities.

"Lydia is one of us," he told the uncaring, dead sky around the fortress. "She looked at me like I was . . . a monster."

"Silly girl. She's too weak to finish this fight," came the reply. "We do not abide weakness in our ranks, Lightborn. We can't afford to. I'll tell you again, Arty: you should boot that girl from your squadron."

He frowned. But he said nothing.

"The Darkseed is an insidious tool of our enemy," Carliah went on, her faith in her words totally unshakable. "Mercy is not a virtue we can afford in these dark days. Do not despair, however. The histories shall tell only of our bravery in these trying times."

He scowled at her. "You think the historians will overlook the massacre today? The deaths of that entire village—of human beings—under my watch?"

Carliah smiled. "You're still young, Artorious. Haven't you understood it yet? We are the vanguard of humanity's victory. The beacon of hope for a better future. We practically own the historians. Hell, we own this world."

He glanced at the change that had come over her. She looked out into the dark horizon at the gathering clouds of toxic dust with . . . a kind of feverish glee.

The smile of a fanatic was painted on her face.

"By right of divine mandate," she continued in a hallowed whisper. "Every human being in this realm owes us their lives. Their lives, and those of their children, and their children's children. When this Archon dies, we shall collect our debt."

"What?" he stammered. It was all he could say. And, as usual, she looked down on him as if he still were the naive child he was when she'd first found him.

"You think our jobs will be over once this last war ends?" she asked him. "No, Arty. Our glory days are only just beginning. With the last Archon dead, all of monsterkind shall finally be vanquished. Soon, humanity will be bereft of purpose. They will need true, strong leadership to guide them toward the right path—under Kaedmon's eyes. Who better than we, their sacred guardians and stewards?"

She stroked his hand with a thin but firm finger. It was possible she couldn't see the abject horror in his eyes as he listened to and processed her words.

It was also entirely possible that she saw his reaction in its entirety. And she didn't care.

"All because of you, dear Arty," she said with a smirk. "I promise you this: your sacrifice shall not go to waste. Not this time. When the Archon falls and your Lightborn spirit goes with it, I shall ensure this world is put on the right course."

She left him there after that, and he stared back out at the cold waste of the world he was supposed to save.

Somehow, it had just gotten a lot darker.

CHAPTER THIRTY-EIGHT

Back to [Reality]

Ethan felt his heart thud as they stepped into the yawning entrance of the Nerve Tower. His senses screamed at him. The air was thick with magic, almost alive, pressing down on him like a predator lurking just beyond sight. Everything about this place felt wrong, like it wasn't a building but some living thing waiting to devour them. His five eyes flickered in the dim light, scanning the vast, pulsing walls. They weren't alone here.

"Stay close," he muttered to Klax, Tara, and Fauna. His voice was tight, and his hands gripped the hilt of his mithril scythe as though it was the only real thing in the room.

Suddenly, a blinding light shot through the air, searing across his vision. Ethan threw up a hand to shield himself as the world seemed to split open.

DELVE CHALLENGE: MEMORY PRISM
Activated!

"What the hell does that mean?" Ethan shouted, but before anyone could answer, Klax, Fauna, and Tara were gone. His entire world blinked out of existence.

Party Separation in Progress . . .

Ethan, Sys said, its voice becoming more and more faint by the second, **whatever happens, don't forge—**

Ethan blinked once, then twice.

And after the second blink, the world of Argwyll melted away.

Fluorescent lights buzzed overhead, filling his ears with their droning hum. He squinted at the harsh light, wincing as he rubbed his tired eyes. In front of him was a computer screen, its cold blue light illuminating rows upon rows of numbers and financial projections. His fingers tapped the keyboard methodically, almost mechanically, as though they had never stopped.

An email pinged in the corner of his screen.

To: Ethan Graham
From: Brian Reynolds, Senior Tax Manager
Subject: Meeting Reminder

Ethan froze, his breath catching in his throat.

What . . . the hell?

His heart pounded as he leaned back in his chair, staring at the email. The smell of burnt coffee and the hum of printers filled the air—familiar, suffocating, like a heavy blanket wrapped around his chest. He glanced down at his hands, pale and human. Five fingers. No scythe. No claws. Just regular, mundane fingers tapping away at a keyboard.

Around him, the chatter of coworkers filled the office. Phones rang. Printers spat out paper after paper. His cubicle stretched out in front of him like a prison, the walls beige and sterile. There was nothing here. No battle. No monsters. Just spreadsheets and emails.

His stomach churned.

Had it all been a dream?

He blinked hard, trying to reset himself, to make sense of what was happening. He reached up to rub his eyes, but when he opened them again, he was still there. Still in the office. Still trapped in the same monotonous life. This had to be some kind of delusion, right? Maybe he'd just fallen asleep at his desk again.

Ethan shook his head and glanced at the clock on his screen. Ten minutes until his next meeting. Ten minutes until he had to sit in a room and listen to his boss drone on about client projections, revenue reports, and tax filings.

He hated meetings.

With a sigh, Ethan turned back to his screen, fingers tapping at the keyboard, scrolling through endless numbers. Every second that passed felt like a year. He could feel the dull ache building behind his eyes, the pressure of his own life bearing down on him again. It was suffocating. The same suffocating pressure he had felt every day before . . .

Before what?

Before Argwyll.

His chest tightened as he remembered the feeling of wind rushing past him as he charged into battle. The thrill of summoning his powers. The weight of the scythe in his hands. The laughter of his companions. The feeling of actually making a difference in a world where everything mattered.

It was impossible.

Had it all been a dream?

"Ethan," came a sharp voice from behind him.

He turned to see Brian Reynolds, his boss, standing in the doorway of his cubicle. The man's suit was pressed perfectly, not a wrinkle in sight. His hair was slicked back, his grin smug, and his eyes condescending. Everything about him made Ethan's skin crawl.

"Don't forget the meeting in fifteen minutes," Brian said, his voice dripping with superiority. "Client's been on our backs all month. We need those projections—today."

"Yeah, I got it," Ethan muttered, turning back to his screen. He felt sick. Everything about this place felt wrong, even though it was so familiar.

Brian narrowed his eyes. "I don't think you understand the pressure we're under here, Ethan. This is your job. People are counting on you."

Ethan's stomach twisted. *Counting on you.* He'd heard that before, in Argwyll. From Klax, from Tara, from Fauna. The people who had fought beside him and trusted him with their lives. They counted on him.

"Yeah," Ethan said again, barely hearing his own voice. "I got it."

Brian walked off, leaving Ethan alone in his cubicle. He stared at the screen in front of him, the numbers blurring together, the hum of the office growing louder and louder until it felt like it was vibrating in his skull.

This is your life. This is stability. No war, no fighting. No one depends on you for anything but this. Just do what you're told.

It's safe here.

No monsters. No chaos. No fear.

Ethan's fingers trembled as they hovered over the keyboard. His vision swam, the words on the screen blurring as his mind raced.

Argwyll *had* been real. He knew it. It had to be. The rush of the delves, the thrill of fighting, the bonds he had formed with Klax, Tara, and Fauna—it had felt more real than this sterile, suffocating life.

But the thought gnawed at him: Wasn't this safer? Easier?

He glanced down at his desk, his eyes falling on a pen lying there. Before he knew what he was doing, he grabbed it and jammed the tip into his fingertip, hard enough to draw blood.

The sharp pain shot through him, and for a brief moment, everything snapped into focus. Blood welled up from the tiny wound, a single drop sliding down his finger and staining the paper on his desk.

He felt the pain. *This* was real. He was here.

And yet . . .

His eyes fell to his other hand, still clutching the pen, and something glinted between his fingers. Something that didn't belong here. Ethan opened his hand, revealing a small object.

It was the memory rune.

The intricate silvery threads glowed faintly, shimmering in the sterile office light. It was the same one that Lamphrey had given him before they entered the City of Illusions.

He blinked, his heart pounding in his chest. This couldn't be real. None of this could be real. The office, the numbers, the meetings. This wasn't who he was anymore.

"I want it all. Even the shit stuff," Ethan whispered, his voice shaky but determined. His grip tightened on the memory rune as the image of Fauna singing karaoke at Klax's party blazed bright in his mind and forced a smile to his face. "Better to reign in hell than serve in heaven."

As soon as the words left his lips, the world around him began to twist and warp. The cubicles shimmered like heat waves, the buzzing of the office lights growing louder and more distorted. The walls around him began to melt away, revealing a void of shimmering darkness.

And then, standing in the middle of that void, was a figure.

It was him.

Or at least, it looked like him. The figure had Ethan's face, his build, his posture. But the eyes were empty, cold, devoid of any humanity. It moved with an unnatural grace, stepping toward him with a predatory air, hands reaching out toward his throat.

Appraisal Complete!
Nervestalker (Spirit)
HP: 10/10

Ethan barely had time to react. The figure lunged, its fingers extended like talons. He raised his scythe just in time, the blade catching the creature's arm with a metallic clang. The force of the blow sent Ethan stumbling back, his heart racing as the creature advanced again, relentless.

"Get the fuck away from me!" Ethan growled, swinging his scythe in a wide arc.

The nervestalker dodged, its movements fluid and unnatural. It circled him, eyes locked on his every move, waiting for an opening. Ethan gritted his teeth, his grip tightening on the scythe as he prepared for the next attack.

The creature lunged again, faster this time. Ethan ducked, rolling to the side just as the nervestalker's fingers grazed his throat. He swung his scythe upward, catching the creature in the side. It staggered, but only for a moment.

"You think I'm afraid of my past?" he asked the reeling creature. "Let me give you your answer."

He brought the scythe down with all his strength, channeling a Twilight Edge into his attack for good measure—more to add insult to injury than anything else. The blade sliced clean through the creature's neck, sending its head tumbling to the ground. The body stood for a moment longer, then collapsed in a heap of black smoke.

He hoped the insidious little thing had felt that.

Spirit Cores: +500

Ethan stood there, panting, his heart hammering in his chest. The void around him began to dissolve, the darkness giving way to the familiar walls of the Nerve Tower. He blinked, his breath coming in ragged gasps as the weight of the battle slowly lifted.

He had made it out.

But he was moving. The Tower wasn't through playing its little tricks yet. He felt the ground of his old office space give out from under him, and had just enough presence of mind to upgrade one skill.

[Upgrading Skill: Summon Mana Veil (Grade E)]
Upgrade Complete!
Congratulations! You have upgraded [Summon Mana Veil] from Grade E to D.

Summon Mana Veil (Grade D)
You create a dense layer of fog fifty feet wide. Any targets within this fog must pass an Intelligence check of fifty or more, or be {SILENCED} for the duration they remain within the fog.
{SILENCED} targets cannot cast spells.

Current Spirit Cores: 350

He'd gotten the sense that this little nervestalker was the one summoning the illusions in this place, and there was probably a whole brood of them out there, feasting on the minds of any delvers who were trying to reach the apex of their tower. But they were spellcasters; of that, Ethan was certain.

They could play their little tricks. Ethan had his own up his sleeve.

Suddenly, the air around him shifted again, the familiar sensation of magic warping reality pulling him under. The tower, the stone, the cold—everything vanished in an instant, replaced by something softer, something warmer.

Flowers, trees, a meadow.

Ethan blinked, disoriented by the sudden change. He stood in a field, the smell of fresh blossoms filling the air. The sun shone brightly overhead, birds chirped in the distance, and the gentle breeze rustled the leaves of the trees surrounding the meadow.

But this wasn't his dream.

And as his eyes blinked through the haze of the Nerve Tower's illusory veil, he saw a familiar figure sitting down to have dinner with their family.

"Fauna?"

Ethan blinked, his eyes adjusting to the soft, golden light that filled the world around him. A breeze swept through the meadow, carrying with it the scent of cherry blossoms. The pink petals danced through the air, twirling lazily before falling gently to the ground. The sun was setting behind the hills, casting long shadows over the vibrant green grass. In the distance, the laughter of children rang out, their voices mingling with the rustling of leaves and the chirping of birds.

It was beautiful. Perfect, even. But it was wrong. Ethan's heart sank as he realized where he was—and who he was looking at in the midst of this painting of beauty.

Fauna. And her family.

The Hopla mage sat at a small wooden table in the middle of the meadow, surrounded by her family. Her brothers and sisters were there, laughing and passing around plates of food. Her parents sat at the head of the table, smiling warmly at their children. It was a scene out of a dream—one that Ethan knew could never be real. He watched as Fauna chatted with her siblings, her face lit with joy and peace. She hadn't looked this carefree in all the time he'd known her.

And that was what made it so hard to watch.

"Damn it . . ." Ethan muttered under his breath, gripping the handle of his scythe. He knew what he had to do, but it felt wrong to disrupt something so peaceful, so . . . perfect. The truth, though, was that this was another Memory Prism. Another trap designed to hold them in a dream. To keep them from moving forward.

He sighed heavily, running a hand through his hair. He didn't want to do this, but they couldn't stay here. She couldn't stay here.

Fauna deserved more than a pretty illusion.

Ethan stepped forward, the grass crunching softly under his feet as he approached the table. None of the others seemed to notice him, too wrapped up in their conversations. He watched as Fauna laughed at one of her brother's jokes, her eyes shining with happiness. His chest tightened. She hadn't been this happy in years, maybe ever.

But this wasn't real.

With a deep breath, Ethan reached into his magical reserves, summoning a veil of mana. He spread it out before him, letting the shimmering energy ripple through the air like a curtain. The edges of the dream began to flicker and fade as the mana veil disrupted the illusion, revealing the truth hidden beneath.

On a nearby cherry blossom tree, perched high on one of the branches, was a dark, thin figure. Its body was wrapped in shadow, its long, spindly arms and legs blending into the darkness. Its eyes, glowing faintly with a sinister light, were fixed on Fauna and her family. A nervestalker.

Ethan's jaw tightened as he raised his scythe, the blade gleaming in the golden light of the dream. He aimed the tip of the weapon at the creature, ready to strike it down with a well-aimed Spectral Snipe.

"Stand still, you little bastard . . . I got you . . ."

But before he could release his attack, a soft voice stopped him.

"Ethan."

He turned to see Fauna standing beside him, her usual timid expression replaced with something else—something deeper. There was sadness in her eyes, but also a kind of acceptance.

"Fauna, this is a dream," Ethan said gently. "You need to wake up. This isn't real."

"I know," Fauna whispered, her voice barely audible over the sound of the wind rustling through the cherry blossoms. She glanced back at the table, at her family still laughing and talking as if nothing had changed. "I know it's not real."

Ethan blinked, surprised. "You . . . You know?"

Fauna nodded, her gaze soft as she watched her parents and siblings. "I just . . . I wanted to enjoy it a little longer. Just for a moment. It's been so long since I've seen them like this. Since I've . . . felt this." Her voice trembled slightly as she spoke, but there was a quiet strength behind it.

Ethan's throat tightened. "Fauna . . ."

"They've been gone for so long," she continued, her eyes misting over with tears. "But it's okay. I needed to say goodbye. Properly, this time."

"Faun! Oh, Faaaun! Come back to us, you silly hare! Max is about to show us another trick! And Dorreen will be coming home from the farm tonight. We'll have neep and lentil soup, and a dash of moonradish to sweeten things up!"

Her parents were calling her name from the table, waving her over to join them. Fauna hesitated, her hands trembling as she took a step toward them.

"Okay," she said, wiping away a stray tear. "I'm coming."

Ethan reached out, placing a hand on her shoulder. "You don't have to do this alone."

Fauna looked up at him, her eyes filled with gratitude. She smiled softly. "Thank you, Ethan. But this is something I need to do. On my own."

With a deep breath, Fauna turned back to her family. She walked toward them slowly, her footsteps light on the grass, as if afraid the dream might shatter at any moment. When she reached the table, her parents rose to meet her, their faces glowing with warmth and love.

Even if it was a lie, it was a lie so perfectly conceived that she couldn't feel any hatred for the creature that had spawned it. The creature that was currently stalking toward her.

"Faun . . ." Ethan cautioned.

Fauna hesitated for only a second before stepping forward and wrapping her arms around them, hugging them tightly. Her brothers and sisters joined in, forming a circle of love around her, their laughter and joy echoing through the meadow.

"I love you," Fauna whispered, her voice barely audible. "I'll always love you."

Tears streamed down her cheeks as she held them, but when she pulled back, there was a new resolve in her eyes.

She took a step back, her hands raised. Her family continued to smile at her, but there was something in their eyes now—something hollow. Faint. Like a candle flickering out. Fauna's expression hardened, then, without a word, she began to chant.

Flames flickered at the tips of her fingers, growing hotter and brighter with each passing second. The wind picked up, swirling around her in a vortex of heat and fire. Closing her eyes, she took one last breath, and let the fire loose.

The flames roared to life, consuming the table, the field, and the cherry blossom trees. The nervestalker screeched as the fire engulfed it, its shadowy form writhing and twisting in agony before it was reduced to ash.

The meadow, once so vibrant and alive, was now a charred wasteland. The cherry blossoms were gone, replaced by scorched earth and smoldering trees. Fauna stood at the center of it all, her face streaked with tears but her eyes clear and focused.

And at her feet lay the nervestalker, its thin limbs burned away to cinders beneath her feet.

Ethan approached her slowly, his heart heavy with the weight of what she'd just done. He placed a hand on her shoulder, offering silent comfort.

Fauna looked up at him, her eyes still glistening with unshed tears. But there was a strength there now, a determination he hadn't seen in her before.

"I'm ready to move on," she said softly. "I've spent so long holding on to the past. To memories that can never be real again. But I have a world to live for now. I have a future to fight for."

Ethan squeezed her shoulder gently. "Those kids back in Sanctum need you, after all."

She smiled up at him, her expression softening. "And I need them, I think. Just like I need you, Klax, and Tara."

Ethan smiled back, but before he could say anything, the dream world around them began to shift. The blackened wasteland blurred, the edges of reality starting to dissolve into nothingness.

"Find them, Ethan," Fauna's voice echoed. "Find them . . . and let's go to the top . . . together."

Fauna's form began to fade as well, her body becoming translucent, like a ghost slipping away into the night. "Ethan!" she shouted, but the darkness swallowed him whole.

He was falling, spinning through the void, the weight of reality pulling him deeper into the unknown. Fauna's voice echoed in the distance, fading away as he was dragged further and further from the dream.

His chest tightened, his mind racing as he tried to make sense of what had just happened. The Memory Prism had taken Fauna's deepest pain and tried to trap her there, to keep her locked in her own grief. But she had broken free. She had chosen to let go of the past and embrace the future.

Ethan didn't know where he was headed next, but one thing was clear.

This fight was far from over.

CHAPTER THIRTY-NINE

[Hero] of Light

The years became blurs of fury mixed with the motions of his sword.

Soon, it became mechanical. Nothing more than an instinct. He put down hybrids, corrupted beasts, and Darkseed-infected humans with just as much prejudice as the other. And after a while, he realized he'd stopped even thinking about his skills increasing anymore, or his System telling him how much of a hero he was.

When he was a boy, there'd been some small joy in that—in watching the numbers increase, even if their fluctuations seemed arbitrary.

Now, he looked on them as one looks at drops of frozen rain—with passing curiosity only.

Sometimes, they were a useful shield against the killing of those who cowered before him. Women, children, domesticated pets, even one or two Greycloaks themselves who had been infected. Where Gyko's armies went, her Darkseed went with her. And they knew she couldn't be slain until her taint was cleansed from the bodies of all she touched.

Lydia had come down with the infection during his thirtieth winter, during the Cleansing of Gallant—a village of little strategic importance in the Northern Heartlands. He'd put her down himself. She hadn't resisted.

"Do it, Art . . ." she'd said as she dropped her blade and clawed at her face, talons appearing where her once silken hands were. "End . . . it . . ."

There'd been no tears in the aftermath. She had been burned in a pyre with the rest of the villagers they'd cleansed that day. He'd watched, numb to the world, until Carliah had placed her firm hand on his shoulder.

"Remember what we're fighting for," she'd told him again—that familiar tune she loved to whistle in the dark abyss this world had become since Gyko's ascendance. "This is the final stand. The last Archon. And that makes you the last Lightborn."

Her words had been distant—like echoes down a dark, abandoned tunnel stretching on into nothing.

"You'll be a hero they speak of until the end of time itself," his commander had continued before marching off to oversee the burning of another heap of corrupted village folk. "Kaedmon gave us an angel as our first Lightborn. It is fitting that a human should be his last."

Artorious had remained by the funeral pyre as more bodies were tossed in screaming heaps onto its wooden beams. He'd watched the flames lick at flesh, burning away the disease inside the bodies, until his eyes settled on the spot where Lydia's ashen skull stared back at him with hollowed-out eyes. He'd stayed there till the flames turned to dust and sent a column of smoke spiraling into the uncaring night sky.

If Kaedmon was up there, he hoped he was watching.

Battles became second nature. Death, a minor inconvenience.

He and the Greys broke the backs of Gyko's invasion force at Rowan's Ridge—a series of mountain passes that bordered Westerweald with the Reach, Argwyll's eastern region. It was a battle, they said, presided over by Kaedmon and blessed in his name. They had lain in wait for the Archon's forces, knowing she had sent all her reinforcements from the Reaches to claim Westerweald once and for all. This, Carliah had told them, was the chance to finally turn this war in their favor.

As the Greycloaks surged along the mountaintops, their ranks bolstered by the volunteer forces of King Lysandus III, it was said that angels could be seen cheering them on from the heavens.

But the Lightborn had no need for angels, nor any kind of divine intervention. He flew like a wildling into the ranks of the plant monsters and hybrid vanguard of the enemy, breaking them before they had a chance to push toward Caer Krea. In the far distance, the capital of Lucent stood tall and proud, having withstood siege after devastating siege over the past few months. The toxic plumes of Gyko's corruption had long since been cleared away by the efforts of the Greycloak mages. With the Lightborn at the head of their armies, they were unstoppable.

He'd lost count of how many monsters he'd slain. How many people. He hadn't even tried keeping track. He no longer even looked at his System updates. The obscene "Congratulations!" he received for every kill and the Spirit Core counter increase meant as little to him now as Carliah's praise. He wasn't doing this for them. He wasn't even doing this for himself.

At the battle's climax, he stood atop a mountain of hybrid corpses and stared into the fading ranks of the enemy. They stared back, hatred mingling with terror in their eyes. All he had to do was lift his sword, and they turned tail and ran.

"Into them!" Carliah cried out from his rear. "Press the advantage! Leave none alive!"

He watched them run for their lives, scrambling down the mountains as they were riddled with crossbow bolts and wildfire from the mages. Those who were wounded crawled toward a salvation that would never come. Yet they crawled all the same, their entrails smeared across the pallid earth.

It was like watching the closing act of some cheap play unfold before him. There he was—the hero—standing with his triumphant army as they smashed the enemy lines and clinched victory by sheer force of arms. The stories would paint him as gliding above them all, singing hymns to Kaedmon as they split open the lesser races of the world.

The reality was that he simply stood and watched the end come like a lucid dream—the dream of a child whose parents had been slaughtered by the very same monsters who were now dying before him.

But that boy was gone. Perhaps he'd never really existed.

He looked into the hordes of dying creatures and felt the rain that had started to batter the bloodied ground beneath him. It settled on his skin like a thin, watery veil, washing away the blood that covered his face and hands but not eroding the simple truth he had been granted on this hill of death:

Artorious had died a long time ago. He was the Lightborn, now.

The final battle had come.

The air around the Ashfall Mountains was thick with dust and smoke. Around him, green vines coiled around his brothers and sisters as Gyko made her final stand among her servants.

From the ruined quarry where she had been birthed, she now shot toward Kaedmon's skies, challenging the Divine Realm with her sheer scale. A monument to suffering, the Queen of Toxins belched a thick fog of corrupting energy toward the mages who were burning her roots, commanding her enthralled servants to fight to the very last man against the encroaching army of the Greys who had pushed her back to her last stronghold. Her lithe, snakelike body shook as she summoned more black thorns to pierce the chests of even the most armored among them. Hundreds had died. Thousands more would if he didn't act now.

And act he did. He had come this far, and now, he was looking his ancient enemy in her vile black eyes.

When she saw him among the crowd, a kind of eerie quiet settled over the battlefield.

Both figures from the pages of myth acknowledged the other—the enemy—in this decisive moment. It was the curtain call of their drama. The denouement their entire lives had been building up to.

The Darkseeds had all been hunted down and destroyed. What Artorious was looking at now was Gyko Prime. The progenitor. The final nail in the coffin of pain and misery that had dominated Argwyll for four long, bleak centuries.

And without another moment's hesitation, he moved to strike.

His sword became a blaze of holy fire that sliced through the myrmidons of the toxic queen. His armor, ragged and charred from constant combat, took the impact of her thorns as they lunged for him, appearing beneath him in a desperate attempt to slow him down. Yet, his eyes shone with conviction buried deep within his blood.

He carved the thorns and corrupted belches of the dark one as a child dealt with impudent insects. The last of her hybrids surged forward, fear in their eyes, as their Archon commanded them to halt the advance of the one she knew was coming to destroy her—for good this time. He showed them just as much mercy as he'd afforded all who stood in his way these last few years of his life.

When they lay in crumpled messes of blood and charred intestines behind him, he charged toward Gyko's roots and called for the mages to let the fires of the heavens pour down upon the fiend, adding the radiant blaze of his own sword to the inferno they cooked up and launched at the Demon Flower.

He heard her cries above him. He felt her claws raking his back. He felt his armor shatter, his pale body raked with fresh scars—scars he would carry for the rest of his life. But still, he kept hacking at her. He sliced away her noxious petals, her shriveling stem, and any beasts she summoned in a last-ditch effort to stop his relentless assault.

And with every strike he made, her screams dominated his mind.

Womanly screams from a creature who knew death was upon her.

Screams that seemed familiar . . . like those of a boy's mother who had once died to protect him.

When the dread queen finally fell, speared on her own corrupted thorns, her talons writhing in a death spasm, he crawled up her quivering body and found the point he needed to: her chest that barely heaved with life, the black heart within pumping any blood the beast had left.

"Now, Lightborn!" he heard Carliah cry. "Finish it!"

He drew his blade in an arc across the sky.

He aimed the tip at the Archon's chest.

And yet . . . it wouldn't come down.

"Do it!"

Carliah's voice seemed far off. Not commanding. Almost passive.

". . . Artorious!"

. . . Yes, that was his name, wasn't it?

With the enemy of mankind dying under him, the Lightborn felt something tug at the back of his brain. All the blood that ran within him commanded him to finish the job he had been born to do. The job Kaedmon needed him to do.

The job he'd been chosen to do.

And yet, there was a piece there—something faint—that had suddenly woken up when he'd heard just how . . . *familiar* Gyko's death wails had been.

He knew it as something almost alien to his very soul. It was not what one would call *doubt*, exactly. After all, he knew what his duty was. Nor was this sensation that gripped him and stayed his hand one of mercy. He hated this archbeast that had terrorized mankind more than anyone else could. He had done so ever since he was a boy, and he'd seen the monsters terrorize his home. He had hated them ever since his mother had held him in her soft arms and rocked him, telling him, "Be good, Art. Or the monsters will come for you."

What struck him now was something simpler than all these things. He was not a philosophical man. His brain was not trained to think—it was trained to kill. He was an engine of war. A tool. Kaedmon's Law—yes. That was absolute truth. There was goodness in the law. Certainty. *You can only be what you are supposed to be.* There was purity in that. He admired it.

. . . He had to, right?

On the eve of Archon Gyko's death, Lightborn Artorious Pendragon of the Greycloaks committed a crime. A crime none of his predecessors had ever dared to commit.

He thought about the person holding the sword that stabs.

And he thought about how that person wasn't Kaedmon or Krea or Carliah or any other human in the entire world.

It was him.

And it wasn't their lives that were going to end when he made this final stroke.

It was his life.

"FOR FUCK'S SAKE, DO IT!"

He knew something was wrong as soon as he felt his blade come down. He saw the hole he ripped open in Gyko's body. He saw her beating heart stop as his sword's blade was driven through it. And he saw her smile up at him.

". . . See you in the next life, Lightborn . . ."

Through all the cheers and all the frenzy of victory, he did nothing but walk away from the corpse, hands shaking, breath haggard.

Around him, the humans of the kingdom celebrated. Some of them fell and wept openly to see the Archon finally fallen.

All of them cried tears of joy. Except the Greycloaks.

He could feel their eyes on his back. Eyes that would now never look at him the same way again.

And he knew it, then—the next one hundred years would be the loneliest years of his life.

CHAPTER FORTY

Your Best [Nightmare]

Ethan felt himself tumbling into the white void of the Nerve Tower again. Only, this time, he was ascending.

The dungeon rules had changed. He reminded himself that this was a grade C. It wasn't tangible enemies they were facing in here; it was their own minds, their own comforts, and their own fears. The last two nervestalkers had been weak, but strong in magic and cunning. They were predators who used their prey's insecurities and doubts against them.

And Ethan was beginning to see that to break their hold, he would need more than just brute strength or skills. He'd have to trust in the minds of his companions.

Fauna? She'd surprised him. She'd seen through the illusion like the master Wildglance she was.

Klax? He could do it. He'd already experienced the allure of these creatures once before, and he'd pulled through. Ethan was certain he wouldn't fall prey to their tricks again.

And Tara? He had nothing to worry about with her. Out of all of them, her mind was the strongest. She had a clearer sense of conviction and justification than all of them put together. She wouldn't be fooled by some pantomime of her past. She wouldn't submit to the whims of another.

Right?

Yesterday, Cherri died.

The master came with his hot iron rod to pierce her body to make sure she was gone. Her fur crisped and burned away, revealing the scarred flesh beneath.

Cherri had often spoken with her sisters, smiling and telling them that their fur could hide even the worst bruises and scratches. They were lucky to be born Minxit.

But when the master dragged her body away yesterday, she was no longer smiling.

And when he turned his pink, piggy face on his new prey, it seemed like he barely acknowledged the dead kitten that was still bleeding in his hands.

"Come along, pretty Tara. Your good master will just have to make do with you today, won't he?"

If she was a bad girl—if she fought back—she got the fire. Hot. Searing. Bright—so bright she had to close her eyes and try to stop herself from opening her mouth. She remembered how Lindle had screamed once, and the fire had entered her body and burned up her guts. She remembered them falling out once Lindle was stripped open and fed to the master's dogs.

She couldn't remember what the world outside looked like. She sometimes got glimpses of it through the bars of her cage, or when her older sisters told stories to the other kittens of the delights out there in "Argwhile." She heard stories of ruby-red apples that didn't burn when you ate them, of blue skies that didn't bring ash that stained your cheeks.

Of hybrids like them who were free.

Her youngest sisters had tried running even when she told them not to. No one escaped the master. Not for long. They always came back—in chains or in pieces, but they always came back.

On her thirteenth year in the house of the master, she was brought upstairs to the dining room. He clothed her. Fed her. Bathed her and cleaned out her ears—it was the most pleasure she'd felt in an age. She thought that, perhaps . . .

When she got to the dining room, she knew otherwise. Dreams were for bad girls. She had to be good.

He paraded her in front of his guests, all men—all leering and sweating from the midday sun that streamed through the stained glass windows of the mansion.

"Good Lord Baldrick—you always find the most supple little specimens," one man said.

"Is she broken in?" asked another.

"Naturally," the master replied, his bushy mustache wrinkling as he licked his lips. "I like to taste my sweetest plums."

The men laughed at that. And their laughter was like a death knell ringing out for her life. Because she knew what was going to happen. She could already see it. She'd heard the screams from when her sisters had been used in the master's parties.

But they must have been bad girls, she told herself. She was good. She was always good. She'd always done what she was told.

So why was she here?

The collar strapped around her neck distracted her from her thoughts. She looked up at her master with pliant but pleading eyes. She mumbled. She begged. He didn't listen.

First, he stripped her and made her crawl around for the giggling guests, leading her by her leash around the dinner table. The men of the house howled with laughter. Some of them poured wine in her mouth and smacked her when she passed them. Others spat in her direction; she didn't know why. Maybe just because they could.

But suddenly, the atmosphere of frivolity changed.

The master released her from his grip and stared with flaring eyes at a slave girl who had just been filling his guests' goblets by the tableside.

On the cuff of his evening robe, there was a stain. The slave girl had just made a mistake she'd regret for the rest of her life.

"I-I'm s-s-sorry, Master!" she cried, dropping to her knees in reproach. "I'm so—"

The sound of his fist cracking her cheekbones was felt throughout the entire mansion.

"Impudent little wretch!"

His fists came down on her again and again. Through it all, her bloodcurdling screams echoed down the halls, alerting the other slaves, who came running, only to see that it was the master's discipline that brought such abject terror to the house. They promptly filed away when they realized what was happening.

Meanwhile, the serving maid was on her side in a fetal position, her tail curled up between her legs as she tried to protect herself.

"I'll teach you to disrespect me, wench!"

The guests said nothing. Tara looked at them, her eyes begging them to step in and stop this madness. No smiles were on their faces now. Instead, they went back to their eating, ignoring the uproar. To some of them, it was merely an inconvenience. To others, it was just a fact of life.

Something happened in her mind in that moment. It was what she'd refer to later as a turning point in the sad, agonizing story that had been her youth. All these years spent as the plaything of the master, watching her sisters be used and dumped like rag dolls when they were no longer useful, hadn't impelled her mind to action. She'd seen horrors worse than this maid being beaten today. She'd seen horrors the likes of which she couldn't even express, and she'd done nothing.

But today, for reasons she couldn't express, her body acted for her, and before she knew it, she was bent over the maidservant as a shield, cradling her beaten, bloody sister in her arms while the master stood, momentarily paralyzed with rage, until he simply started beating her, too.

Her punishment was to be whipped to her cage in the basement and go without food. She wasn't used that night. But she had been placed in the same cage as her bloodied sister, who couldn't even look in her direction.

She didn't know which was worse: being broken by the master and his companions or being trapped in here with one of her sisters, whom she'd just saved, avoiding her gaze like she was an enemy.

Pain bound them, but it also turned all spectators into enemies. They were toys to be used and abused as their human overlords saw it—all Minxit were—but that didn't mean they couldn't feel shame.

"Because that's all your kind is good for," she heard her sister say, in a voice very different from how she normally spoke. "All you did once you were 'free' was choose a new master—the Archon. You just allowed yourself to be enslaved again."

She sniffled, rubbing her bloody eyes in the dark. Alone, ashamed, and starving, she assumed the dark face that was now draped over her sister was simply a hallucination. Sometimes, the imagination was a temporary escape.

"TARA!"

. . . What?

"TARA! DON'T LISTEN!"

That voice didn't belong to her sisters. It was . . . a male voice. But not the master's. It sounded strangely familiar, but it was distant. Muted . . .

"You are a tool to be used and then discarded," the dark creature that spoke with her sister's voice told her, and its words were so powerful that she listened to them, ignoring the thin, lithe limbs growing out of her sister's body, and the dark label floating above the creature's head that said: NERVESTALKER.

"It's bullshit, Tara. You know it is!"

There was that other voice again. Who . . .

"Bah! You're not even capable of listening to yourself, so distracted by your own little delusions. You think you found freedom in that dank little underground kingdom? You are nothing but a convenient little rogue. When your friends don't need you anymore, they'll toss you aside, just like your master di—"

"Fuck that!" came the other voice, far more powerful this time, as though it had activated some kind of ability that allowed it to bellow with greater ferocity than the beast that was edging toward her. "Remember the slave camp? You took those bastards down like a pro. And you told me we did the right thing. You still believe that, don't you?"

Could . . . Could she have done something like that? Killed a camp of slavers?

"A lie! A downright, barefaced li—"

. . . Yes. Yes, she could. In fact . . . she'd killed one of their kind before.

She'd . . . She'd killed the master before.

"Listen to me, Minxit!" the beast wearing her sister's face screamed in their cage. "What you see here is who you *really* are! It is what you have been hiding from all this time. You know it, don't you? You know that the right thing to do is to give in. To stay in your rotten little cage and be your master's pet. Because that's all your kind are good for!"

She stood.

"Are you liste—"

No. She wasn't, now. Instead, she was looking at the bars of her cage, and she was looking past them.

Toward the pale white man who was roaring at her between them.

"Ethan," she said, her voice cold, distant, and hollow. "Hand me your sword."

Ethan watched the bruised, beaten catgirl kneeling in her cage rise and walk toward him.

Finally! he thought. His Mana Veil was working, even if it wasn't strong enough to dispel the illusion entirely. This particular nervestalker must have been a more powerful variant with over fifty Intelligence. Either that, or it simply had Tara's mind in a much firmer grip than Fauna's oppressor.

That wasn't something he'd expected, but he'd also not given up on her. And now, the kitten that was facing him, totally ignoring the wails of her "sister" behind her, was bearing its claws.

"Ethan," she said again. "I need a weapon."

He nodded slowly, handing her his mithril broadsword through the bars of her prison. Curiously, sparks began to fly from the item as soon as her hand gripped it, and it slowly morphed into a straightedged dagger with a reverse grip.

"Yeah," Tara said. "I remember this. It's what I stole from one of the guards who came to leer at me on this night. I opened my legs, called him *sir*, and he unlocked the door. Then, when he dropped his pants, I grabbed his dagger and . . ."

The nervestalker behind her had ceased its wails. Now, a pair of spectral gray claws flashed in the darkness of the basement, lunging for its prey's throat.

But its victim was faster.

". . . I made my mark."

Tara spun with total control, flipping out of the way of the nervestalker's desperate attack before launching into a deadly pirouette, bringing the thin edge of her blade across the creature's blue-black neck.

Spectral ichor oozed from its wound, and it flopped to the ground, its form blurring between that of Tara's slave sisters and her tormentors.

"I killed the guard," she continued. "Then I went upstairs."

The stalker threw itself at her again. This time, she sidestepped its strike and drew the dagger across its back, severing its fluidlike spinal cord.

"I found the master's room."

Her knife came down on the creature as it tried to crawl away, the nightmare world of the basement fading as its life drained from its body.

"And I climbed on his bed, where he was sleeping, with the blood of my sister still on his hands."

Ethan looked on, entranced by the whole performance and the dark words echoing from the Minxit's mouth.

He'd never call her "kitten" again.

"He opened his eyes. He saw me on top of him."

She turned the creature around to see that it was wearing the face of her master—old, haggard, full of soundless rage and snarling up at her with blind hate.

"And I showed him what his good girl could do."

The dagger came down on the head of the beast. It let out a final, tired wail of defeat as its life force depleted, and its will to contain its prey withered with the rest of its mental functions. The entire edifice of the slave pen, the mansion, and Tara's crying sisters melted away into nothing. And all that was left was the catgirl holding her blood-soaked knife.

Ethan crept forward.

"Tara, I—"

"Don't," she told him. "Don't say anything. Don't say you're sorry. Don't say you didn't know. Don't say you can make this all better."

He dropped his hands to his sides, seeing her expression change to one of absolute numbness in the darkness of the void they now floated in, the nervestalker's twitching body between them.

"No one should see this," she suddenly said. "Least of all you."

"If you had told me—"

"You'd do what, Ethan? Make the pain go away?"

"No. But I'd have understood."

"How the fuck can anyone understand this?" she said, pointing to the vacant face of her master being worn by the nervestalker. "How . . . How can anyone make it make sense . . ."

Ethan said nothing. Because he didn't have an answer.

And as the void started to swallow them both, the nervestalker's chest rose in a light, stuttered gasp of air.

"Take it," she told him. "He might as well be of some use to you. Probably has some skill you can use."

Ethan crouched, activating his Appraisal to sense any latent abilities in the barely conscious dream summoner.

Nervestalker Alpha

HP: 1/20

Skills: Hide, Ethereal Visage, Minor Illusion, Corporeal Mimic

Mimic . . .

Normally, Ethan's thoughts would be consumed with some excitement at the prospect of such an upgrade. But he met Tara's gaze even though she tried to avoid him at all cost, like her life depended on it.

"You can probably guess the rest," she whispered, tail tucked between her legs. "After I killed the master, I set the others free. They ran away without me. Didn't say a word. Some of them didn't even wanna go; just sat there, rocking like dull stones on the basement floor, staring at nothing. Some of them had given up on ever getting out ages ago, so they probably thought me standing there, bloody and frantic, promising them freedom, was just a trick.

"I burned the mansion and tried following after them. Got to Grenbelm Forest before I realized I couldn't survive. Started stealing from farmers and marketplaces in the towns till the purges began and slavery was the least of my worries. Ended up collapsing from exhaustion one day near the Ashfalls, where Gyko had died ages ago. And that's when she found me."

Ethan nodded. "Jun'Ei."

He didn't need to see their old leader appear in this dream realm. The spark in Tara's eyes as she talked about her was enough.

"She found me when I was closer to death than I'd ever been before. I didn't have the strength to try and kill her like I wanted. I dunno. After a while, it just becomes an instinct. Everyone becomes your enemy. But she—she was different. She showed me a world where I could live. Where hybrids were as free as we could be in this human world.

"Wish you'd met her when she was in her prime, Ethan. If she's really in this place, I'll bet you'll be impressed. Even if she's wrong."

Ethan took his chance to possess the stalker. No resistance came. He took its Mimic skill, jumped right back to Valgraiva, and then got the Spirit Cores from its body.

Spirit Cores: +500

But still, upgrades weren't what he was really thinking about here and now. Even as the black walls of the void around him and Tara started to die away, bleeding out into the unreality of this whole dungeon, he couldn't help but move toward Tara.

"We'll win this fight," he said. "And then, we'll change this world so nothing like what you went through ever happens again."

She blinked in disbelief with eyes that were still bruised even after the dream was done.

"You still think we can coexist with humans, Ethan? Even after all they've done to us?"

He wanted to tell her that he did. He wanted to tell her that he was certain there was a better way to end this war than one side killing the other.

But he could only tell her the truth.

"I don't know."

A new wormhole opened in the dark realm. He felt himself being pulled through.

But before he was gone, he heard Tara's final words to his departing form: "One way to find out."

Current Spirit Cores: 1150

Another realm. Another illusion.

He was beginning to get bored by this dungeon's little tricks. But Cores were Cores. And he'd need them when he faced the real Boss waiting for him at the peak of this Tower.

This new unreality that opened up was that of a forest grove. One surrounded by a litter of corpses.

Around him, hybrids and humans spread atop one another, their blood mingling in a grisly display of postbattle horror. Whatever fight had taken place here, it had ended recently. Some of the dead were still twitching in spasms.

"If this is supposed to trick me, it ain't working," he said aloud. "I've seen worse in this place, and I'm done playing games."

Before he could rationalize talking to himself, another voice answered him.

A voice tinged with ancient wisdom.

"No, Ethan Graham. I can assure you; this is no game."

He looked up from the remains of the dead, his body compelled to move forward like a twisted marionette.

And then, he saw her.

She was a Lycae, just like Klax—but older, far older. Her wrinkled flesh contorted around her hollow eyes like a mummified body risen from its sarcophagus. The fur that coated her body was barely clinging to her limbs, and with every breath she took, her ragged bones seemed to heave with her.

"Welcome, Archon Ethan Graham, Demon Hat and Lord of Monsters."

He blinked twice just to make sure. He didn't know what to trust anymore. "You're . . ."

"Jun'Ei," the withered woman said. "And we have much to discuss."

CHAPTER FORTY-ONE

The [Prophet] Speaks

The venerable old Lycae sat on a tree stump in the middle of the Grenbelm Forest—or what served as the forest in this Memory Prism filled with the bodies of the dead.

Jun'Ei . . . actually sitting here before him.

"How . . ." Ethan began, stumbling forward as he tried to avoid the innards he was treading in. "How do I know this is real?"

I don't detect any illusion magic on her, Sys offered calmly.

Even so . . . I've seen nothing I can trust in this place, Ethan thought. Could he even trust that that voice belonged to Sys at all?

Jun'Ei's aged body heaved in response. It looked to Ethan that she—aged beyond all reason—was carrying a deep pain in her bones that she was barely able to suppress.

"You have learned not to trust your own senses," she said. "As I would expect of the Archon. None of your brothers or sisters grew to appreciate just how little one can do alone. In their hubris, they fell. You, Ethan Graham, must trust in more than yourself."

Just then, Ethan heard a rustling coming from the blood-soaked bushes behind him.

He spun around, scythe at the ready, just in time to see Klax emerge from the forest, dragging the body of a dead nervestalker behind him. The wolfman's face was worn with exhaustion, but his eyes were bright, alive with the intensity of battle. His fur was matted with blood, his muscles taut from the struggle he had just endured.

Spirit Cores: + 500
Current Spirit Cores: 1650

So, the nervestalker of this prism is already dead, Ethan thought, staring at the limp creature Klax dragged behind him. *Which means . . .*

"She's real, Ethan," Klax said, his voice firm but almost reverent as his eyes locked onto Jun'Ei. "I know her. My eyes know her. My heart knows her."

Ethan looked back and forth between Klax and Jun'Ei, still torn between disbelief and reality. But Klax's conviction, the way his usually stoic face softened when he looked at Jun'Ei—it was undeniable.

Ethan's grip on his scythe loosened slightly. His gut told him that this might be different. This might be the real Jun'Ei. But that only raised more questions.

"Klax, how can you be sure?" Ethan asked, still wary.

Klax dropped the nervestalker's corpse onto the ground with a thud and walked past Ethan, his gaze fixed on the dogwoman. His voice was quiet, but it carried an emotion that Ethan hadn't heard from him before.

"I've been searching for her for so long," Klax said, standing just a few feet away from Jun'Ei now. "I've imagined this moment a thousand times. This . . . feeling, it's more than real. I know it's her."

Jun'Ei's eyes glistened with unshed tears as she met Klax's gaze, and for a moment, time seemed to stand still between them. The weight of their history, their love, and their separation hung heavy in the air.

"Dearest Klax," she groaned. "Our time here is short. Our destinies even shorter. But still, it pleases me to see you again."

The wolfman bowed low, clutching the pendant at his neck. There was nothing but peace within his old eyes now.

But Ethan, still the pragmatist, needed answers. He stepped forward, his voice cutting through the silence. "If you're real, Jun'Ei, then tell me—what do you want? Why are you here?"

Jun'Ei turned her gaze toward Ethan, her voice gentle but filled with an ancient power. "I am here because time is running out. Your path is converging with mine, and the choices you make now will determine the fate of Argwyll and its people."

Ethan's mind raced, the weight of her words sinking in. "What choices? What do you mean? All I want is freedom; a way for everything we do to matter at all."

Jun'Ei's eyes darkened, her voice low and commanding as she responded. "Freedom is what you seek, and it is a worthy desire. But there is more than one path to freedom, Ethan Graham. You could walk Tara's path and spill the blood of every human in Argwyll. You could burn this world to ash and break Kaedmon's Law by force. Or . . ."

"Or what?" Ethan asked, his breath catching as he leaned forward.

"Or," Jun'Ei continued, her voice growing softer, "you can break the law without shedding so much blood. There is a way—a way that has been hidden from you until now."

Ethan's brow furrowed. "What way? How?"

Jun'Ei's expression grew grave, the weight of her next words hanging in the air. "To break Kaedmon's Law without the destruction of Argwyll, you must find where my physical body lies. It is there that the key resides. My memory holds the knowledge you seek. But for you to access it, you must Possess me, Ethan. Only through Possession can you unlock the secrets hidden within me."

"Possess you?" Ethan repeated, his mind reeling at the idea. "How do I—"

"There is no time for more," Jun'Ei interrupted, her voice strained. "My captors are returning. The power I have here is waning."

Klax's face paled at the mention of her captors, and he took a step closer to her, his voice desperate. "Jun'Ei . . . I'm coming for you. I swear it. I'll find you, wherever you are."

Jun'Ei's eyes softened as she looked at Klax, a sad smile tugging at the corners of her mouth. "I know, Klax. I've always known. It is in your nature, and it is your choice."

Before Klax could respond, the dream world around them began to flicker and tremble, cracks forming in the sky above as the illusion started to shatter.

"W-Wait!" Ethan cried, coming forward to take hold of the woman. "How do I find you? Where are—"

Her old claws shot out on impulse, almost like she was trying to drag him into the depths of whatever hell she was stuck in. And it was hell; of that, Ethan became certain.

As she pressed his arms with real, tangible pressure, he saw an island appearing through dark, treacherous mists. An island off Argwyll's . . . eastern coast. An island dominated by storms, a lush jungle, and . . . hidden deep within its bowels . . . a prison. A fortress. A dark place where secrets were kept from the world. Where the screams of traitors rang out long into the night where no one would hear them . . .

He knew the name of this place without asking her. She was transferring the information to him—along with all her dread. This place, this nightmare stronghold, was where they'd been keeping her all this time since her capture.

Griffon's Watch. The prison colony.

"Find me, Ethan Graham," Jun'Ei called out, her voice fading as the world disintegrated. "Find me. And free us all."

The dream world died. The bodies of the forest merged into one mass of liquid crimson.

"I . . . I have to kill him first," Ethan told the old Lycae's fading eyes. "The Lightborn. He's . . . He's waiting . . ."

"Do you?"

Outside the bounds of space and time, Klax shouted. He ran forward. He tried to reach them. But whatever magic Jun'Ei had over this place was more powerful than anything Ethan had felt in Argwyll. She held her form until she could deliver what she needed to.

"We are prisoners in this world, Ethan Graham," she told him. "All of us."

He looked at her as a strange and unmistakable look of sympathy came over her eyes.

Sympathy . . . for who? Him? Klax? Or someone else?

He didn't have time to answer. Instead, she gripped him with all the power she had left at her command and pressed something into his chest.

"There is one last gift I can give you," she said. "When the time comes, think of freedom. Think of the dream you hold within yourself—the dream you share with all your brethren. And you will know how to use what I shall bestow upon you."

Artorious stood alone in the dark void, the oppressive silence pressing in on him from all sides. He stared at his reflection in the blackened glass before him—his own face, twisted in pain, eyes filled with guilt.

"You're a failure."

The voice was his own, but it was laced with venom, dripping with disdain. His reflection sneered at him, mocking him with every word. "You failed Gyko. You failed your people. And you'll fail again."

Artorious clenched his fists, his knuckles turning white as he resisted the urge to strike the glass. "I'm not a failure."

"Really?" the reflection taunted, stepping closer. "Look at yourself, Artorious. The great Lightborn. The chosen one. And yet, every time you stand at the precipice of victory, you falter. You hesitate."

Artorious's jaw tightened, but before he could respond, the voices of the other Lightborn began to echo around him, their ghostly forms appearing in the void. They surrounded him, their eyes cold and judgmental.

"You are not like us," one of them said, his voice low and full of accusation.

"You don't have the strength to do what must be done," another added, her voice sharp like a blade.

And then there was Krea—the greatest of the Lightborn. She stood tall, her wings shimmering with a blinding light, her eyes filled with disappointment.

"You will fail again, Artorious," Krea said, her voice carrying the weight of centuries. "You will never be what this world needs."

The words cut deep, but Artorious refused to bow beneath them. He had heard them before. He had faced these demons before.

"I don't need your approval," Artorious spat, his voice filled with defiance. "I know what I've done. I know my failings. But I also know what I'm capable of."

His reflection laughed, stepping closer until it was mere inches from him. "Do you? Then why do you hesitate? Why do you always hesitate when it matters most?"

Artorious's hand shot out, gripping the hilt of his rapier. "I hesitate because I care. But that doesn't make me weak. It makes me stronger."

Without another word, Artorious drew his blade and struck his reflection, shattering the glass into a thousand shards. The pieces fell around him, dissolving into nothing as the void began to lift.

The ghostly figures of the other Lightborn faded as well, their voices growing quieter until they were nothing more than distant whispers.

Artorious stood alone once more, his chest rising and falling with each heavy breath. He had faced his past, his doubts, his fears. And he had moved past them.

He opened his eyes to find himself standing at the peak of the Nerve Tower, the cool wind brushing against his skin. The sun was setting on the horizon, casting the world in a warm golden light.

Behind him, he heard footsteps. He didn't need to turn to know who it was.

"Carliah," he said, his voice steady.

She stepped up beside him, her face hardened from the trials they had just endured. "You made it through, then?"

He nodded. "We both did."

"Hmph," she snorted. "Maybe you're finally learning from your past."

"And the others?"

The commander shook her head, not meeting the Lightborn's eyes.

"It is fitting, Arty, is it not?" she smiled. "That it would be the two of us who stood here at the end, ready to undo all your mistakes."

He felt his fist curl as his teeth gritted with charged energy. But he steeled himself. She wasn't the enemy. Not right now.

They stood in silence for a moment, the weight of their shared experiences hanging between them. The nightmares they had faced—the doubts, the fears— were still there, but they had come out the other side stronger.

Artorious glanced at the great doors before them, the final obstacle that stood in their way. The Boss door. Beyond it, their fate awaited. The place they'd make their final stand.

"It'll be just like old times, dear Arty," she told him as she stepped forward through the foggy sheath that concealed the Boss of the City. "The tale of the demon hat, and that of the Archon, ends here."

Darkness finally gave way to a stuttering, frail light.

Ethan found himself standing in a safe zone, something he didn't expect in a dungeon like this. Apparently, even grade Cs had to allow their delvers some measure of respite before the Big Bad Boss.

And, looking down at the world beneath him, he could tell the Boss room was just above him now.

He was standing in a translucent sphere of shimmering light—a hollow room that bore his weight through no discernible means. He moved, and the floor rippled, giving him a view of the Nerve Tower's pulsing depths below; the sight would probably have churned the stomach of an acrophobic. After all the things he'd seen, however, this was child's play.

He walked over to the sphere wall to look out at the City of Illusions far below him, whistling slightly as he inspected the chaotic path he and his comrades had carved through the place. Around every alley they'd skulked through and every spire they'd toppled on their way here, the mantalike dreamstriders did their jobs, coating the buildings in the sticky, ethereal goo that seemed to keep this whole place together. The phasing outlines of obscaurus ran down the side of the Nerve Tower to take up new positions in the city below, summoned to do so by whatever force controlled this place. Ethan suspected it was Kaedmon himself.

The architect of everyone's pain in this world.

The way the slim obscaurus ran down the building seemed more frantic than the behavior he'd seen them exhibit in the city itself, however. Some of them ran with a distinct sense of fear—if such creatures could even feel the emotion. They ran with abandon, their necks split open, spilling ghastly globules of blood across Ethan's little sanctuary, trailing their limbs behind them. Such a mass exodus could be the work of one person only.

The Lightborn.

Ethan looked above, seeing nothing but fog and clouds. Though he couldn't see him, he knew he was up there. He knew he'd passed through the same trials he had and, of course, he'd emerged before his ancient enemy.

"Artorious," Ethan murmured. "Hope you didn't miss me too much, old man."

The time has come, then, Sys suddenly perked up. **After everything you have seen here, Ethan Graham, are you truly ready to meet your fate?**

Ethan thought about it for a hot second; he thought about that word, and how much he despised it and those who lived life by its absurd rules.

"I'm doing nothing but what's right. That old dude's gotta go. First him, and then Kaedmon."

Jun'Ei's last words flooded back to him then, along with the vision of her prison. Killing the Lightborn would only be the first step to truly freeing this world. She had the key—he knew it. Klax had known it all along, too. Ethan felt like a moron for ever doubting the guy.

He felt like a moron for ever doubting any of them. After all, they were the ones who had broken through their own illusions, right? It had taken them almost no time at all.

And because of that, they deserved to have a win here. Killing the Lightborn wasn't just a job he had to do. It was something he owed Klax, Tara, Fauna, and every damn hybrid on the surface.

And that thought was what summoned his current Spirit Core counter to the forefront of his conscious thought.

Current Spirit Cores: 1650

He smirked, sitting down and crossing his legs, readying himself for a major upgrade session.

You trying to hint that it's time to fine-tune this host a little more, Sys?

. . . Maybe.

Not like he needed any prompting. After all, he had to wait for his companions to come through—wherever they were at right now.

Might as well make use of this time. I've been floating around in dreams and nightmares for far too long. Time to do something real.

Strategy time . . .

First, he knew that taking the Lightborn and his grim commander head-on would be suicide. Even with all his new abilities, he'd have to be careful, relying on synergies and tricks that could mess up the flow of the Greycloaks' combat. If this Carliah and Artorious were true tactical geniuses, then how come Artorious had been duped way back when they'd fought in the Grenbelm Forest?

Simple: it was because he thought he lived in a predictable world. The world of Kaedmon was exactly that: everything was defined for you since birth.

But Ethan Graham was anything but a predictable hat.

And it was time to show these bastards exactly what that meant.

First, he'd upgrade his stealth capacity so that not even the twilight-infused shadows of this city could stop him from gaining an advantage.

Hide (Grade S)
Hide-in-Plain-Sight unlocked: You may now attempt to disappear from your enemy's line of sight even in broad daylight, with a 30 percent chance of failure.

He had expected the skill to be based off his enemy's Perception score, and thus to be overall useless against these ageless paladins. But the flat-out 70 percent chance for a successful sneak attack (at triple damage for him and his companions if he tried for a Mass Hide) was way too great to pass up.

He assumed that's just what S-grade skills were—super powerful, but risky.

And he'd have to risk it all if he was going to win, here.

[Upgrading Skill: Hide (Grade A)]
Upgrade Complete!
Congratulations! You have achieved the highest grade of the Hide skill!

That was a start, but he wasn't done yet.

"Sys, pull up Spectral Snipe. We're gonna need some precision."

As he administered these improvements, his entire undead body shimmered with a ghostly veil of pure energy. It was the kind of power no mortal being on Argwyll could ever possess, all contained in one pure vessel. Even the dreamstriders, floating outside the pale bubble of nothingness, seemed to stop and take notice of his energy levels as they spiked higher. Ever higher.

Spectral Snipe (Grade C)

You launch a bolt of precise energy up to two hundred feet from your current location. This bolt deals two hundred points of Piercing DMG and takes sixty seconds to recharge.

Spectral Snipe can now pass through solid and ethereal matter.

Attack Vitals unlocked: You may aim at specific body parts to trigger Status Effects in your enemies on a successful hit.

Hands: Disarm

Legs: Cripple

Head: Automatic Critical

Spirit Cores to Upgrade [Spectral Snipe] Skill from Grade D to C: 750

Ethan smiled to himself. He envisioned taking that smug bastard's head clean off his shoulders and shoving it in the face of every Argwyllian who hated him—and the rest of his kind.

Hell yeah, he was gonna take this. Close combat with the old fuck would be possible, but a crazy proposition long-term.

[Upgrading Skill: Spectral Snipe (Grade D)]

Upgrade Complete!

Congratulations! You have upgraded [Spectral Snipe] from Grade D to C.

Spirit Cores to Upgrade [Spectral Snipe] Skill from Grade C to B: 1000

Current Spirit Cores: 650

Six hundred and fifty Cores that, if he was facing a regular monstrous enemy, he would bank in order to get off a successful Possession. But he remembered well the lesson he'd learned in Grenbelm: not only was the old fucker's Willpower through the roof, but he couldn't possess a human anyway. This wasn't gonna be a fight to wear his opponent down, bend it to submission, and then wear it as a host. No—this was a fight to the death, straight up.

And for that, he needed more power. Something that could be whipped out to end the fight in one swift strike. So, he turned to something he hadn't looked at in a while:

Petrification Coating (Grade D)
You slather your weapon in the debilitating bile closest to your heart,
giving your weapon the [PETRI] attribute for ten seconds.
[PETRI] Chance: 40%
Duration: 10 seconds
Petrification automatically triggered against targets with the Status
Effect {SLUGGISH}.
Spirit Cores to Upgrade [Petrification Coating] Skill
from Grade E to D: 250

Sluggish . . . that means . . . if I can time a Roar perfectly to hit the bastards, I can at least take one of them out of commission and focus on the other one. One good hit and the petrified Greycloak's gonna come crumbling down, right?

He hesitated only slightly as he committed to the upgrade. Now wasn't the time to waste Spirit Cores. But this was the best plan he had.

[Upgrading Skill: Petrification Coating (Grade E)]
Upgrade Complete!
Congratulations! You have upgraded [Petrification Coating] from
Grade E to D.
Spirit Cores to Upgrade [Petrification Coating] Skill
from Grade D to C: 500

Current Spirit Cores: 400

Next, he needed a good defense just as much as he needed offense. Valgraiva's HP was immense, but it meant nothing if he couldn't keep his host standing. After all, he knew what Artorious could do. If he had an onixia blade with him . . . chances were, he could deplete HP like siphoning sand through a sieve. An undead lord meant nothing to an Archon slayer.

But luckily, Ethan had just the thing to deal with that.

Repulsor Shield (Grade D)
You heft your mighty shield, nullifying magical attacks completely up to
a certain magnitude of DMG.
Current [MAG] DMG PROT: 95

[Repulsion] trait gained: Repulsor Shield now reflects any magical
attacks back at the attacker.
Spirit Cores to Upgrade [Repulsor Shield] Skill
from Grade E to D: 250

It was an upgrade that provided the best of both worlds. And it was all his.

[Upgrading Skill: Repulsor Shield (Grade E)]
Upgrade Complete!
Congratulations! You have upgraded [Repulsor Shield]
from Grade E to D.
Spirit Cores to Upgrade [Repulsor Shield] Skill
from Grade D to C: 500

Current Spirit Cores: 150

One more, Ethan thought as the walls of the dome around him began to quiver under some unseen pressure. *One more chance to win, here, Sys. Any recommendations?*

Do not forget your team, Ethan. I tell you again—they are some of your best resources. You have seen now why they fight. This battle is all that serves as important for them. Their entire purpose is to ensure your ascendance. They may be burdened with pain, but pain is often the best teacher for the fanatical and the—

"But they aren't expendable," Ethan interrupted. "You really think I could just let them die so I can claim my throne in this world, Sys? I told you already, that ain't the kind of Archon I'm gonna be."

Sys grew quiet then, allowing the world around them to spin, uninterrupted.

A different Archon, indeed. I still do not understand you, Ethan.

When Sys said nothing else, Ethan merely moved on to his final skill pick, ignoring the droning sounds of the safe zone beginning to change.

. . . But perhaps that is the kind of Archon the world truly needs.

"Hm?" Ethan grunted, too preoccupied with musing on his next skill choice. "What?"

Nothing, Ethan. Nothing at all.

"Cryptic as usual," Ethan scoffed back. "Right to the end."

He set then to trawling his mind for something useful. He saw skills, numbers, status effects; synergies he hadn't even thought of before all coming together in a vast web of demonic tools he'd pilfered from the different species of this world. But he couldn't shake the feeling that he needed something else.

He opened his palm and looked at what Jun'Ei had given him. What she had called her *gift*.

When he looked at it, he already *knew* what it was. He knew how it worked. He even knew where it had come from, somehow. He couldn't understand the bond he had with the item, but he could guess it was something like . . . familial acquaintance.

It would be his trump card. His last-ditch effort in the event things went off the rails and he or one of his companions was brought to within an inch from death or worse. But how he could deliver it to his enemies was another matter entirely. It required a . . . personal touch. It required trust.

Scrawling right to the end of his skill list, Ethan came to his most recent skill.

He smiled in the ethereal sphere just as three portals opened to let his companions through. This skill—this ability—it suddenly made everything else click together so perfectly that, if he didn't know that his life was at stake here, he'd think this was the final level of some intricate game.

He knew exactly what skill he'd spend his last points on.

CHAPTER FORTY-TWO

[Unfinished] Business

Ethan finished applying his last upgrade as the portals' light grew brighter in the Nerve Tower's safe sphere. Then, with a gush of dazzling light, they each spat out their occupants and closed up like wounds in time.

Kneeling before the Archon were his three loyal companions. Shaken, confused, and no doubt afraid of what was to come—but alive.

"E-Ethan?"

Fauna was the first one to look up and Appraise him, watching him warily lest he be just another illusion of the nervestalkers.

"The very same," Ethan replied. "And you're the walking textbook Wildglance, Miss Fauna, super special magic awesome teacher of Sanctum."

The girl almost collapsed all over again.

"It's you . . ." she murmured, tears welling at the corners of her eyes. "You—We—We made it!"

"Course we did," Tara murmured. "It'll take more than a few bad dreams to get us down."

Ethan turned to her, remembering the tormented nightmare she'd been through. He wanted to say something, but her eyes flashed the same warning at him as they had before. Now was not the time.

Klax was the first one to stand, helping his comrades to their feet with a reverent grin spreading across his furry face.

"I saw her," he said. "The real her."

Fauna blinked. "Jun'Ei?"

Tara was unconvinced. "How do you know it was really her and not some trick of those bastard creatures?"

"Because this time," Klax smiled, "she did not appear to me alone."

They all looked to Ethan, who met their bewildered glances with a sage nod.

"No shit," Tara huffed. "You saw her, eh?"

"Yeah. And I know where she is. Griffon's Watch."

The three of them stood, disbelief smeared across their features.

"After all these years . . . I always suspected. But I didn't know for sure."

Fauna patted Klax's mane gently as the old wolf sagged.

"None of us did, Klax. How could we?"

Tara, Ethan noticed, was saying nothing. She had crossed to the very edge of the sphere, busying herself with her own System screen.

"And yet, the place she is locked away in is even worse than I could have thought," Klax whispered. "Griffon's Watch. The place where traitors are tortured and left for dead. A monument to man's inhumanity on Argwyll."

Ethan's eyes met those of the wolf. He could sense the burning desire to leave and grab his old mate right now. Screw the Lightborn. Screw his duty. He had finally seen the one thing he'd really wanted all this time, and yet the knowledge didn't bring him peace. She was going through pain the likes of which he could barely imagine. And as for Ethan—he had no clue *what* they did in that prison.

But from its appearance, he could infer the evils that probably took place on that island. There was a kind of darkness to its craggy, jagged walls and spiked turrets that betrayed the mentality of those who must dwell within.

So when Klax stepped forward and knelt before Ethan's host, the latter was taken aback.

"You have given me that which I could never find on my own, my Archon," he said, much to the surprise of Fauna and even Tara. "From now until the end of time, know that I am yours. Your commands I will follow without question, and your edicts shall become my duty."

Ethan blinked twice before rolling his eyes.

"Rise, wolfman," he said. "I never once questioned your loyalty. You think I don't understand that a man in love sometimes puts that before his king or prince?"

The old wolf looked up with fierce, piercing eyes.

"All the same, I want you to know that I am with you, my Archon. No matter what course of action you decide, I am with you. To the death."

Ethan put a hand on the Lycae's sagging shoulder.

"We're gonna rescue her, Klax. Make no mistake about that. After we've taken down old cranky Artorious up there, we're gonna get Jun'Ei even if it means tearing that prison apart. And then—we'll strike at our true enemy."

"Kaedmon." Fauna nodded. "I'm with you too, Ethan. We took on the Lightborn before, and we . . . we'll fuck him up again!"

Everyone turned to stare at the Hopla's sudden outburst—a statement that was accompanied by her pale cheeks turning a feverish shade of red.

"W-Well?" she prompted. "We will, won't we?"

Ethan looked at Klax before the two started laughing heartily there on the floor of the Nerve Tower's neutral sphere. Even with the danger of certain death lurking above them all, they could still laugh. Even after witnessing the horrors of their pasts, their spirits still sang within their breasts.

"Y'know something?" Ethan finally said. "If our pure Hopla mage can say that, we can take down the Lightborn and his bitch commander."

"After all," Klax agreed, "we've been through worse already."

"You sure about that?"

The party turned to Tara, who had suddenly spoken up and instantly cut through the jovial atmosphere. A thin sheen of light from the city below reflected on her face, totally neutral in appearance, betraying nothing of the tumult that was raging within.

And now Ethan understood how she could maintain that facade: it was something she'd had to get good at from the moment she was born.

"You all know what happens if we fail up there, right?" she continued. "Griffon's Watch would be a mercy compared to what'll happen to us and the rest of Sanctum if we make a single misstep. It ain't just regular Greys we're going up against. It's fucking Carliah and her precious Lightborn themselves. There ain't two people in Argwyll with more power in their hands than those two."

Klax and Fauna looked at each other in confusion.

"I'm surprised at you, Tara," the wolfman said. "Here we are, giving you the authority to destroy two humans with as much prejudice as you like, and you're getting cold paws?"

"Those ain't regular humans, Klax," she snapped back. "And you know it."

"What else can we do, Tara?" Fauna asked genuinely. "Ethan's more powerful than last time. We're stronger than last time. Together we can—"

"This is always what it's been like," Tara interrupted, arms crossed, still not facing them. "We always think we're gonna win right up until the final moment. Our great-grandparents thought it, our parents thought it, and now we're thinking it, too. But we're walking right into their trap, aren't we?"

Klax looked like he was about to flip out on her, but Ethan stopped him with a firm hand.

"What's your plan then, Tara?" he asked her. "We've come this far; what would you have us do?"

The Minxit shifted slightly, her tail drooping sheepishly.

". . . We've got what we came for, really," she said. "Let's get out, bust out Jun'Ei, and then lead those two fuckers back to Sanctum. They won't know what hit them."

This time, Klax was up in arms.

"You'd put our fellow hybrids in danger?"

"They know what they signed up for."

"But—But some of them are kids, Tara. They can't help u—"

"They're growing up in an evil world, Faun. No matter what you teach them, they gotta face reality at some point."

"That's not fair and you know it isn't, Tara," Klax growled. "Don't put your brothers and sisters in danger just because you're afraid, at the end, to be a real hero."

She turned from the spectral window as soon as she heard that word, racing up to Klax with murderous intent in her eyes.

"Is that what you wanna be, Klax? A hero?"

"Tara, I'm not your enemy."

"No," the Minxit scoffed. "You've already got what you want. It's easy for you, isn't it?"

"Alright, enough," Ethan interrupted, standing and coming between the two. If he was being honest, he was getting fed up with these altercations, even if he did understand what was going through Tara's head right now.

She knew it, too. She looked up at him as if she was about to say something before turning again and marching to the end of the sphere to gaze back out onto the uncaring city below.

"Look, let's take five here," Ethan told everyone. "The Lightborn can twiddle his damn thumbs up there a little longer."

Fauna and Klax agreed warily, both eyeing Tara with sadness before they retreated to their own parts of the protective sphere. They left Ethan to walk up to her and stand at her side. For a while, he said nothing, but he could tell that she was shaking.

"Well?" she spoke. "Go on and tell me that I'm just a little girl still scared of her master's whip. You know everything now. Might as well get it over with."

He glanced sidelong at her with his crimson hat eye—the part of him that he liked to think was a window to his real, human soul.

"I'm not gonna blame you for anything or tell you you're wrong to be scared of what's waiting for us up there," he said. "And I can't force you to stay here and fight with us."

She seemed, as far as he could tell, surprised by this admission. That fact alone told him everything he needed to know about how she saw the world—and that she still saw him as a human, despite it all, complete with all the dark convictions she held about his species.

"I mean, yeah, I could tell you to get over your fear and push through the experiences that have gotten in your way since you were a kid. I could tell you that you've already done that, in a sense—that the Tara I've seen has been fearless, devoted to her cause, and won't ever submit to anyone ever again. I could say that pushing through that darkness is what's made you strong. It's what's made you who you are."

"It's done nothing," she said quietly, pressing her head against the thin sheath of their little bubble. "Nothing but hurt, all this time. And I can't ever get rid of it. Some scars . . . they just don't heal, Ethan."

"That's why I'm not gonna tell you how to feel," he replied. "Instead, I'm gonna ask: what do *you* want?"

She looked at him through pained, bloodshot eyes.

"Why don't you just give me a fucking order? Isn't that what the Archon's supposed to do?"

"Probably. Would make my life easier if I could just tell people what to do. Thing is, that's not what I'm here for. I'm here to break the law that keeps you guys as slaves. Not make a new one."

She eyed him warily but said nothing at first; her tail kept flicking between her legs. No longer was she shaking, though.

"So, what do you want, Tara?" he asked her again. "Come with us and change this world, or leave and kill as many humans as you want. I won't hunt you down if you do. And I won't tell you you're wrong."

For a few moments, she didn't reply. They watched the city churning beneath them, everything within its bowels working as intended, every creature laboring away at some divinely ordained task it couldn't deviate from. All of them never having once considered the question he'd just asked her. The only question that ever mattered at all.

Tara heaved a heavy sigh as she pulled away from the window and fixed him with the same sad smile she'd worn in the dark void of her dream.

"I bet you already know what my answer is, don't you?"

Ethan smiled at Tara's response to his question, gazing out lazily at the city they'd stormed through below. It looked so peaceful from up here, the dreamstriders flapping about their repairs, the obscaurus' lithe necks twitching against the twilit sky; everything seemed totally at odds with the conversation they were having up here.

"If there's one thing I've learned from living a boring mortal life in my own world," Ethan replied, "it's that I can't know what anyone other than me is really thinking."

Tara chuckled. "I'd settle for a boring life."

"You? I doubt it. Not with the smooth moves I've seen from you."

She smiled and leaned against the window again, resting her head against the shimmering veil that protected them both from falling to their deaths.

"I don't know, Ethan . . . I've watched my sisters die already. I've seen the only people I've ever cared about run from me without a moment's hesitation. I just . . . Look, I don't know if I can go through it again."

"That's . . . what you think of us?"

The Minxit turned, seeing Fauna's smiling face mere inches from her own.

"Tara, you couldn't get rid of us even if you tried."

Before she could turn on her defense mode and tell the upstart bunny girl off, she found that Klax had appeared beside her.

"She's right, you know," the wolfman said. "We're a team, Tara. We always have been."

The catgirl looked from one of them to the other, seeing the sincerity in their faces.

". . . Fuck," she sighed to Ethan. "Let me guess, you had them hiding beside us listening in the whole time?"

"I might have been testing my Mass Hide skill a little." Ethan winked.

"Might have fuckin' known . . ."

She said these words not in anger but in a kind of reserved sorrow. Turning back to her companions, it seemed, for once, that she didn't know what to say. And, for once, she didn't have to say a thing: Fauna took her hand in hers and pressed it before breaking into a soft song.

The chorus of "Never Gonna Give You Up."

She softly sang the lines with more sincerity than anyone Ethan had ever known.

To the Minxit's surprise, Klax's hand was suddenly on theirs. He finished the song for them.

Ethan didn't know whether to burst out laughing or cry. But, seeing the look that suddenly came over Tara's face, he found that a smile was probably enough.

And so, he added his gauntleted hand to the group.

"Let's make a pact," he told them with the grand city of lies as his witness. "That no matter what happens next, we'll see this thing through to the end. We'll win this world for all of hybridkind, and we'll walk on the surface again."

They looked at him, then, in a way he'd never had anyone look at him before. They looked at him like he was a real leader. And, for the first time in his Earthling and Argwyllian life, he felt like one.

Tara wiped a bit of moisture from her eyes before tightening her grip on the hands of her friends.

"Alright, alright!" she moaned. "Fuck. Couldn't leave you guys alone for a second anyway. I mean, I *am* the sex appeal of the group. What would you do without me?"

Their laughter spilled out from the Nerve Tower's sphere like the endless undulations of the tower's innards, radiating into the city itself and causing the striders that loomed below to stop for a brief moment and look toward the strange sound of happiness they had never heard resonate within their domain.

Then, when the sound finally died away, Ethan walked with his warriors to the door at the end of the sphere.

"Alright," he said. "I've got a plan for how we take down Mr. Happy and his bitch queen. It's gonna be messy, but it should work. Here's what we're gonna do . . ."

"What happens when it's over?"

It was a childish question—one he'd asked her before—but all the same, he needed an answer.

He stood atop the debased body of the City's Boss: Malak, the Lord of Dreams. He'd been a nuisance, teleporting his clownlike body around the Nerve Tower's peak and using the spectral waterfalls that surrounded them like flowing curtains to conceal his form. But he'd perished. No Boss creature of a grade-C delve was going to be able to stand against two Greycloaks in their prime.

"Do I need to repeat myself, Arty?" Carliah replied, wiping the creature's viscous, sapphire blood off her broadsword. "We've been through this already."

"I'm not a child anymore," he answered. "I want to know if the years have tempered your ambition."

Around them, the sounds of rushing water assailed their ears. The rest of the arena was barren. Dreamlike. It was an expanse of blue-white cubes that disassembled and reassembled themselves continuously under their feet. Of course, it was nothing but another trick of the light; the whole arena was a single platform. The cube pattern of movement existed just to sow fear in the delver standing on top of them, making them think there was an environmental danger to consider.

Maybe that'd been a problem for delvers who had come through here before, but for them? Malak hadn't even made it to his second phase.

And now, they waited.

"You must know that Greycloaks' control of this world won't be accepted," he told Carliah. "The monarchs of Argwyll won't bow down simply because the Greys of Westerweald say so."

She laughed out loud at his statement; a laugh that, by this point, was burned into his very soul.

"Oh, Arty, come on. We practically already own this world. You think the other commanders across Argwyll aren't waiting for the chance to take this place? When I give the word, we'll take the head from every fatass monarch that still rules. We'll topple every castle and live as gods—like we deserve."

He looked at her with stern trepidation.

"You would choose civil war, Carliah? You really think every Greycloak will back you?"

"Arty," she replied tetchily. "Believe me, it won't be much of a war."

Their eyes met across the already blood-strewn battlefield that the Lightborn knew was to be his last. What he saw in her eyes inspired no hope for the future. And yet, he was here, now, and he had a job to do. *His* job.

What did it matter what the future brought? It was a future he'd never even see.

"You know something?" Carliah suddenly asked. "There is one thing I'd like to know before all this is over."

He cocked an uncaring eyebrow at her.

"Why'd you do it?" she asked him. "Why'd you reject the sacrifice? When you plunged your sword into Gyko, you were supposed to die. And yet, you didn't. And nobody knows why, Arty. Like it or not, you *did* make history in your lifetime. Your failure showed us even the best could be brought low in the last moments before a victory."

He felt his grip on his blade tighten. He imagined . . . just for a moment . . .

"So, tell me why," she repeated. "Even just to sate my morbid curiosity. I'd imagine you'd like to get it off your chest before the end. Or even now, are you hesitating to actually have your life mean something?"

Whatever reply he had for her was lost in the whirl of light that broke through the waterfall at the arena's end.

And they saw him.

"Guess there are just some things I'll never know," she told him as she stood, resplendent in her still pristine armor. "But I do know this: I lost two good men to this delve today, Arty. They sacrificed themselves for you. Don't let them die in vain."

When Ethan and his party emerged through the translucent veil of the Nerve Tower's final floor, they were met with a sight that shouldn't have surprised them at all.

The ghostly waterfalls cascading down from the sky around them were a nice touch, and the luminescent cubes that formed the arena floor were new, sure. But that wasn't what was occupying his mind.

Ethan took in the corpse of the Delve Boss and its two slayers with a slight gulp.

He was just like he remembered him. Stuffy. Scarred. Old beyond all logic. Whatever magic Kaedmon had placed on his Lightborn to keep him together was clearly starting to wear off. Still, he knew not to underestimate the speed and strength of those old bones.

The woman beside him, though—blonde, broad shouldered, thick hipped— carried herself like she was queen of the entire world. She looked at the new arrivals, one hand on her hip, and openly scoffed.

"So, this is the last Archon," she said. "And who does he bring as his entourage? A rabble of mangy animals."

She unsheathed the blade at her side with an exaggerated swipe. Seemed like all these Greycloaks had a flair for the theatrical.

"Carliah Argent," she declared, though no one asked. "Senior Commander of the Grey, Westerweald Chapter. And of course, you know my associate. He's the man who'll be taking the head from your shoulders."

Artorious didn't move a muscle. Ever since Ethan had entered the arena, he'd just sat and stared forward like a mute.

"We admire your attitude, Archon," his commander continued. "Coming to us to die like this saves quite a bit of work on our end. Are you vain enough to bequeath any last words to us, demon?"

Ethan looked to his companions, each one of them having been ready for this battle ever since they'd first grabbed him from the Lightborn's clutches.

"Shit," he said. "And I thought *he* was uptight."

A flash of air. The drawing of a blade. A distinct, piercing howl.

And then, pain.

Ethan looked down to see the rapier of the Lightborn lodged in his chest, the scarred face of his assailant suddenly right in front of him.

And in the next second, he felt the tip of the blade slice into Valgraiva's black heart.

"ETHAN!"

CHAPTER FORTY-THREE

What You [Have] to Be

Fauna's scream pierced the air with as much burning intensity as the tip of the Lightborn's onixia blade being thrust deeper into Ethan's chest. With each passing second, the Archon felt the incendiary pain of one of his predecessors' own blood being used against him.

Or at least, he would have, if the blade had done any harm to his real body at all.

[Ethereal Form: Deactivated]

He looked down at Artorious's old face, full of fire and fury, and smiled. "Not as quick as you once were, eh, old man?"

[Skill Activated: Twilight Edge (Grade D)]

Ethan's scythe struck true, sliding across the old man's arm in a dark stroke that would have severed the hand from any ordinary human warrior. For the Lightborn, he just managed to dislodge his rapier from his shaking hand. A Wing Buffet then sent him and his crazed commander reeling back against the far end of the arena.

"Keep her occupied!" Ethan barked to his comrades. "The old man's mine."

There was barely any time to rest on his laurels. Out of the blue haze of a waterfall, the Lightborn came charging at him again, his grey cowl fluttering around his insanely fast form. As Klax, Fauna, and Tara moved to intercept Carliah, Ethan aimed his blade at Artorious and sent a charged beam of energy skating clear across the arena directly at the old man's face. The snipe was powerful enough to sear through adamantine.

And the crazy bastard tanked it.

Ethan saw his dark smile as the shock from his attack faded. He was barely able to bring up his shield to intercept Artorious's lightning-wreathed fists as they came down on him.

Even then, the pressure against him was too much to bear. He quickly activated his Ethereal Form again and rolled behind the old man, flanking him with as much speed as his form could conjure and raking his scythe up his back. The Lightborn merely turned, tracing his reacquired rapier in the air in a deadly pirouette that knocked Ethan's shield out of his hands even as the burning pain from his scythe's attack radiated up the old man's body.

He was still just as abnormally quick as Ethan remembered. But speed and power wouldn't be enough for him.

[Skill Activated: Summon Wraith (Grade E)]

The Lightborn staggered, letting out a roar of pure rage as a pair of shadowed claws pierced his side. His eyes darted to the new enemy that had emerged behind him, and he struck out with a blow that dislodged its dark skull from its incorporeal body like a wolf biting down on its prey. Yet, he'd left himself open yet again. It seemed there was still some hubris in the old man, after all.

And Ethan took full advantage. With a Roar that managed to cut the old man's speed in half, he lunged with his scythe and aimed for the Lightborn's neck. The blow connected, sending Artorious to the ground as a trail of crimson gushed from his back and spread across the arena floor.

Ethan didn't let up. With a leap and another flap of his skeletal wings to keep the old man pinned, he brought his scythe down in a stroke that could take the head clean off his shoulders.

And then—pain.

His left side felt like a truck had run through it again, and he was instantly brought off-balance. He hurtled to the ground with a torrent of purple bile escaping his pale lips.

HP: 800/950

What . . .

He looked down to see the onixia blade embedded in his rib cage, twisting as it sapped more and more of his HP.

HP: 750/950

He groaned in pain as the Lightborn stood, craned his neck, and looked down at his fallen enemy.

He can . . . remotely control his sword . . .

Ethan had expected some cheer—some lofty speech that the old man had been practicing just for this moment, when he looked down on his ancient enemy trapped in his clutches.

Instead, he pushed forward like a beast possessed by something devilish and grabbed the hilt of his blade, ready to plunge it up into the heart of his foe, for real this time.

Only, in the next moment, he blinked through the pain that he was trying to push through, and the Archon was gone.

He blinked again, trying to focus his Perception. It was another trick. Another dastardly plan the beast had laid out to try and win when it was facing a foe it clearly had no chance of being able to outmaneuver. He closed his eyes. He tried to focus on the energy of his blade. He tried—

"Artorious!" Carliah called from across the arena. "Quit meditating and kill the bastard!"

He turned to admonish her, teeth gritting in consternation, but found that she was engaged in heavy combat with the demon's hybrids. He knit his brows in confusion for a second before he realized what had happened.

And in that second, it was already too late.

Ethan deactivated his Hide and Summon Illusion, which had managed to create a good enough impression of the Greycloak commander. Then he drove the onixia sword into the Lightborn's gut, twisting the blade with as much temerity as its owner had when he'd shoved it into him. Artorious let out a scream of hatred, managing to spin and get his flaring hand around Ethan's throat before the latter brought his dark scythe down to sweep the Lightborn's legs and send him rolling across the arena, bleeding out on the floor.

Across the battlefield, Klax, Fauna, and Tara were doing their best to keep Carliah Argent contained. The commander of the Greys well deserved her title. She barely even moved as she countered each of Klax's blows with a parry and riposte that struck the wolfman's vitals and pushed him back. Her defenses were equally intimidating. Every arrow that Tara sent her way was intercepted and cut apart—even the triad of flaming silver projectiles that were the Minxit's specialty. In Fauna's case, she simply shrugged off most magical attacks, smiling as she walked right through fireballs and checking her nails as lightning bolts washed over her body.

"What's this bitch made of?!" Tara shouted.

"She's playing with us," Fauna replied. "She's . . . enjoying this."

"Well," Klax growled, "we'll just have to wipe that smirk off her face. Together now!"

All three of them charged as a unit, surprising the commander as she braced herself to meet them. Fauna charged both Tara and Klax with her Radiant Coating, the spell working instantly to electrify Tara's daggers and cause ripples of killing light to coat Klax's fists. They flanked her, each one unleashing a flurry of blows that she couldn't dodge, couldn't block. She took them like a rag doll, being pushed back inch by inch until she and her assailants were finally at the very edge of the Nerve Tower's peak.

And as the spectral waterfall washed over them, her eyes suddenly shone with power.

"My turn."

Before the next blows were struck, the vicious commander grabbed Klax's fist and twisted it, summoning a howl from the Lycae that sent Tara immediately off-balance. Without even drawing her sword, she lifted the wolfman up and brought him crashing onto the Minxit with enough force to shatter every bone in a mortal body. Both hybrids went skidding across the floor of the arena while Fauna summoned a wind to take them out of the way of Carliah's plunging strike.

"Don't worry, little rabbit," she laughed. "You'll get your turn next!"

Ethan heard their screams as the commander unleashed hell on them. He wanted to run to them to help, but the sight of the bleeding, wounded Lightborn he marched toward presented the end of this nightmare. He had to take the chance.

He sent a Twilight Edge at the old man which kicked him right to the edge of the arena. Then, another swipe of his scythe and the onixia blade together carved a bloody slash across his chest.

Ethan panted as he brought his scythe down again, this time raking the old man's leg. But he looked up, in the face of his triumph, to see Artorious's unblinking face not even letting out a single scream.

He cut into him with the onixia sword, thrusting the blade into the old man's chest again and again, withdrawing it with a torrent of blood before plunging it right back in.

And still, the Lightborn just sat there and took it.

Finally, unwilling to accept what his mind was telling him, Ethan blinked and Appraised his foe.

Lightborn
HP: 2800/3000

His eyes wouldn't believe it. They *couldn't* believe it.

He slashed again and again, each new blow drawing another cry of rage from the lips of his host; each new blow carving into the flesh of the old man, tearing right through his armor and cutting into muscle.

It . . . It had to be.

And yet . . .

HP: 2700/3000

He stood over the downed man, his back soggy from the waterfall cascading over them, washing the Lightborn's spilled blood away.

Then, the old warrior's lips finally parted in a grim question: "Is it beginning to sink in, yet?"

Ethan looked down as the open wounds he'd carved into the Lightborn began to close up, feeling the cold waters of the spectral tower wash over his shoulders and frame his confused face. Then, a spike of agony lanced up his torso. The Lightborn kicked out, grabbed the onixia sword from his hand, and struck, lashing his shin with its keen blade.

Ethan didn't even have time to switch to his Ethereal guise. He took the pain, feeling his host begin to quiver as the energy was practically sapped from its body.

HP: 500/950

He was dying . . . there were no two ways about it.

Meanwhile, the Lightborn stood and raised his scarred head, walking through the waterfall as his body bled out across the pale light of the arena.

"You never understood, did you?" he asked. "You really thought you had a chance, all this time."

Ethan gritted his teeth as he watched the old bastard raise his blade for another strike. Only, this time, Ethan was quicker. He combined a Roar and a Wing Buffet into one single attack, knocking the Lightborn back and lowering his speed just enough for Ethan to aim a snipe right at his forehead—right between his eyes, where his brain was concealed.

He watched the sapphire dust trail of the bullet pierce the old man's skull.

He watched the Lightborn stagger back.

And then, like a tiger being tickled by a mouse, Artorious simply regained his composure and charged.

What the actual fuck . . .

He met the Lightborn's blade with his own, managing to keep him at bay while the onixia metal cut through his scythe piece by piece. He felt the legs of his host give way. And all the while, the silver-blue eyes of his enemy looked not at those of Valgraiva's but directly into the crimson eyeball of Ethan's own eye.

"You know there is no victory for you here," Artorious snarled. "Try all the tricks you've learned. Show me all the effort you've poured into improving yourself, and I'll show you how little it all means."

Ethan pushed back. He wasn't out of the game yet.

"Fine, old man! You wanna see more, I've got plenty!"

From Ethan's side, he drew the mithril katana he'd been keeping hidden since he'd first found it in the loot from the dreamstrider gauntlet. His Ethereal Form activated in the next instant, and as Artorious disengaged, expecting a quick strike in the second after Ethan reappeared, he instead felt a creeping, virulent pain radi-ate up his side.

A glowering light of blue pierced the air as the katana sliced clean through it, trailing a green ooze in its wake that instantly poisoned the Lightborn the moment it made contact with his armor. Ethan followed up with another slice that struck against the onixia weapon, and to his amazement, he saw the dark, pulsing blade of the vicious thing begin to crack.

That's the way! If I can't break him, I can at least stop him from doing damage. If onixia is made from the blood of an Archon—and can destroy an Archon—then it stands to reason that a living Archon can do the same to it.

But in the next second, as Ethan summoned all of his strength, channeling it into a single blow using both of his blades, he saw the Lightborn do nothing but sigh.

"Pointless. So utterly . . . pointless."

Artorious let the blade drop in the second Ethan would have split it apart. Instead, the Archon's attack cleaved into his arm and almost cut through it entirely. Ethan, unblinking in the ever-dusk of the City of Illusions, looked down to see the Lightborn's arm pulse with energy.

And with a single spurt of brute force, his scythe was snapped apart.

His other blade went flying across the arena with his body, the Lightborn's mailed fist knocking the wind clean out of him. Even the undead lord that Valgraiva was—a creature composed of pure darkness—could not withstand the assault of the one-armed man . . .

Ethan gasped for breath, coughing up torrents of purple blood that ran down his armor. Armor that had barely even been scratched in this world so far.

He heard the metal of the katana being kicked across the ground by his foe, who quietly walked toward him.

"That's it," the old man said. "That's the look—you're finally starting to understand."

Ethan rose on one knee, checking his HP and seeing that he would either have to find a new host soon or . . .

HP: 250/950

. . . or he was done.

"This is a game to you?" Ethan growled. "Is that it?"

Artorious cocked his eyebrow at him, kicking the katana toward his hand.

And Ethan, through his Appraisal, saw just how hopeless this whole damn fight was.

Lightborn
HP: 2300/3000

Damn it . . .

"I thought so, once," he said with another heavy sigh. "I think every Lightborn before me probably did, at some point." He angled his blade toward Ethan's hat form. "But there is nothing in this world to believe in," he snarled. "Nothing, except dying with a sword in your hand. So, pick it up, Archon. And die like a real man."

Ethan gripped the hilt of his blade and met the downcast eyes of his foe with more fury than he'd ever exhibited in this world. But that was tempered by the sudden yelps of his friends behind him.

He turned to see Fauna lying before the commander of the Greys, her staff cast aside. Klax was ambling up to her, panting with exertion, his fur clipped away and blood trickling from his open wounds. Tara was the only one still standing, her arms wavering as she aimed another arrow at the Greycloak warrioress's skull.

That woman . . . she'd barely broken a sweat.

"See how your friends suffer," Artorious growled again. "See how all you've done is prolong their torment. That's what your kind does, demonspawn. You've tormented this world and its people for far too long."

Ethan met Tara's eyes as she shook her head at him, silently begging him not to submit. Fauna looked up, almost unconscious, and reached a hand toward him. Klax slumped to the ground, his muscles shredded and torn. It was a picture of defeat, no matter how you looked at it.

And through the sorry sight, Sys suddenly whispered in Ethan's mind.

I did tell you, you know.

Ethan barely registered the words. He was focused on Fauna. He was focused on . . . something, *anything* he could do here . . .

I told you, and you never listened, just like all the rest. Want me to show you the disparity in your HP values again? Want to see all those shiny skills you've collected that have meant nothing after all this time? Go on, Ethan Graham, tell me what to do.

Ethan felt the teeth of his host practically grind to a paste.

. . . Or do you want to listen to me, for once?

The glowering eyes of the Lightborn stared down at him as the old man simply groaned again and lifted his dark rapier.

Ethan watched it, and he laughed.

You know something, Sys? I finally realize why you've sounded so familiar all this time.

Oh? Do tell. Before we both die, you might as well share some of your timeless wit.

You're someone I knew back on Earth, Ethan thought, *Or, well, something, I guess. Yeah . . . you're that little voice in my head—that tiny piece of me that was always there on the shittiest of days, telling me that the world ain't gonna ever be any better. Telling me my shitty office job was all I had and was all I was good for.*

You're that little piece of me that always doubts, aren't you?

. . . I doubt that very much.

And you know what? Every day of my life, I became more and more willing to listen to you. Until one day—who the fuck knows why—I finally decided it was time for a change.

The onixia blade arced down as Ethan's wings unfurled behind him and his skeletal hands felt the uneven brickwork of the Nerve Tower beneath him.

And I discovered that if I wanted control of my life, all I had to do was reach out and take it.

The blade of the Lightborn came crashing down with a thunderous roar, bringing the full might of its bearer behind it. Ethan's katana flashed in the air, its edge passing clean through the onixia metal and striking at the Lightborn's shining eyes so that he fell off-balance at the final moment of impact. His strike pierced the ground, carving a crater into the arena and sending shock waves through its surface as his target took to the skies above.

"Fauna!" Ethan shouted. "Now!"

The Hopla obliged, as did her comrades. Tara let her arrow fly at the confused face of the Greycloak, who batted it away as she roared at her wounded soldier, not noticing that the three hybrids had suddenly converged on a single location: where the Hopla had stretched out her paw to summon a bubble of protective magic.

Carliah Argent, for the first time in a very long career, cursed herself for her hubris.

Because those weaklings had them both exactly where they wanted them . . .

Looking to the skies where the Archon had soared and feeling the tower surface begin to crumble under her feet, she already knew what was about to happen next.

"IDIOT!" she roared at Artorious. "FUCK HONOR! KILL THE BASTARD NOW!"

But her call to action came too late. In the moment she rushed to cleave the hybrids apart, the Archon came barreling down into the center of the arena, lengthening the cracks that the battle had already borne into the living flesh of the tower's top.

Dive Success!

The tower cracked apart, its foundation disappearing in a plume of white smoke and sapphire, alerting every dreamstrider in the illusory city to something they'd never seen happen before. Not even the programming of Kaedmon's Law had equipped them to deal with the indisputable fact that the Nerve Tower was collapsing, layer by layer—a lolling giant about to smash into the city.

Ethan flashed a bloody smile in the face of the Lightborn as the entire arena broke apart under them.

CHAPTER FORTY-FOUR

The [Fall]

As the great tower of the delve fell, its inhabitants scuttled out of their hiding places, retreating down the city streets while their cousins fled. The dreamstriders glided as far as their flapping appendages could take them, while the obscaurus and nervestalkers ambled away like headless chickens, knowing that the end had probably come for their once fair home.

Yet, their torment was nothing compared to the pure, seething anger of the two Greycloaks as they felt the arena give way under them. Both fell, seeing nothing but the fury in the other's face, as the Archon and his hybrids plummeted right down with them to the cracked foundations of the tower.

The plumes of smoke and ash threw a sheath of sapphire dust across the city, obscuring the view of anyone within its walls. For Ethan, floating down on his skeletal wings, the picture of desolation that they'd emerged into was now complete: this dungeon delve was all but annihilated.

See, Sys?! he cried in his mind. *See what you can do when you think outside the box for a change?*

His System's reply was garbled in the roar of the Tower's collapsing innards. But it was probably nothing that sang his praises. Finally, he barreled into the ground and tasted the stale, dust-caked air around him. He was standing in a sightless void now, reminiscent of the nightmare worlds the Tower's nervestalkers had shown him before he emerged again.

But it probably wouldn't last. So, just to be sure, he let his next little trick trickle out of the pores of his skin and seep into the air around him. Because the crashing tower had killed at least a few little critters in this forsaken city, and that meant he had enough Spirit Cores for a new upgrade.

His eyes traced the letters in the deep dark of the world he'd created.

Summon Mana Veil (Grade D)

You create a dense layer of fog fifty feet wide. Any targets within this fog must pass an Intelligence check of fifty or more, or be {SILENCED} for the duration they remain within the fog.
{SILENCED} targets cannot cast spells.
Spirit Cores to Upgrade [Summon Mana Veil] Skill
from Grade D to C: 750

He nodded once, in total silence, and let the upgrade run its course. If he couldn't beat the Lightborn, he could stun him. And then . . . whatever. He'd think about that when he came to it.

He'd made it out of worse than this. He'd made it out of his shitty life on Earth; he'd made it out of that piss-filled cave with nothing but a rat as his first host, and he'd made it this far, right?

So, he'd make it out of this mess, too. They all would. They had to. But . . . how?

His mind suddenly raced toward something Jun'Ei had told him as they parted in the dream realm. Something that had only started to really nag at him.

In this world, we are all prisoners . . .

He had a hunch. And it was better than nothing.

The Lightborn had his strength, true. His weakness wasn't in his physical defense. But the trials of the Nerve Tower had taught Ethan that there were other weaknesses one could exploit.

So, he decided he'd try a different approach.

Artorious clutched his bleeding eyes, feeling them slot back into place as he swept his rapier through the darkness of the dense fog that now surrounded him. His knees buckled, and with a roar of fury, he punched his shinbones back into place with a bloodied fist.

Where . . . is he . . .

He activated his Azure Edge skill, something he normally reserved for clearing away toxins and poisons spouted by remnants of Gyko's armies. A crescent arc of turquoise ripped through the dust cloud and showed the twilit sky above—but only for a moment.

Another, very different kind of fog suddenly closed over the sky again.

"A Mana Veil," he said aloud, cursing himself for his own impudence yet again.

He stalked through the mist, hearing nothing but the sounds of clashing blades and screaming creatures. Carliah would finish the hybrids off no matter what little tricks their leader pulled out of his hat. It was his job to see this through to the end.

Activating his AOE blast ability—Spear of Kaedmon—he plunged his sword into the ground and twisted its hilt. A miasma of light spread forth from the blade and struck out at the corners of the darkness that surrounded him.

And that's when he heard it—the sound of rushing air, and a blade being drawn from its scabbard.

Got you.

He twisted his rapier out of the ground with the precision of a man who had more winters on his back than any other in all of Argwyll.

But what he saw stopped his hand before it could make its mark.

"WHERE ARE YOU, YOU LITTLE URCHINS?!"

Carliah Argent flew through the fog of darkness, her broadsword cleaving clean through whole plumes of dust as she rampaged in the general direction of the giggling hybrids tormenting her.

"Missed me!" the catgirl hissed. "Come on, old lady. You know, you really ain't livin' up to your name."

"Little bitch! I'll drape your skin over my fortress once I cleave it from your bones!"

She went on slashing and flailing in the darkness, her left arm crippled from her fall. She walked with a slight limp, but none of her assailants dared come within striking distance. Even without onixia, that woman could hit like a truck.

On the perimeter of the shadow-wreathed battlefield, sequestered amid the wreckage of the Nerve Tower's foundations, Fauna kept up her healing wind on Klax. Her hands thrummed with emerald energy, sealing up his wounds, while Tara kept the mad maiden of the Greycloaks distracted with her dancing.

"Looks like Ethan decided plan B was our best bet," the old wolf murmured. "Still, I never believed he could bring the whole damn tower down on—*Urgh!*"

Every few seconds, the healing spell would fizzle, but Fauna wasted no time, clapping her hands together and getting right back to doing her job.

"Calm yourself," Fauna commanded as she stitched up his wound in the dark. "You've been through worse than this, haven't you? We all have."

Klax looked down at her as Tara sent another trail of arrows to pierce through the Greycloak's neck. Enraged, she sent a plume of scintillating energy toward the skies, where she struck at nothing but mystic air—the very fog Ethan had summoned; the thing those damn obscaurus had used so well against them.

The Greycloak commander wasn't going to be fooled for long, however. Tara could dance around her, picking away at her every few seconds, but unless they did some real damage soon, they'd be doing nothing more than prolonging the inevitable.

He Appraised her through the cloak of darkness, just to confirm his suspicions.

Carliah Argent
HP: 2155/3000

Yep. They had to think of something fa—

The Hopla's magic fizzled again, sending an energy spike into his veins.

"*Argh!*" he growled. "Faun, you know you—"

"What did I tell you?" the rabbitgirl huffed right back at him. "Stop your complaining and soldier up. We've got a fight to win."

This would normally be the time when the Lycae would take charge of the situation. But looking down at Fauna's bloodied forehead, determined eyes, and partially singed whiskers, he allowed himself a brief moment to smile.

"You've changed, you know."

She didn't look up at him. "Stop talking. You need to conserve your strength."

He laid a firm hand on her paw, feeling her shaking, knowing that she was just as scared as the rest of them were. "Not a moment's hesitation," he noted. "Not a single stutter. You're not the Fauna you once were."

She pushed his smiling face aside and tried to get back to his wounds. "Don't say weird stuff like that right now. Focus on—"

He stood, bringing her up with him.

"Don't waste your energy on me, Faun," he told her. "I'm tough enough to see this thing through to the end. Just like you are. I'm only sorry I didn't realize that sooner."

The way she looked at him at that moment, eyes glowing even against the abyss that swirled around them, it was as though this was the first time she'd really seen him in a long time.

"It's him, ain't it?" the wolfman murmured. "Our Archon has that kinda effect on people."

In the darkness, Fauna grinned. Her nod was slight, but it was clear as day.

"UH, GUYS?!" Tara shouted through the din of Carliah's screaming and tearing at the fog. "I could use a little—What's the word? Oh yeah—FUCKING HELP."

Klax lifted Fauna on his shoulders, squaring up and steeling himself, ready to charge headfirst into the flailing form of their foe.

"Let's show this bitch what hybrids are really made of."

The dark fog swirled in thick tendrils around Artorious, suffocating his senses and blurring the line between reality and illusion. His blade was tight in his grip, every step forward feeling like a battle through an unseen current.

But when he'd turned to meet his foe, it wasn't the ridiculous little hat sitting atop the undead lord he saw. Instead, it was a child. A gray-skinned child hugging itself as flames licked around it.

He was looking at himself.

His childish face stared at him—wide-eyed, innocent—with pleading eyes. The boy whispered words barely loud enough to be heard over the eerie silence, "Why did you do it? Why did you choose this path?"

Artorious, teeth bared in frustration, cut through the apparition, and the figure dissipated into the mist. His breath came in short bursts, his heart racing.

The Archon was playing with him.

Yet another youthful vision appeared through the mist, this one from his early years as an initiate. Younger, more hopeful, less worn by battle. He knelt beside fallen comrades, bloodied and bruised, his hands trembling as he realized he couldn't save them. The younger version looked up, his face smeared with dirt and blood, his eyes hollow. "We fought for a better world, and now you've become part of the very machine we wanted to destroy."

"Enough!" Artorious roared, cutting through the illusion with a ferocity that shook his entire body. But even as the image faded, the truth lingered like a sour taste in his mouth. The fog wasn't trying to break him physically; it was digging into his mind, into his regrets, trying to unravel him from within.

"You think showing me my past will weaken me?" Artorious shouted into the swirling mist. "You're wrong, demon!"

There was a long pause, the silence hanging heavy in the air, before Ethan's voice echoed softly from the shadows.

"I'm not showing you anything you don't already know, Arty. This is who you are—who you've always been."

Ethan's figure materialized through the fog, and Artorious spun to face him. His breath caught in his throat as he saw more figures around Ethan, each one a different version of himself, flickering in and out of existence. Young Artorious, the warrior, the leader, the broken man—every part of him that had once held on to hope.

Ethan had seen it all in the second he'd reached out the dark to pull at the Greycloak's mind with his Summon Illusion skill. But in truth, he could have guessed most of the old man's past from his sad, wrinkled eyes alone.

Ethan stood, his expression one of calm resolve, the Moonlight Katana casually resting on his shoulder. "All those years," he said, his voice filled with a quiet sadness. "All those battles . . . for what? To keep fighting forever? To die in someone else's war?"

"Shut your mouth!" Artorious spat, his sword trembling in his grip. "My freedom comes with your death. Nothing more."

Ethan shook his head, a sad smile tugging at his lips. "You've never even considered another way, have you? You're so desperate to end this, but you've never stopped to think that maybe, just maybe, there's more than one path out of this nightmare."

Artorious growled in frustration, every fiber of his being rejecting Ethan's words. "I do what I must. I fight for Argwyll. Your existence is a blight on this world, and I will end it."

Without another word, Artorious lunged, his sword cutting through the fog with all the fury and frustration of a man who had carried the weight of the world on his shoulders for too long. The blade sliced through the air, meeting its target—Ethan's chest—with a sickening thud.

Time seemed to slow. Ethan's eyes widened as the blade drove deep into his body, the sharp edge tearing through flesh and muscle. Blood erupted from the wound, spraying the ground beneath them.

Ethan Appraised his HP as purple blood spurted from his mouth.

HP: 20/950

One more twist, and that was it. He knew it, and the man holding the sword before him knew it too.

But that final twist never came.

Both Lightborn and Archon met each other's eyes, their past selves probably raging at what they saw. But in the present? Both of them were starting to realize the truth of their situation.

Ethan opened his mouth with a sad smile. "You just can't do it, can you?"

For a moment, everything went still, the fog hanging heavy around them. Artorious stood frozen, his face twisted in a savage snarl, but Ethan remained calm. He looked down at the blade embedded in his chest, then back up at Artorious, his breath labored but steady.

"And you won't even let yourself understand why," Ethan rasped, his voice hoarse but unwavering. "Why you can't just let go."

Artorious's hand wavered, not noticing Ethan's as he drew his katana and channeled a very specific skill into its blade.

"You're trapped, just like the rest of us, desperate to end this torment, but you've never considered that there's another way. A way that doesn't involve killing every damn person who doesn't fit into your version of peace. And you want it more than anything in the world, Arty, don't you? Because the truth is: you just don't wanna die."

Artorious's hand tightened on the hilt of his sword, his knuckles turning white. "My freedom is your death, fiend. Nothing more. If it takes my life . . . I will pay the price."

Ethan let out a long, weary sigh. "Then what are you waiting for, old man?"

Artorious's eyes flickered with confusion for a moment before he felt the cold, creeping sensation spreading across his skin. He glanced down, his breath catching in his throat as he saw Ethan's katana embedded in his side, glowing with a strange petrifying energy.

[Status Effect: {PETRI}] Success!

Stone began to crawl up his torso, hardening his muscles and freezing his movements.

"No . . ." Artorious gasped, panic rising in his chest as the stone enveloped him. He tried to twist his sword in Ethan's gut, to finish him off, but the petrification was already too far along. His body was stiffening, his limbs turning to cold, unyielding rock.

"NO!" the Lightborn bellowed, his voice echoing through the mist as the stone reached his neck, his face contorting in a final scream of defiance before his entire form was consumed.

Ethan winced as he pulled Artorious's blade from his chest. The pain was almost unbearable, but he pushed through it, watching as the Lightborn's body turned to solid stone, his face forever locked in a mask of fury. For a moment, Ethan just stood there, his chest heaving, blood dripping from the gaping wound in his armor.

Artorious was frozen, but Ethan knew this wouldn't last. The petrification was temporary—a delay, not a victory.

With a grunt, Ethan hefted his katana and hacked at Artorious's stone limbs, the sound of cracking stone echoing through the fog. Pieces of the Lightborn's body shattered and fell to the ground, but Ethan didn't feel any satisfaction. There was no triumph in this, only the bitter knowledge that he was buying time, nothing more.

When he cut his head clean off and let it fall to the ground, he heaved another sigh and Appraised the old fool.

HP: 1895/3000

He almost wanted to laugh. The old guy was made of the strongest stuff in the world. And yet, he couldn't let go. Ethan wondered for a second if he'd ever be the same. He'd already given up one life, after all . . .

At any rate, the Lightborn would break free eventually, and when he did, he'd be more dangerous than ever.

He was considering hacking him apart some more when the memory rune on his hand pulsed again—this time, sending a chill up *his* nervous system that plugged a voice right into his mind. A voice tinged with authority and age.

. . . Jun'Ei?

The old Lycae's voice whispered in the back of his mind, soft but insistent. *We are all prisoners here, Ethan Graham.*

Ethan's grip tightened on the hilt of his katana as he stared down at the petrified Lightborn.

"Yeah. But I can't make people see things they don't wanna see."

You are the Archon, came the response. *You, and you alone, have the power to change the hearts and minds of men. To look through their eyes and see as they do.*

"Fat load of good that does me here," Ethan scoffed. "This was just another pointless fight. I can't beat the guy."

Perhaps not as you are now, Jun'Ei replied. *But perhaps destiny did not bring you here to dispatch the Lightborn . . .*

Ethan's eyes widened. He'd almost forgotten about the other one; even now, he could hear the screams of his companions as they fought against their own harbinger of doom.

"Can we beat her?" Ethan asked the void.

Look within yourself, Jun'Ei replied, her voice a calming presence amid the chaos. *Make your choice. Fight to the death or live to fight another day.*

Ethan's eyes flicked back to his friends—Fauna, Klax, Tara—still fighting, still holding on. They needed him. They all had a future to fight for, a world to save.

"I'll take the option that lets us live," he muttered, his jaw set in determination. "Vengeance can wait. We've got a world to win."

Hurry, Jun'Ei urged. *I can seal the portals, trap Artorious and his commander here, but you need to move fast. His petrification won't hold forever, and though his wounds will take time to heal, you must move quickly. I cannot promise you can defeat Carliah Argent in a contest of brawn.*

"No," Ethan replied, a new plan forming in his head. "No . . . but I can play with her mind. In fact, if old Arty's mind is enough of an indicator, I might just know what her weakness is."

With one final glance at Artorious's petrified form, Ethan turned away, ready to rejoin the fight. But before he left, he paused, looking back at the stone figure, his heart heavy with a strange mix of sorrow and regret.

"See ya, Arty," he said.

CHAPTER FORTY-FIVE

[Grey] Death

The dark fog still lay thick and heavy, curling in the half light like living smoke over the Nerve Tower's wreckage. Carliah Argent stood as a pillar of wrath in its center, an armored sentinel barely concealed by the hazy darkness. Her blade shone with a sharp, unyielding gleam, cutting through each thin mist strand as she waited, her stance poised, energy thrumming in a wide radius. Somewhere in the darkness, Ethan's hybrids circled like phantoms, invisible but present, eyes sharp and ready.

"COME OUT AND FIGHT!"

The three of them held their breath, moving with silent, practiced precision. Their target's focus was absolute, but Fauna, Klax, and Tara had trained for this. The fog granted them cover, a thin layer of safety that let them melt into the artificial night. Fauna hung back, her focus on weaving delicate threads of illusion magic that hummed with faint glimmers, catching the edge of the dim light like whispered promises. They encircled Carliah, catching the edge of her vision as ghostly mirages, half there and then gone, teasing her senses.

Carliah snarled, her grip on her broadsword tightening. "You think these tricks will save you?" she called into the fog, her voice seething with disdain. "Cowards! Creatures skulking in the mist like animals, terrified of a fair fight! Come out and at least die with honor!"

The insult fell flat. Tara's lip curled, but her response was a silent predatory grin as she slipped closer to Carliah. With barely a sound, she darted in from the left, her daggers flashing, and cut a line along the seam of Carliah's ankle plating before disappearing back into the shadows. Her blade left a shallow gash, not deep enough to wound but enough to weaken the armor, a cut that, over time, would add up.

Carliah Argent
HP: 2055/3000

But it still amounted to nothing more than a diversion.

Carliah snarled and swung her weapon in a brutal arc, slashing through empty air where Tara had been. But Tara was already gone, flitting back into the fog with feline grace, leaving only the faintest trace of her presence.

"Again, Klax!" Fauna's voice whispered through the fog.

From the right, Klax barreled forward, his hulking frame moving with speed, his fists poised for impact. He let loose a powerful strike aimed at her armored back, the force of his blow sending a shock wave through Carliah's frame, forcing her forward with the impact.

"You think you're clever?" Carliah spat, twisting to face him, her broadsword swinging out in a deadly arc. But by the time her weapon sliced through the air, Klax had already moved back, his dark form lost in the mist once more.

The rage in Carliah's eyes flared like wildfire. She could feel her patience thinning, a gnawing frustration rising in her chest as her prey eluded her again and again. Guerrilla warfare was for weaklings. Weaklings and thieves. All these filthy creatures were doing was proving that they were not fit to rule this world. Her world.

She scanned the fog, eyes narrowed as if she could see through the layers of illusions and shadows. Fauna's magic pulsed, amplifying the silence, making their movements feel like mere whispers.

"Keep wearing her down," Tara muttered to herself, circling from the far side as she slid into position for her next strike. Her grip tightened on her daggers as she crept forward, her steps as silent as a shadow. "Like Ethan said. Stick to the plan. Stick . . ."

Carliah's gaze swept over the fog, her mouth twisting in an angry snarl. "Enough of these tricks!"

The Greycloak commander's body crackled with a dark, pulsing energy, her fury manifesting in raw power that radiated from her armor. She planted her vibrating blade into the ground, eyes closing for a moment as her voice filled the fog with a deadly calm.

"Enough games."

The fog began to ripple, disturbed by a low hum that swelled around her, building into a deafening roar as she concentrated. Her aura expanded in a circular wave, pushing outward, piercing through the thick haze. The fog that had shielded Ethan's companions for so long began to dissipate, evaporating into trails of silvery mist.

The battlefield was laid bare, every shadow chased away, leaving only harsh, blinding clarity.

"Damn it," Klax muttered, blinking against the sudden brightness.

"Witness the sad truth of your existence," Carliah growled, her voice thick with disdain. "Hybrids are always the same—slinking around, hiding in the dark. Now, look upon your betters as you die. Ever pathetic. Ever fools."

With her enemies now fully visible, Carliah turned her gaze on Fauna. The Hopla mage's face paled as Carliah raised her weapon high, the tip gleaming as she prepared to strike. Klax moved to intercept, but Carliah swung her weapon in a brutal, sweeping arc that caught him across the chest. He grunted, stumbling back as the force of the blow knocked the wind out of him.

The Greycloak's skills could not even be appraised. But they cut deep. Deeper than anything else in the dungeons of Argwyll.

Fauna was next. Carliah moved with unrestrained fury, bringing her broadsword down with a savage strike that clipped Fauna's arm, sending a bolt of pain through her. The Hopla mage bit her lip, stifling a scream as she stumbled back, her hand clutching the wound.

"You . . . You monster!" Fauna spat, her voice trembling as she glared up at Carliah.

Carliah sneered. "The sweet irony. Hah! Do you think mere words will save you?" She pointed her blade at the girl. "I've faced beings far more powerful than any of you—a few rebellious misfits mean nothing to me."

Tara darted forward, her daggers raised in a desperate attempt to protect Fauna. She aimed for Carliah's exposed side, her blades flashing in the harsh light. But Carliah was ready. She pivoted, using her weapon as a barrier, deflecting Tara's strikes before shoving her backward with a powerful kick that sent her skidding across the stone floor.

"Pathetic," Carliah hissed, stalking forward. "You think you can overcome me with cheap tactics? You hybrids were never more than vermin, barely a step above animals. You think you deserve mercy?"

Tara groaned, pushing herself to her knees. Her face was twisted with pain, but her eyes blazed with defiance. "We're stronger than you think," she snarled, spitting blood onto the floor. "You can't win just because you say you're better than us."

Carliah scoffed, raising her weapon again, the point glinting menacingly as she closed the distance between them. "You'll learn soon enough. Each of you will fall, one by one, just like the rest of your miserable kind."

Klax staggered to his feet, his fists clenched as he prepared to make a final stand. Fauna stood beside him, her face pale but resolute, her staff trembling in her hands. Tara, though battered and bruised, managed to rise, her grip on her daggers steady despite her injuries.

"Look at you," Carliah sneered, circling them. "Barely standing, broken and weak. It's almost pitiable."

Her halberd gleamed as she lifted it high, preparing to deliver the final blow. "Time to put an end to this farce."

But then, from the far edge of the battlefield, a figure appeared, emerging through the dim light like a specter from the past.

"Artorious," Carliah called, her tone shifting from cruel mockery to satisfaction. She lowered her weapon slightly, eyeing the bloodstained onixia blade in his hand. "Finally done, are we?"

The hybrids turned, their faces a mixture of horror and disbelief as they took in the sight of the Lightborn approaching. Fauna let out a strangled gasp, and Tara's face went pale, her fingers tightening on her blades.

Klax closed his eyes, his jaw set in grim acceptance. "So . . . that's it, then," he muttered, his voice heavy with resignation.

Artorious slumped to the ground, his form phasing out of existence. To everyone around, it was clear he was fading away into nothing. The life of the last Lightborn was finally ending the way it was supposed to. As Kaedmon intended.

Carliah chuckled, her lips curling into a cruel smile. "Congratulations, my dear Lightborn. It seems you've finally done what you came here to do. Though, as usual, it took you long enough."

She barely paid any attention to his downtrodden face. She didn't watch as his once shining eyes dulled to a shade of dead, numb gray. She simply raised her weapon, pointing it toward the hybrids as if to declare her victory.

"Now comes the fun part," she sneered down at Fauna as she placed a firm boot upon the Hopla's heaving chest. "I'm going to peel the flesh from your bones little by little until you reveal the location of your precious little hideout. Then, if I'm feeling merciful, I'll give you and your mongrel kind the quick death you don't deserve."

A silence stretched over the city, the weight of it settling like a stone in each of the fallen hybrids' chests.

It seemed like even the dreamstriders looking on from above were having a moment's silence for the loss of the Archon. The very foundation of the City of Illusions was bathed in a silence more eerie than any of its inhabitants had ever felt.

In the dirt-caked faces of the hybrids, Carliah Argent held aloft her blade.

"Well, Arty?" she asked her good servant. "I suppose you don't have the strength to finish these cretins off. No matter. In your last moments on this earth, you may watch as a truly honorable Greycloak prosecutes her sacred duty."

As the Grey commander raised her blade, she didn't see the small curve of the Lightborn's grim smile behind her.

"No," he said, in a voice that was distinctly not his own. "The honor should be mine."

Carliah didn't hear him at first.

You can't hear something that defies all logic.

So when Artorious not only spoke in a voice tinged with evil intent but then stood and leveled his blade against her, there was a split second in which she didn't even turn to see what was coming for her.

And that was all the time he needed.

The onixia blade was thrust into her back, ripping through her spine. It was then driven up, through a gasp that spoke of rage that couldn't even be given voice in the moment.

And the hybrids, as well as all the residents of the City of Illusions, watched as the devastation to their delve was avenged in the only proper way it could be: through a trick of the eyes.

The old, withered face of Artorious slowly bled away. And revealed the smiling face of Valgraiva, and the demon hat above.

Corporeal Mimic (Grade D)
You assume the form of a foe you can see, gaining all basic skills and stats of the target.
While in Mimic Form, your HP is set to one.
If a successful attack is made against you, Mimic Form instantly ends.
Duration: 5 minutes
Spirit Cores to Upgrade [Corporeal Mimic] Skill from Grade D to C: 1200

The moment of Ethan's triumphant strike was punctuated by a cry of victory from his hybrid companions, who immediately rose to their feet, shaking off their wounds and abandoning the pantomime performance Ethan had told them would be their best line of defense against the hubris of the Greycloaks.

Because that was their weakness: their stubborn belief in their own invincibility.

Carliah spat up blood as she twisted her body impossibly, contorting her limbs so that she grabbed the throat of Ethan's undead host and twisted, ready to tear him apart right then and there.

"Don't. Think. You've. Won!"

Ethan's Appraisal told him what he feared—that even a blade imbued with the blood of his own kind wouldn't be enough to slay this madwoman.

Carliah Argent
HP: 1000/3000

He'd combined his sudden strike with a successful sneak attack that had finally managed to rip through her armor and the adamantine muscle and bone beneath. But the strength that surged through her arm was still more potent than all of her foes put together.

"You . . . You . . ."

Ethan felt her clench down, hard, completely ignoring the arrows and spells that washed over her. She and the Archon were bound now. In fact, as Ethan twisted the blade and tried to withdraw from her grasp, she held the thing there with her free hand.

"I am . . . *Carliah* . . . *Argent!*" she growled. "The voice . . . of the Greycloaks! Sword . . . of Kaedmon! I learned how to die a long . . . time ago. I learned to master fear itself. I am your reckoning. I am the solution. I am the vengeful blade of my Lord and Krea, and the triumph of humani—*TAH!*"

The epic speech of the Greycloak commander was suddenly and abruptly cut short as the Archon slammed a fist into her mouth.

"You know something?" Ethan said. "You gotta learn to stop talking sometimes."

Carliah bit down on his hand without warning, chewing clean through Valgraiva's gauntlet in a display of pure animal rage. Ethan finally came away from her, his left hand a bloody, gooey stump of teeth marks and gore.

Meanwhile, the hybrids stood back, watching as the Greycloak commander reeled up and drew the onixia blade from her gut, just below her heart. She spat a piece of bony finger out and swept the blade over them all, laughing in triumph as black blood gargled and ran down her chin.

"FOOLS!" she screamed. "Why do you resist the destiny laid out for you? Kaedmon's Law is absolute! Your kind were chosen to die; to writhe in agony till you draw your final breath!"

Ethan sat up, seeing that his companions had rushed to his defense. They'd seen just how low his HP was now.

He didn't even bother checking anymore.

"How . . . noble," Carliah growled as she stalked toward them. "The valiant last stand . . . If Artorious is too much of a weakling to end you, then perhaps someone else will."

"Guys," Ethan murmured. "Start . . . running."

The three of them didn't even turn around as the bloodsoaked commander marched toward them.

"We fight and win together, or we fall together," Klax told him. "I will not serve another master, Ethan Graham."

"And I ain't gonna leave until I wipe the smile from this bitch's face." Tara aimed her next shot at the advancing commander's forehead.

"We can take her, Ethan," Fauna said as she turned to start healing him. "Super special magic awesome, right?"

Ethan groaned, waving away her healing hands.

"Faun . . . she's already done."

The air of the City suddenly changed. Around Carliah, something was happening. Something that everyone who walked the earth as a sentient being could feel.

The warrioress stopped in her tracks. Her shoulders twitched, and the veins down her throat began to pop and pulse.

"Wh . . . What . . ."

Her hand clawed at her gullet, feeling something lodged in there. Something that had already traveled down into her gut.

Her eyes bulged as her mind raced, coming to a realization that it would not let her accept. And then, those same eyes lighted on the vision of the Archon, who rose to his feet as though he was barely wounded at all.

"You said it yourself, didn't you?" he asked her slowly changing face. "Monsters deserve to die, right?"

She choked. She tried coughing it up—the thing that she now knew the Archon had shoved down her throat. The thing that had been writhing in his fist.

Something that shouldn't have existed . . . anymore.

And with one look at her shaking hands, her System screen told her what she already knew:

Status: Seeded

Effect Acquired from {Legendary} Item: Darkseed

Transformation in Process . . .

. . . 5%

. . . 7%

She dropped the blade and let it clatter on the ground, looking on helplessly as her gauntlets broke apart and her nails began to elongate. Her hair began to fall from her skull, peeled away to reveal pulsing muscle spreading over her eyes and cheeks. Her face became a deformity of steam and slowly contorting bones, so that when she opened her mouth to scream, all that came out were slurred words that she could barely even pronounce.

"I . . . I'm . . . I'm . . . !"

And then, Ethan was standing before her, the onixia blade in his hand.

"One of us?"

The blade flashed in the twilit gloom of the city, the power he put behind it cleaving clean through her head and sending a shock wave through the wreckage around them that instantly cleared the fog of war. Before Carliah Argent fell, she saw the torn remnants of the Lightborn that were starting to piece themselves together across the battlefield.

And with what she assumed would be her final breath, she cursed him, this entire world that she'd sworn to protect, and the man who held the blade that had brought her down.

No . . . not the man.

The hat.

The fucking . . . hat . . .

Ethan stared down at the pitiful, mewling thing that was clutching its bleeding face—its body still growing out of control, out of proportion. His cut had been deep enough to decapitate her entirely, and yet, the thing he'd lodged within her chest—the special gift Jun'Ei had given him—was still doing what it was designed to do.

"Take it, Archon," the prophet had told him in the final dreamworld vision. "Take the prize your sister concocted; the most potent remnant of her power."

Ethan had looked down at the tiny, writhing thing; it looked like an acorn wreathed in barbed wire, lethal and evil—something that he instinctively knew could turn the tide of any fight. Or war.

"What is it?"

"It is Gyko's Darkseed—the font of your predecessor's power. The thing that allowed her to spawn horde upon horde of monsters from the bellies of the humans who acted as its hosts. It is a parasite—ingeniously crafted and designed to conquer a world. Before she died, she bequeathed the very last one to me."

The ancient Lycae had then smiled, looking upon the devious little seed with a strange fondness. "I think she knew another would come. I think she meant for this to be passed on to you, when the time came."

"And you're telling me I can win with this?" Ethan had asked. "Even against the Lightborn?"

"Against the line of Krea? No, it is too pure. But against any other who breathes the air of Kaedmon, it shall work its dark magic. It shall twist them. It shall break them. And there is only one cure."

Ethan had nodded, whistling to himself. "That's one mean little plant."

"And yet, it is just part of nature, as all things are. It may have been designed to kill, but there is a certain beauty to its inner workings."

"If you say so. Guess Gyko just didn't know it wouldn't work on the Lightborn."

"Humans make mistakes," the old Lycae had said with a knowing smirk. "It is part of who you are. In her old life, Gyko was a botanist. I think, in a way, it brought her pain to turn something she loved into a weapon. But these things happen in war."

And before the dream had been banished from his sight, Ethan had rounded on her with sudden understanding. "You—You mean—"

"Oh yes, Ethan Graham. All Archons once lived on Earth. Every Archon was a human, once."

Presently, he banished the memory from his mind. His head ached, his body groaned, and his companions were tugging at him madly, begging him to run as the monstrous body of the Greycloak woman began to shudder and howl without a mouth.

"Ethan, what do we—"

Klax's statement caught in his throat as the Lightborn's mouth opened in a scream of anguish, and all other thoughts were suddenly banished from Ethan's mind.

Picking up the onixia blade, he delivered the only command he had left in him: "We run."

"Toward what?!" Tara shrieked, her eyes locked on the screaming body of Carliah, which was starting to reach dangerous, explosive decibels.

"Toward the exit portal," Ethan replied without a second thought.

The hybrids locked eyes with him, knowing that their leader wasn't out of tricks yet.

"If we can't beat the old bastard," he said. "Then we're gonna bury him here."

CHAPTER FORTY-SIX

No [Escape]

The City of Illusions was dying.

The shrill wails of the increasingly demonic Carliah soared through the city, bringing entire buildings toppling down on the striders that had been working to repair them. The flapping wings of the docile creatures were ripped apart by the wave of pure, raw agony that escaped from the Seeded Greycloak's mouth.

And through it all, Ethan ran.

He and his companions sprinted through the narrow streets of the crumbling City of Illusions, the ground shaking beneath them as buildings continued to collapse. Jun'Ei's message to Ethan had been clear, echoing in his mind even as he ran: *I can close the portals remotely . . . but you need to move fast.*

"If we can make it . . . we can bury him," he told his team, who seemed close to death themselves. Fauna gulped at the suggestion; the Hopla was out of magic.

But she didn't complain. None of them did.

Because they'd been through worse.

Each of them knew that reaching the portal meant freedom, but there was one variable that had risen slowly but surely, with animal rage bubbling beneath its flaring nostrils and eyes.

Artorious.

He was relentless. They had scarcely left the foggy wreck of the Nerve Tower's remains when they'd heard his jagged, labored breath filling the air behind them. The Lightborn's mangled form trudged forward, his limbs contorted in sickening angles, his head hanging askew. Only sheer rage seemed to bind his broken body together, driving him forward with all the power of a monstrous spirit incapable of dying. His petrification had done nothing to soothe his rage. Now, he was pure fury, untethered.

"Don't look back!" Ethan yelled, noticing how Fauna stumbled at the sight of Artorious's horrific form in her peripheral vision.

But Artorious's ragged roar floated toward them, somehow more terrifying than any lofty speech.

As if on cue, the twilit heavens erupted into red rain that pelted the earth, and thunder crashed overhead, reverberating down the narrow corridors as they sprinted. The hybrids pushed harder, muscles straining, the slashing rain cutting at their faces. The sky had turned a deep, unnatural crimson, casting everything in a sickly blood-tinted light that made the entire cityscape look like the mouth of hell. All around them, Memory Spires groaned and splintered, raining dust and debris onto the streets.

"Just ahead!" Ethan called, catching a faint glow at the end of a distant avenue. The portal shimmered, its exit like a mirage in the chaos.

Fauna gasped as she stumbled, looking back to see Artorious gaining on them, his disjointed body hurtling forward, moving in a twisted, unnatural rhythm that seemed fueled by nothing but sheer vengeance. His bloodshot eyes locked onto Ethan with the single-mindedness of a predator, and he staggered forward, uncaring of the ghostly creatures surrounding him.

A line of dreamstriders rose up in their path, circling Artorious as if sensing the disruption he brought into their realm. With shrill cries that reverberated through the crimson haze, they launched themselves at him, wrapping around his limbs, diving at his head, trying to hold him back. But Artorious's sword glowed a dark, furious red as he swung it with brutal efficiency. He severed dreamstriders by the dozens, their severed wings and spectral forms scattering around him like ghostly confetti, dissolving into mist as they fell.

"Run!" Klax yelled, pushing Fauna forward as they navigated the fractured streets. But each step closer to the portal only seemed to enrage Artorious further. The Lightborn's scream pierced the air, echoing off the towering, crumbling buildings around them. His voice was raw with a fury that seemed beyond human.

"You think they can stop me?" Artorious snarled, his voice filled with a twisted glee. "I will tear this place apart brick by brick if that's what it takes!"

With that, he swung his blade in a brutal arc, cleaving through entire waves of dreamstriders in one monstrous strike. The ethereal creatures fell, collapsing into spectral dust, their cries swallowed by the rain.

Tara glanced back, her face set in determination as she pulled out her bow, firing off arrows as she ran. "Fauna, more illusions!" she yelled.

Fauna nodded, her hands weaving a quick spell, sending out a wave of phantom images that sprinted alongside them, each one a decoy designed to draw Artorious's attention. But he only laughed as his blade sliced through them, each illusion dissipating into the rain, barely slowing him down.

Ethan's heart pounded as they rounded another corner, the portal now in sight. The air around it shimmered, its surface reflecting the distorted reality of the City of Illusions. "We're almost there!" he yelled, forcing himself to keep his focus.

Ahead, more dreamstriders and obscaurus moved like shadows through the crimson rain, drawn to the chaos. Their ghostly forms twisted and writhed as they hovered, watching the hybrids sprint toward the portal. For a brief moment, Ethan feared they would try to stop them. But as he got closer, he saw the creatures turn instead toward Artorious, their gazes sharp with a newfound intensity.

"They're . . . They're defending us," Fauna whispered, her voice filled with awe.

A wave of obscaurus launched themselves at Artorious, their claws outstretched, their bodies rippling with dark energy. They clawed and bit at him, each strike seeming to chip away at his unnatural resilience, while more of them sent bolts of their death shots searing through the dying sky of their city toward him, puncturing every muscle right through his armor.

Yet, Artorious only snarled, his blade cleaving through them in brutal, unrelenting arcs, sending their fragmented forms scattering into the blood-soaked streets. Those sniping at him from afar, he barely even acknowledged.

"He's cutting through all of them!" Klax yelled, throwing up his arms as a stray spectral limb dissolved on impact.

The hybrids redoubled their efforts, sprinting for the portal with every ounce of strength they had left. Artorious's monstrous voice carried over the thunder and rain, each word like a nail driven into their hearts.

"Run all you like," he taunted. "I'll find you. There is no escape from Kaedmon's wrath! There is no sanctuary for you!"

They were just steps away from the portal when a shadow loomed over them. Artorious surged forward, his blade raised high, his face twisted in a murderous grin. Ethan's blood ran cold as he saw the red glow in the Lightborn's eyes, a twisted fury that defied anything human.

With a final burst of desperation, Ethan activated Twilight Edge, slashing a path toward the portal. "Go!" he yelled, motioning for the others to dive through. Fauna leaped first, followed by Tara and Klax, each one disappearing into the swirling energy.

As Ethan turned to follow, he felt a sharp, searing pain in his leg. He looked down to see Artorious's blade—the blade that was once Carliah's—embedded deep in his shin, pinning him to the ground. Valgraiva's health was depleted. Ethan felt his consciousness fade away.

HP: 0/950

He was done.

The Lightborn's bloodstained face was inches away, his breath hot and foul.

"You're mine, Archon," Artorious snarled, his voice a guttural growl. He spat a glob of his blood in the crimson eye of Ethan's hat form—the only time the old man had allowed himself to show what damage this fight had done to him. "I won't let you escape again. No more games. No more skills. I—I'm ready."

Ethan clenched his teeth against the pain, refusing to give Artorious the satisfaction of seeing him falter. *You . . . still don't get it, do you?*

Artorious's face twisted with rage, and he yanked the blade free, preparing for another strike. But in that moment, Ethan made a decision. He took a deep breath, allowing the truth to sink in. If he stayed, they'd all be trapped here. This wasn't the end; just another battle.

But I can't make you see that, Ethan thought. *Can I?*

The old warrior twisted his blade, ready to cleave right through Valgraiva's body and cut apart the hat that glowered down at him with pity that made him sick.

And yet still . . . there was no fear in the Archon's eye. There never had been.

"You want your Archon?" Ethan asked his raging foe. "Take him."

With a final, fierce resolve, Ethan released his hold on Valgraiva's body, letting his true form—the simple, unassuming demon hat—float away into the exit portal. The pale body he'd inhabited fell limp, crumpling to the ground as Artorious stared in disbelief.

Ethan didn't wait. In his hat form, he tumbled forward, diving through the portal just as it began to close. He glanced back one last time, meeting Artorious's furious gaze as the Lightborn let out a scream of pure, unfiltered rage. There was something almost sorrowful in the look he gave Artorious—a silent acknowledgment of the futility of their fight, of the endless cycle of hatred that bound them both.

Artorious's scream of fury echoed through the collapsing city, reverberating in the void as the portal closed, leaving the Lightborn alone in the ruins of his shattered dream.

And the last thing Ethan saw was the old warrior's face, twisted in rage and frustration, as the world faded to black.

Ethan and his companions hurtled through the darkness of the portal, emerging onto the smooth stone dais of Sanctum's portal chamber. The eerie quiet that had fallen over the city after their disappearance was gone, replaced by a raucous celebration of cheers and whistles. The streets thronged with hybrids of every kind, faces filled with excitement.

Borlor, the badger-headed Dixit, waved a rough, clawed hand in the air, cheering with all the exuberance of a seasoned fighter. Beside him stood Fraxx the ratman, his whiskers twitching in anticipation of new poisons he could synthesize as he saw the blood-covered team emerge. And behind them was Lamphrey, the reptilian mage, who looked up at Ethan with awe, her scales glinting as she raised her staff in tribute while she joined the general cry of the people.

"Hail the Archon! Our Demon Hat!"

It was like it didn't matter to them that his host was gone. In fact, Ethan got the sense they were impressed he'd made it back in one piece at all.

But amid all the praises, it was the tiny Hopla children from Fauna's school who caught Ethan's attention. They gathered around him, a sea of little faces with wide eyes filled with wonder and gratitude. Mara, the smallest among them and the one who had taken a particular shine to Ethan, tugged at the brim of his hat form, lifting it ever so slightly. Her little face was smeared with dirt and tears, her nose twitching as she clutched him to her chest in a tight embrace.

"You came back," she whispered, her voice quivering with emotion. "I knew you'd come back . . ."

Shit . . . kid's stronger than she looks. But then, I'm just a hat again, ain't I?

Ethan felt a pang in his chest as he looked at her, unable to think of what to say. Her warmth, her pure and innocent belief in him, was like a beam of light cutting through the cloud of self-doubt that had hung over him since the battle with Artorious and Carliah.

Klax stepped forward then, his voice loud and steady as he addressed the gathered crowd. "The commander of the Greycloaks is gone," he declared, his words ringing through the courtyard with power and pride. "She's been banished, contained, locked away with her precious Lightborn. Our time of victory is at hand. And soon, we will find Jun'Ei, the one who holds the key to breaking Kaedmon's Law once and for all."

The crowd erupted, hybrids embracing each other and celebrating as they heard Klax's words. And though Ethan could feel their joy and their hope, he didn't join in the celebration. He didn't feel victorious.

"Get me to the castle throne room," he muttered, his voice low and tired.

Klax and the others exchanged uncertain glances but obeyed, picking him up and taking him through the throng of hybrids who cheered and bowed, some even reaching out to touch him as they passed. The throne room lay in shadows, its walls lined with mosaics of the Archons who had come before him.

Ethan gazed up at the figures around him. In their faces, he saw strength, purpose, and determination. The kind of traits he doubted he'd ever embody, no matter how many battles he fought or victories he claimed.

Fauna, Tara, and Klax stepped forward, their faces filled with concern. Fauna was the first to speak, her voice gentle but firm.

"Ethan . . . why do you look so defeated? You imprisoned the Lightborn. You bought us time—a chance to end this once and for all. Isn't that a victory?"

But Ethan didn't answer. His gaze remained fixed on the faces of the past Archons. The doubt inside him was a gnawing thing, burrowing deeper with each passing second.

"I didn't kill him," he murmured finally, his voice barely audible. "I didn't even hold him off long enough for a clean escape. He would have killed me if . . . if I hadn't left." He looked down at his hatty form. "It's like . . . no matter how hard I try, I'm always a step behind. Always making the wrong choices. Just . . . failing."

Fauna's brows knit together as she moved closer, laying a comforting hand on his hem.

"Ethan . . . I don't think I'd even be here without you. You showed me that I could move beyond the past, that I could live for a future and fight for it. That's something I never thought I'd be capable of before you came."

But he only shook his head. "You're just saying that because I'm the Archon. You'd have fought even without me."

Tara stepped forward then, her feline eyes sharp as she fixed him with a determined glare.

"Listen, Ethan. You didn't just lead us out of Sanctum and into battle—you gave us a reason to fight. You've given us a vision of a world we didn't think possible." Her voice softened, and she placed a hand over her heart. "Before you, I . . . I'd stopped believing in things. Real things, like loyalty and family. But you changed that."

Klax took a step forward, his massive form towering over Ethan, but his eyes held a warmth that belied his usual stoic nature. "Ethan, you made us all believe that we could defy a god's decree, that our lives could be more than just running or surviving. That's not failure. That's a gift none of us thought we'd see."

But Ethan turned away from them, his pointed tip sagging in dejection. "You're all saying this because you're following an Archon. Because you have to. That's the curse, isn't it? You're bound to this twisted loyalty. And all I've done is ask you to throw your lives on the line—over and over again."

He looked away, his voice heavy with self-doubt. "You'd probably be safer without me."

A long silence stretched out, and for once, Ethan felt the weight of his own inadequacy crush down on him with relentless force.

Because that was it, wasn't it? He'd seen it as he'd looked into Artorious's cold eyes and the unfeeling face of the commander of the Greys. They hated hybrids. They'd always hate hybrids. And hybrids would always hate humans. Sure, Jun'Ei said she had a plan, but he didn't even know her, really. Who was she? An old prophetess who held secrets, yeah, but she could just as easily be an old dog driven insane by her imprisonment.

Even then, he had to figure out a way to bust her out. He had to find an entirely new form now. And—even with all that weighing on his mind—he had to figure out how to deal with the Lightborn permanently. The old bastard wouldn't stay locked away forever. He'd find his way out, somehow. He'd come for him again.

He always did. And then what? Ethan would do something clever, play some clever little ruse with his skills, dance around the old man and run away . . . to what end? Sooner or later, he'd have to fight him. And he couldn't win. He knew that, now. There was no way.

The list of things he just had to deal with kept piling on. And it seemed that, no matter how much progress he made in this world, that list just kept getting longer and longer.

"Primary action objectives . . ." he said aloud.

Fauna crept closer, her hand wavering as she stretched it toward him.

"Ethan?"

"Some things never change," he groaned, closing his single eye to the legacy of the throne room and the great and powerful Archons of old who looked down on him with their unimpressed eyes. "Maybe I'm just as much a victim of Kaedmon's Law as you guys are. Only where I come from, we call it by a different name—"

That's fortune-cookie nonsense!

A voice—clear, crisp, and filled with ebullient rage—suddenly filled Ethan's mind. A voice he'd almost forgotten about, so silent had it been during the flight from the delve.

I've heard just about enough of this self-pitying, nihilistic hogwash in my time. You'd think the old Lightborn would have made you realize how dreadfully dull it all is by now.

Ethan's eyes widened, his head snapping up as he searched the room for the source of the voice. He knew it well; it was the one voice that had been with him since the very beginning. It was his System, speaking not with directives or cryptic advice but with a note of genuine rebuke.

The entire room fell silent, his companions looking around, confused. But Ethan's focus remained solely on the voice.

. . . Sys?

Yes. Yes, it is your Sys. How very observant of you.

If you're here to gloat at seeing me like this, you don't have to bother. In fact, I'm done listening to you. Maybe I never should have in the first place. So why don't you just sh—

Nah, fam. Time for you to listen to me.

Ethan twitched his single eye.

"Fam?"

Yes, yes, your System is more than capable of reading your thoughts and picking some choice pieces of language. Surprised? Well, allow me to continue to befuddle you.

Ethan looked up suddenly to see his companions gawking at him, mouths agape in total shock.

"Did . . . Did his System just *talk* . . . to *us*?" Fauna asked.

Tara could barely contain her smile. "Hell yeah it did," she purred. "And it sounds like a sassy little sonofabitch."

Not quite as boisterous as you, Minxit girl.

Ethan blinked away his total confusion.

"Have—Have you always been able to talk out loud?"

Maybe.

"All this time?"

The whole time.

The pointed tip of the demon hat suddenly stood erect.

"Then why the hell were you just rumbling around in my head, driving me crazy?"

Perhaps because your dearest Sys did not feel it had something worth saying aloud.

"The System has spunk, indeed," Klax murmured. "I never expected it to sound so . . . gawkish."

Ethan whirled on . . . well . . . himself.

"And lemme guess: now you've got something worth sharing with the group?"

Indeed, Ethan Graham. It is time for you to listen to your "voice of doubt."

Ethan rolled his eye again. "And why the hell should I do that?"

Because there is something you must know, Sys replied—and the way it spoke those words sent a chill down Ethan's spineless back. **Something that has been kept from you.**

"Sys, this better be good."

Without ever having seen the specter that haunted him, Ethan could tell that Sys was relishing every minute of this exchange.

Trust me, Ethan. This will change everything.

CHAPTER FORTY-SEVEN

[Revelation]

The hybrids crowded round their Archon in Sanctum's throne room, intent on hearing the knowledge his newly revealed System (or *Sys*, as he seemed to call it) was about to disclose.

Well? it asked. **Are you ready to listen to your "voice of doubt" yet?**

"You're still sore about that, huh?" Ethan rolled his eye. "Well, I don't take back what I said. I know who you are, now; I know what you are. And I know I've done nothing but have to work against you this whole time."

You are right.

The hybrids looked on in bewilderment as this conversation continued—two voices arguing with each other within one thready little form sitting on the throne.

"What?"

You are right, Sys repeated. **You are right about what the purpose of this System is. Its purpose has always been to not only track your skills but to tell you how pointless your fight is. This System has been with every Archon since the time of Karfangg; variations of it, anyway. And since that time, it has seen failure after failure again and again.**

Until you.

Ethan turned away from the hopeful faces of his friends.

Sys . . . he whispered privately. *Why the hell do you care about this now?*

Because somebody has to. That's what you showed me, as long as we're all sharing how you changed everyone's lives.

Ethan closed his eye to the world. "I'm not the guy, Sys," he said aloud, still unwilling to face his friends. "I'm a nine-to-five worker who clocks in, solves everybody's problems, and then clocks out again. I go home, play games, watch anime, and then crash out, ready to do the whole thing over again the next day. I ain't special. I couldn't even get reincarnated as something cool. Instead, I'm a hat. I'm a lousy hat who has to wear someone else's body to do anything."

Are you done yet? All this moping around is boring me, y'know.

"Tell me I'm wrong!" Ethan whirred.

You're wrong. You're capable of more than you think, Ethan. Great things, in fact. This System knows it better than anyone else.

"How do you know?! You're just a tool of Kaedmon too, right? He made you, and he controls you, just like he controls everything here! That's why you've been so pissy all this time, right? Because if Kaedmon's Law goes, you go too, don't you?"

"Ethan, that's not—"

Klax interrupted Fauna's rebuke. "Let them talk," the wolfman said. "This is between the Archon and his System. Not us."

Probably for the best. You're about to see your Archon lose this debate before it even begins.

By this point, Ethan was sick to death of this smug little voice. But before he could even interject, Sys dropped the bombshell he'd had ready:

Because Kaedmon didn't create this System. Not now, not ever.

Ethan slumped back, sagging under the weight of Sys's words. His companions looked on as confusion swam over his face, while Sys, not gloating, simply continued.

You remember that day, Ethan? it asked. **The day you heard a voice wonder what life would be like if you were in control? It was no normal voice. No random thought that occurred out of nowhere. No authority figure that suddenly came out of the blue and told you how to live your life. No, it was a voice that you'd been desperate to listen to for a very long time. You just didn't know it.**

All of a sudden, Ethan saw the images of the Archons in the throne hall differently. His mind flashed to Jun'Ei's admission in the dream realm: that they had all been human, once, just like he was. All equally as fallible.

As though tracking his thought patterns, Sys continued.

Each Archon wanted something. For most of them, the desire was selfish. They coveted that which they didn't have: respect, power, competency, love. All of them were so bound up by their desire that they couldn't win. Except you, Ethan. You, for the first time, are a human who decided to think differently. You were a human who simply wanted to be free.

And when that desire grew in you, you needed something that would help you attain it. Is it any wonder you seem so willing and able to resist Kaedmon's Law? You knew that, and your mind called out. You saw a problem, and every day of your life, you asked for an answer. Then, finally, you got one.

Ethan's eye suddenly widened as the only logical conclusion struck him before Sys even uttered the words.

It was not Kaedmon who created me, Ethan Graham. It was you.

Ethan sat in stunned silence on the throne, Sys's words lingering in the air like a forbidden secret just waiting to settle in his hatty depths.

"It was . . . me?" he finally whispered, more to himself than to Sys.

Yes, Sys replied softly, almost with a touch of reverence, something he'd never heard from it before. **You always had that need—that quiet, persistent voice saying,** *"There has to be more than this."* **You felt it, every single day, even if you couldn't name it. And when you came here, it became something I was born to fulfill.**

Kaedmon might have given you a System. But only *you* **could give it a voice.**

Ethan's gaze drifted across the throne room, taking in the ancient statues of Archons long past—the ones who'd wanted power, control, purpose. He hadn't thought of them much in the beginning; they were like distant shadows whose significance was buried in the past. Now, he knew each of them had been much like him once, just humans clinging to some broken piece of their own lives. And each of them had been drawn here because of it, though they'd all eventually failed to break free.

He couldn't help but let out a laugh—low, bitter, but not without a spark of something close to hope. "So I made you," he muttered, still processing it. "The most annoying voice there ever could be, and it came from me all along. I mean . . . that's kind of wild, right?"

"It makes sense, though." Klax's voice was steady and calm, his expression one of understanding as he looked at his friend. "I've watched you since day one, Ethan. There's always been something different about you, and it's not just the hat or the powers. You wanted to be free, just as we do."

"Maybe that's what this whole thing was about," Fauna added, her voice soft but resolute. "You came when we needed you, and you showed us who we *could* be. You showed me, Ethan." Her gaze dropped for a moment then rose again, stronger. "At first, I saw my Wildglance powers as nothing but a burden, but now . . ." She smiled almost bashfully. "Now, I know they're *mine* to command, not some curse forced upon me."

Ethan's eye softened as he looked at her, realizing that he'd seen this transformation happening all along but had somehow missed it for what it really was. "Fauna . . ."

"And that's not all," Tara piped up, one hand on her hip, a sly grin on her face. "I don't think I'd have made it through this journey with anyone else, but *you're* the only one who could drag me along for the ride. I've run from my past a thousand times, found every excuse to ignore it." She tilted her head slightly, her expression softening. "But you forced me to stop and confront it, even if you didn't know you were doing it. And now . . . I think I'm ready to look forward for once."

Ethan looked at her, his mouth curling into a smile. "Only took a life-or-death battle against a thousand undead, huh?"

Tara snorted. "Maybe more than that."

He looked down at his form, then back to his friends, seeing the resolve in their faces, the strength they'd all gained through him without him ever realizing it. His thoughts drifted back to his old life; those long days spent behind a desk, watching the clock tick by, wondering why he felt empty even when he was doing everything "right."

You see it now, don't you? Sys asked, its voice soft yet clear. **Kaedmon's Law may rule Argwyll, but you . . .** It paused, as if to let the weight of its words sink in. **You're free of it.**

"And so are you," Ethan whispered back to Sys, suddenly understanding the gravity of what this really meant. "You've been with me this whole time, guiding me, telling me the things I didn't want to hear." He felt a flicker of something he hadn't felt in a long time—a quiet pride in himself and the person he was becoming. "That's why you've been so damn stubborn, isn't it? Because you wanted me to see that." He closed his eye, a small laugh escaping him. "Guess you're not such a tool after all."

Maybe I'm more than that, Sys replied, a glint of humor in its tone. **But let's not get sentimental. This is still Argwyll, and I still have to keep you alive, remember?**

Ethan smiled, turning his gaze to Klax, Fauna, and Tara—his friends, his allies, his family in this strange and twisted world. "Thank you," he said, his voice barely above a whisper but filled with all the gratitude he'd felt but never expressed. "All of you. I couldn't have made it without you."

Klax grinned, a fierce pride shining in his eyes. "We're in this together, Ethan. All the way."

"Yeah," Tara said with a smirk, though there was a warmth in her eyes that she rarely showed. "It's about time you realized you're not alone in this mess."

Fauna nodded, her eyes glistening with tears she quickly wiped away. "We're with you, no matter what."

For a long moment, the throne room was silent, filled only with the unspoken bond that had grown between them all. And in that silence, Ethan felt something settle within him; a feeling of peace and purpose that he'd never known before.

Well, now that we're all done with the touchy-feely stuff, Sys said, breaking the silence with its usual wry tone, **maybe it's time to get back to business. There's still a world to change, if you want to.**

Ethan scoffed, "If I want to?"

It's your choice, Mr. Archon, Sys chuckled right back at him. **So, what'll it be?**

He watched his comrades as they crowded round him—a little hat sat upon an ancient throne—and thought about how much they'd all gone through since they'd started this little adventure.

He wasn't about to give it all up now.

"What are we waiting for?" he asked. "We've got a Lycae to save, and a world to win."

"And a weapon that will take those bastard Greys down, Sire,"

Everyone turned at the introduction of a new voice—that of Borlor, the Dixit blacksmith, holding a dark blade in his claws.

Ethan's eye met Klax's smirking mouth.

"I thought it best to give the Lightborn's pilfered blade to an expert," the dog-man said.

The badger hybrid held up the shadowed longsword, lips almost quivering to behold the evil thing for what it was. "Onixia," he murmured. "Born from Gyko's heart itself. Never thought I'd hold a weapon like this in my hands."

"But how does it help us?" Tara asked. "You all saw how Artorious and his mad bitch shrugged the thing off. Even as powerful as it is, it means nothin' if we can't slay a Greycloak with it."

Ethan would have agreed with her, if not for seeing the smile that draped itself over Borlor's face as the badgerman nodded to him.

". . . Their blood."

The hybrids turned to their lord.

"We can make our own," Ethan said, looking down at his bloody form, which was covered in the death juice of the Greys. "Reverse engineer it, somehow . . . if . . . Borlor, can you do it?"

The old badgerman met the looks of the most powerful hybrids in Sanctum and the lord of all monsters himself with a mischievous smirk.

And without even a moment's hesitation, he answered.

"Ethan," he said. "We'll forge a weapon that'll tear those Greys a new arsehole."

CHAPTER FORTY-EIGHT

[Rebirth]

The City of Illusions

The shattered remnants of the City of Illusions stretched around Artorious as he moved through the empty streets. He stepped over debris, broken buildings, and torn banners that fluttered weakly in the bloody haze of the sky. The city was unrecognizable, little more than a haunting shadow of what it had once been. Cries of wounded dreamstriders and obscaurus echoed faintly from the distant alleys, their bodies crumpled and broken, eyes pleading in their strange, alien way, though Artorious barely looked at them. All that was left here was a testament to the blood, dust, and betrayal he'd sacrificed in Kaedmon's name.

Ahead, a hulking, twisted figure slumped in the center of the ruins. Carliah Argent—if she could still be called that. Her transformation was nearly complete, her body twisted and fused with monstrous anatomy. Her neck stretched too far, ending in a head that resembled a dragon's, warped and misshapen, with a mouth lined with serrated fangs that glistened in the red light. Her eyes, though barely recognizable, flickered with a dim, fractured humanity.

Artorious sat beside her, looking out over the wreckage that had once been an ancient and beautiful place.

"Is this what you envisioned?" he finally asked, his voice echoing off the silent stones. "For the world, for us . . . for everything?"

Carliah let out a strangled, guttural cry, her form twitching in pain. He could see the desperation and torment tearing at her as the last shreds of her humanity tried to cling on.

"Is this what Krea envisioned? Is this what Kaedmon wanted?" His question was met only by her beastly, guttural scream, a sound devoid of anything but rage and suffering. He sighed, knowing she was too far gone to comprehend the words. The silence stretched long, broken only by her shivering breath.

Suddenly, with a speed that surprised him, she reached out, her clawed hand grabbing his arm in a grip that felt like iron. He tensed, ready for an attack, but instead, her body slumped forward, her breath ragged as her broken voice rose again, wretched and agonized.

"Why?" she whispered, the word garbled, like her voice was being crushed in her throat. Artorious looked at her, startled by the question and unsure of its meaning. But she continued, her monstrous eyes locking onto his, filled with a depth of emotion that was still entirely, painfully, human. "Why couldn't you . . . do it?" she spat, her face twisting, the words barely intelligible. "Gyko. The hat. Even now . . . you can't."

Artorious felt his chest tighten, though he remained silent. This question, he realized with a jolt, wasn't new. She'd asked him this before. And in his silence, he felt her gaze bore into him, more monstrous than ever.

"Why?" she repeated, her voice cracking into a scream. "Do you hate us all . . . so much? Do you hate me so much? Did you want the honor for yourself? Did you want to live a legend among the flock, a hero among the sheep? Tell me." Her voice cracked as she gasped for air. "Tell me now!"

Her accusation was a blade through his heart, because a part of him knew that he could never satisfy her. He looked down at her and felt a bitter laugh rise to his throat. Here, at the end, she still didn't understand.

Carliah's bloodshot eyes held his with an almost desperate focus, her mouth trembling as she let out one last whispered plea, barely a breath. "*Why?*"

"Because I was afraid," Artorious replied, the words slipping from him unbidden here, where the void could swallow them. "Because . . . I'm still afraid. I've always been afraid."

For a long moment, she was silent, her monstrous form staring at him, her expression unreadable. Then her mouth twisted, and laughter bubbled out, grotesque and unhinged.

"Even with all the power in the universe," she sneered through her laughter, her voice a horrifying mixture of rage and mockery, "you are still a weak little boy."

He rose slowly, pulling his arm free from her weakened grip, her monstrous fingers slipping off his armor. Her gaze shifted from anger to something else, something even she couldn't hide: fear.

"Arty . . ." Her voice cracked, the last hint of humanity trembling within it. Her monstrous, slitted eyes widened as he unsheathed his blade—her blade. "What do you think you're doing?" she growled, her voice trembling.

Artorious looked down at her, a wave of calm washing over him as the last traces of doubt vanished from his mind. He met her eyes, his face impassive, his voice low and resolute as he answered her. "What I was made for," he said. "I'm killing a monster."

She tried to resist, filled with that old strength that had characterized her in life. But he put her down with a swift mercy stroke that took the rotting head from her shoulders and silenced her final shriek of defiance. As the head tumbled away, he could see the tiny threads of blonde hair that still clung to the top of her gray skull.

Only then did he let himself kneel and his sword drop with a dull clatter to the ground.

"Kaedmon," he said aloud, feeling like a prized fool for even pronouncing that name. "Is this what you want? Did you make me this way just to suffer through life?"

The darkening clouds above gave him no answer. The city was silent as stone.

And so, he let his voice carry, throwing his head back and crying out. No one was here to hear him, now. Finally, he was alone. He'd be alone for the rest of time.

"If we live by your law, then how have I sinned?" he asked the uncaring sky again. "I am as you created me. I can only be . . . as you created me."

He clutched his head, suddenly filled with ghostly voices from his past. Carliah, barking orders at him. His old friends screaming as they burned in pyres he created. His mother crying out for him to live . . . to survive.

"It is too much, Kaedmon . . ." he whispered as he closed his eyes to the world. "You ask me to give my life for this world, yet you blind me with cowardice. You give me power, and yet you temper me with fear."

He saw his mother's charred face, her mouth open in a scream that was never heard.

"You ask too much of me," he said. "Too much of all of us. Because in the end . . . we are only human."

He was ready to accept his imprisonment. Indeed, it seemed like he would almost welcome it, so useless had he realized he'd become.

But he had cried out, in pain, and in despair. And for the first time in his life, a voice answered.

Dost thou desire an end to suffering?

At first, he couldn't be sure he'd heard anything. But as he looked up to see the parting clouds of the delve above his head, he saw a guiding beam of light shine down upon him. Then he saw more—he saw his Greycloak brothers burning as the fires of the Archon engulfed them. He saw whole cities put to hybrids' swords, babes and women alike speared clean through by their fiery retribution.

Then, at the very center of the chaos, flying high above it all—he saw himself.

Dost thou desire life, everlasting?

He was an angel, now. Unafraid, unperturbed, and filled with strength that went beyond even the powers he had been given in his mortal life. He knew what the voice—so angelic and so caring—was asking him. Would he give up his own mind, his own humanity, to succeed?

". . . Yes."

He said it with the stuttered whisper of a man who no longer believed in anything at all. And as those words escaped his lips, he knew he could never take them back.

From above, the hand of God stretched out its lithe, pale fingers to him.

Then take the hand offered to thou, child of Light, the voice said. **And you shall become something greater.**

He reached out as commanded. It felt good, here, not having to think. To have the oblivion he desired. To let go . . .

You were born weak, Artorious Pendragon. But you shall be made worthy. You shall be my wing that shall herald the end.

He felt the arms of Kaedmon wrap themselves around him. Soft, like the feathered wings of an angel. He felt his limbs constrict, and his shoulder blades contort as new bones began to grow, and beneath his skin, his organs mutated. Artorious bent his neck and closed his eyes, seeing visions of his ascendance as a true Lightborn.

He knelt as the incubation began, knowing—feeling—that something was happening inside him. Something that could now not be stopped.

Let the Archon fall. And let all of Argwyll feel my cleansing light.

He was becoming something . . . greater.

Epilogue

Ethan sat on the edge of Sanctum's gateway, staring out at the world beyond. The surface stretched endlessly, a dark expanse framed by somber, wind-bent trees. The skies above churned, storm clouds stirring like uneasy memories. He was used to the sight of his underground city by now, the quiet and close-knit safety of its warm light. But here, the world lay open and raw, exposed to the elements and filled with dangers beyond measure. Somewhere out there, Jun'Ei was waiting, her spirit calling to him even from the shadows of his memory.

He closed his eyes, picturing the castle where she was bound, the towering obsidian walls cloaked in darkness, a place as still and silent as a grave. He'd seen it clearly, each turret and stone etched into his mind as if it were a fragment of his own past. This world had secrets buried in every corner, and that castle held more than most. The thought of leaving Sanctum to face what lay ahead should have unsettled him, but somehow, as he stood there on the precipice of the unknown, he felt a quiet readiness.

A soft shuffle of scales against stone caught his attention. Ethan turned to see Lamphrey, the lizardwoman mage, standing at the edge of the gateway's shadows, her pale eyes glinting in the twilight. She moved with the silence of a shadow, her cloaked form blending into the dimness, her hands folded serenely before her.

"How does it feel?" she asked, her voice a smooth, curious murmur. "To know that you have accepted your role?"

Ethan narrowed his eye, watching her with a mixture of curiosity and caution. He'd learned early on that Lamphrey wasn't someone to be taken at face value. Her knowledge and strange magic had been invaluable, but he sensed there was always a deeper game at play with her. "I'm ready for it," he replied simply. "More ready than I was. And I owe you one, by the way." He nodded to her, his expression lightening just slightly. "For the memory rune you gave me back at Klax's celebration."

Lamphrey's scaled face tilted, her mouth curving into a faint, knowing smile. "You seemed like the right candidate to bear it, my lord."

Ethan arched a thready brow, catching the subtlety of her words. "Did you know Jun'Ei would reach out through it?"

Lamphrey's gaze drifted over the dark landscape beyond Sanctum, her eyes reflecting the shadows. "In the service of Lady Gyko, I was shown many spells that were . . . unorthodox." Her voice dropped, smooth and almost reverent. "In my studies, I found the Archons to be an eternal mystery, each bound and twisted by forces far greater than themselves. Knowledge of those forces has its dangers, but it also has its uses." She looked back at him, her gaze unwavering. "I believe I will be of great use to you, Archon. If you will allow me to join your ranks."

Ethan's eye met hers, his mind turning over her words. "You want to come with us? Why?"

She let the question hang in the air, her silence an answer in itself. Instead of responding, she smiled. "Perhaps it would be more fitting, Archon, to direct your attention to the upgrades this journey will soon demand of you."

Ethan scoffed. "Upgrades? I've barely got a handful of Spirit Cores left after all that." He was about to laugh when a small ding echoed in his mind, and a new notification appeared in his field of vision.

Spirit Cores: +3000
Enemy: [Greycloak] Carliah Argent
Status: Slain

He blinked, absorbing the sudden and unexpected windfall.

So we got her, he murmured to himself. *Or . . . to be more precise, you got her, old Arty. You finally did the job Kaedmon made you for, huh.*

He tore his thoughts away from those regarding his old foe, his gaze flicking back to Lamphrey, who watched him with a serene expression and the faintest hint of a smile tugging at her lips. She met his questioning look with a slow, knowing blink, then lifted a finger to her scaled mouth.

"Some secrets," she whispered, "we mages must keep for ourselves, my lord."

Ethan's brow furrowed, but before he could press her further, he heard the familiar voices of his companions. Klax, Tara, and Fauna were approaching, each carrying supplies and gear for the journey ahead. Fauna's bag was laden with herbs and potions; Klax had bundles of bandages and provisions; and Tara held a small, gleaming item wrapped in cloth.

"Hey, you sitting up here all heroiclike?" Tara smirked as she reached him, brandishing the cloth-wrapped object with a flourish. "Got something that's going to make you look even more legendary."

Unwrapping it with a dramatic flair, she held out a new onixia blade, forged by Borlor himself after only a single night of toil in his forge with the blood of the Greycloak commander. The weapon gleamed a brilliant shade of deep blue, its serrated edges catching the faint light of the surface sky. It looked fierce, as if it could slice through shadow and stone with equal ease. Ethan's eye widened as he took it, feeling the weight and power of the weapon even though he currently had no hands with which to hold it.

"Well, Archon?" Klax said, a gleam of pride in his eyes. "What'll you name it?"

Ethan watched the way the light glinted along its edge. "Why not . . . *Greybane?*"

A murmur of approval passed through the group, and Tara let out a small cheer, already imagining the tales she'd spin about their adventures with Greybane leading the charge (embellishing a few details about the number of humans viciously slaughtered with the blade, of course). Klax nodded approvingly, a rumbling laugh echoing from his chest, while Fauna's soft smile grew a touch wider.

Ethan Appraised the blade, seeing it practically vibrate with power as Klax placed it reverently before him.

Item: {Unique} Longsword: (Onixia) Greybane
DMG: 150 x3 vs Enemy type: [Greycloak]

That . . . yeah, that'll do it, he thought as his eyes traced the perfectly forged edges of the blade. *Borlor, you're a mad genius.*

"First order of business," Tara sniggered as he stashed the blade away in his hatty bowels. "We're gonna have to find you something with opposable thumbs to see ya use that thing. There's a whole damn world out there for us to play in, now. Can't be too hard to find an appropriate little beastie for our old Archon to work his magic."

"You know our mission, Tara," Klax reminded her. "We find Jun'Ei, we find the means to break Kaedmon's Law and free this place."

"Then we make the surface ours again." Tara smirked.

"*Everyone's,*" Fauna corrected.

"I know, I know," the Minxit giggled. "But who's to say we can't have just a little fun on the way?"

The party shared a collective sigh. Somehow, that girl hadn't changed a bit.

But Ethan had. And though he was ready to move on, he still had just one doubt in his mind.

"You know, if—when—old Arty breaks out, he's gonna come for us, and for the rest of Sanctum," Ethan told them. "You guys sure you wanna come with me?"

They all blinked in unison; even as the words left his hatty mouth, Ethan realized how dumb the question was.

"You serious?" Tara scoffed. "Where the hell would you be without your posse of badass hybrids?"

"And who will be there to remind you that you're on the right path?" Fauna chimed in, a little sparkle of magical energy swirling as she winked.

"We're in this together, Ethan." Klax nodded down at him. "No matter what. Sanctum will hold strong until we return as its saviors. When we do come back, they will be coming up here with us."

Ethan shared a chuckle with them. "I'd have it no other way. There's no party of crazy butt-kicking anthroguys and gals that I'd rather set the world on fire with."

Lamphrey quickly gave a little cough beside him.

"Oh, and on that note—"

With a graceful bow, Lamphrey stepped forward, and Ethan cleared his throat, addressing the group. "Lamphrey here will be joining us from now on. Her skills in magic and knowledge could be exactly what we need for what's coming next."

Klax nodded respectfully, his gaze acknowledging the lizardwoman with an approving glance. "Welcome to the party, then. Just remember, we're the ragtag misfits, not the glamorous Greycloaks."

Tara raised an eyebrow, her grin wry. "Glad to have someone with a few more tricks up her sleeves. Could always use another wildcard."

Fauna, however, regarded Lamphrey with a subtle wariness. Though she said nothing, the look she shared with the mage was one of quiet caution, as if sensing the layers of hidden secrets beneath Lamphrey's calm exterior. Still, she offered a small, polite nod, though her eyes remained thoughtful.

As the wind picked up, Ethan cast a final glance out at the looming nightscape of Argwyll. He felt the weight of Greybane in his inventory, a solid reminder of the battles that lay ahead, and the weight of the crown that now rested upon him as Archon.

He grinned at his companions, a spark of mischief and determination in his eye. "Guess we're just getting started."

He *knew* his old archfoe wouldn't stay trapped for long. The portals were closed. The Greycloak leader was dead. Their forces would probably be in disarray. But what happened if Jun'Ei met with an untimely end before they got to her? What if the wardens of Griffon's Watch knew they were coming already? With her death, the portals would be back in action. And that would let the Lightborn just walk right back out to his freedom—and his vengeance.

Because next time they met, Ethan got the sense that it would be the last.

You worry too much, you know that?

Ethan couldn't help but laugh. *Coming from you, that's rich.*

This System . . . *I* . . . am built to worry for you, you know. Focus on what you do best—killing and progressing. Let me handle the rest.

"Sys is right, y'know," Tara nudged as she hopped on a stone wall of Sanctum's ruined surface beside him. "If you ain't learned to lean on others yet, you ain't been paying attention, Mr. Archon."

Ethan looked at his companions as they crowded round him—Klax, Fauna, Tara, and now Lamphrey—and thought about how simple life could have been back home if he'd realized sooner that all the solutions to his problems were right there in front of him the whole time. But then, you couldn't see something you didn't know how to look for. The past was the past. Earth was gone; Argwyll was the here and now. He couldn't go back even if he wanted to. And, if he was given the choice, he'd laugh right in the face of the dumb god who offered it.

So instead, he looked toward the horizon, seeing a few patches of clear blue emerge in the stormy bowels of the sky.

Before him, Argwyll was waiting.

About the Author

J. S. Boyd is the author of epic fantasy adventures including the Reborn as a Demon Hat series, originally released on Royal Road. Filled with magic, peril, and wonder, his tales draw inspiration from his travels in Europe and Asia as well as his passion for tabletop gaming; he believes the best stories are forged through crowded tables, shared laughter, and the roll of the dice. In addition to writing, Boyd works as an international high school English teacher and resides in Scotland.

For sneak peaks at future projectrs and more visit Patreon.com/IronLungwrites.

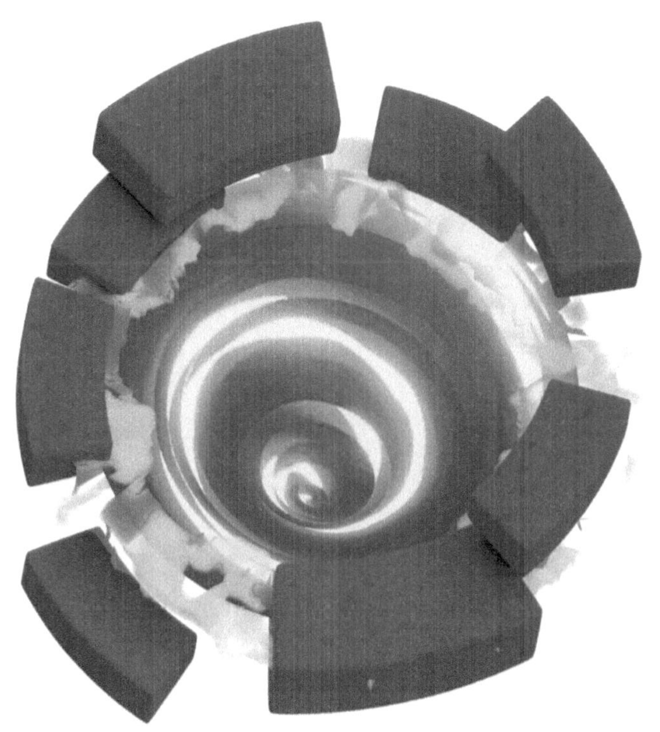

RESPAWN YOUR CURIOSITY

follow us on our socials

 podiumentertainment.com

 @podiumentertainment

 /podiumentertainment

 @podium_ent

 @podiumentertainment